THE ANACHRONISTIC C⌚DE

Happy Reading!

The ANACHRONISTIC CODE Series

Available Now
BOOK ONE: DÉJÀ ME
BOOK TWO: the COMEBACK KID
BOOK THREE: MEMORIES from TOMORROW
BOOK FOUR: ESCAPE from TOMORROW

Coming Soon
BOOK FIVE: the FUTURE-PAST COLLATERAL

and three more to be named later…

Also by DWAYNE R. JAMES:

amuzings

Gingers & Wry

Obsidian Fire

For more information on these titles, visit
www.dwaynerjames.com

The ANACHRONISTIC CODE

BOOK ONE:
DÉJÀ ME

and

BOOK TWO:
the COMEBACK KID

DWAYNE R. JAMES

First Printing: Nov 2019
Second Printing: August 2020*
Third Printing: February 2021

A note from the author:
I'm unapologetic about the number of *pop culture references* that I make in this book. Please note that I give credit for each and every one and that it is not my intent to claim any of them as my own, or to incorporate aspects of their mythology into my story other than in a manner that is either referential or reverential.
Indeed, it is my goal to pay tribute to the positive impact that they've had on my life, and the lives of so many others.

*The second printing introduces a totally revamped first chapter. If you read the first version, then allow me to apologize for throwing so much detail at you all at once. The new format is a lot easier to read, and a lot more fun too!

The folks at *Merriam-Webster* define an **ANACHRONISM** as:

AN ERROR IN CHRONOLOGY; *ESPECIALLY* : A CHRONOLOGICAL MISPLACING OF PERSONS, EVENTS, OBJECTS, OR CUSTOMS IN REGARD TO EACH OTHER.

Which is all well and good until you actually become an anachronism yourself.

TABLE OF CONTENTS

BOOK ONE

BOOK TWO

FOR JOSH DOMEGAL, THERE'S SOMETHING OUT OF PLACE IN THE 80s THIS TIME.

THE ANACHRONISTIC C⦶DE

DÉJÀ ME

DWAYNE R. JAMES

CHAPTER 1
Awakening

S wallowing awkwardly, I looked at the date on the newspaper again.

Wednesday, April 17, 1985.

"Is this yesterday's paper?" I croaked, addressing somebody who, until just a few minutes ago, had been dead for more than twenty years.

My mother came up behind me and, as if to prove that she wasn't an incorporeal ghost, leaned lightly against my lower arm as she looked down at the newsprint that I was holding, rather unsteadily, in my hands.

"That's the one," she said, before commenting on the subject of the paper's main headline, the imminent launch of *New Coke*. "I can't believe that it's really going to happen. They're actually going to change *Coke*."

I swallowed again as, somewhere off in the distance, I could hear the voice of somebody else who should be dead. "What *I* can't believe is that it's front page news," my father muttered from the kitchen table, his coffee mug halfway to his mouth. "It's a geedee soda pop."

He continued to speak, but I wasn't listening because I was staring at the date again.

1985.

My mind struggled to do the math, already overwhelmed with the absurdity—the ludicrousness—of everything that had happened to me since I had been awakened earlier by an oldies song on the radio that was, at least according to the Disc Jockey, being played for the first time.

It had been November of 2035 just last night, and I had been sixty-seven-years-old. That's what ... fifty years?

So, that would make me seventeen... again.

By the time I figured out that the words my father were currently speaking were, in fact, directed towards me, it was too late to do anything other than look over at him as nonchalantly as possible and play dumb.

"I'm sorry, what?"

Dad swore under his breath as he repeated himself. "I said you'd better start getting ready if you want to catch the bus."

"The bus..." I parroted, distantly.

"Yes," my father replied patiently. "The bus. To school. It's where you're going today... Because it's a *school* day." He was speaking slowly now, as you would to a dim child, making it clear that, in 1985, my family's penchant for sarcasm was alive and well. "And if you're going to wash that filthy mop that you call hair, then you'll need time to shower."

"Shower... For *School*..."

Both of my parents were staring at me as if concerned that I was on drugs — admittedly a common concern for parents in the 80s as much as it was one for me in the 2010s when I had checked (or *would* check) Matheson's pupils for excess dilation whenever he was acting unusually weird, which was often.

Teenagers in any decade I guess.

I still hadn't truly accepted that what was happening to me was real, but if there was the *slightest* possibility that the two people in front of me were actually my long-dead parents, then there was no way in hell I'd do *anything* that might distress or worry them (even if I was technically older than them). This meant that my course of action was clear: I had to try and play along until I could figure out how I got here and — perhaps more importantly — why.

So, rather than arguing, I simply said, "Gotcha," stuffed what remained of my breakfast into my mouth, slipped away from the table and willed my seventeen-year-old body up the stairs.

"And get your lazy-ass of a brother out of bed too wouldya?" my father called after me. "I'm not driving him to school again when there's a perfectly good bus..." Mercifully, I didn't hear the rest of his rant, because I'd already entered the bathroom and closed the door behind me.

For a moment, I contemplated the door knob. With my hand still gripping it — as if touching something physical in the new reality that I now found myself in would somehow ground me within it — I took a deep breath and finally articulated the only possibility left as to what was happening to me, no matter how ridiculous it might sound.

"I've travelled back in time," I whispered, not wanting to entertain the thought very loudly, lest more volume make something so insane sound somehow more credible. It was funny how, despite a lifetime diet of science fiction movies, books, and TV shows with that exact theme, I was still resistant to the concrete reality of the idea.

"I've travelled back in time," I repeated, slightly louder this time and with more confidence, letting go of the door knob so that I could turn and face the mirror. At this point, any desire to repeat the phrase flew out of my mind at what I saw in the reflection. It was me, well … kind of. It was the me that I remembered. The me that I saw in the few remaining pictures that I still had of my youth. A teenaged version of my form, with a single chin, a ton of hair, a face covered in tiny swollen red marks, and an overall physique with an enviable body fat percentage.

Seriously. When had I ever been this skinny?

For the longest time, I just stared at myself in the bathroom mirror of my childhood home, as if seeing myself like this made the entire fantastic experience that much more convincing. Admittedly, I had actually been getting swept away by the fantasy earlier when I'd been eating breakfast in the kitchen of the house that I had grown up in, with two people I still missed dearly, I completely forgot to be skeptical about any of it, and just accepted it as real for no other reason than I wanted it to be that way.

But now, well, this familiar-looking, acne riddled stranger smirking back at me from my own reflection, reminded me that I had some tough choices to make.

In the first place, just what the hell am I supposed to do? Not just about the shower, but for the rest of the day. At school.

Well, what were my options, really?

Was there anything wrong with me just throwing caution to the wind and actually going to school? I mean, this whole time-displacement thing could end at any moment, so couldn't I just enjoy it while it lasted?

Can't I just play along?

Chuckling to myself, I realized that, if this experience actually *did* continue for any length of time, I wouldn't really have a choice *but* to do just that, and the main reason as to why was literally staring me right in face.

The reflection I was gawking at even now was the perfect reminder that, to the rest of the world, I was a seventeen-year-old boy. I really wanted to say that it was actually the reflection of a young man, but the sixty-seven-year-old soul inside me knew better. *I was a boy.* A boy who couldn't easily buck the system. I had limitations—even more limitations that had been imposed on me in the *Pucks*. If I tried to step away from any of the standard conventions that limited a seventeen-year old's freedom, like school for instance, then the consequences would be just as real as everything else I was experiencing at the moment.

I'm a boy.

A boy with no real resources to speak of that were solely his. I would have a bank account but, if memory served, it would barely be enough money to get me to Toronto. Sure, I could steal a credit card. Maybe "borrow" a vehicle. Try and make it on my own. But then what? How long could I get by? Where would I go? Yeah, maybe I could use my knowledge of the future to my advantage, but I could do that from here just as easily. Probably even more easily.

And then there was the impact on others that I had been thinking of just earlier, especially in relation to my mother and father. If that really was them downstairs, and I really *had* travelled in time, then I simply could not do anything that might hurt them or cause them any level of stress, and running away from home punched hard on all of those buttons.

My internal soliloquy was interrupted abruptly by a knock on the door and Dad's gruff voice asking me to hurry up. "What are you doin' in there anyways? There are others who use that washroom occasionally too y'know!"

I answered him while pretending that my mouth was full of toothpaste. "Just brushen my teef!" I said loudly, even as I scrambled to find my toothbrush. I remembered enough to look for it at the holder to the right of the sink, but there were four brushes hanging there beside the plastic Tupperware cup that we collectively used to rinse our mouths. Mom and Dad's brushes were pretty obvious, leaving only two and, since that made it a fifty/fifty chance either way, I grabbed the one closest to me and then set about locating the toothpaste.

As I brushed my teeth, I continued my internal contemplation. *Can I tell somebody that I'm a time-traveler?*

Well, in the first place, who would believe me? Unless I could find a way to prove it beyond a shadow of a doubt, but what would I even say?

I began to think about just how such a conversation would go with my parents, and I started to laugh to myself as I came to see its inherent role reversal. Like many of my friends, I'd grown up in a generation when our elders went on at great length about just how arduous had been their pasts compared to our, generally rather cushy, present. They were forever complaining about such things as how far they had to walk to school, or how they had to make do with nothing during the hard times of either the depression or the World Wars.

And here I was in the unique position of genuinely being able to make the claim to one of my elders that my past had been just as grim and challenging as theirs had been, perhaps even more so, even though, strictly speaking, it hadn't even officially happened yet.

You had to laugh. What else could you do?

When I was done with my teeth, I rinsed what I hoped had been my toothbrush, stripped out of my night-clothes, and stepped into the shower. It took a moment to figure out how to operate the faucet and direct the stream to the showerhead, but once the water hit me, I was inundated with another sense that convinced me even more deeply that this could not possibly be some kind of illusion, or dream, or advanced holodeck simulation. It was the smell of the water, the same earthy smell I remembered from my childhood. It was water with a taste, texture, and smell that was unique to Northern Ontario and it made me teary eyed as the scent filled my nostrils. How could that level of detail be replicated? Had I ever had a dream so vivid that I could smell something this strongly?

As I was shampooing my head (while mentally agreeing with my father that this was way too much hair) and trying to remember exactly how to use conditioner, I began to contemplate some popular movies and stories concerning time-travel, since that was where most of my knowledge on the subject seemed to originate.

Will time flow normally from today forward?

Could I find myself jumping around in time like the main character in *The Time-traveler's Wife,* or like Captain Picard in the series finale of *Star Trek: The Next Generation?* Alternatively, what if I kept repeating the same day over and over again like Bill Murray's character in *Groundhog Day?* Both of these questions were pretty easy to dismiss from further contemplation though, since I wouldn't notice either of those effects until they actually started happening to me.

Could this time-travel trip end at any minute, returning my mind to my proper period?

If memory served, in the movie *Somewhere in Time*, that's pretty much what happened to Christopher Reeve's character when he saw an anachronistic artifact—something that didn't belong in the past there with him—that broke his hypnotic link to that era. I hadn't seen any such anachronisms yet, but I made a mental note to watch out for them. Still, like the previous question, the answer to this was something I couldn't possibly find until it, too, actually happened.

Could I make changes to the future if I did things differently in the past?

There were so many examples of stories and movies where the protagonist is given the opportunity to go back in time to a pivotal moment and change the future for the better. A good example of this would be *Quantum Leap*, where Sam Beckett "leaps" through time and into a different body in every episode in order to right a wrong that had been done historically. Then there was CBCs *Being Erica*, one of my favourites from the 2010s, where Erica Strange walked through a doorway into her past every week and tried to make better choices for herself. In both cases though, none of the changes that either characters made, although significant, ever seemed to alter the present all that much, at least not nearly as much as had killing a single butterfly in Ray Bradbury's seminal time-travel short-story, *The Butterfly Effect*. In fact, almost every other time-travel movie or story that I could think of, from *Back to the Future* to the *Star Trek* episode *City on the Edge of Forever*, involved the heroes trying to mitigate the damage that their own time-traveling had wrought in the first place.

This segued quite nicely into my next question.

Can I get back to my own time?

I had mixed feelings about this one. 2035 wasn't anywhere near a utopia worth returning to, and although I most definitely missed my children and Celeste, I'd resigned myself to never see them again anyhow when I'd escaped the *Pucks* in my search to find out...

My thoughts were interrupted by a hard rap on the door and a loud reminder from my father that I'd been taking too long. "If it takes this long to wash your hair, then it's definitely time to consider cutting it," he added in a voice that faded as he walked away down the hall.

I shut off the water immediately and had to admit that, with wet strands of hair hanging down past my nose, my father wasn't wrong about it being too long. Still, I hadn't had hair in decades, and I just really wanted to enjoy the hell out of it. Maybe I'd even get it dyed or styled or something, simply because I could.

I grabbed a towel (after finally remembering where they were stored), wrapped it around myself (amazed at the fact that it reached all the way around me comfortably), and zipped out of the bathroom and down the hallway to my room.

After all the contemplation about time-travel that I'd just done, the only real solution that I had arrived at, other than that I should just act out my part for now, was that, if my current experience actually were a book, or a movie, or a TV show, then it certainly wasn't all that original was it? It seemed to me that it had all been done before.

I began to crave something at that point - something that I knew would be off limits to my seventeen-year-old body: coffee.

B ack in my old bedroom after my shower, I was standing in the middle of the room, towel still wrapped around me, spinning in place. I was like a deer in headlights, enraptured by everything around me, looking at it as if I'd never seen it before.

The walls were that faux-panelling style that was all the rage in the 70s, but you could barely see any of it since every square inch of it seemed to be covered by one kind of pop-culture memorabilia or another (all of it attached with father-approved thumbtacks, since tape would damage the fake wood design easily).

There was the *E.T.* poster with the diagonal crease that had happened when it had been bent almost in half just twenty minutes after I'd bought it when I had jumped out of the way of an Ottawa transit bus that had gotten too close to the sidewalk. Then there was the classic *Raiders of the Lost Ark* poster by Amsel that looked like a monochromatic sketch on a tan background, the one I'd stared at for hours as a youth while trying to figure out how to replicate the drawing style.

There were also quite a few smaller pictures and pin-ups, like a star chart, a world map identifying all the places I had wanted to visit (but never actually had), and a portrait of the *Greatest American Hero* with William Katt as Ralph Hinkley in his red super-suit flexing his non-existent bicep.

Then, dwarfing the rest of them, were three of my prized possessions: an authentic theatrical poster from each of the original trilogy *Star Wars* films that I'd bought from the guy who owned my hometown theater at the end of each film's local run. I smiled ruefully as I stared at the still-creased pieces of paper remembering how, just when these posters were starting to be worth something, Clay—my one-time best friend and roommate when I lived in Toronto—would sell them without me knowing for drug money.

The feelings that were flowing through me were admittedly at odds. As I looked up at the posters and remembered the betrayal they represented, it made me angry at first, but this was followed almost immediately by confusion when I realized that I was getting upset about something that, from my current perspective, hadn't even actually happened yet.

So, I moved on, shifting my drifting gaze enough so that I was now looking at my old desk, the sturdy kind that every teacher used in the 60s and 70s, the kind with a thick, solid-oak surface and three sturdy drawers to the right of the opening where your knees went. There had been drawers to the left too at one point, but my father had cut them off in order to fit it in my room.

Resting on top of the desk, against the back wall where it was out of the way, was my beat-up old tape deck piled high with cassette tapes, some of them actually in their cases. Beside this sat my beloved Commodore 64, with its huge monitor directly behind it, and a monster dot-matrix printer on a make-shift shelf attached to the wall to the right.

Behind and above the desk, there was a corkboard that was mostly covered with pictures, notes, and newspaper clippings. Then, hanging high above it all, were a few large models of the *Enterprise*, *Millennium Falcon*, and the *Battlestar Galactica*, arranged to look like they were heading off on the adventure together, just like my friends and I had always talked and written about, long before such homemade stories became called "fan fiction."

Finally pulling myself away from the room survey, I went to the closet to find something to wear for the day. Inside, I saw a bunch of shirts hanging there that I barely remembered, along with a bunch of extraordinarily thin ties suspended from a hanger that I'd bent into a rudimentary hook. Although I was relieved to find clothing that hadn't been influenced by *Miami Vice*, there was still a little too much pastel for my current taste, a taste that could best be described, I decided with a wry grin, as "futuristic."

Eventually, I slipped on a basic red t-shirt and covered it with a black and white plaid shirt with the sleeves rolled up. For pants, I decided on the pair of jeans that I found on the floor at the foot of the bed, even though they had clearly been worn the day before. Once I'd slid them on and buckled them up, I checked the pockets and I found a few coins (all dated appropriately), a set of keys (although I couldn't remember what they were for), as well as a familiar looking wallet with a few pieces of ID and a single ten-dollar bill.

According to my clock radio (currently playing *Careless Whisper* by Wham!), it was almost 8 AM. I couldn't recall what time the bus usually picked us up, but since my father hadn't been yelling of late and Patrick still hadn't made an appearance, I could only assume that I still had time.

OK, I wondered, standing the middle of my bedroom and looking around at a room that was rapidly becoming comfortable again. *What next? What about books?*

I finally located my school bag it under my desk. Perhaps predictably, the bag was the same kind of red and blue Adidas athletic tote bag that The Barenaked Ladies would immortalize in the late 90s in a song called *Grade 9,* a nostalgic recreation of a high school experience that would be roughly contemporaneous to my current temporal venue.

As I dropped the bag on my chair and zipped it open, it occurred to me that I could have figured out today's date simply by looking at the class notes that were in the binders inside of it. I took a quick mental inventory of the objects inside the sack, such as a pencil case, a math kit, an agenda that I'd fashioned out of a small notepad, a box of pencil crayons, and what might have been a chocolate bar, before pulling out my old binder.

The first thing I noticed upon flipping the binder open was a plastic sleeve that conveniently held my schedule, a tabular graph with each time period clearly marked and colour-coded, although I had no memory of what each colour signified, or what the little triangles in the corners of the cells meant. Thankfully, the schedule listed the room numbers for each class, although it completely failed to list my actual grade-level this year.

I rifled through the papers and notes looking for a mention of this fact, but eventually had to conclude that it probably wasn't listed because it was assumed that I should already know what grade I was in, so there was no point spelling it out. My best guess was that it was tenth grade, but that was a fuzzy estimate since I couldn't remember exactly how ages corresponded to grades in this time period, mostly because school conventions changed completely after the events of 2025. I had just begun to mentally chart out a table of school grades in relation to my birthday, when I could hear my father's voice in the hallway complaining loudly to Mom that we were both going to miss the geedee bus, and if we did, then he was going to drive slowly behind each of us to make sure that we walked the whole way to school.

Chuckling at what even my original seventeen-year-old self would have known was an empty threat, I threw everything into my bag, hoping that I wasn't forgetting anything, and managed to quietly slip past my father and down the stairs when he was looking the other way.

Not a minute later, and right on schedule, I could hear my brother Patrick explode out of his bedroom and sprint down the stairs with my father trailing right after him, haranguing him with each step. Out of the corner of my eye, I could see Dad stop short when he saw me sitting at the table beside my mother, innocently looking through the contents of the lunch bag that she had prepared for me. I glanced up at the two of them, prepared to look smug, but froze when I saw my brother.

I think my father was still speaking, but I wasn't paying him any attention, because I was too busy staring at Patrick. This was the first that I'd seen him since my unexpected arrival in the past this morning and I was momentarily taken aback by his size. Hell, I grew up with the guy, yet I had still somehow managed to forget just how tall and broad he was in comparison to the rest of the family, even at the still-tender age of nineteen. Not surprisingly, his unusual size — especially in comparison to mine — had led to a lot of good-natured ribbing over the years from people wondering who his real father had been. In fact, several years from now, the two of us would team up for an anniversary card for our parents and position ourselves to look like Arnold Schwarzenegger and Danny DeVito in their classic movie-poster pose from the movie *Twins*.

Patrick had the classic build of a football player, which was all the more ironic considering that our high school didn't actually have a football team. I never knew all the details, but the whole sport been cancelled in the entire Northern Ontario region a few years before I'd gotten to high school after some kind of tragic accident at a tournament or something. Patrick had been disappointed, to be sure, but it didn't hold him back. He was the kind of natural athlete that did well in pretty much any sport.

Patrick saw me staring at him as he pulled a couple of bananas off the bunch on the counter. "What?" he asked, an unspoken challenge clear in his voice. "Were these bananas part of one of your geeky science experiments?"

Unfortunately, my relationship with my brother had never been what you could call *easy*. Oh, sure it was cordial, but where my interests ran more intellectual, my brother's were clearly the opposite, and he was currently on track for what would turn out to be a very bright future in professional sports before he eventually shifted into a career as a firefighter for the city of Ottawa.

In his youth though, Patrick had been a jock through and through, and had not always been that kind whenever he teased me about being a geek. Still, I knew better than most that underneath the bluster, there was a genuine heart of gold.

Of course, I wouldn't really see much of that golden heart until our late twenties when we finally were able to truly connect and get past years of sibling rivalry. It was then that he finally revealed that he'd resented me throughout most of our teen years because I was always outdoing him. What's more, he'd had a great reputation at high school until I came along grabbing all of the attention and the glory with my academic awards.

Perhaps worst of all though, he was justified in feeling that I had been aloof towards him in our teen years. I *had* let my successes go to my head, and I *had* been pretty judgemental of his lower grades. If he felt stupid around me, it was at least in part because I actively tried to make him feel that way.

The distant squeal of brakes from outside the house triggered some kind of latent memory in me, and I knew without needing confirmation that the bus was here. Patrick was already moving towards the door, grunting a goodbye to our parents. Gathering my Adidas bag, and slinging it over my left shoulder, I began following after him. As I passed Mom, I stopped quickly to hug her.

"Thanks for packing my lunch, Mom. I'm sure it will be as delicious as always," I said as I kissed her forehead. When I turned around, it was to see my father and brother staring at me. Apparently, this expression of appreciation was something else that was out of character for teenaged me.

"Suck-up," muttered Patrick so that only I could hear him, even as he called out over his shoulder, "Thanks for the lunch, Ma!" before pulling the front door open and sprinting out across the driveway towards the bus. He covered the distance quickly and even though I ran after him at a pace that was much faster than anything that I'd run in years, I was still left in his dust. By the time I'd climbed the stairs and nodded a good morning to the bus driver, Patrick had already settled into a seat about half-way down the long vehicle.

As I carefully moved down the aisle, not used to a bus that had row seating and that wasn't wholly dedicated to being used as a living space, I casually wondered again about what I was doing here back in time. If there was even a slight possibility that I could use it as an opportunity to fix past mistakes, I was going to start with my relationship with Patrick.

The way he stared at me after he reluctantly moved his legs to let me take the space by the window beside him, made it more than a little obvious that this was not a normal state of affairs.

"So," I began tentatively as Patrick shoved half a banana in his mouth and began chewing loudly. "How's it going eh?" I was pretty sure that *SCTV's* Bob and Doug McKenzie were popular around this time period, and I seemed to recall that everyone was mimicking their speech patterns and Canuck-based expressions.

"Can I ask you a strange question?"

Patrick stopped chewing long enough so that a viscous thread of spittle escaped from the side of his mouth and slid slowly down the side of his chin. From the confused, quasi-belligerent expression on my brother's face, I was clearly violating some kind of communication protocol by attempting to engage him in conversation. How could he have known that, from my perspective, he and I hadn't actually seen each other in some fifteen years? How could he know that I dearly wanted to have one of our deep conversations, the kind we had standing vigil over my father's death bed when we both desperately needed to feel a strong connection with a family member while another member of that family was quietly slipping away. We'd waited decades to find out that there was more that connected us than held us apart.

How could Patrick know that I wanted to start that process of discovery earlier in our lives? Now that I'd inexplicably been given the opportunity to do so.

As the bus picked up speed and bounced its way down the road, Patrick finally grunted a non-committal response to my question, before immediately going back to chewing his banana, making it very clear that he wasn't open to a game of Q and A. So, I went in a different direction and made a few feeble attempts to get a conversation going, but each one of his responses was a little more remote than the last. Not that it mattered much by this point anyhow because, once the scenery began to change, my attention got pulled away entirely.

I was now staring out the window at my childhood hometown of Robertson, Ontario. The bus was just now in the process of passing out of the town's rural surroundings and into the regular system of streets, a division traditionally marked by the truck stop on the edge of town with a Canadian flag the size of an Olympic sized swimming pool flying from a pole that was at least three-stories tall. It was this flag, perhaps more than anything else, that made me realize that I was well and truly in my hometown because it had always been the first thing I had seen whenever I had been coming home, no matter what time of day or night.

When I was a kid, my father had turned this flag into a game that would signal an end to our road trips. When we had been approaching Robertson, driving home from wherever we'd been traveling together as a family, he'd have us all watching for the flag. The first person to spot it and call out "I see the maple leaf!" won a prize, which was never more than him running his fingers through our hair afterwards and saying "Good job." Those moments of praise and affection were, to this day, some of the sweetest prizes that I'd ever been awarded.

As we passed the gas station, I whispered wistfully out the window as tears began to flow, "I see the maple leaf, Dad. I'm home."

Patrick must have heard what I'd said and had likely noticed that I was crying, because he was looking at me with an expression I would come to know well years from now—one of genuine concern. My brother had never been one to ignore genuine distress. It was what would make him such a good firefighter, I suppose. As much as he had teased me as a child, he had also always been there with a joke or something equally distracting to lift my spirits when I was clearly distraught.

"What is it?" Patrick finally grunted, almost reluctantly. "What's your strange question?"

I sniffed a few times and wiped at my eyes before responding through a broad smile. "Actually, I don't have one yet. I just wanted to know that I could ask it when one finally occurs to me."

Despite himself, Patrick laughed. A quick snort of his nose accompanied by an almost imperceptible smile. "You really are a freak," he said, almost affectionately as he pulled a Sports magazine out of his bag and began thumbing through it, effectively signalling an end to all further conversation.

I didn't mind so much though. The ice had been broken, and that was enough for now. I just really wanted to get back to looking out the bus window at a town that I'd never thought to ever see again, much less as it was in 1985.

Robertson was a mining town in Northern Ontario, with a population of roughly five thousand, and located about an hour north-east of Timmins, and about eight long hours north of Toronto. It was originally a tiny trading outpost for the Hudson's Bay Company, being located where two large rivers merged into one before flowing into James Bay some three hundred kilometers to the north. The outpost had been pretty much completely abandoned in the mid-1800s until a huge silver deposit had been discovered close-by in the early 1900s, at which point it exploded into a full-fledged town almost overnight.

Robertson's biggest claim to fame, other than the silver mine that ultimately ran dry in the 1960s, was that it was named after an ancestor of the guy that invented the Robertson screw driver. At least that was one theory. I'd also heard that, way back, it was actually called Robertstown, named after Obadiah Roberts, the prospector who discovered the silver deposit, but was changed because of a clerical error on a legal document that was too expensive to redo.

And I was back in it. Back in Robertson.

Yet, to my chagrin, I wasn't getting a chance to see that much of it on this ride because the route that the bus took to get to school, although slightly circuitous, wasn't all that comprehensive. I could get a feel for the town now, with its dwarfish trees, and its single-storey structures and occasional row housing, but a thorough tour would have to wait until later, because a building that played such a large roll in my teenaged years was just now coming into sight.

The high school in my northern Ontario town of Robertson was a sprawling brick structure with a squat two stories and a student population of about five hundred, distributed over five grades from nine to thirteen (Ontario wouldn't eliminate the thirteenth grade until a few years after I'd graduated.) There was only one high school in Robertson, as the town really wasn't big enough for more than that. Like most of the communities in Northern Ontario, Robertson had a vibrant Franco-Ontario population, but it still wasn't quite big enough to support a dedicated French secondary school, so we had been grouped together into a single bilingual high school, making the small-town stereotype of everybody knowing everybody else even more pronounced. If all the kids didn't know each other directly, they at least knew *of* each other. What's more, the teachers knew our parents, and in many cases, the teachers *were* our parents. We couldn't get away with much, although we certainly tried. Well, some of us anyhow. Mostly my brother.

I had had some excellent times in this building, and met a few life-long friends along the way too.

And then there was Andi.

I sighed as I thought about my first love, Andi Petras. In Grade 11, she and I made it our mission to explore every nook, cranny, or hidden area of the high school for tender moments that seemed to last forever no matter how briefly they might actually have been.

Andi had been equal parts smarts and passion, two things that had fueled her rebellious nature and headstrong attitude, something she had always claimed was owing to her Greek heritage. Her unique name was actually an abbreviation of the much longer and more traditional one that her parents had given her, one that she hated so much that she hadn't even told me what it was until we'd been seriously dating for well over a year.

At the same time, she revealed that she had actually been in the process of defying her parents by changing it legally, because the abbreviation was too much of a boy's name. But then she had seen *The Goonies,* and had been excited to be introduced to Kerri Green's character "Andy," and suddenly, she hadn't felt so alone anymore. But even that excitement paled in comparison to the unbridled euphoria she felt a few years later when her favourite actress, Molly Ringwald, played a character named Andie Walsh in *Pretty in Pink,* a movie by her favourite director, John Hughes. Suddenly all of the planets were in alignment, and, as far as Andi was concerned, hers was the best name ever.

It doesn't take a time traveler to appreciate how funny it is how things turn out. The universe is playing the ultimate long game.

Truth be told, I was relieved that I wasn't going to be running into Andi today, because her family didn't move up north until the beginning of Grade 11. As much as I'd have loved to see her again, she'd be a lot to handle right now with everything else that I'll have to adjust to, both today and beyond (if this time-slip thing persists, that is.)

The school bus had come to a stop in front of the school in a line with four or five other buses, and the kids were all clamouring to stand up to be the first off. Patrick waited until everyone else had moved out of the way before easing his muscular bulk into the aisle. Pulling my Adidas bag from the floor, I followed after him.

The last one off the bus, I could hear the doors hiss shut behind me as I took a step onto the school's lawn and stared at the red-brick building in front of me. Patrick had stopped to wait for me, as if sensing that I was out of sorts today. For a moment, it seemed like he was going to walk with me, until somebody in the group of sports-jersey clad jocks by the nearby student parking lot called out to him. My brother narrowed his eyes at me searchingly, before punching me solidly on the shoulder and striding away.

"Keep your honey-stick in your pants," he said to me over his shoulder, before adding, "Geek."

With Patrick gone, I took a few tentative steps away from the bus, after making a mental note of the route number beneath the big side mirror so that I knew which one to board at the end of the day. All around me, dozens and dozens of excited teenagers, many of whom I could just barely recognize, were streaming across the grass aiming for a handful of school entrances. I merged with the moving throng as I watched Patrick join up with his hockey buddies and lumber off collectively towards a group of girls, one of whom I recognized from a distance as his long-time girlfriend, Monique (she was actually his beard, but I wouldn't know this for another couple of years). I hadn't expected to rely on Patrick today, but I did feel a little vulnerable without him with the rush of nostalgic feelings making me feeling a little more sentimental than usual. If I wasn't careful, the teens around me would smell my fear, and turn into the pack of uncivilized animals that they were always on the brink of becoming.

Anybody watching me walk through the doors to my old high school must have thought that I looked like a tourist or something, the way my head was zipping around looking at everything as if for the first time. With the pressure of so many of us streaming through the metal fire doors and into the school, I couldn't stop and look and touch as much as I wanted to. When I finally entered the main hall — the one that was lined on one side by large windows and the other side by lockers and classrooms — my first reaction was that the place seemed *tiny*. Far too small to have been the same hallways from my memory. Far too small to have occupied that much space in my mind all these years.

Clearly, my first, and perhaps biggest challenge today would be remembering where my locker was and what its combination was. I had been here for five years of high school. That meant that I had been in at least five different lockers, not including the number of times that I'd moved without asking permission. I could find no mention of either in my binder, nor hidden anywhere in the Adidas bag that I was currently wearing like so many other students were, as a backpack.

Where the hell had my locker been in Grade 10?

With every step closer to a problem for which I had no potential solution, I kept thinking back to Oskar's philosophy on life. We'd spent hours in his makeshift bar in the Pucks exchanging stories and viewpoints, and he had definitely impressed me with his ideas that staying in the moment in any situation and looking for both opportunities and inspiration was the best way to live. He even had a computer animation playing on a loop on an old iPad on the wall behind the bar that showed a wise old monk leaping into the sky, seemingly at nothing, before miraculously landing on a cloud that supported his weight long enough until he could leap again into the void, where he'd conveniently find another cloud. Oskar told me that the animation represented the ultimate leap of faith. That each time that monk jumped, he wasn't jumping *towards* an existing cloud, he was jumping knowing without a doubt that one would be there just when it was needed.

I may have scoffed at the idea initially when he told it to me, but after several years of it being reinforced, usually with copious amounts of bitter tasting alcohol, I began to see it working in my own life, and his too. I mean, how the hell else could you explain the microbus appearing when it did?

So, here I was, walking into my old high school, fully present, and full of the faith that the very thing that I needed would appear to me just when I needed it the most.

And that's when it hit me: I didn't have to wander around aimlessly trying to figure out where I belonged, I already knew where I belonged.

I'm not really sure how it started, but sometime in my second year, those of us who didn't quite fit with the "in" crowd because of our mutual love of everything that wasn't mainstream in the 80s (like science fiction, or comics, or video games, or Dungeons and Dragons, to name a select few) started meeting before and between classes in front of a large window on the second floor. We'd exchange ideas, trade comics, get excited about upcoming movies, or even re-enact the plotlines of genre television programs that some of us may have missed the night before (this was in the days before it became commonplace to record television shows on video tape or, later, TiVo and PVR).

This area was where I'd finally heard all about what had happened in the pilot episode of *The Greatest American Hero*, how Indiana Jones had known to keep his eyes closed during the climax of *Raiders of the Lost Ark*, or even how he'd hitched a ride on the outside of a submarine, and it's where I'd first been told about a little upcoming movie named *E.T.*

Eventually, this meeting area became known as *geek window*, and us geeks had it to all to ourselves, not because we discouraged others from joining us, but mostly because nobody wanted to be associated with the likes of us. It was a lot like the couch in the *Central Perk* coffee shop on *Friends* in that everyone knew it was our spot and to stay away from it.

As I exited the stairwell that emptied onto the school's second floor and turned down the hallway that led to geek window, I could see that there was a group of about a half dozen kids already gathered there listening intently to something that Calvin Ferguson was saying. I smiled when I saw Calvin. It's not so much that I'd forgotten about him, it's just that I hadn't actually thought about him in years. He was our unofficial nerd King, a position that was well-deserved because he was most assuredly the most passionate and unapologetic geek that I'd ever had the pleasure of knowing.

He was currently talking about something that had him so excited that, even from halfway down the hallway, I could see his arms waving animatedly. I wasn't the only one who noticed him either. A couple of dudes were walking beside me and speaking loudly enough for me to hear one of them refer derisively to Calvin and my friends gathered around him as "Fucking fairy-tale freaks."

I really wanted to both praise the guy on his clever alliteration as well as to correct him by pointing out that, strictly speaking, they were actually fans of fantasy and science fiction and *not* fairy-tales, but I was pretty sure that such distinctions were beyond his pay grade.

More importantly though, the dude's derogatory comments made me want to tell all of my geek friends not to let idiots like this Neanderthal get to them, because there would be a day in about twenty-five years when being a bona fide geek would become something to aspire to. That's when superhero movies would become all the rage, and books like *Harry Potter* and *Game of Thrones* would dominate, and all of the popular kids that shunned and mocked nerds like us in high school would suddenly embrace our culture and start claiming on social media that they too had always been geeks at heart.

Especially women.

This was something that had always confused me. Around about the 2010s, at the peak of geek culture, I started having conversations online with some of the girls that I'd known in high school and, suddenly, they were quoting my favourite movies and TV shows, or telling me about the books we had in common, or sharing their theories on how Boba Fett might have escaped the Sarlacc pit, or how they'd cried during the lighting of the beacons in the third *Lord of the Rings* movie, *Return of the King*. When I had asked these women how long they'd been interested in geek culture, they claimed that they had always been nerds, even in high school!

But, here I was, back in the hallways of that very high school, and I was looking at incontrovertible evidence to the contrary. The group currently gathered in front of geek window was exclusively male, just as it always had been, and just as it always would be. Right now, in 1985, geeks were still girl-kryptonite, and being seen associating with one was clique suicide.

I'd almost reached the window by now, but was slowed by the throng of kids bunching up where two hallways intersected. As I brushed by so many people, I found myself wondering, for the briefest of moments, if perhaps I wasn't the only one who had mysteriously slipped through time last night. I began to search faces for others, like myself, who might not belong here. Somebody looking lost, or confused, or over-nostalgic. I hadn't been looking very long when, soberly, I realized that I very likely had to have been the only one to have shifted in time from 2035, for the simple reason that pretty much every single person I was looking at in this school would be dead in some forty years.

For just a few seconds, despite being surrounded by dozens of other people, I felt completely alone. Sighing, I pushed through the last of the crowd and walked over to stand beside Calvin, who was, even now, making it more than a little obvious that he was NOT a time-traveler.

"...heard it from my cousin in Sudbury," he was saying to a chorus of impressed oooooo's from kids who were clearly under the impression that Sudbury was the 'big city,' and everyone who lived there was so much more in the know than those of us who lived in the backwater of Robertson. "Hey Josh," he said parenthetically to me before continuing. "So anyway, he has it on good authority that George Lucas wants to go back and film the first three *Star Wars* stories... (there was a loud chorus of murmurs at this, but Calvin ignored them all in favour of pushing through to the next part of his news) ...maybe even continue Luke, Leia, and Han's story in the next three chapters, and — this is the best part — it's gonna happen soon. Like in the next few years."

It was all I could do to suppress a laugh at how far off his projection was, and the fact that everyone else in the group was reacting with excitement to what he was saying led me to suspect that none of them knew what I did, and this meant that none of them were likely fellow time-travelers either. While the others were expressing their delight at the news, one of the youngest members of the group (whose name I just couldn't quite recall) made the mistake of asking out loud, "The first three?"

Immediately, everyone stopped talking. I hadn't seen Calvin in years, but nonetheless I joined everyone else in wincing at the tirade that this innocent comment was bound to evoke from our King who thought that everyone who hung out at geek window should already be aware of the most well-known parts of *Star Wars* trivia. Calvin surprised us though, and very calmly replied, "When Lucas had first begun to write *Star Wars*, he realized very early on that he had way too much material for one movie, so he split it all up, eventually sketching out nine in total. Then, when it came time to make the first movie, he decided to start with the fourth episode in the story, since, at the time, there was no guarantee he'd be able to make more than one movie. He figured that Episode four, more than any of the others, could stand on its own if it had to."

As the kid was asking more questions about what happened in the first three episodes (nobody knew yet that such a thing was called a "prequel"), and just as Calvin was telling him about how Obi-Wan had apparently defeated Anakin Skywalker and left him for dead in the volcanic sith pits, which is what turned him into Darth Vader, I was abruptly distracted by a pair of hands suddenly blocking my eyes and a voice beside my ear saying "Guess who?"

Seriously? Today of all days?

I decided not to even play the game, so I playfully grabbed the hands and moved them from my eyes and spun around. I was about to say "Hey you," to whomever had been familiar enough to play this guessing game with me, only to find my mouth unable to function due to the sudden application of a pair of lips that appeared to belong to a young, dark-haired girl.

I froze right up, but she didn't seem to notice. Eventually, she stopped kissing me and pulled me into a hug. "I've missed you," she said.

Andi.

Wait. What? Andi!?

Oh shit.

"Andi!" I blurted without thinking. "What are you doing here?"

"I should ask you the same, Mister," she replied good-naturedly. "We were supposed to meet at my locker this morning, remember?"

I blinked a few times as the obvious occurred to me. Unless Andi was a temporal anachronism, this was Grade 11.

If Andi noticed how stiff I was or that I wasn't exactly returning her hug, she didn't say anything. Instead, she whispered quietly into my ear so that only I could hear her, "Hey babe, wanna make *in* at lunch? My parents are still down in Toronto."

Oh My God. I'd completely forgotten about the very unfortunate expression that I'd made up in my teens. Basically, *making in* was just like *making out*, but it involved getting *in*side of each other's clothing.

I know what you're thinking, I thought in my best Magnum P.I. voice, *I was a real Hemingway with the way I could turn a phrase back then.*

Frantically, I did the math in my head, adjusting now for the fact that I had been off by a year in my earlier estimation as to what grade I was in back in 1985. It was April. This meant that the Petras family had just moved to Robertson from the Danforth area of Toronto the previous August (although she and her parents still travelled there often to visit family, which is where Andi had obviously just returned from on her own). Andi and I had met the previous Autumn, become very good friends, with our relationship finally becoming self-aware in February when we'd fallen off a ski-doo together into a snowbank with her on top of me, and we'd just started kissing. That meant that she and I had been dating for what, about two months? We'd just started getting physical, mostly by sneaking over to her house at lunch while her parents were away or at work.

When I hadn't responded to her proposition, she eventually stepped back and glared at me suspiciously, giving me my first really good look at her.

Fuck. Had she ever been that young?

I blinked back at her, even though I knew that I had to respond soon but… well, she was just so goddamned young! Sure, we were the same age bodily, but mentally, I had every single person in this school beat in that regard. Even the ancient English teacher Mrs. Cloutier, who retired (or rather, was about to retire) at the tender age of something like 64. To make matters worse, strictly speaking, I was still married, kind of, and it would feel like I was cheating on Celeste. I had to find a way…

"Josh?" Andi said, concern finally creeping onto features that had never in my memory shown anything else besides geniality and affability.

In response, I did the only thing I could think of doing, and I just kissed her. It was the only way that I could buy enough time to figure out how to rebuff her offer but also soften the rejection enough so as not to insult her. It was a slow, lingering kiss, mostly because I needed that much time to think.

From the unfocused look in her eyes as I pulled away afterwards, I had to assume the desperate ploy to distract her had worked, thanks in large part to the fact that, since I'd last locked lips with this young woman, I'd literally had decades to practice kissing and, at one point, had even had a most excellent teacher. Her name had been Heather, and we had dated off and on in University for a couple of years.

When we had first gotten together during Frosh week though, she'd told me in no uncertain terms that I had no idea how to use my lips, so she took it upon herself to teach me "for the sake of your future lovers" (which was ironic since she actually became one of those future lovers when we met again in Toronto a few years after we'd graduated, and had gotten married shortly thereafter).

But, during those first few weeks of University, with Heather as my new teacher, I had been a very enthusiastic student. And, from the dreamy look on Andi's face now (not unlike the look on Lois Lane's face after Clark kissed her in *Superman II* and magically modified her memory to make her forget that he was Superman) and the fact that her mouth was still hanging open, my lessons with Heather had indeed paid off.

"Hi Andi," I said warmly, having finally found the words to speak to her, as well as a plausible excuse for not going over to her house at lunch. "I'm so sorry, but … well, I can't come over today. I have to practice my, … um, music. Rain check? … Please?"

In response, Andi blinked weakly a few times, and then smiled. "Um, sure," she finally said as she leaned in closer for a hug. "But only if you promise to kiss me like that again."

Thank heavens she didn't ask how it was that I suddenly knew how to kiss.

At the same time, we both noticed that the group gathered at geek window was no longer making any noise and neither was Calvin's voice sharing the prevailing *Star Wars* theories of the day. Andi and I broke out of our hug and looked over to find that every single one of the boys were staring at us wide-eyed, clearly not used to such overt displays of affection in a high school corridor.

Andi giggled at the attention, the fugue brought on by my kiss having finally dissipated, before grabbing my hand, and pulling me down the hall and away from our appreciative audience. As we walked away, I could hear Calvin calling after me, so I turned back towards him even as I tried to keep up with Andi.

"Hey Donegal," Calvin said loudly so he could be heard over the sea of chatting kids all around us. "It's your turn to host next week, right?"

The blank look on my face hadn't lingered very long before he realized that I had no idea of which he spoke, so he immediately followed up with, "...for the next Video Recital. I've got *Blade Runner*, and I've been practicing!"

"The Director's Cut?" I asked without thinking. That took the smile off his mouth as he looked at me dumbly in response. I could barely hear him calling out, "What's a director's cut" as Andi pulled me away through the throng of students. "You and your geek friends," she said affectionately as she rolled her eyes. "What's a Video Recital again?"

"Um," I answered hesitantly because the answer was quite frankly coming back to me just as quickly as I was delivering it to Andi.

"It's a video party where we, uh, play popular science fiction movies," I began to explain even as I smiled bittersweetly to myself. In the future, I'd told my kids about the video party phenomenon a number of times. It had become my generation's version of the tired old "you kids don't appreciate how hard things were when I was your age" story. I had tried to tell them that they didn't know how lucky they were to be able to pull up pretty much whatever movie they wanted at any time they wanted, on whatever hand-held device they wanted. Because, "in my day", I had told them, the only way to watch a movie was when it was scheduled to be shown, either in a theater or on TV. And you had to take what was offered too, since there was no such thing like being able to make a movie request like you could with radio stations for songs.

This all changed when video stores came along and rented out movies on video tape. The only problem though, at least in the beginning, was that the machines on which to play these video tapes were very expensive to own, but you could rent them for short periods, so that's where the idea of video parties came from. This was when we'd pool our money and rent a VCR video machine for a weekend, along with a whole bunch of movies, and invite a big group of friends over to stay up late together and watch them all one after the other, along with a small country's GDP worth of soda pop, chips, and popcorn.

By 1985 though, most of our families owned VCRs, but it was still fun to get together as a group to catch the latest releases anyhow. I knew that Andi was familiar with the concept of the video party, but what I was trying to explain to her now was that, because my geek friends and I had seen all our favourite movies multiple times over, we put a twist on the video party convention by turning it into a *recital*.

"While we watch the movies, well... we call out the dialogue in time with the ... um, actors. We watch three movies at a time, and the guy who knows the most dialogue wins the, um, crown. It's best two out of three."

Andi laughed, but not derisively. "Sounds like fun," she said. "Are girls allowed?"

"Well... I can't remember. I don't think we ever had a girl who actually *wanted* to come."

"It's a good thing I'm babysitting then," she said. "Otherwise I might come and challenge you all to do a John Hughes film instead."

I laughed at the image of my high school geek friends being in the same room as an attractive young woman like Andi. "They wouldn't be able to speak. A smart and gorgeous girl like you would definitely have the advantage."

Andi looked at me funny, as if this kind of compliment was unusual for me, then the moment passed and she asked, "You guys have an actual crown?"

"Yeah, it's the inside straps from a hard hat; the part that tightens around your head. Calvin Krazy-glued a couple of action figures around the top, and each winner gets to write his name and date when he won it in black Sharpie, and he gets to keep it until the next party. Kinda like the Stanley Cup. It, well, um, it gives whoever has it special magical powers at our Dungeons and Dragons games too." I made a mental note to check and see if I had the crown at home before the next video party. Ironically, although I didn't know where it was right now, I did recall that I ended up with the crown after high school (after my triumphant recitation on our celebratory final recital of *Back to the Future*, *Wrath of Khan*, and *Raiders of the Lost Ark*, during which it seemed like, even to me, that I had been channelling the movies) and had even gone so far as to build a glass display case for it.

The whole time that we'd been talking I'd been letting Andi lead the way to my locker since I had no precise idea where it was until we got close enough for it to finally come back to me.

"Oh," Andi continued. "Are we still on for Saturday night? Phoebe and Brock want us to confirm."

Inwardly, I groaned. Phoebe had been Andi's best friend when she'd lived in Toronto, before the Petras family had moved up north, and they'd kept in touch.

"Oh sure," I answered as enthusiastically as I could (the last thing I needed today was for Andi to get insecure about our relationship all of a sudden, especially since I'd just turned her down for a *make in* session.) "Absolutely. I'd almost forgotten that she was in town," I lied.

"Yeah, her parents will be visiting my parents for a few days, and she thought it would be nice to have a double date. I told you all this already," a hint of irritation in her voice. "Remember. She's bringing her fiancé Brock to meet us."

Oh God.

Now it was all coming back to me. I remembered meeting the two of them when they were on this, their engagement tour, showing off a diamond ring the size of a baby's fist to all of Phoebe's old friends. If memory served, Phoebe was about a year older than Andi (who, like me, would have been seventeen now), and Brock was a few years older than that, and was the heir to some huge Canadian beer company or something, which made him practically royalty. They were both the epitome of yuppies, a term that I'm pretty sure hadn't even been invented yet.

The only thing more noteworthy about Brock, aside from the fact that he was quite shameless in showing off how rich he was, was the way in which he mangled the English language in an obvious effort to appear more macho. Even in the 80s, I was convinced that his whole act was nothing more than a transparent ploy to mask his evident homosexuality, something that I'm pretty sure was closeted only to him — and maybe Phoebe. In fact, it was something that was confirmed several years later when I ran into an adult Andi at a reunion, and she told me that Brock had finally left Phoebe and their kids for a man, and everybody was a lot happier as a result.

We had arrived by now at my locker, so I pretended that my arms were full (in anticipation of this ruse, I'd unslung the Adidas bag earlier, and had been surreptitiously grabbing books and things out of it as we walked). So, I asked Andi, "Would you mind, um, getting the lock? My hands are, um… full."

"Sure," she answered brightly to my great relief. I'd forgotten how much Andi loved opening my locker for me. For her, it was a form of intimacy that she knew my combination when nobody else did, and that she even had her own area on the makeshift shelf that I'd built above the locker's bottom so that there would be room for wet boots. In high school, these two aspects were akin to living together, even though it wasn't all that visible to the casual onlooker. If you *really* wanted to advertise the fact that you were in a committed relationship in Northern Ontario in the 80s, you would sit right up beside each other on the bench seat of a pick-up truck like you were crowding the steering wheel, even when there was plenty of room closer to the passenger's side. Naturally, this led to more than a few pranks amongst the teenaged boys if ever there were three of them crammed into a truck. When the truck passed a group of people, the one by the passenger door would bend over to hide, thus making it look like the other two boys were sitting right up beside each other, and were, by extension, a couple.

As Andi spun the tiny dial on my combination lock, I watched carefully over her shoulder. The code that I watched the pointer land on felt familiar, but I repeated the numbers in my head a few times just to cement them in my memory anyhow. I was greatly relieved to have things work out so perfectly this morning in respect to access to my locker, because my only other option would have been to go to the office and ask to have my lock cut off, once I had been forced to admit that I didn't know where said locker was.

Thanks Oskar!

With the locker open, we didn't have much time to linger, because the crowds in the halls were obviously beginning to thin as students began to make their way to their respective home rooms. As if noticing this fact too, Andi excused herself, pulled me in for a quick kiss, and was off down the hallway a moment later saying, "See you in third period, Josh!"

"Um, Sure," I answered, waving weakly at her back. I had time to pull my binder out of my Adidas bag, hang it up in my locker (with one strap on each the coat hook on either side of the locker so that the bag was suspended just below the top shelf), close the locker and click the lock into place (upside down, I realized too late) and head off in the direction of the room whose number I'd thankfully noticed scrawled in the margins of my schedule this morning.

Entering my homeroom classroom as the national anthem was playing over the speakers, I was finally face to face with another challenge that I'd knew I'd be facing multiple times today: figuring out where I normally sat. Thankfully, there were only a handful of seats available, most of which were along the back row. I knew for a fact that I never sat all the way in the back (I was too much of a keener for that), so chose the only seat left in the front row.

As I sat down, I nodded at my home room teacher, remembering as I looked in his direction never to actually stare at him. Until I saw Alphonse Grenier, I'd all but forgotten about his distracting, and oh-so-obvious combover, and now it was all I could do not to squint at it wonderingly as I puzzled out (again) exactly how and why he styled it the way he did.

The kids in my school had debated long and hard over the years as to exactly what concoction Monsieur Grenier used to secure the coiled strand of hair to his scalp, with our best guess being that it was equal parts motor oil and industrial-strength adhesive. Not that it mattered all that much in the end though because whatever it was had never actually worked all that well. Despite the poor man's best efforts over the course of the school day, his hair would inevitably (and frequently) fall out of place, eventually ending up as a snake-like clump of glistening hair that hung down at least as far as his shoulder.

True to form, whenever this happened, Monsieur Grenier never acknowledged it beyond mechanically coiling the hair back into place, before pulling a semi-translucent handkerchief from his suit pocket to wipe the oily goo from his fingers.

Personally, I'd never actually had a class with Grenier (I'm pretty sure he taught welding, which was surprising considering how much incendiary liquid his head was bathed in), which I always considered to be a good thing, because I was distracted enough by his head in my home room alone. Years later, when my own hair was rapidly receding, it was thanks to Grenier's ridiculous antics of trying to fool others into thinking that he still had hair, that I decided to forgo ego, and simply shave my entire head instead.

As Grenier took attendance, I was trying to remember when the man had retired. I was pretty sure that this would be his last year at the school because, if memory served, in next year's Christmas assembly one of my classmates will get himself in trouble with the administration for performing a sketch about a recently retired teacher who, dressed as an evil scientist and working in a basement chemistry lab, created a powerful epoxy to permanently glue his obvious toupee to the top of his head. The character then proceeded to get high from the fumes coming off his chemistry experiment and destroy his lab as he hallucinated that his former students were coming back to haunt him as demons.

Naturally, the student got into trouble for his performance, not for so obviously skewering Grenier, but instead for the drug references. It was because of that student that the school administration thereafter insisted on signing-off on all sketches and performances at school assemblies.

With the attendance and announcements finished, there were about five minutes left in homeroom so, for lack of anything better to do, I browsed through my agenda. My father had always taught me to only buy something when you couldn't make it yourself, and my agenda was certainly proof of that concept. It had started out as a small coil notepad that I had gone through and calendarized by splitting each page into two days, each of which was clearly labelled. In school, I had used it to keep track of milestones that were coming up, when homework was due, and what to expect in each subject.

Perhaps most amusingly, I had also jotted down a comment at the end of each day that best summarized something that I'd learned in the course of it. Titled simply the "PTOTD" (for Profound Thought Of The Day), the recorded observation was never more than a line or two. Skimming back a few weeks in the agenda, I read a few of the pithy observations, marvelling not only at how much they resembled tweets but mostly how they were neither particularly profound or thoughtful. Well, not to the mind of a sexagenarian anyhow. Still, they were an interesting insight into the psyche of a seventeen-year-old white male who didn't realize just how privileged his pasty ass was.

Putting the agenda aside, I scanned the list of today's upcoming classes in my binder, as I deliberated what to expect from today, a prospect that was all the more complicated now that Andi was back in the picture. Andi said that she'd see me in third period which, according to my schedule, was History. I chuckled as I thought about studying a topic like that as a time-traveler. If those who forget history are condemned to repeat it, can the same be said of a time-traveler who forgets that which, to everyone else, hasn't even happened yet? Would I be condemned to repeat it myself?

Now, how's that for a Profound Thought of the Day?

It was at this moment, that something occurred to me about a possible side-effect if this time-slip experience persists.

Will I start to forget my own past? Will I begin to forget the future?

I had no idea how this time displacement thing worked. Presumably, my future consciousness somehow installed itself into my past body and, in the process, superimposed itself over my existing consciousness. What had happened to that consciousness? Was it still around somewhere? Would it slowly start to reassert itself? Was it possible, the longer I spent in this particular timeline, that I would forget about my future because it no longer existed? Would things readjust?

I had no idea.

What's more, there were also stories about time-travel that I'd either read or watched in which the travellers eventually "disremembered" their former lives through some fail-safe mechanism in the universe as it healed itself after a disruption in the space-time continuum. If this were true, then it was entirely possible that, even within a few short weeks, the entire fifty years that I'd lived since I was back in 1985 the first time would feel like little more than a vaguely-remembered dream.

I could think of only one solution to this possibility: I was going to have to write things down. I was going to have to start a journal that, among other things, documented a history that hadn't actually happened yet.

CHAPTER 3
Excerpt from Josh's journal

I've never kept a journal before. Am I supposed to write it informally, or compose it like I'm writing a story—with punctuation and dialogue and everything like that?

I dunno, so what say I just start jotting stuff down and see where it takes me.

I'm using this journal to record details of the future as I remember them. I have no idea what in hell's going on with me, but I'm concerned that, if this time-displacement experience persists, my memories of everything might start to fade, so I feel that it's important to set them down before that happens.

By the way, if you're reading this without my permission, it's just a science-fiction themed story that I'm working on. If you've ever pissed me off, then there's a good chance that I've either named or based a character on you, so happy reading trying to figure out which one it is.

Oh yeah. SPOILERS. Nobody knows who River Song is yet, (hell, nobody knows what a "spoiler" is yet) but that word makes more sense if you can imagine her saying it.

Well, let's start with how I got here...

So, last Thursday morning, I woke up in my own past, awoken abruptly by music that even my slumbering mind knew was out of place.

Just to be clear, my temporal displacement wasn't immediately obvious to me, not by any stretch of the imagination. At first, as far as I had been concerned, I was still in the *Ensee* cell that I'd been "invited" to move into a few weeks earlier. Which is why I found it odd that there was suddenly music in a room that I knew for a fact was devoid of electronic devices capable of broadcasting sound.

Then, there was the choice of music. Somehow, I found it highly unlikely that my captors were into 80s soft-pop, although I briefly entertained the idea that they were playing it to torture me, which would never have worked anyhow since I'd always preferred music that was slow and sentimental.

In any event, I pretended to be sleep anyhow, hoping that if my captors thought I was still unconscious, I could catch them talking to each other again. Maybe I could have learned something new. Maybe I could have finally found out if Casey had managed to transmit a message before they had...

I can't even finish writing that sentence without the risk of replaying the scene in my mind, again. What I had watched them do to the little guy was horrific. In fact, one of the things that had kept me going in the long hours in solitary confinement was the hope that maybe, just maybe, there'd be some kind of reckoning for Remmus and his ilk for what they had done, not just to Casey, but to all the others too. Funny how that's all a pipe dream now, eh? How can you possibly hold somebody accountable for heinous crimes that he hasn't even committed yet?

So, anyhow, after the music had woken me up, I had been focusing so hard on pretending to be asleep that it took me way too long to become aware of certain, oh let's call them, INCONSISTENCIES.

For one, once the song was over, a very jocular Disc Jockey announced that the tune had been REO Speedwagon's LATEST song: *Can't Fight This Feeling*. It was so new, he'd said, that this had been the first time he'd heard it, and he "loved, loved, LOVED it!"

"This song's gonna be huge," he had added. "Mebbe not Michael Jackson huge, but huge nonetheless."

At that point, curiosity got the better of me and I had decided to risk opening my eyes a little, at which point I was presented with the second inconsistency: I was looking up at the ceiling. This meant that, unless the laws of gravity had somehow repealed themselves while I had been unconscious, I had been sleeping on my back. This might not seem too unusual to most people, but you have to understand that as a heavy-set man pushing seventy, my mild to moderate sleep apnea hadn't let me sleep on my back for decades.

The third inconsistency presented itself to me when I tried to brush something off my forehead only to find out that it was hair, something else that hadn't been a part of my life for decades. Indeed, for the last thirty or forty years of my life I'd been completely bald—not including that time in my early forties when I'd heralded the beginning of my mid-life crisis by trying to grow a ridiculous looking pony-tail out of the back of my head with the scattered follicles that were still loyally clinging to it.

At this point, I gave up all pretense at feigning sleep, and sat bolt upright (something that almost caused me to tumble out of bed completely since there was much less of me to move than usual) to stare in bewilderment at what appeared to be my childhood bedroom.

The scene that greeted my eyes defied belief. It was the bedroom in which I'd grown up, just as I had remembered it having been in my teens, sometime in the 80s. There were the posters on the walls from genre movies like *E.T.*, *Star Wars*, and *Raiders of the Lost Ark*. And, across from my bed, there was a beat-up old desk with my Commodore 64 sitting on it, and hanging from the ceiling above that were models of my favourite starships. Then, in the far corner was an overflowing clothes-hamper that smelled, even from here, like a teenaged boy.

Despite what I was looking at, seeing was definitely not believing, at least at first. The first thing I did was to contemplate whether it was some kind of *Ensee* trick.

First, I theorized fleetingly that they had simply put me into a room that looked exactly like my old bedroom, but I dismissed this possibility almost immediately. Even if the *Ensee* could have known exactly what this room looked like some fifty years ago, how could you explain the position in which I had been sleeping, or the fact that I clearly now had a much smaller physique, or the hair that was, even now, hanging down in front of my eyes. No, this went beyond a cleverly built set. Wayyyyyy beyond. Like the *Twilight Zone* beyond.

Secondly, I wondered if perhaps I was inside some kind of super-advanced OVUM simulacrum. That was pretty easy to dismiss though. All I had to do was pick up the Rubik's cube off the bedside table and give it a few spins. Even with haptic gloves, there was no way to replicate that kind of physical sensation, one that was both comfortable and familiar.

Next, I considered whether it was some kind of simulated reality like the Matrix or, more appropriate to the era I appeared to be in, Tron. Both of those movies had plots where real people were digitized and put inside a computer-generated simulation that couldn't be distinguished from reality.

The *Ensee* certainly had access to all kinds of advanced technology, but that? And, even if they *could* fool me like that, why bring me *here*? Why *this* period of time? I could understand them putting me in a familiar environment where I might let my guard down and tell them what they wanted to know, but why go through such an elaborate ruse to make me think I was back in my childhood bedroom? They'd want to know about my life on the Pucks wouldn't they? About the Resistance? This bedroom had nothing to do with either one of those.

The fact was, I had already given up pretty much everything I knew during the interrogations, since I really hadn't known that much about the Resistance in the first place, having just recently been made aware of it. It's what made me so perfect for a mission that was bound to end in my capture. I couldn't give up secrets I didn't know.

Eventually, I figured the best way to test whether it was some kind of simulation was to scrutinize everything in the room in excruciating detail in the assumption that no replication could possibly know so many intimate details about the room in which I'd spent the first twenty years of my life. So, I began to crawl around the room (because I was way too nauseous to stand) examining everything closely.

By the time I was closely studying the wooden *Coca-Cola* box that served as a night-stand, I came to the sudden conclusion that there was no way that it could be an *Ensee* trick to get me to reveal Resistance secrets. My reasoning was that the only way for them to pull off a simulation of this complexity would have been for them to tap directly into my memories, and if they could tap into my memories, then they could have just as easily taken whatever else they had wanted from my brain, including everything I knew about Oskar's band of merry men.

Indeed, if they *could* read my mind, then what was the point of the numerous "question periods" over the last few weeks with Remmus Kemp himself?

By this point, I was finally able to stand, and was looking at the more adult-themed posters on the back of my door when I discovered that the mysterious temporal-displacement experience extended beyond the room itself.

Vibrating faintly through the closed door was a deep, regular thumping sound. Like drums off in the distance, or...

... the deep bass from music coming from a cabinet radio in the living room downstairs.

The same radio that my father would turn on every morning when he got up at around six to prepare breakfast for himself and get ready for his day while waiting for the rest of the house to rouse. So absorbed had I been in experiencing my childhood bedroom, that it hadn't honestly occurred to me that there might be more to this fantasy beyond those four walls.

There might be people.

People I'd lost a very long time ago.

I swallowed hard and slowly opened my bedroom door. I was greeted by the smell of freshly brewed coffee wafting up the stairs and down the hallway, bringing with it the distant sounds of clinking dishes and cutlery. That's when it truly hit home what might lay waiting for me.

Mom? Dad?

As if to confirm my wondering thoughts, the deep sound of my father's gravelly voice called out.

"I won't ask again!" it said simply.

His voice went straight to my tear ducts, and I actually sobbed out loud despite myself as the tears began to flow unhindered. How appropriate that this was the first thing that I would hear him say in some thirty years. He had said that exact phrase multiple times every morning of my teens as he struggled to coax me and my brother out of bed in time to get ready for school. Every fifteen minutes or so, he'd tell us that he wouldn't ask us to get out of bed again even though we both knew that he would. Especially my brother, Patrick who, seemingly every morning, would wait until he couldn't wait any longer, leap out of bed, throw on his cleanest clothes and run out to catch a bus that would be just about to pull away, while grabbing a banana and his lunch from the kitchen counter along the way.

I lurched forward in the direction of my late father's voice, suddenly no longer caring whether or not this was real, just as long as I could see and talk to him again.

I didn't get far. Still not used to moving my new body, I miscalculated, and walked it right into the door jamb. It smarted a bit, but it didn't slow me down long. Readjusting my trajectory, I moved jerkily down the hallway towards the stairway, correcting for my lighter frame with every step so that, by the time I had reached the top of the stairs that led to the kitchen, I was pretty much used to things. I stopped there for a moment so that I could compose myself and wipe the tears from my eyes and cheeks with the bottom of my t-shirt. Then, taking a deep breath, and holding tightly to the bannister just in case, I descended the steps one at a time.

When I finally saw Dad, I didn't really mean to start crying again. I just couldn't help myself. It had, after all, been over thirty years for me since I'd last seen him, and he hadn't looked anywhere near this young at the time.

He froze, sitting at the breakfast table, his toast halfway to his open mouth and dripping with liquid honey as he stared at me.

Suddenly, my arms were around him, and I was cradling his very confused head against my chest. My father had never at all been affectionate, and the only time I finally got comfortable enough to truly let my guard down with the man and express my own affection towards him was in that hospital room in 2004 when I stroked his head and held his hand as he had struggled in vain to form words.

"Josh, what the hell," my father muttered into my shirt. "What the hell's the matter with you?"

If this actually were some kind of dream, then he felt so damned real. Hell, I could even smell him—that unique combination of Irish Spring soap and the stale sweat that always seemed to permeate his work clothes no matter how much Mom washed them. I was still crying, still trying to answer him through a voice that was overburdened with emotion, when my Mom entered the room. Then, the scene pretty much repeated itself, only with her this time. Mercifully, she didn't act nearly as surprised as had my father by my sudden and intense display of affection.

"Well, look at you," she sputtered as I squeezed her, my chin on her head. "You're just... well... full of hugs this morning aren't you." Then, after it was clear I wasn't about to let her go, she added, a little more warily, "Are you all right, Josh?"

Finally, I pulled away from her while explaining my odd behaviour with the first mollifying excuse I could muster, "Sure, sure. It's just... well, I got some good news this morning. I'm very excited about it." Turning away, I dried my eyes again as best I could and rallied to get my bottom lip from quivering and the tremor out of my voice. When I turned back, it was to find both of my parents staring at me again, even more confused than before. My father actually glanced briefly at the phone before asking, "From where?"

Oh right.

With no access to the internet in the 80s, the only news from the outside world was delivered via phone, television, mail, or newspaper—none of which applied to this situation since I'd only just come downstairs, and I didn't have any of those things in my bedroom.

"I mean... um, yesterday," I stuttered. "I got it yesterday. I just didn't get a chance to tell you about it then. What I mean to say is that I got good news yesterday, and it's put me in a very good mood this morning."

<Well, would you look at that. I just stopped to read what I'd been writing, and somewhere along the way, I've started writing it like a story. I didn't do it on purpose, it just seemed like the best way to express everything. So, let's keep it up shall we?>

Anyhow, I was feeling awkward standing in the middle of the room with them staring at me, and thankfully, chance saved the day—literally. In response to a scratching noise from the front door, my father said, "Let Chance in, wouldya?"

Holy fuck. Chance? I'd completely forgotten!

I bounded to the door and swung it open to let the yellow blur that was my childhood dog, Chance, into the house. I dropped to my knees and enveloped the excited Golden Retriever in a huge hug. As she licked me excitedly, we tumbled to the floor and I pretended to hide my face in my arms as she tried to force her nose between my arms to lick me some more. It didn't take much to get Chance excited, and I'm pretty sure that she could sense my own glee at being able to play with a dog that I hadn't actually seen in some forty-five years.

"Chance, old girl," I muttered through a mouthful of fur. "I've missed you."

We'd gotten the dog as a puppy just a few years before this, my father having surprised us out of the blue with her one day. He'd already decided that we should name the puppy Chance and none of us knew why he'd chosen that name until we were eating steak one night and my father, through a barely suppressed grin said, "Don't forget to give Chance a piece."

I swear lightbulbs appeared over each of heads at that point as my father cackled at his own humour. He'd been a huge *Beatles* fan in his youth and he also loved wordplay like this. He'd told us that he'd apparently considered calling the dog Yoko, but figured that it would be too cruel a name, even for a dog. Dad would tell this same joke over and over again through the years, pretty much every time we talked about our dog, thinking that it never got old. We all begged to differ.

After a few minutes of rough-housing with Chance, I began to feel like somebody was watching me. Pulling the dog's licking snout away from me, I looked up to see both my parents staring, my Mom's eyes wide and coffee mug halfway to her mouth. I had to assume from their expressions that this wasn't the way I typically greeted our family dog every morning in my teens.

Had they heard me say that I missed a dog that I'd presumably just seen yesterday?

Deciding not to even broach the subject, I pushed Chance off of me, got to my knees and said, "Ok Chance, it's time I got some breakfast." Taking the cue, the dog skipped over to her dish and lapped noisily at some water while I thought about cereal. I mean, that *was* what I ate for breakfast in the 80s right?

Now, where in hell do we keep the cereal? I wondered as I brushed dirt and dog hair off my clothing.

I walked over to the cupboard that was my best guess, opened it, and was rewarded with a selection of various sugar-delivery systems disguised as breakfast substitutes. I wouldn't have let my kids eat this junk when they were young, but I figured that, since I was in Rome I should render onto Caesar—or something like that. I chose a box of Honeycombs, pulled it from the cupboard, and turned around to find that both of my parents were still staring at me expectantly.

"What?" my mother asked finally as she pulled a couple of heavy paper bags (that were presumably our lunches) out of the fridge and set them on the counter. "What was the news?"

Oh shit. They would call my bluff wouldn't they. At least they didn't ask about my comment to the dog.

As I thought about how to answer my parents, I carried the cereal box to the counter and opened a cupboard door to get a bowl and then closed it again immediately when I found only glasses and mugs within.

What the hell year is it? I thought as I tried another door. *My bedroom is right out of the 80s, but when? My best guess was early to mid-decade—maybe. What was I into back then? What was going on at school? Shit Josh, think!*

I had guessed right with my second kitchen cupboard, and was pulling a bowl from the shelf (and trying not to get distracted by the fact that I'd forgotten that they had ever made bright orange Corelle dinnerware designs) as a solution occurred to me.

"I found out at school yesterday that a drawing I'd entered into the annual art department at show won a prize," I said,

My mother's response was effusive. "That's wonderful, Josh," she said while my father grunted grumpily, making it clear that he didn't think that this kind of good news warranted the tears and the clingy hugs that I'd just subjected both of them to moments earlier.

I ignored him, and, as I poured milk into my bowl of cereal, I asked them about their coming day in what turned out to be a successful ploy to change the subject. Hopefully, they wouldn't want to follow up on my white lie later and start asking where the prize was. As they spoke, I briefly wondered which chair was traditionally mine until I spotted Chance already sitting beside one waiting for me.

Now, that's a good dog. A dog who knew how much of a mess I made in my teens when eating, but still a good dog.

Sitting down at the table in the chair beside Chance, I looked over at my parents as I put a spoonful of Honeycombs in my mouth. I struggled to contain my emotion all over again as the flavours hit my system. It had been years since I'd tasted Honeycombs, and it was exactly as I remembered it.

Off in the distance, Mom and Dad were discussing their plans for the day and my mind was split between soaking in as many details as I could (just in case this whole time-displacement thing actually did suddenly end without warning), and trying to figure out exactly what year it was and—by extraction—how old I was in it.

The radio in the living room helped a bit. The news had just come on and, although I couldn't hear many of the details, I did catch the fact that it was a Thursday. They didn't mention the year of course, and I couldn't very well ask my parents for that detail. I might be able to get away with the date, but asking for the month would raise eyebrows, and asking what year it was would probably get me tested for drugs or alcohol.

I need a newspaper.

As casually as I could, I asked my Mom, who was just now pulling some toast out of the toaster. "Where's the latest paper, Mom?"

"It's where we always keep it, Josh," she answered as she pointed me towards the pile of magazines on the bench by the broom closet. "Did you want some toast while I'm here?"

"Well, of course I do," I answered jovially, jumping at the opportunity to taste Mom's home-made strawberry jam again. I stood up and walked over to the bench that Mom had indicated and started rifling through the stack balanced there. It was obviously spring or summer, otherwise all of this paper would, by now, have been burnt in the woodstove. On top were a few supermarket tabloids like the *National Enquirer* and the *World News Weekly*, my mother's main source of the original "fake news" before Trump redefined the term.

It didn't take long to find a copy of the *Northern Lights Focus*—our town's weekly newspaper, but it took me a moment to be able to read any of the print beyond the headlines. In the first place, I wasn't wearing glasses, and in the second I no longer had presbyopia. For the first time in forever, I didn't have to hold the paper on the other side of the room to see the small print—I could actually hold it at a reasonable distance. Once I got used to the new visual perspective, I could clearly see that the date and on the front page was: "Wednesday, April 17, 1985."

Before I had a chance to truly react to this news though, my father was reminding me that it was time for me to get ready for school, and the roller-coaster ride that was a trip to my own past had begun in earnest...

CHAPTER 4
Reruns

P erhaps predictably, my first day back in high school after a fifty-year absence was a tad rocky, although I suppose it could have been a lot worse. The biggest problem was that I had enough of the same classes with the same people, that more than a few of them were looking at me and asking what kind of drugs I was on when I kept "forgetting" where I sat in whatever classroom I was in, or when I drew a blank in the review of topics that we had apparently been discussing only yesterday. More than once, I found myself reflexively reaching for the pocket where I'd have normally kept my smart phone so that I could look up the answer I needed on an internet that wouldn't even exist for another decade.

There was also my attitude that was apparently different too. For one, I was treating my classmates and friends like, well… children. For another, I was talking to our teachers (who were, to my perspective, just as much like kids as the actual teenagers) as if they were my equals. It was coming off as arrogant, and people were beginning to talk, not so covertly, behind my back. Not that I cared about what they said. Hell, maybe at one time I would have, but not under these circumstances.

Still, I knew that it wouldn't help to draw undue attention to myself so, at lunch, with Andi right beside me, lightly rubbing my upper thigh under the table in a very distracting way, I threw myself into conversations about current music trends, gossip about popular entertainers (even though I secretly knew what the future held for each and every one of them), and behind the scenes trivia for blockbuster movies. This last was something I was particularly well-versed in, thanks to the simple fact that the almost-elderly (like I had been just yesterday) didn't need as much sleep as did the young, and I had solved my decade-old problem of waking up at 3AM and being unable to get back to sleep by streaming movie after movie with the commentary tracks on.

A smaller problem was names. There were just so many kids, and so many of them had been people that I was supposed to have known. Tonight, I would have to locate my yearbook from 1984 and start memorizing.

Speaking of all those kids, it was when I was interacting with so many smiling, gleeful faces, that I began to notice something else, a feeling in the air that was a lot harder to define, much less describe. To put it succinctly, things were just a whole lot *lighter*.

I'm not saying, like Doc Brown, that there was a problem with the Earth's gravitational pull in the future, but I knew from personal experience that things were certainly about to get a lot more *anxious* for everyone. Starting pretty much with the 9/11 terrorist attacks in 2001, into the 2010s with the climate crisis scare, and right on up past the events of 2025, the people of the future were going to be constantly on edge, especially the kids. Yet here, in 1985, there was just a feeling of hope, in that the future held so much promise. It was definitely contagious, and actually a little intoxicating. I was definitely starting to feel like making a go at blending in had been worth it.

Until I saw Clay Peterson.

I spotted him for the first time at lunch, and was grateful that we hadn't known each other all that well in Grade 11, so that I wouldn't have to actually interact with him at all. In 1985, most of my friends were either geeks or the same ones I'd had in grade school, and Clay and I wouldn't become friends until next year sometime when we'd meet in Martial Arts classes. From there, luck would put us in the same residence at Western a few years later, and we would eventually become roommates in Toronto when I was doing my graduate studies in the mid-nineties.

It was around this time that Clay had… or rather would, steal my *Star Wars* memorabilia and sell it for drug money. This would lead to a falling out that would end with me kicking him out of my apartment. With nowhere for him to go, he'd eventually end up sleeping on the kitchen floor of his buddy's run-down townhouse. It was the beginning of a downward spiral for him, one that would eventually land him in jail, first briefly for possession, and then for a longer term for armed robbery.

It was the kind of betrayal that had stuck with me for years, and still kind of hurt even now. But, there was a bigger emotion in play, one that I hadn't really become aware of until a many years after I'd thrown him out: guilt.

Clay's personality had always been both addictive and reactionary. I eventually came to realize that he hadn't stolen my stuff with malicious intent, but instead to feed his addiction. It had never been personal, even though I'd certainly taken it that way. At the time, I'd washed my hands of him, and blamed his decline on his own demons, but, eventually I began to think differently. Could I have done something to help him? If I hadn't evicted him, and instead got him help — the kind of thing that a true friend would have done — could things have turned out differently for him?

This was a topic that Oskar and I had discussed at great length in his bar on the Pucks. His older brother had been an alcoholic and had pickled his brain and squandered a bright future despite several interventions and the support from a large and loving family. Perhaps predictably, Oskar's opinion had been unforgiving.

"You did the right thing, Snowflake," he had said to me. "If you'd have kept him around. He just woulda stolen more. There ain't nothin' can help an addict 'till he's ready to help himself."

Except, perhaps, time-travel, I mused as I finished off my peanut butter and honey sandwich. Mentally, I was putting Clay Peterson on the list of things that I wanted to do differently, assuming, of course, that this time-slip experience persisted.

In general today, I think that I managed to mask any obvious signs that I'd been temporally displaced, at least for the casual observer. Andi, however, was more than just a casual observer. Beyond our History class, she and I had a number of courses together, and I could see her looking at me funny every time I forgot a person's name, or when I needed direction as to which desk was mine. In English class, I was pretty sure I had it right, but then it turned out that I was remembering where I sat in a completely different class from a completely different grade even though it was the same room.

It didn't get any better when I tried to sneak off by myself for the remainder of the lunch break to go to one of the music practice rooms. I hadn't completely lied to Andi this morning when I told her why I couldn't go over to her house. It wasn't so much that I needed to practice my music, as I needed to *relearn* my music. Naturally, she wanted to join me, which is when it became exceedingly obvious to Andi, with her playing the flute and me the clarinet, that I was doing a pretty lousy job reading music and had only a very vague recollection about how to finger my instrument.

Andi wasn't the only one who noticed either. Later that day, in music class, our teacher, Monsieur Rand, pulled me over afterwards, and in a heavily French-accented voice that was one part sympathetic and two parts sarcastic, asked if I wanted to take my instrument home to practice tonight.

It was Monsieur Rand's broken English that had inadvertently given me one of my most hated nick-names a few years earlier in Grade 9. It had been early in the semester, and he had asked us one at a time which instruments we most wanted to learn how to play. I told him that I wanted to play the trumpet, but he said I couldn't because the mouthpiece was small and you needed thin lips to play it properly.

"You cannot play the trumpet, Josh," he had said so that the entire class could hear. "You have too big lips."

Naturally, everyone else in class heard this differently and thought he was saying that I had two big lips, and thus my unfortunate "Big Lips" moniker was born. I can't recall why, but in the 80s, telling a male that he had big lips was an insult, so I had been shackled to one of the worst nicknames possible, all thanks to Monsieur Rand's tenuous grasp of English syntax.

That was neither here nor there at the moment though, so, in response to Rand's sardonic request that I get some practice tonight, I, of course, simply said, "Oui, Monsieur."

That had been the last class of the day and, as I said goodbye to Andi—who was about to start her walk home while I headed for my bus (which thankfully appeared to be right where I expected it to be, in a line with a bunch of others just beyond the student parking lot)—she asked, "Are you feeling all right today, Josh?"

I smiled as reassuringly as I could muster and shrugged my shoulders. "I've been working on a new computer program," I lied. "I've been staying up way too late, and it's been occupying all of my attention during the day. I'm sorry if I've seemed out of it today. My Mom always says that, sometimes, I'm just like an absent-minded professor."

She had, in fact, always said this, I imagined Ron Howard narrating, as if this were an episode of *Arrested Development*.

That seemed to placate the young woman, and she leaned up to kiss me full on the lips and I found myself welcoming the gesture.

I'd forgotten how soft her lips were and how her hair smelled like cherries. When she was done, Andi nuzzled her head against my chest for a moment while I hugged her, then she pulled away so that she could catch up with her friends.

"Bye Josh," she called over her shoulder. "Call me tonight?"

"Um, sure," I called back as I walked towards my waiting bus. It was then that it occurred to me that I had no memory as to what her phone number was and, I was pretty sure that "speed dial" was still a few years off.

"What'd I tell you about your honey stick?" asked a familiar voice from behind me.

"Fat lot of good you were today," I replied without even looking back at Patrick. "I didn't see you at all."

"Basketball tourney," replied my brother simply, as he climbed onto the bus ahead of me. "But you wouldn't have noticed a tournament that big with your head up your own ass...orted science experiments."

Chuckling at Patrick's wordplay, I followed him up the steps. He wasn't wrong. I had had no idea that there had been a tournament going on today, but I guess that explained the buses from the other schools in our district parked over by the gymnasium.

On the bus, I went out of my way to be genial to Patrick, a gesture that he was thankfully reciprocating this time and, about a half-hour later, we were getting off the bus and getting tackled by a very excited Golden Retriever. We played with Chance together for a while, tossing her favourite chew toy back and forth and out for her to fetch, before eventually heading into the house chatting fairly comfortably. Mom was making supper and told us that we had about an hour before it was ready, which was more helpful than she knew since I had no recollection as to what our normal after-school schedule was. While my brother turned on the TV to watch reruns of *I Dream of Jeannie*, I headed towards my bedroom, Chance in tow.

As I walked upstairs (after hugging my Mom tightly and asking about her day), I found myself singing "Time Warp," one of the songs from *The Rocky Horror Picture Show*.

"With a bit of a mind flip, you're into the time slip, and nothing can ever be the same..."

Yeah, that sounds about right, I mused.

Back in my bedroom, I powered up my Commodore 64, as well as the disk drive that sat beside it. Then, I made sure that TV set that I used as a monitor was set to channel 3, and flipped it on as well. After a moment, the familiar blue boot screen faded into view with large blocky text across the top of the screen identifying the system. Below this, in the same blocky text was the word "READY", beneath which was a flashing rectangular box that indicated the location of the text prompt.

```
READY.
▮
```

I stared at the flickering prompt for a few minutes, confused.
Ready? Ready for what?
I'd completely forgotten what to do. A computer system that didn't offer me choices by way of icons was completely foreign to me now. With this ancient computer, I actually had to know what I wanted to do ahead of time, and then know what command to type in, as well as how to properly compose that command.

It was so strange to be looking at this familiar machine yet feeling so lonely. Partly because it wasn't connected inherently to a World Wide Web of any kind like we'd all start to take for granted in the future, and partly because even that kind of World Wide Web would itself eventually disappear. I was being nostalgic for both my future and my past at the same time and had to smile at the oddness of it all.

On a whim, I entered the question:

```
WHERE THE HELL AM I?
```

I was half thinking that, were I living some kind of 80s time-travel adventure movie, the computer would actually be in on it, and reply with something kind of smarmy like "Don't you mean *when* the hell are you?" but instead the immediate response was one that was all too familiar with me now that I was looking at it:

```
?SYNTAX ERROR
READY.
▮
```

Yeah. That sounds about right.

Pulling open one of the desk drawers, I found my cache of floppy disks, hoping to locate a game that I could play to pass the time. These were the original floppy disk—a five-inch square of protective material with an oval window on its side that exposed a portion of the magnetic circle that stored some 700 odd Kilobits of data. It was a shape that would be familiar to generations of people for years to come, even those who had never seen a real floppy disk, when it becomes the universally-recognized SAVE icon.

I flipped through the floppies looking for something light to play, so I passed on the opportunity to run the text-based *Hitchhiker's Guide to the Galaxy* because I really didn't feel like dying over and over again today. I used to play that game so much as a kid, and knew how involved it could be; it wasn't the kind of game you could just slip into for a few minutes as a distraction.

Eventually, I found a disk labelled "GAMES", and slid it into the drive. Nothing happened. As I stared at it, I seemed to recall that you had to type a command to load the disk directory or something, and that directory would tell you what programs were actually on the floppy. Then you had to type a command to tell the machine to load that program and then, once it was in the machine's memory, you would tell the computer to run it.

Damned if I could recall the proper syntax of the directory command though, and this system seemed to be all about syntax. I pulled the well-worn manual off the shelf above my desk, flipped through it until I found what I needed, and then just followed the instructions. Within ten minutes (most of which was spent waiting for the program to load, during which I was cursing and asking "How long can it take to load a program that is obviously less than 64K into memory?") I was playing *Choplifter*, one of my favourite games from the time. The game was fairly straight-forward in that I used my joystick to pilot a tiny helicopter from right to left across a series of screens to rescue hostages, even as I fought off the enemy in their tanks and jet planes. The nostalgia made manifest by the sights and sounds of playing this old game helped me with my feelings of loneliness.

After a few levels though, I began to get restless and a little bored. Although I wanted to engage my mind, I still wanted to explore the physical environment I found myself returned to and soak up every detail. So, I quit the game and turned off the computer. Then, I sat there in my rickety old office chair—a hand-me-down from my father—and spun in place slowly as I took in my room again. Nothing appeared to have changed, meaning that, at least so far, this time displacement thing was being consistent.

Deciding to explore my desk a little more, I pulled open a few drawers and looked through them. The long one that was right above the desk's leg opening, not unexpectedly, held pens and pencils and the like, as well as a couple of film canisters with undeveloped cartridges in them, so I closed it and shifted my attention to the three drawers to the right. This particular exploration however proved to be a little more difficult, because Chance was assuming that, since I was bent over in my chair towards the ground, I wanted to play. I scratched her behind the ears until she settled down out of the way.

The top drawer was a bit of a catch-all, containing a couple of old cameras, an envelope full of participation ribbons from track meets (unlike Patrick, I never got anything from a sports contest beyond a token to prove that I'd actually been there), novelty souvenirs from Robertson's winter carnival, a number of science fair medals (all gold, naturally), a bag with an old watch that I'd taken apart but couldn't figure out how to reassemble, a few electronic circuit boards, and an old transistor radio. In addition, rattling around on the bottom of the drawer, were some random pieces of Lego, some assorted screws, a dozen or so silver dollars that my Great-Grandfather had given me (one every year since the early 70s), a couple of puzzle games, as well as some old rocks that I'd kept because I'd thought that they had been culturally modified.

They had not been culturally modified, said Ron Howard's voice, once again.

The second drawer held paper and envelopes and other stationery products, while the one directly below it was locked.

Oh right! My secret stash!

I couldn't for the life of me remember what was actually in my secret stash, I just remembered that it was secret enough that it needed to be kept locked. Sucking at my teeth in thought as I resumed spinning in my chair, I tried to remember where I kept the drawer key hidden. It wasn't on the ring in my pants pocket, so I tried my other secret stash: the little cardboard box that I'd placed inside the heat vent in my early teens before I got this desk. I was just about to stick my hand down the pipe in the floor when I remembered that, by 1985, I wasn't using this hiding place anymore, not since my father had cleaned out the heat vents and miraculously found, among other things, the pen that he'd lost just a few months earlier — the one where the woman's bathing suit slid off when you tipped it upside down, revealing her naked body beneath.

The next place I checked for the key was the bookshelf in my closet. When I'd been about a dozen years old, I'd been home sick one day and had asked my mother to buy me a new book to read. I told her that I preferred a *Hardy Boys* mystery, but she couldn't find one, so she returned with something else entirely: a book about some kind of mutiny on a Victorian sailing ship. The story was grittier than I was used to and I gave up after a few chapters, hating it so much. It was at that point that I decided that I would turn the book into the perfect hiding place, in much the same way that Andy Dufresne modified his Bible to hide his rock hammer in *The Shawshank Redemption*. I cut a large rectangular hole through each of the pages, leaving just enough paper around the edges so that it would still look like a book to a casual observer, then I glued the pages together, and just like that, I had a space big enough to hide small things — like a key.

Sure enough, I was right. The key to my desk drawer (attached to a key chain charm that looked kinda like E.T.) was hidden in the book along with a few old coins from the 1950s and a note from a girl I'd known in grade school telling me that she had a crush on me.

Using the key to finally open the bottom drawer that held my secret stash, I was immediately surprised to find that there weren't nearly as many things in it as I thought there would be, or at least not as many things as I'd thought needed to be kept secret.

Oh sure, there were some very descriptive (and in places X-rated) love notes that I'd exchanged with Andi over the last year, but I couldn't understand why I thought to lock up the old cloth that my Mom had used to bathe me as an infant. Beyond that, there was a sketch book with a number of nude sketches that I'd done (all very artistic and tasteful of course) as well as a pad of yellow lined paper with my handwriting on it, locked up because I'd once made the mistake of leaving my intimate thoughts lying around for my brother to find. The document currently visible on the top page of the pad appeared to be a letter that I had been writing to Andi apologizing for something I'd done recently. I couldn't recall what it had been, and I couldn't force myself to read past the following line:

"The only thing I can offer by way of motivation for my behaviour is that, in my short life, I've learned how to fly, but have yet to perfect my landings."

OMG. Seriously?

My entire teen years should have been preceded by a warning: Mind the Melodrama!

I put down the pad like it was on fire, and picked up the most lurid thing in the whole drawer: a box of condoms. From the condition of the box, it looked like I'd had it for a long time, which wasn't surprising since, in a tiny town like Robertson, you couldn't just go to the local pharmacy to buy condoms all that easily because the cashier knew you and would tell your parents. Instead, you had to make arrangements to go to nearby Timmins (or better yet, have a friend go instead) where you were pretty much anonymous. This kind of subterfuge may sound a little funny from the perspective of a few decades down the line when condoms were distributed for free in many schools, but in 1985, you still couldn't even show condoms on TV without having to blur them out.

I put most of the things back the way I had found them in the drawer and locked it up again, but kept the key, winding it onto the set in my pants pocket (minus the E.T. figure). This drawer would be the perfect place to store the journal that I was definitely going to buy so that I could record my memories of the future, and I wanted easy access to it from now on.

I had just gone back to staring at the room, and was just standing up to get a closer look at the model of the *Enterprise* to see if the running lights in the saucer still worked, when I heard my Mom's voice calling us all to supper which, I found out a moment or two later, was spaghetti.

This wasn't just any old regular spaghetti, mind you, it was my Mom's spaghetti—from the 80s. Oh, I've tried to replicate the recipe over the years, but nothing has come anywhere near as good, which is why I actually moaned out loud a little with the first mouthful. If either my parents or my brother noticed, they didn't say anything, and everybody just kept eating while chatting about their day.

What is it that makes this spaghetti so good? I wondered. *Is it the tiny canned mushrooms? Her blend of spices? The fact that she uses regular ground beef instead of lean? Or is it just my taste buds?*

I'd remembered reading somewhere that taste buds faded as you aged. Maybe that was it, but I wasn't sure if it was the buds that I was currently using were newer than the ones I'd left behind in 2035, or if it had just been so long since I'd tasted my Mom's cooking, but, between this meal and the strawberry jam this morning, I was in heaven.

This actually got me thinking about something else. If my consciousness shifted into my younger body, was it my consciousness that was doing the tasting or was it the taste buds themselves? I didn't get far pondering this because my interest was piqued by my father talking about how his new motion sensitive light wasn't working the way it was supposed to.

Still distracted by the deliciousness that was my Mother's spaghetti, I wasn't really thinking when I said, "It's probably just electromagnetic interference. This generation of motion sensors used passive infrared systems that were notoriously inaccurate, especially if the motion in question was either lateral or slow, but it was the interference that was the biggest problem. I should be able to shield it properly with some filters and feed-through capacitors." I spun more spaghetti onto my fork without noticing that I was now the only one actually eating. "I'll take a look at it tomorrow, but I'll have to make a trip in to Radio Shack to get the parts."

I put the food in my mouth and stared back at three blank faces, forks either midway to mouth or food in midchew.

Oh right. My seventeen-year-old self didn't know anything about electrical engineering.

At first, there was a lengthy period of silence, where the only thing anybody could hear was the sound of air whistling through my father's preternaturally large nostrils, before everyone slowly resumed eating. They were all still glaring at me though, my mother wearing a shocked expression and my father looking apprehensive.

"This spaghetti is delicious, Mom!" I started effusively, trying to deflect attention away from what I'd just said. "I've always wondered: what spices do you use?"

Almost coldly, my mother answered, "None."

"Ah, I see." Well that hadn't worked, but had finally explained why my own sauce had never tasted like hers. I rallied and tried something new. "Did Patrick mention that he single-handedly won the basketball tournament with a six-pointer?" I was offering my brother two opportunities here to speak up. One to talk about his game performance, and the other to correct me. Thankfully, he rose to the occasion.

"Well, that's not exactly right," he said in his slow drawl before launching into an animated play-by-play of the game's final moments. Within mere minutes, my mother was "oohing" and "aahing" over Patrick's narration even as my father continued to glower at me. I went back to enjoying the spaghetti, only speaking up a few times for the remainder of the meal to prompt Patrick to keep talking.

The moment dessert was done, I helped clean up the dishes before zipping upstairs, saying that I had a ton of homework to catch up on. It wasn't a lie. If I was going to succeed at this masquerade, I was going to have to relearn a ton of stuff that most adults took for granted. Some classes, like Math and Science for instance, likely weren't going to be a problem with my level of education, but History? Who could remember all those dates and events fifty years gone? I needed to do some research, and it was going to be a lot harder to do without access to the internet.

Shortly after 8 o'clock, I called Andi. It was actually surprisingly easy to figure out her number, thanks to a wonderfully archaic invention called the *telephone book!* In 1985, when extra phone lines were expensive and cell phones hadn't taken over, there was usually only one phone per household, and its number was almost always listed in the community phone book. I was lucky that, in a small town like Robertson, Petras was a unique enough last name so that there was only one listing for it in the directory, because I didn't remember her father's given name until I saw it on the page.

Dialing the old rotary phone hanging from the wall on the kitchen was another experience entirely as I waited for each turn of the dial to click its way back to the beginning. When had I last used one of these? I mean there had to have been a last time right? Had I known it at the time?

Andi and I spoke for close to a half hour. Mercifully, she had completely abandoned her earlier concern about my well-being, and went on breezily about what had happened to her in Toronto over the last few days while I drifted along happily listening, having forgotten just how much I enjoyed the melodic, almost sing-song, sound of her voice.

My father walked by twice while I was on the phone, the second time making a judgmental snort that made his displeasure clear that I'd been on it for too long. He used the phone for business and got most of his inquiries in the evening when people weren't at work, so he didn't like having it tied up. Before I could interrupt Andi to tell her that I should go, it was as though she was somehow expecting that very thing.

"Well, I'm guessing your father has about had enough of you tying up his phone," she said by way of winding down the conversation. "And I've got some work to catch up on from missing three days of school, so I'm gonna run. See you tomorrow, Josh. I love you…"

I hesitated, but only for a moment. How had I usually responded to a declaration of love from Andi? "Um, I love you too, Andi," I said finally, assuming that she wouldn't have offered it if she wasn't at least fairly sure it would be reciprocated. This wasn't our first such avowal was it?

There was a crackling silence on the line for a moment before Andi's bright voice simply said "G'nite, Josh," before the line went dead.

Putting the phone back on the hook, I stared at it for a while and was surprised when it rang.

"Hello," I said into the receiver after I'd picked it up, wondering if it was Andi calling back but, as it turned out, it was a client of my Dad's. After instinctively searching in vain for a mute button on the phone, I covered the mouth piece with my hand and called out for my father.

"He's in the workshop," I heard my mother's voice yell from downstairs, so, hanging up the receiver on the little notched shelf that my father had built for just such a need, I sought him out in the garage that was attached to the house.

"I'll take it out here," he answered, so I went back to the kitchen and hung up the phone properly when I was sure that he'd picked up the extension in his workshop. Then, I meandered downstairs to find Patrick (on the couch with Chance cuddled on top of him) and my mother in the rec room, partway through the Thursday night "Must See TV" lineup of *Cosby Show*, *Family Ties*, *Cheers*, and *Night Court*. I'd normally be watching with my family, but I'd seen them all. Several times. Reruns and repeats were all we had on

Prince Edward Island in 2035, as there wasn't much in the way of new content with Hollywood and the major TV networks all gone.

I watched for a while as Michael J. Fox, as Alex Keaton in *Family Ties*, sat up on the counter and sipped orange juice as he delivered his zingers and one-liners. My mother and brother laughed at all the right places, but I was having a hard time paying attention to the actual plot, because I was instead musing about the fact that Michael J. Fox was Canadian, which somehow segued into thoughts about Canadian culture in North American popular media in the 80s.

About a decade earlier than this, there had been an effort by the Canadian government to combat the cultural onslaught from the south by instituting rules on Canadian content. No longer could TV programs pretend to be American in order to appeal to the US audience, they had to be, at least in part, noticeably Canadian. This was no problem with old shows like *King of Kensington* (even though its frail sets, that seemed to shake every time a door was closed, made it exceedingly obvious with even a cursory viewing that this wasn't an American production), but other shows had to try a little harder, leading to some unintentionally hilarious results. SCTV, for example, reacted sarcastically to the request from the CBC, their broadcast network, to increase Canadian content by a couple of minutes each week, by introducing two characters that were stereotypically Canadian. The writers introduced these hosers who would wear toques and do quintessential Canadian things like drink beer and eat back bacon during the segment that was, perhaps predictably, only as long as CBC had decreed. Against all odds, the *Great White North* would become a hit, and Bob and Doug McKenzie would become celebrities here and abroad, demonstrating that being unapologetically Canadian was actually kind of appealing.

The episode of *Cheers* that followed *Family Ties* was one that I'd seen a number of times, being the one where Diane goes off to Europe to marry Frasier, and Sam hires an older, unattractive waitress to replace her. I was halfway tempted to start quoting lines of dialogue before they were spoken just to freak out my mother and brother, or just tell them how the whole Sam/Diane relationship would eventually end with Shelley Long leaving the show to be replaced by Kirstie Alley, but I resisted. It would definitely take some explaining, especially after what had just happened at supper.

I really wanted to go upstairs and practice my clarinet, but I was concerned that suddenly walking away from shows I typically enjoyed watching would be seen as being out of character for me. It had only been one day for me in April of 1985, and already things were getting complicated.

I began to crave something at that point - something that I knew would be off limits to my seventeen-year-old body: alcohol.

The strong stuff.

CHAPTER 5
Meltdown

I n the rare moments that I was able to hold onto sleep last night, I dreamt of a future that was now my past. The rest of the time, I would lie there wondering if I had shifted in time again, but then I would see the stars through my bedroom window, and feel better.

Then, around 3:30AM, I woke up so completely that I gave up even trying to stay in bed any longer, mostly because I was tired of the internal analytical monologue that had been running pretty much all night long in the background. Indeed, from the moment that my head had hit the pillow last night (around 11:30, after I'd spent over an hour silently relearning how to play music and finger a clarinet), my brain had seemed to figure out that this was the first real chance to actually think about what was happening to me. I certainly couldn't have been expected to focus on it during the day, what with everything that took place—from seeing my dead parents alive, to kissing my high school sweetheart again. What's more, around 9:30—like a loud irritating noise that you only notice once it stops—I finally started to realize that I had actually been in shock the whole day.

So, what had last night's running session of reasoning and rational contemplation resulted in? Well, no matter how I spun it, I kept coming back to the exact same conclusion that I'd already reached yesterday morning: I had to play along and pretend to fit into my own past. And, this last bit was the most important part, I had to do it *surreptitiously*. No more slip-ups like the one at supper.

Pulling myself out of bed, I stood up and stretched a little, once more marvelling at a body without any aches and pains, or muscles that got pulled simply from the act of coughing, or a back that got thrown out by an over-enthusiastic sneeze. I turned the light on and looked around the room casually, giving it a cursory examination. Nothing appeared to have changed, so I probably hadn't shifted to a different time period in my sleep again. My school bag was still on top of my desk, and my clarinet case was sitting on top of it: just the way I had left both before I'd gone to bed. Still, I couldn't be absolutely sure that I hadn't traveled even a day or something without knowing the precise date, but I couldn't check this as I normally would have on my smartphone, nor could I simply turn on the radio, because it would still be playing generic overnight programming—with no record of the date and time.

Man, the 80s suck, at least insofar as continuous access to information goes.

Finally, it occurred to me to check my school books, where I found the class notes that I'd made the day before, just as I remembered them. I hadn't moved temporally; this was still my new reality, and I wasn't stuck in a *Groundhog Day* situation where I kept living the same day repetitively.

I had a few hours to kill until I could safely move around the house without the risk of waking anybody up (most especially Chance, who slept downstairs in the recroom), so I pulled a few binders off the shelves above my desk to see what was in them. Most of them contained notes from last year's classes, but what I found in the papers for my Grade 10 course, *Man in Society* was a huge surprise. It was one that, I was confident, would be very useful in figuring out how my peers in this time period would be expecting from me in terms of my temperament and behaviour.

I had pretty much forgotten that, at the very beginning of the course in September of 1984, our teacher had told us that she'd be giving a full ten minutes at the beginning of every class to make a journal entry. She had instructed us to use this entry to record how we were feeling about the things that were happening in our lives so that we could hopefully look back at it later and see how much we had grown during the tenth grade, a time that she said was one of the most formative of our lives. My goodness, was she ever right, because what I read in that binder was eye-opening to say the least! I'd completely forgotten about this insecure child that I used to be and how aloof I had been to those around me, especially Patrick.

It really is amazing how a single year can change a person. The boy who started journaling in September was feeling superior to all the close-minded people in his school, resentful that he had basically been ostracized because of his intellect, and claiming that he hated everyone about as much as they hated him. In the entries, this almost-stranger was clearly overcompensating for his sense of loneliness by saying repeatedly that it didn't bother him at all, at least not as long as his teachers were happy with him, because, in school, that was all that really mattered.

Over the next two hours, I read as my younger-self yearned for a girlfriend who understood him, friends who shared his passions, and teachers who praised him. I read about all the changes he went through as he joined clubs, found new interests, met new friends, learned to talk to girls, and grew as a person. And, perhaps most amazingly, I watched as my younger self went from blaming his temper on others, to learning that his mood didn't have to hinge on external circumstances, or something that this version of myself had called "fate". Amazingly, long before the self-help movement popularized such messages of self-empowerment in social media memes, I had discovered them for myself.

Slowly, almost reverentially, I closed the binder and sat back in my office chair. For the longest time, I just sat there, spinning slowly and staring at the walls of my bedroom as they slipped gradually by, contemplating what this journal had to say about the man I had eventually grown into, before that same man had become a boy again.

Around 5:30 AM, I decided to head downstairs so that I could surprise my father by having his coffee ready for him when he got up. When he came down a short while afterwards and saw me standing in the kitchen (surreptitiously putting away the coffee mug that I myself had just used), he stopped short and glared at me warily before eventually eyeing the steaming mug that I'd just set out for him with the jar of liquid honey sitting beside it.

"Hmph," he snorted, moving past me as I stood there beside the fridge, grinning.

"I hope it's the way you like it, Dad," I said through a mischievous smile, knowing that it was *exactly* the way he liked it, having learned a long time ago how to brew it to his precise specifications.

Wait. Did I used to call him 'Dad' in my teens? Or was it 'Daddy,' or 'Father,' or even 'Pa'?

Crap, it wasn't 'Sir' was it?

My father took a sip from the mug. "It's fine," he grumbled. From him, that was high praise indeed, and I beamed.

Yeah, my Dad had always been a tough nut. Raised on a depression-era farm in the Ottawa area of Ontario, he inherited his tough-as-nails attitude from my grandfather, who I'm told once killed a deer with a pitchfork because he didn't have time to go home and get his gun.

This was the family legacy I inherited, even though I often wondered if it was wasted on me, as I have been known to cry during Disney cartoons, and the only time I've ever handled a pitchfork was when I hung an old one up on my wall because I thought it looked pretty.

Turning from the table, I opened the cupboard door where the coffee and tea supplies were kept. I'd barely had time for more than a few sips of coffee before I'd heard Dad on the stairs, and I knew that I couldn't suddenly start drinking it in front of him, but thought that I might at least be able to get away with a tea. I started sorting through what I thought would be a selection of teas, only to find that the only variety available was the vanilla of teas: orange pekoe. My family wasn't much for anything that might be at all exotic, like herbal teas — or spices either, for that matter.

"What are you looking for, dear," asked my mother who had come up behind me while I'd been looking in the cupboard.

Without thinking, I asked her, "Do we have any green tea?"

There was silence for a moment before my father asked, "What the hell's a *green* tea?"

Later, sitting on the bus beside Patrick (with *Every Breath You Take* by The Police playing on the bulky vehicle's staticky radio), I discovered that he seemed to think that, with my being polite to him yesterday and then peppering him with questions about his tournament at supper, that I was finally coming around to liking sports. So, naturally, he had taken it upon himself to give me a crash course in… well, pretty much everything to do with the subject. As I listened to him intently, asking the occasional question (especially about the concept of being "offside", since I'd never really truly been able to understand it), I really wished that I could have remembered which team would win the Stanley Cup this year, because it would have been nice to blow his mind with advanced knowledge like that.

The funny things was, I had once known this guy when I was living in Toronto who used to memorize things like that. He could tell you who had won each of the major Academy award categories, or what team won whatever major tournament for the last two decades. To others — whenever he'd perform it as a party trick — he'd explain that he had committed this information to memory just in case he was ever thrown back in time and needed to make a lot of money, but he had privately revealed to me that he was just exercising his memory muscle. For whatever reason, I sure could have used some of those facts now that I, myself, had been unexpectedly thrown back in time.

The only piece of analogous sports trivia that I had at my disposal was that the Toronto Blue Jays would win back to back World Series in 1992 and 1993. Which didn't really mean much to me now, since I couldn't recall if the Jays had even been around in 1985. Like I said, I didn't much follow sports. Still, this meant that, if I could wait seven years, I stood to make a fortune betting on the Jays to win it all.

Managing the school hallways this morning was a little easier than it had been the day before thanks to the time that I had taken last night to study the yearbook, meaning that I could put more names on faces today and greet people a little more properly. I was a little more relaxed this time around too, which is probably why I was noticing the smells in the building more. At the core was the high school's distinctive aroma, a unique combination of a hospital and the gym change room. But layered on top of it, in new and unique combinations depending on where I walked, were the various student-supplied scents. Perfumes and colognes permeated the air so thickly in places that they made my eyes water and I could feel them sticking to the back of my throat like an aerosol spray. I had to suppress the urge to cough as I worked my way through the crowds to get to Andi's locker, only to find that she wasn't there.

We had agreed to meet here hadn't we? Have I got the right floor?

Scanning the crowd and not seeing her, I eventually gave up waiting, went to my own locker to drop off my jacket and school bag, and then wandered off in the direction of geek window. Amazingly, that's actually where I found Andi, deep in conversation with Calvin, and clearly not having even been to her locker yet since she was still wearing her jacket and carrying her school bag.

"...let me get this straight," Calvin was saying incredulously, glancing up at me as he spoke. "You want to come to our next Video Recital?"

"Yep."

"But you're a girl!" he protested.

"I am aware of that fact," Andi replied through a cheeky smile.

"Group bylaws require that we confirm it nonetheless," I interjected.

If I was expecting my comment to discomfit Andi, it failed, because she immediately shot back, "I'm sure that Mr. Donegal, a group member in good standing, can attest to the fact that I'm a female. He is, by now, an expert witness in this regard."

Ah yes, I'd forgotten about Andi's playful side. I'd missed this. She always gave as good as she got – sometimes even better.

Calvin's face was colouring a little and, while Andi pulled my face to hers for a quick kiss, he said, "All right you two, break it up. What do you think Josh? Andi wants to come to the next video recital."

"She mentioned something about that yesterday, come to think of it," I said, before turning to Andi. "I thought you said you were busy."

"My plans changed," she answered. "The Babcocks don't need a babysitter after all. And I think your little party sounds like fun."

"Well then, I have no objection," I said. "I too think it'll be fun."

"Done," concluded Calvin. "Welcome to the group Andi. Next weekend, we're meeting at Josh's place, and we'll be watching *Blade Runner, Temple of Doom*, and *Superman: the Movie*, so you've got a week to practice."

"I want to choose one of the movies," Andi said, her grin once again looking cheeky.

By this time, a few of our other friends had begun to gather around us, and had figured out what was happening. Collectively, they gasped at what Andi had just requested.

Calvin wasn't exactly angry, but he was certainly affronted. "You want to choose a movie? That's never been done before! The movies are always chosen by the last person to host."

"That'd be you?" Andi asked innocently, batting her eyelashes impishly.

"Yes."

"Ok Calvin, let me put it this way," said Andi sweetly. "I'll be the first girl to come to one of your typically male-only parties, right? But, if you let me choose a movie this time, then I'll make sure that I'm not the only girl at *future* parties."

The group of geeks that now surrounded us started murmuring excitedly. "Girls?" I heard one squeaky voice stammer breathlessly. "There could be *girls* at our party?"

Calvin was smiling now, knowing that he'd been outsmarted, but he was obviously loving every minute of it. There was no way he could very well say "no" now, not when so many in the group were obviously so thrilled about seeing an honest-to-goodness girl at a traditionally male geek get-together. Not when there was a possibility that there could be even more of these seemingly alien creatures at future parties.

"Fine," Calvin said finally. "You can choose one of my movies. *One!* And no garbage by John Hughes, no Disney, or anything with Tom Hanks. Let me know by end of day so that I can let the others know so that they can prepare."

Andi was bouncing up and down on her feet now. "Oh, no worries, Calvin," she said. "I know just the movie. You're gonna love it."

The others were staring at Andi now like she was some kind of celebrity, and they weren't far off. Seeming to understand the old show business adage to leave them wanting more, the young Greek woman said, "Ok, gotta run and get ready for home room." Then she spun around, gave me a knowing wink, and practically skipped away down the hallway, deftly avoiding the crowds of kids milling all around us.

Calvin was still smiling when he called after her, "And no Muppets either!" Then, turning to me, he said, "I'll blame you if I have to give up my crown to a girl, Donegal."

Shrugging my shoulders as if to say that things were out of my hands, I turned and headed off towards my own home room. Behind me, I could hear the others in our group chattering happily about the prospect of actually being at the same party as a girl.

"What do girls eat?" I actually heard one of them ask.

I was just about to walk into my homeroom classroom when Andi caught me by the arm to stop me. Slightly out of breath, she pulled my head down so that she could whisper in my ear.

"Please let me know when you'd like to conduct that examination, Mr. Donegal. Y'know, the one to confirm that I am, in fact, a female. My schedule is pretty tight, but I'm sure I can fit you in." Then she kissed me lightly on the lips, and was off down the hall without another word.

I stared after her in wonder as she walked away, trying not to ogle, and shifting my legs uncomfortably at the sudden pressure I was feeling south of the border. Another side effect of the shock of my time displacement wearing off was that I was suddenly aware of a healthy amount of age-appropriate teenage hormones, and Andi was sparking every single one of them. The little voices in my head were still telling me that I was actually an old man and that it was wrong to lust after Andi like this, but those voices were getting weaker and weaker by the minute. This, by itself probably wouldn't be all that bad if it weren't for the fact that they were the combined voices of Heather and Celeste, and they were making me feel guilty that I wasn't missing them and our children more than I was.

It took me a few minutes to come back to myself, and, when I did, everyone in my homeroom was staring at me expectantly, including Monsieur Grenier. Sheepishly, I held my binder to cover my crotch, crossed the threshold into the classroom, and took my seat just as the announcements began. I didn't really hear what was being said over the PA system though, as I was too busy contemplating the fact that I was entering an impossible love quadrangle with three women, one who was ostensibly fifty years my junior, one who hadn't been born, and another that I'd yet to even meet. This had all become exceedingly complicated. If there actually was a person responsible for my spontaneous trip through time, he or she was going to get an earful if we ever met!

My first class of the day was Math with poor Monsieur Lagacy, who had a grasp of the English language that was even more tenuous than was Monsieur Rand's. This meant that, every time he mispronounced the word "polynomial" or "hypotenuse," (by putting the emphasis on the wrong syllable) his class of already restless teenagers would break out into gales of laughter, which would just serve to enrage the man to the point that his already high-pitched voice got shriller and squeakier.

Personally, I liked the man, and I had learned a lot from him and his class, and not just about math. For instance, it was here that I first started to break through my once debilitating shyness and discovered that, if I could be entertaining, others could look past my freakishness enough to stop laughing *at* me and start laughing *with* me. This epiphany had come to me when I had been asked to stand in front at the black board in front of the whole class and explain a concept, but I had been so nervous that I had spoken so quickly that nobody could understand anything that I had said. When Monsieur Lagacy told me to do it again, but slower, I had obeyed, but not in the way he had been expecting. I began to talk like a tape machine with slow batteries, just as I had once seen Robin Williams do on an episode of *Mork and Mindy*. To my great surprise, the class erupted in laughter. I can remember standing there at the front of the room, soaking it all in, thinking that this was much better than getting teased.

This had been the day that I had discovered that, if I kept my bullies and tormenters laughing, they wouldn't harass me. It worked surprisingly well, and with time, I learned to balance being a smart-ass with being genuinely funny. With more practice, I even learned to be flippant without being sarcastic so that nobody got hurt feelings, and it eventually became my goto state for dealing with uncomfortable situations.

Today though, for the first time since I was pretty much forced to go back to school in 1985, I found myself actually enjoying a classroom lesson. Even though I'd taken advanced math courses in University that had greatly expanded on the concepts that Monsieur Lagacy was now teaching, it was a thrill to relearn the basic building blocks all over again. I also had to admit that Lagacy was doing an excellent job, despite the children making his task all the more difficult, and I told him as much as I was leaving class. Although, by the expression on his face in response, I'm pretty sure that he thought I was being sarcastic.

In my next class, Andi sat behind me, and I had a hard time concentrating on the subject because she kept tracing huge hearts on my back with the end of her pencil whenever Mrs. Cooper wasn't looking. It was much the same thing in Geography afterwards, only this time we were far enough away from the front of the class that she could pass me notes that described, in fairly graphic detail, what she wanted to do to me this coming weekend. The frankness of the content was blunted somewhat by the fact that she'd topped many of her lowercase 'i's' with little hearts, but it still had the desired effect on me. I spent most of the class in a heated sweat, replying to Andi as briefly as I could get away with, hoping against hope that Mr. Drummond didn't ask me to stand up to answer any questions.

Lunch was actually a bit of a reprieve from Andi's targeted onslaught of affection. Although we were sitting beside each other, and she was sitting close enough so that our thighs were touching, she was sufficiently distracted by our friends. I spent most of time just listening and soaking it all in, amazed at the young woman's ability to engage so many people at once. Her curiosity and desire to ask questions turned what would have normally been banter about gossip among teenagers into a deeper conversation about wider topics. She wasn't talking about people, she wanted to talk about *things*. It was no wonder that she would eventually get into broadcasting, and be so successful at it too.

Fuck. She's not making it easy to keep her at arm's length.

It wasn't something that I wanted to admit — with me noticing things about Andi seemingly for the first time — but I was becoming enamoured with her all over again. This, in and of itself, wouldn't have been that big a deal, were it not for those two imaginary voices in my head who were still mocking me and telling me to act my age. I knew that those voices were nothing more than a projection of my conscience and that I (probably) wasn't going insane. It was just that, the negative thoughts were coming a little more often now, and they'd also expanded into new, shame-inducing, territory. Now, pretty much every time I found myself actually enjoying myself as I relived my own past, I started to feel genuinely guilty. Guilty that I had escaped from a terrible future, and that everyone else that I had known there — at least as far as I could tell — had not. Was there an alternate timeline where they still existed? If so, then why had I been allowed to escape into the past and relive my youth while they were stuck in the dystopia that I'd left behind? What had I done to deserve such a sweet reward?

The kind of survivor guilt that I was feeling right now definitely wasn't covered in your run-of-the-mill psychology text books.

This whole train of thought was really starting to irritate me, and I could feel a bitter mood descending on me that just got worse each time Andi smiled at me. As classes resumed after lunch, I started to get more and more withdrawn, eventually getting to the point that I fervently started wishing that I could have even just a little bit of privacy. Ironically, this desire to be left alone actually helped me stick to my plan of not drawing attention to myself, at least until the last class of the day, when it all fell apart. Spectacularly.

The class was Science, and it had actually started out well, mostly because I was finally able to focus clearly without Andi in the room to distract me. I sat listening to Mr. Hamm drone on about the wonders of science in a tiresome tone of voice that made it seem anything but wondrous.

Seriously. How had I fallen in love with science in high school with this guy as its ambassador?

It was at this point that Hamm started talking negatively about renewable energy and how it just wasn't going to be sufficient because of its limited power output and the extreme cost, meaning that it just couldn't ever be an appropriate alternative for our future power needs. In other words, he lectured, by the turn of the millennium, we would all be completely and totally screwed.

"We're going to need another source of energy if we are going to be able to survive the glacier advancement and downturn in global temperatures that many scientists have claimed are on the way," he preached. "And unless aliens arrive out of the blue and offer us a magic solution, we'll be out of luck."

Inwardly, I laughed at what Hamm was saying, remembering now his frequent lectures on the subject. He was one of those environmentally-minded teachers who wanted to scare us all into fearing the future so that we'd be more motivated to do something about it. I hadn't liked it then, and I liked it even less having actually lived in that future this guy wanted us to fear. Oh sure, it was bad. But not for any of the reasons that this idiot was freaking out over.

That's when, without thinking, I put my hand up and, without even waiting to be called on, I said, "What about the more distant future? Won't things change with technological advancements?"

Hamm sputtered self-importantly in response, clearly not used to being interrupted, much less challenged, before answering, "Well… um, perhaps, but it would take centuries. If not more. And we don't have nearly that long."

"No," I said curtly, cutting across him. "It's more like a couple of decades," My voice was growing louder now, driven in part by the frustration that had been building in me all afternoon. "The growth in renewable energy technology will be exponential once the costs start to come down, and those costs will drop in inverse proportion to the efficiency. Once this starts to happen in earnest, then we'll start to notice a significant reduction in the greenhouse gas emissions that are *warming* the Earth, not cooling it."

I'm not sure when it happened, but somewhere in the middle, I stopped talking about hypotheticals, and started talking about what actually had happened.

"Solar cells will remain about as efficient as they are now in terms of conversion rates, but we'll find ways to make them smaller so we don't need such large arrays, and we will even start to use lenses to focus and direct the strength of the sun. Then, once we have the kind of high-efficiency batteries that can store the power being generated, we can finally get past the problem of solar only being useful when the sun is actually shining.

"As for wind, the real advances will be with turbines that are designed specifically to operate only occasionally during typhoons where enough power to sustain a city for a year is released over an afternoon. Those will be quite common by the early 2020s. Then there's the tidal energy of places like the Bay of Fundy where they will eventually build an underwater grouping with the potential to power a large portion of the Maritimes.

"And then there are other power sources right under our very noses that we'll eventually learn to tap into, like turbines on large water mains in cities, or even on our taps at home. Then there's wave, geo-thermal, and thermoelectric energy — just to name a few. In time, each one of these parts of the solution is going to contribute to a larger whole."

All around me, things had frozen more solid than that time I found out that an aging body needs a healthy intake of liquids to keep the digestive system moving. Nobody in the lab so much as stirred as I ranted, and Hamm himself was standing there slack-jawed at the prospect of an upstart seventeen-year-old lecturing him in his own classroom. The same seventeen-year-old that had been too shy to say much of anything at all just a few days before.

"You're right in that there is not just one solution," I continued unabated. "There are *many* solutions, and they will all have to be used co-operatively." I was beginning to slow down, well aware that I'd already crossed a line but, off in the distance I could hear him trying to interrupt me by telling me that I was just an ignorant kid and didn't know what I was talking about. This just fired me up even more so I held my hand up, palm facing him to silence him, the way I used to do it with my kids. Amazingly, it worked — at least for a moment.

"All in all *Sir*, you're just part of a problem that's gonna get worse before it gets better. You could be using your position of authority to inspire these kids. To work to improve the future, but instead, you've decided to have an ego trip, and you're *scaring* them instead.

You're making them fear the future, so that the only way they'll be able to prepare for it is by following your example and stuffing their collective heads up their collective asses!"

Perhaps predictably, at this, the kids that I'd just referred to as a collective, gasped collectively. I ignored it and plowed on.

"The truth is, you can't always prepare for what's coming, but you can *inspire* this generation to be optimistic that things will turn out well no matter what takes place. Engage and inspire them, don't berate and belittle them!"

Hamm's shock was finally melting away, and he was walking towards me now, telling me to stop, but I just kept talking over him.

"I mean, don't get me wrong, I know what you're doing. Or, at least what you think you're doing. You're trying to scare people into doing something about the environment. You figure that fear will motivate them, but it doesn't and it won't. All you're doing is planting the seeds for a generation of people who will be scared of everything and paralyzed by the expectation of impending doom. People like that can't be reasoned with. People like that can't be motivated. People like that will flock in droves to the mouthpieces that deny that there's anything wrong."

I was packing up my things now, knowing even as I spoke that I'd gone too far to walk back on it now.

"Inspire them sir," I pleaded. "Give them something to hope for, something to aspire to."

Everyone was applauding now, but I only heard part of it because I was already walking out the door in the direction indicated by Hamm's bony finger. The last thing I heard him say as he shut the door to his classroom loudly behind me was, "You don't know the future! Nobody does!"

"You're wrong about that too, you myopic asshat," I muttered quietly enough so that none of the students and teachers who had been gathering outside the room to hear what all the yelling was about could hear me, and stalked off down the hallway, a decidedly intemperate mood settling comfortably onto my now-slumping shoulders. Were I still in my sixties, my disposition would have been described as "curmudgeonly" and I had to admit that it suited me. All at once, the thrill of being back here in my own past gave way to the frustration that I was no longer being deferred to because of my greater age and experience, and that I was lacking even the most basic of freedoms.

So much for being surreptitious and playing along quietly, I thought, but I was well past caring that I'd blown my cover at this point.

I spent the rest of the last period in the vice-principal's office with Mr. Barker staring at me, not sure what to say since this kind of thing was, suffice it to say, completely and wholly out of character for my younger self. I didn't help things by sitting there sullenly, arms crossed and answering his questions in a manner that was detached and aloof, making me seem, perhaps ironically, like a petulant teenager with a chip on his shoulder. He was trying to lecture me, but I'd tuned most of it out because I was still technically older than this wet-behind-the-ears Vice Principal, and this whole thing was a waste of my fucking time.

Besides, there wasn't much he could say to make me feel worse than I was making myself feel. I had broken my own pledge to keep a low profile today, and my outburst would have repercussions, especially once my father found out, and I didn't want him angry at me. So, when I finally left Barker's office in time to go to my locker to get my things before catching my bus, my mood was even more unpleasant.

I was grabbing my jacket and unhooking my book bag from my locker when Andi walked up with a grim look on her face.

"You heard?" I asked her as I angrily shoved a binder into my Adidas bag.

"*Everybody's* heard, Josh," she said in response as she reached out timidly to put a hand on my bicep, even as she tried to lighten the mood. "From what I hear, Hamm's locked himself in his office and is yelling at his DNA model. I've even heard talk that people want you to run for Student Council now."

I snorted at this.

"How was Barker?" she asked.

"Says he was lenient considering this is a first offense and so out of character for me," I said, scoffing. "He's 'letting me off easy' with a week's worth of detentions."

Letting me off easy, my wrinkled ass.

"Well, it could have been worse, I suppose," offered Andi, gently.

Rounding on her, I barked, "Worse? Getting kicked out would have been a hell of a lot better, believe me! This whole masquerade is a waste of my fucking time!"

Instead of backing down, or responding in kind with an outburst of her own, Andi stood her ground, and asked me, sternly, "What's going on with you, Josh? Really." There were tiny tears forming in the corners of her eyes, but instead of inspiring sympathy in me, it just enraged me more.

Why the hell couldn't she just leave me the hell alone? This is difficult enough as it is, without her throwing herself at me every time I turn around!

All at once, I realized what frustrated me the most about Andi, the beautiful young woman standing in front of me who was, even now, struggling not to cry. *She was just so goddamned perfect!* Everything about her was just so fucking faultless! She was the epitome of the "Mary Sue" stereotype that you hated simply because she was absurdly competent and was an expert in things she had no right being an expert in.

Part of me knew that it was irrational to blame her for my being tempted to break wedding vows that, strictly speaking, I hadn't even made yet, but a different, darker part of me was in charge at the moment. This darker part of me was telling me that I'd already had my chance, and that breaking up with her all those years back had been my biggest mistake. And, for some reason, it just made the mistake I'd made today all that much worse because it had a companion.

Seriously, this dark voice was saying, who cared if this was an opportunity to go back and do it all over again when I could still remember how I'd screwed it all up the first time! My whole life had been a pale comparison of what it could have been if I hadn't dumped Andi all those years ago. I had married Heather because she kind of reminded me of Andi and, although we'd had some good times, I had always—ALWAYS—secretly wished it had gone differently.

All at once, being back here was just a reminder of just how selfish and short-sighted I had been in my youth, because so far, almost everything I'd experienced being back here had been a stark reminder of just how goddammed idyllic this young woman was, and how enamoured she was with a boy who just wasn't worth it.

I just couldn't stand seeing Andi right now, and I could only think of one way to get rid of her so, sighing irritably, I finally answered. "Trust me, you wouldn't understand, and I really don't have the energy to explain myself to a child."

Beside me, Andi froze, the tears fully-formed in her eyes, her hand gripping my arm tightly enough to bruise it.

"You really are an arrogant son of a bitch sometimes, Donegal," she said, coldly, before spinning in place and charging away down the hall.

I watched her go out of the corner of my eye, already regretting what I'd said, but still too incensed to do anything about it other than glower at her.

This just keeps getting better and better.

The bus ride was quiet. Patrick had, of course, heard all about my meltdown and, instead of bringing it up, he just let me stew in silence, even going so far as to shoo away other kids who wanted to ask me about it.

When I got home, my father was waiting for the bus, standing outside the open overhead door to his workshop. He was eerily calm, which was his worst state of anger. As a kid, it had scared me silly, but now, well... mentally, I was older than he'd ever be. He might look like the authority figure at the moment, but from my perspective, he was Matheson having a temper tantrum. In fact, as I moved closer to my father, this was the first time that I fully appreciated how much my son had grown up to look like his Grandfather. What's more, that look of heated disappointment on Dad's face was almost a carbon copy of the look on Mat's face back in 2035 (at which point, Mat would have been about the same age that my father was here in 1985) when I told him that I was leaving the *Pucks* on Oskar's hair-brained scheme to follow the power cables.

Dad sent Patrick inside and stood glaring at me, ignoring the "Oooooo, you're in trouble now..." that my brother had directed at me before slipping inside the house. What my father hadn't seen was the thumbs up that Patrick had flashed me before he closed the front door behind him. It was his way of giving me some much-needed moral support.

"What the hell's up with you lately, Josh?" Dad growled quietly. "Are you on drugs?"

I actually laughed out loud at this. "Dad, no. It's not that. It's just ... well, Hamm's an idiot."

"I *know* he's an idiot," my father said, surprising me. "I used to play poker with him. We all know he's an idiot but that's not what I'm worried about. It's you. Since when do you talk back to your teachers? For that matter, since when do you hug me and your Mom in the morning like you haven't seen us in years? Since when do you know how to fix a motion sensor? Since when do you …" he paused, not sure what words to use. "Well, do you do whatever the hell it was you were doing this morning?"

As I stood looking up at my father, who was clearly disappointed in me, I suddenly didn't feel old anymore. All at once, I was a reckless teenager again and, like a pricked balloon, my anger deflated completely and absolutely. I still hadn't fully decided if this whole damn time-slip was permanent, much less real, but suddenly it didn't matter. Illusion or not, this version of my father cared for me, and what I was doing was concerning him. It was causing him pain. I didn't want to cause any incarnation of my father pain, not when we'd finally been reunited, against every conceivable odd in the universe.

I let out a long breath and finally relaxed my shoulders.

"Dad, I'm sorry. I'm not on drugs it's just that… well, do you know what an epiphany is?"

"God damn it kid, I know what an epiphany is."

I smiled and put my hand on his elbow as I looked directly at him. "Well, I've had one. A *big* one. And I'm having a hard time sorting out what it all means. There are so many new possibilities for me, and I'm feeling a confidence I didn't have at seventeen." He cocked his eyebrows at my gaffe, and I tried to backtrack. "…*before*. I mean confidence I never had *before*. Please. I just need some time to find my feet again. I'm not doing drugs. I'm not going to run off to find Jesus or join a circus."

He stared at me a moment. "There have got to be better ways to express this … this new 'confidence' of yours," he countered finally, emphasizing the word as if he didn't believe it.

"Well, maybe," I answered. "But you raised me to trust my own judgement and to stand up in the face of bullshit." My father's mouth twitched a little at this as if it wanted to form a smile. "Well Hamm personifies that, and I just couldn't take it anymore. I spoke my mind today, just like you always do when you know someone is lying, or trying to take advantage of you." This was true. My father had an acid tongue when he felt he was being played for a fool, and a biting wit when he was fired up and inspired. With my bedroom above his home office, I could always tell when he was typing an angry letter, because he hammered each key of the manual typewriter so forcefully that I was sure that every single embossed letter was breaking through the paper. Alluding to this aspect of his personality to justify my having done something similar and, in effect, turning it back on him was a desperate gamble, but it appeared to be mollifying my father, who was finally looking a lot less irate.

"I promise," I continued. "Next time I express my newfound confidence, I'll be more subtle about it."

My father stared closely at each of my eyes in turn, giving me the impression that he was studying them closely to see if they were suspiciously dilated. Finally, he said, "Fine. Just no more phone calls from Hamm. He's an idiot." Then he turned and started to walk back into his workshop before speaking over his shoulder. "Your mother doesn't need the car tonight. You can take it to work."

"Work," I answered, as if I had just invented the word. "Right. I *work* tonight." It was supposed to sound like I was stating the obvious confidently, but inside I was freaked out. Add this to the list of the many things that I'd completely forgotten about since my recent time-shift. In my teens, I worked part-time at *Duckies*, a local convenience store. Apparently, I was in for a crash-course tonight on how to operate an 80s-era cash register.

Son of a bitch. This just kept getting better and better.

The last thing I heard my father mutter before firing up his table-saw were the words "collective asses." And then, I swear to God, the man actually smiled.

W ell, this morning marks the beginning of the third day in my own past. When I woke up, the first thing I did (again) was to check to make sure I hadn't come unstuck in time while I had been sleeping. And, as far as I could tell, time was proceeding, if not normally, then at least predictably and consistently in the correct chronological sequence and pace.

Last night's sleep was actually the best that I'd had in a long time, and it even included an added bonus, something I hadn't experienced since my teens: a wet dream. These teenage hormones might have even been fun to feel again at any other time, but now they were just so frikkin' distracting! I was having a difficult enough time fitting in at home and at school without my mind drifting off every six or seven minutes to fantasize about things like the swimsuit models on the back of my bedroom door coming to life and showing me their gratitude. And I wasn't alone either. It was like the entire student population was swimming naked in a vat of a powerful military-grade aphrodisiacs, and they were all just letting their bodies follow their natural, primal urges as they…

See! There I go again. Knock it off Josh! Focus already!

My shift at *Duckies* yesterday evening had gone pretty well, all things considered. Interestingly, the hardest part hadn't actually been figuring out how to use a cash register again as I'd expected, but had instead been remembering how to drive the car to get there! From my perspective, it had been over a decade since I'd last operated a real car, or at least something that hadn't been part of an OVUM simulacrum. Luckily, it was a lot like riding a bike, in that it came back to me pretty quickly.

When I got to the corner store, I chatted for a while with Charlotte, the employee I was taking over for. I guided the conversation to make it seem like we were commiserating about the downsides of part-time shift-work, while casually prompting her to offer up examples of her experience with various aspects of working retail. In the course of the discussion, I admitted to her that I'd never really gotten the hang of the tax button on the cash register, and sometimes wasn't sure what items we were supposed to apply tax to and which ones were exempt. As I'd hoped, this motivated her to demonstrate the proper technique on the machine, a process that involved revealing a great deal more about how it worked. Charlotte also encouraged me to refer to the instructions again, which was a great reminder that we actually had documentation that the owner had prepared so that each of the employees knew what they were doing.

Once Charlotte left, I immediately pulled out the instructions and scanned them quickly to make sure that I wasn't in over my head. There were customers in the store at that point, but I was feeling pretty confident, especially once I found the last page with the list of phone numbers that I could call with questions.

A few customers later, I found that, just like driving, it all came back to me pretty quickly. It was about this time that I noticed something else. My foul mood, that had mostly disappeared during Dad's lecture, had actually turned into an excited exhilaration, due entirely to an idea that had occurred to me once I had been afforded an opportunity between customers to contemplate the potential of my situation.

The whole experience of standing up to Hamm by telling him that his prediction of the future was wrong because I secretly knew better had got me thinking about something that I'd only heretofore briefly considered. If I knew what the future was bringing, and if this time-displacement of mine was permanent, then could I use my knowledge of the future to effect positive change in this timeline?

The possibilities actually kind of excited me. How much could I do? Could I curb climate change? Stop 9/11 and the litany of wars that followed it? Keep Trump from getting elected?

Oh God. Could I actually stop the events of 2025? Could I stop the pandemic?

My eyes actually teared up a bit as I thought about this last possibility. This was all the balm I needed to assuage the festering sores that were the negative, self-punishing thoughts of guilt that had tortured me earlier that day. The voices went away completely once I had begun to consider that maybe the reason that I had slipped back in time when nobody else had, was because I had some significant role to play in fixing the future.

Once I began to feel better about that problem, I turned my attention towards what to do about Andi. Clearly, I had let my frustration get the better of me earlier in the day, and I had taken it out on her, mostly, out of reflex. It wasn't something that I liked admitting, but this wasn't something that was out of character for me because, it had, in fact, been exactly how I had treated Celeste in the first five or six years of our marriage.

To be fair, when Celeste and I had been joined in 2027, we'd both recently lost loved ones. Celeste's parents had perished in the events of 2025 and my first wife, Heather had lost her battle with breast cancer just eight months before that. In those early years of our time together, Celeste harboured a certain animosity towards me because I was significantly older than her. As for me, well I resented her … well, simply for not being Heather. It hadn't been easy, but we persisted, and even developed a certain fondness for each other — eventually.

And now, it felt like it was happening all over again for me, no matter how many times I told myself that it was different. I knew deep down that the biggest part of the reason that I was pushing Andi away was because of the perceived age difference of fifty years between us. It was making me decidedly uncomfortable although, admittedly, this discomfort had taken a remarkably short time to fade as I'd gotten more and more used to being physically seventeen again.

Could a marriage bond even survive time-travel? Not that it mattered really because, as I reminded myself, for the second time in as many days, Celeste and I had said our goodbyes with the expectation that we would likely never see each other again. Once she found out what Oskar had asked me to do, she'd told me to go — begged me even — even though she knew that it meant that she would have to go into hiding. She told me that she'd be fine on her own and that she had Mat, Suki and the kids to watch out for her.

I knew that I couldn't very well tell Andi any of this, but it did help me to understand how I was feeling about her, and also how to potentially resolve the quarrel that I'd created. So, a few hours later, after I'd locked up the store and gone through the closing procedure according to the, somewhat familiar, instructions, I called Andi from the store phone. It had been something that we used to do all the time because it had been our only real opportunity for a private conversation, or at least one where my father wasn't checking in on me every ten minutes to see if his line was still tied up. Andi picked up right away, as if she had been expecting the call.

"Josh?" she said quietly.

"It's me," I answered.

"I'm sorry for upsetting you today," she said before I had a chance to say anything. This was typical Andi, always apologizing for things that weren't her fault just to keep the peace. It was a defence mechanism that I now know she adopted to deal with two emotionally distant and narcissistic parents, but it didn't make me feel any better knowing that I'd taken advantage of it more than a few times in our relationship. But not anymore. I was determined to do things better now so, before she could say anything else, I interrupted her as gently as I could.

"Andi. Please... just stop right there. You've got nothing to apologize for. This was all on me. I'm the one who should be sorry. I was wrong, and I apologize." From the gasp I heard through the line as I spoke, and the silence that endured afterwards, I knew that I'd just shocked Andi. The seventeen-year-old me that she knew didn't like to say sorry. He didn't like being wrong. Being able to admit wrongdoing was a skill that had taken me decades to learn.

Andi still hadn't said anything, but I could hear her breathing so, taking advantage of her loss for words, I just kept talking and told her the truth about why I'd barked at her in front of my locker, having decided that the truth (or at least a small portion thereof) was the best course of action. I explained that my outburst was due in large part because I was angry at myself for losing control with Hamm and she was the closest target, but it was also paradoxically because she was just so perfect and that I was constantly feeling like I wasn't worthy and couldn't live up to her, and couldn't be everything she needed.

Abruptly, she spoke up, cutting across me. "Josh. Just stop talking and come pick me up, OK? I can still go out for a while, especially if it's with you. I can't ... I can't have this conversation over the phone."

I didn't hesitate. "I'll be right there."

Ten minutes later, Andi was sitting beside me in the car, and we were driving around town aimlessly. We didn't really have much to say about our argument at first, and instead just enjoyed being together. Eventually, we found ourselves in the parking lot above the Hermann gravel pit a few miles east of town, uncharacteristically empty of party-goers tonight, and put the back seat of the hatchback down so that we could look up at the moon and the stars through the back window — at least until it fogged up. As we held each other, I apologized again and we both cried. There in the dark of the car, her olive skin glowing in the soft pale light of the moon, I finally felt fully present in my own past. No longer was I feeling torn between my future and my new present. In fact, until Andi was holding me, I hadn't even realized how very lost I'd been feeling the last few days. I was literally a man out of time. I was in a place where I didn't really belong anymore and, despite how familiar it was, I was still a stranger to it, and it to me. Andi's embrace had finally grounded me, giving me shelter and welcoming me home.

We eventually stopped talking entirely and just started kissing, and I felt like I was tumbling through time all over again at the sensation of it all.

About a half hour later, I was kissing her goodbye reluctantly outside of her door, cursing inwardly at having to accept the rules that a teenager living at home had to abide by, like curfews. I had been resisting Andi's affections for so long, but suddenly, I couldn't get enough of them. The porch light flashed, signaling that it was time for me to go, so I hugged Andi one last time and said, "Goodnight Andi. I love you."

"Love you too, Josh," she replied. "See you tomorrow at 5? Phoebe and Brock will be here at the house, and we can go to the restaurant in Brock's car."

Nodding by way of an answer, ignoring something that was tickling the back of mind in reference to Brock's car, I gave her one last peck on her check, and slipped away down the porch steps.

This resolution of our conflict had certainly helped me get a better night's sleep, and this morning, I actually slept-in until around five-thirty, proving that my mind was definitely adjusting to the body of a teenager! I started the day with some stretching and Tai Chi movements, something that I hadn't actually had an opportunity to do for … how long had it been? Months, at least for my mind, but it was definitely the first time I'd ever done anything like it with this younger frame. This body was definitely a lot softer in terms of musculature, but the focus and the mindfulness of the exercise helped center me nonetheless.

A short while later, I went downstairs and joined my father for breakfast. The moment I appeared at the base of the stairs he glowered at me a little, even as Chance bounded over to welcome me enthusiastically. After yesterday's conversation, things were still kinda tense with Dad, and me being up this early of my own volition was still, as far as he was concerned, wholly unheard of for me.

"'morning Dad," I said as I sniffed at his coffee covetously (maybe I could sneak a full mug later when he was gone). "What's on your agenda today?"

My father cleared his throat as his eyebrows furrowed briefly. Yes, I knew that this would have been out of character for me fifty years ago: me talking to my father like this. How could I tell the man that, after losing him some twenty years in my past, I would have been happy just to spend every waking minute with him in this freaky alternate reality, just asking all the questions I wished I'd have asked him before he'd died?

As my father told me about the work he was planning in the workshop today, and the errands he had to run, I went to the fridge to pull out some eggs.

That's when it hit me.

We had bacon!

How is it that it's taken me two whole days to realize this?

"We have bacon!" I announced excitedly, interrupting my father, who had started to glare at me again, no doubt beginning to disbelieve my claim at being drug-free again.

"It's just that I haven't had bacon in years!" I added without thinking. Again, I was just happy to be able to have conversations with my father again. I still hadn't figured out what I should and shouldn't say. He was, after all as far as I was concerned, some twenty-five years younger than me.

Dammit, he should be respecting his elders, not contemplating grounding them!

"We had it last weekend," he said suspiciously.

"Well, it just *seems* like years then," I countered defensively as I did the math in my head, trying to figure out the last time I'd eaten it. From my perspective, it had been about eleven years. All pork products had, of course, all but disappeared after the pandemic of

2025, for obvious reasons. "It's bacon. We should be eating it every day!"

I almost started crying again once the bacon started cooking and I could smell it, and I could barely wait for it to cool before I started sampling it. When I sat down beside my father a short while later, my plate was loaded with several fried eggs, some home fries, and every piece of bacon that had been in the fridge—close to half a package. Naturally, Chance was sitting right beside me, her envious eye on my overflowing plate, hoping that some of it would find its way accidentally to her. I tried not to swoon as I ate it all (Spoiler alert: I did ultimately share some of it with my faithful Golden Retriever who had the cutest set of puppy dog eyes in the world), because I was pretty sure that my father was watching me suspiciously again.

"Hey," I said, between mouthfuls, while also trying to distract from my table manners. "Do you mind if I use the car this morning? I have a few errands."

"Check with your Mother," Dad answered. "She might need it to get to her *coffee club*." My father said these last two words as if they were somehow distasteful. The coffee club was a group of women that met several times a week at the local *Stedman's* lunch counter. Dad disliked them, assuming that they only ever got together to gossip.

Sure enough, when I asked my Mother a couple of minutes later, she did have plans to meet up with her friends, but not until about noon. That would give me plenty of time to run my errands first thing in the morning, and be back to give her the car.

When I got into town a few hours later, I went straight to the lone stationery store in Robertson. The moment I walked into the building, and saw the reams of paper against the back wall, I stopped short. Paper was one of the many things that we had to ration on the island, so it still felt unfamiliar to see that much of it in one place, so inexpensively priced and with nary an armed guard in sight.

As I stood there gawking, an older woman I didn't recognize greeted me like an old friend and started asking me familiar questions that I probably should have been able to answer. I muddled through some feeble replies, wishing beyond hope that I had had a smartphone in my pocket that I could pretend was ringing to get out of the situation. Eventually extracting myself for the conversation, I grabbed a couple of nice pens (a long time ago, I had learned to despise cheap pens, because, if I was going to write something, I might as well be using something that feels good in my hand while I'm doing it) and picked out a thick hardcover notebook (a long time ago, I had learned to despise cheap notebooks, because, if I was going to be putting my ideas somewhere, it might as well be on a product that was well-made). The notebook was more expensive than the more basic varieties there on the shelf beside it, but I was planning on using it for something important, and didn't think that a spiral notebook had the right amount of gravitas.

It was when I got to the cash, standing under the handmade sign advertising the store's new "Faxing Service" that I opened my wallet and looked at the very lonely looking ten-dollar bill within it.

Nuts, I wondered at a completely inopportune time, as I stared into a near empty wallet. *How am I going to pay for my date tonight with Andi?*

It had completely slipped my mind that I had to have enough physical money to be able to pay for my purchase as well as go out tonight. This kind of basic budgeting was suddenly very alien to me. For the last decade of my life on the island, physical money didn't really exist. In fact, our economy was almost completely barter for anything that the *Ensee* didn't provide.

Standing there with the cashier wondering what I was doing, I realized that I'd completely forgotten that debit transactions were a thing of the future. In 1985, you went to the bank in person on Friday to withdraw all of the money that you anticipated that you would need for the weekend. If you didn't withdraw enough, then you were out of luck.

Oh crap – banks.

How the hell did you take money out of a bank in 1985 before ATMs? I seemed to recall that you went into the actual building, filled out a form with your account number (something that I'd have no hope in hell of remembering) and all the pertinent details, and then waited in line to present it to a teller who would then ask how your mother was as she counted out your money.

It was at this point that I was rescued by the cashier, a young woman who I had finally figured out, by what she'd been saying to me, was a friend of the family. Hell, Robertson was such a small town, that everyone was a friend of the family in one way or another. I was likely insulting her by not using her name.

"Did you want to put this on your father's account?" she asked, having obviously been looking into the same near-empty wallet I was dumb-foundedly holding open in front of her. "Like last time?"

My father ran a construction business, and had accounts at most of the stores in town. In fact, he'd admonished me once for buying a three-holed punch on my own and not putting it on credit at this very stationery store so that he could have claimed it on his taxes. Naturally, in response to this request, and much to his regret, I immediately went out and charged a very expensive scientific calculator to his name. I'm guessing that this past event had actually happened fairly recently if this, increasingly familiar looking young woman, was asking me to do it again.

"Um, sure," I muttered as I returned my wallet to my back pocket, happy that there was nobody else standing behind me in line.

As I stood watching the cashier pull out some kind of ledger from under the counter, I wondered if I would be able to borrow money from my father for tonight. Or, maybe my mother instead, since Dad would no doubt want to lecture me on the importance of financial planning. If he only knew that such planning was a complete waste of time with what awaited us. But that was in the future, and this is now. How much would I need for Chinese Food and a movie in 1985? Would $80 be enough? While I was in town, I was going to have to check out some prices so that I would know what to expect.

Wait, do I even have to pay tonight? Did Brock pick up the tab in the original timeline? Damn, I can't remember. In fact, my only clear recollection of the evening was that the annoying yuppie needing us to sit at a table by the window so that he could keep an eye on his Jag in case a passer-by looked at it too intently or something. Oh, and there was something about the actual Jag too, but that wasn't completely clear.

I thanked Melanie for her help (serendipitously, somebody had called her by name from the back of the store while she was doing the paperwork for my purchase), and walked out of the stationery store and onto the street. It was a bright sunny day, and I stood on the near-empty sidewalk sniffing at the spring air and marvelling at just how much sky there was here in Robertson. Trees didn't get very tall up north, and neither did the buildings, something that had always made me feel exposed to the elements whenever I'd come back to visit the town in my adulthood.

After stashing my recent purchases in the car, I decided that, since I had enough time left, I'd wander around a bit. The stationery store was on a side street that intersected with Robertson's main street, the chief thoroughfare through the town that also acted as the business core. This three-block section of town housed most of its storefronts, commercial businesses, and public gathering places, meaning that you could usually find a very large percentage of Robertson's population milling about here, especially on a Saturday morning when most people were off work.

It took me about a half hour to walk up one side of the street and down the other, during which I browsed in store windows and nodded at the people I passed on the sidewalk, and even stuck my head into our town's sole Chinese restaurant to take a quick look at the menu so I knew what to expect in terms of both food and prices tonight. It was when I was approaching the town's local library that it occurred to me that I might be able to get some answers to some of my questions, mostly about what the *Ensee* was up to in 1985. One of the things that I wanted to detail in my new journal was the critical role that the *Ensee* would play on the island in the wake of 2025, so it made sense that I look into their history. What better way to do that from here, some fifty years back into that very history?

The "*Ensee*" was an acronym that had pretty much universally been adopted in reference to the huge corporation known officially as "*The Naffarium Collective.*" Personally, I hadn't really become aware of them until sometime in the 2010s even though they had apparently been operating quietly in the background of North American corporate culture since the 60s. As for what they actually did as a company, well that was another topic altogether. They were most famous simply for acquiring and assimilating other companies into their greater whole. In fact, the *Ensee* would eventually became known colloquially as "the Borg," in reference to the infamous race of augmented beings from *Star Trek: The Next Generation* that would absorb other species into its hive mind to make the collective that much stronger. This association was made dangerously explicit on the island when the underground Resistance first began to publicly defy the *Ensee's* authoritarian rule by covering walls with graffiti declaring, "Beware the Borg".

It was only after I'd walked through the door and into the library, and was staring at the squat stacks behind the welcome desk that I realized that, without an internet search engine, or at the very least, some kind of dedicated library computer terminal, I was at a loss as to how to search for something.

There used to be narrow drawers full of index cards right?

Trying not to look conspicuous, I meandered into the stacks while nodding robotically at a few of the patrons as well as the woman behind the counter, all of which had me at a disadvantage in that they knew who I was, but they were but an unfocused memory to me.

Damn. What I wouldn't give for a smartphone with facial recognition software right about now.

I browsed a few of the shelves that were obviously dedicated to new releases (from the likes of Sidney Sheldon and Danielle Steele) as I scanned the room for the drawer system. Once I finally spotted the cabinet, my memories of having used it came back to me immediately. Not so much *how* to use it mind you, but definitely the memory of once having used it.

After about ten minutes of fruitless searching, the librarian (whom I eventually figured out was named Madame Beauclair) came over to offer her assistance.

"*The Naffarium Collective*," she said after I'd explained what I'd been looking for. "Can't say that they sound familiar at all. They're a company?"

"One of the biggest," I answered. "Or at least they will be."

If she noticed my temporal gaffe, she ignored it. "Have you tried the *Who's Who of Companies*?" she asked as she tottered off towards the Reference area. I took the huge tome she eventually returned with and retreated to a table in the corner of the book-shelved room to browse through it. Over the next hour, Madame Beauclair fed me a steady diet of books and magazines that she thought might have the information I was looking for but, in the end, I had to admit defeat. I couldn't find any reference anywhere to the Collective, nor any of the major corporations that Oskar would one day connect to the larger whole. Even the CEO, Remmus Kemp, was unknown.

From what little I knew about the *Ensee's* history, I was pretty sure that, in this time period, the company was operating out of hundreds (if not thousands) of small, decentralized hubs spread out around the Globe. None of them shared the same company name, so none of them could be associated with any other, yet they all worked in tandem, like a flock of birds murmuring. It was a mystery how they managed to act so cohesively and in concert in an era that was decades before a communications and information system like the World Wide Web had appeared.

Thanking Madame Beauclair, and promising to give my best to my mother, I left the library, blinking at the bright sunlight that greeted me after the dimmed environment of the book stacks. Continuing my walk along the street, I soon found myself standing in front of *PJ's* arcade. For a moment, I stood in front of the squat, slightly run-down building, not sure whether I should go in.

Although I had never been very good at arcade games in the 80s (or ever, really), I absolutely loved going to *PJ's*—the cultural hub of my teen years—and watching others play. This wasn't where I saw my first saw arcade games, mind you. That would have been on a trip to Florida in the early 80s, when I'd seen an *Asteroids* console and begged my father to give me a quarter so that I could play it, even though I had no idea how. As he watched each of my tiny triangular ships (which I would later find out were called vector graphics), get blown apart one after the other in short order by jagged, irregularly shaped, polygons not more than a minute or two after I'd started the game, he famously quipped, "Well, that was a good use of my quarter now wasn't it?"

The funny thing was, this wasn't the only time that this kind of thing had happened to me. I'd had an almost identical experience with *Pac-Man* a few years later, but this time it was my own quarter that I'd sacrificed as I ate my way through the maze with absolutely no idea why I kept dying when the ghosts touched me and why they occasionally turned blue. I had never been one to read instructions ahead of time, much to the chagrin of both my wives.

Although there were four or five dedicated arcades in Robertson, *PJ's* was by far the most popular and was owned by a young man who wasn't really that much older than me. He'd graduated a few years back and had decided to open an arcade and give it the nickname that he himself had been given in Grade 10 when he'd worn pajamas to school one day.

PJ's arcade really was the best. Not only did it always have the best selection of coin-op games that changed monthly, but it also had an awesome lunch counter with the absolute best fries in town. In high school, it was where my friends and I hung out. When we weren't playing in the arcade, we were eating fries and burgers at the counter in the next room and planning out our next Video Recital.

When I finally walked in (figuring I still had most of an hour left), it was the smell of delicious hot grease that hit me first and, without even thinking about it, I was ordering an extra-large order of fries from PJ himself. While I waited for it, I wandered into the arcade where I was overwhelmed by computerized beeps and sound effects mixed with the din of excited kids arguing with joysticks. The place was busy even on a Saturday morning, full of teen-agers I kinda recognized, but who were thankfully too involved in their games to challenge me to name them. I walked around the room and looked at everything like it was my first time there, even though it had almost been my second home for a time. This was the first place I'd seen the awesome graphics of *Donkey Kong* and *Pole Position*, or a person using the *Pac-Man* pattern, or watched a friend master *Joust* by not straying from the sweet spot, or watched somebody loose a ship on purpose in *Galaga* in order to get more firepower when he got it back later in the game.

For years, I'd harboured the fantasy of being able to walk into this arcade with a whole ten-dollar roll of quarters and just go nuts. I never did it though, because I knew it wouldn't last nearly as long as it should have, what with my lousy hand-eye coordination, so I just spent most of my time here watching others play. Maybe now I would finally have a chance to live out that simple fantasy, even though the appeal was somewhat diminished because I'd come from a future when I'd been able to play each and every one of these games for free online as much as I'd wanted to. Not that this made me any better at playing them though, which dashed my other fantasy of coming into this arcade with skills I'd honed in the future and become some kind of arcade hero.

When I left *PJ's* a little while later, I was grinning ear to ear as I ate fresh-cut fries out of a box-board container covered in grease stains that was wedged between the two front seats of the car for easy access. The fries were moist, and covered in an almost obscene amount of salt and ketchup — dressed up in a manner I'd loved as a kid, but avoided as an adult, especially once I had become aware of something called "blood pressure." I savoured each and every fry, even though this particular vegetable certainly hadn't been in short supply on Prince Edward Island in the future, unlike some other foods.

I took my time getting home, knowing that I still had a full half-hour. I rolled the windows down to let in the crisp spring air, and toured my hometown of Robertson, waving at people who were getting more and more recognisable every hour, and seeing places and things that triggered one fond memory after another. Apparently, the person who said that you can't go home again didn't know about time-travel.

Every square inch of this town had some kind of memory associated with it and, as I drove, it was like I could actually see my former self there, physically acting out each one of those memories. I could see my juvenile figure out on *Shelter Bay* in winter stumbling around awkwardly on skates, and in summer learning how to swim and being scared to death of the high diving board. Here I was a little older and carrying a guitar to the community center for lessons (which brought with it the olfactory memory of the sweetly acrid, yet totally addictive, smell of photocopies in the 70s), and there I was going door to door selling chocolates, candles, or apples to raise money for one school activity or another. I was riding my bike through a dusty field, building a fort in a secluded area of Hilltop park, getting bullied on a street corner, slipping into a corner store to get an ice cream cone, cramming way too many friends into a tiny car, or standing high up on a snowbank watching the big carnival parade go by while catching candy being thrown by a clown.

There were so many ghosts here. All of them my former self at one point or another in my life and now, through some kind of trick of fate, I was actually one of those ghosts, remembering things that had happened to me even though many of them had yet to actually occur.

Now, I'd never really been one to wax nostalgic, even more so in a future where looking back on an idyllic past was actually quite painful, but I had to admit that I was enjoying being back in Robertson, for the first time in some thirty years. The closest I'd been to driving these familiar roads was the time I'd used Google maps, back when there was a full-fledged internet, and when it was still world-wide. At the time, I struggled to remember a lot of what I was seeing. I wasn't sure at the time if it was because I'd forgotten it, or if it was because it had just changed so much. Now, back in time, with things exactly the way they'd been, I'm realizing that it was a bit of both.

It's a goddamned shame that this quiet little town, like most of the rest of the country will be a ghost town in some forty years after the events of 2025. It's hard to think about that right now though, when I'm being inundated with unfiltered nostalgia made manifest.

I actually started to cry when I drove by the bandstand where Andi and I would linger most Friday nights on our way to supper on our weekly date, (and where I ultimately broke up with her because I didn't want a long-distance relationship in University). We never did have long to linger there before getting to the Chinese food restaurant, mind you, as we had to make the most of our time together between the end of school and the start of my shift at *Duckies*. But it was usually long enough for me to sit her up on the railing or lean her up against one of the columns so that I could explore her mouth with my own.

I actually had to pull over completely when I saw the fountain where she and I had first met. Well, of course it wasn't the *first* time we'd met mind you — everyone knew everyone in a town the size of Robertson, even though she'd just moved here a few months before — but it was the first time we really talked to each other without the distraction of other kids. We'd happen to run into each other one gorgeous Autumn day at the fountain and, well … we *fell* into each other. I have no idea how it had happened, because I was normally just so, well… weird and withdrawn around girls. Normally, I clammed up and got all self-conscious, but Andi somehow got past all of that. Somehow, she shared some of her self-confidence with me, and we found out that we had a lot in common. I'd made a wish that day to be with Andi, and it had come true for two glorious years, until we went our separate ways after high school.

Funny how I was feeling nostalgic about this girl when I was, even now, in the process of living out my own history with her again. In my memory, Andi had grown into something of mythical proportions. She had been my first … well, she had been my first *everything*: My first kiss, first love, first time, first breakup, and first regret all rolled into one. The young girl who was Andi in the past didn't seem like the same person, even though I knew that she was.

She just seemed so, … damn, there was no other word for it but, *young*.

Maybe it was because I knew her potential. Maybe it was because I knew about the distinguished career that lay ahead for her in broadcasting, and that was somehow fusing with her incarnation in the past. In my mind, I still saw the face I would come to know on my TV screen, the face that was wearing an expression of deep concern that last time I saw it as she implored a scared population to remain calm in the face of a ruthless virus that was racing across the world like a wildfire.

After a few minutes of staring at the tumbling water in the fountain, I dried my eyes and pulled carefully out into traffic, heading in the direction of the big Canadian flag towards home. When I got there, Dad's truck was gone, and so was Patrick's motorcycle (I seemed to recall that he was away for the weekend at some kind of team-building retreat), and Mom was sitting in the kitchen waiting for me.

"Did you have lunch?" she asked as I tried to hide the greasy bag of fries behind me, which was made all the more difficult because this just made it easier for Chance to get at it. "There's some leftover lasagna in the fridge if you're hungry."

"Thanks Ma," I said, shooing the mischievous Golden Retriever away. "Have fun."

She was almost out the door when she turned back. "Are you OK on your own? Did you need me to drive you somewhere?" That was typical Mom. She was probably already late, but was still willing to delay further to make sure that I was properly fed or to drive me somewhere.

"Nah, it's all good," I said. "I've got my bike if I need to go anywhere."

When my mother was gone, and I finally had the place to myself, I brewed myself a pot of coffee and put a plate of Mom's lasagna in the microwave (with a healthy helping of freshly-shredded cheese piled on top). As the large machine hummed, I couldn't help but be reminded of my father's first reaction to a microwave oven. It had been at supper a friend's place when our hosts put a bag of buns in the microwave to warm them up. Perhaps predictably, my father had panicked, thinking that, because it was an oven, the plastic bag would melt. A month later, we had this unit, retrofitted into a hole that my father had made in the wall beside our conventional stove.

When the lasagna was warmed through, I filled a mug with some coffee, and headed out onto the back deck where I set up shop at the picnic table. Once I was seated and comfortable, Chance leapt up on the bench seat beside me to rest her head on my lap. I took my first sip of coffee as I stroked her fur affectionately and looked out over the fields in behind our house. It wasn't all that cold, but I shivered at the pleasure of it all nonetheless. Then, with a mouthful of lasagna, I opened my new journal and wrote my name on the inside cover, mostly to test the pen and to get the ink running. This done, I turned to the first page.

Looking back out across the meadows, my new pen poised to compose the first line of the journal, I paused, unsure where to begin with my story.

That's when it all became clear…

CHAPTER 7
Excerpt from Josh's journal

THE FUTURE AS I REMEMBER IT.

In my last journal entry, I wrote all about how I found myself in here the past. This one will be a tad confusing. It will be about what my future, but it will be something that's already happened to me, so from that perspective, it will be my past. Got it?

Good. Then let's begin...

WARNING: SPOILERS BELOW!

STOP READING IF YOU DON'T WANT TO KNOW THE FUTURE!!

****

When I was growing up, the old folks used to tell me that they just didn't understand the world anymore, and that the only thing that made sense to them was the past. Now that I've lived through both the past and the future, I understand what they mean because, now that I'm back in my own past, I can't help but feel that the only thing that makes sense to me now is the future, the thing I've just come from, the time that hasn't happened yet.

Anything makes sense when you've had time to think about it afterwards. Nothing makes sense when it's happening, especially when it's happening to you for the second time and you don't know why.

It's been a full two and a half days in my own past, and it doesn't seem anywhere near close to ending. This is my reality now, as far as I can tell, but I'm no closer to understanding how, or even why, it's happened. Fitting in has certainly been challenging, if a little fun at times, and I keep going back and forth on whether I should even try. For now, I'm rationalizing that the world believes that I'm a seventeen-year old boy and that has certain limitations to it. If I push things too much, or tell people too much, I may end up getting put away, or worse, forcibly medicated.

Which is why I'm taking a really big chance with this journal I suppose, but it's a risk worth taking. I think.

Here, in a nutshell, are all the major events in my life B.P. (Before Pandemic):

After high school, I went to Western University for my undergrad, and then University of Toronto for grad studies, eventually getting my Ph.D. in Electrical and Computer Engineering. Somewhere in the middle of that, I met and married Heather Hudson, and our son Matheson was born in 1995. We settled in Vaughn,

Ontario eventually, with me working at Canada's Wonderland and her at a not-for-profit organization that offered free legal advice for battered women.

Life in the city wasn't really a good match for us though, and we moved north to Haliburton around 2000, where I worked from home for IBM and Heather set up her own law practice. Life was pretty good for us. Heather built quite a legal team, and I set up a helluva workshop on our property where I supplemented our income with the sale of various made-to-order electronic devices of my own design. Oh sure, there were the sad parts, like Dad dying in 2004, just a couple of years before Heather's father did, and Mom following about a decade later. But there were the happy parts too, like Matheson marrying his high school sweetheart, Suki, in 2020.

Heather and I had planned on retiring up North eventually, but Heather's health decided otherwise. Diagnosed with breast cancer in 2023, she would be gone within a heart-breakingly short one-and-a-half-years. One small comfort was that she got to hold her newborn grand-daughter, Wilson, before she died.

My late wife's last request was that we take her ashes to her hometown of Summerside, Prince Edward Island, and toss them into the ocean that her ancestors had fished and where she herself had come of age, having been practically raised on a fishing boat. So, in the spring of 2025, I rented a huge RV, and set out for the Maritimes with Matheson, Suki, and Wilson for a long-overdue family vacation, during which we would say goodbye to Heather while we honoured her wishes.

Needless to say, something came up.

<I just stopped to get more coffee. Damn, it's good. I also played fetch with Chance for a bit to compose my thoughts. Now, where was I?>

Sometime in the not too distant future, Michael J. Fox, battling Parkinson's Disease for control of his own body, will famously say that it's rarely the worst-case scenario that you've been dreading that will get you, but something else entirely. I can't, of course, confirm the exact phrasing of this quote without access to the internet, or a time machine, but it's something like that, and it's an eerily accurate prediction of what's coming for all of us.

People today—or well, maybe not so much in 1985, but in a few decades—will come to believe that the biggest threat to humanity's future will be climate change, but it isn't. Well, I mean, yes it's still going to be a threat, but by 2025, it won't really matter that much anymore.

Anyhow, a few years before that, two political schools of thought will go head to head, one of which had been operating pretty much secretly even as it had been guiding public policy for at least two decades.

The first ideology was one that everyone was already familiar with. It was the group that had been saying for years that environmental degradation was a species-ending problem, but it wasn't too late to do something. Even though massive changes in worldwide weather patterns seemed to be too widespread to influence, they suggested that, if we poured all available resources into technologies and techniques, we could reverse the effects of climate change. They used public money to help those affected, and espoused green technology over the traditional, dirtier variety.

It was the other political ideology that finally made its genuine intentions clear, even though they had been pretty much obvious all along for those who were paying attention. This included big-oil companies like ExxonMobil who knew about the threat of climate change decades before it was publicly acknowledged, and actually hired think-tanks to release data that knowingly misled the public in order to foment skepticism.

Then there were the political parties that had always denied climate change. Well, the time finally came when they simply couldn't maintain that charade anymore, so they made a big deal publicly about suddenly caring, even as they enacting useless legislation that still somehow managed to channel the money towards the richest one percent.

Anyhow, what finally emerged into public knowledge was the fact that these far-right administrations had actually long believed that it was far too late to fix things. So, they had decided that it was better to plow full-steam ahead, exploit every resource, and secretly channel as much money as possible into building a worldwide network of massive underground complexes in which a small segment of the population (aka: the rich) could survive.

Once this fact was finally made public, people freaked out, but not in the way you might expect. Sure, some were outraged at the deception, but a larger portion (ironically, mostly the same ones who were duped into believing the conspiracy theories that the majority of the world's scientists were in cahoots) were clamouring to be included in these communities.

I'd love to tell you which side won, but I can't, because something more important happened first, something that nobody saw coming. It was an event that had decimated a full quarter of the Earth's population before anybody even had a chance to give it a proper name.

It happened so quickly that everything changed in about a minute. Those of us who survived did so mostly because of geography and dumb luck. For me and Matheson, Suki, and Wilson, it was because we just happened to be on Prince Edward Island spreading Heather's ashes when the first case of what came to be called the "Yellow Death" (named after the first symptom to manifest in a victim: yellow skin) was recognized in New Delhi. Then, two days later, when the 100,000th milestone death was reached, with the disease rocketing west across the Mediterranean into Europe and East across Asia before jumping across to British Columbia, that what remained of the Canadian government appeared on the island, surrounding it with about two-thirds of the Canadian Navy and most of its air force, declaring martial law. They closed down the Confederation bridge that joined PEI to the mainland, and ordered every civilian boat off the water and every aircraft out of the adjacent airspace.

Then, they took control of all the resources on the island. Every scrap of food, gas, and alcohol was locked up and rationed out to an increasingly jittery population. To their credit though, they found shelter for everyone who needed it, and vowed to do everything they could to keep us all safe.

For the next month, while the rest of the world died, the Navy patrolled the waters and the Air Force the skies all around the island both night and day. If any other vessel came anywhere near the shores, they were escorted far enough away until it was clear that they weren't infected and, if the occupants of the boat ignored these instructions and tried to make landfall anyhow, they were unceremoniously blown out of the water.

Dumb luck and geography. That was the only thing that saved my life and separated me from my friends and family, many of whom I would never see again until, unusually, some fifty years in the past. Mat was convinced that it was more than luck though. He swore that Mom had reached out from beyond the grave and saved our lives. I couldn't disagree. It was Heather who, more than a year earlier, had suggested the specific time frame for our visit. Just a few days either way, and it's hard to say if we would've survived.

Oskar had a different spin on it. He used to tell me that we owed our lives to the God of Irony because we were saved by the very fact that the disease was TOO deadly. If it had spread any slower than it had. If the incubation period was anything more than eight hours and the death rate was anything less than the 99% it was, then it would have spread everywhere in the world without exception: even PEI. Sick people would have gotten on flights without knowing that they were sick, and it would have gotten here—somehow. But then he put his typical conspiracy theory spin on the whole thing as he asked how a disease that killed in a matter of hours spread across the ocean from Asia to North America in the first place.

"Obviously," he stated matter-of-factly, "If the shortest flight between the two areas is about ten hours, then something else is goin' on."

As it was, many was the time I would stand on the wharf in Summerside, looking across the Northumberland Strait at the mainland, and pray that the winds weren't strong enough to carry an airborne disease across fifteen kilometers of open water.

Another ironic aspect of the whole sad tale was that, in the information age, information was exceedingly difficult to get ahold of. We were told it was a pig disease, much like swine influenza, but deadlier. A FUCK of a lot deadlier. Naturally, the moment this news broke, every pig on the island was destroyed and their remains, along with any and all packaged pork products, were loaded into large tanker ships and dumped into the ocean about a hundred miles offshore.

It was quite simply staggering how quickly everything broke down globally, I mean beyond the pandemic. We were told that something big had happened in Russia. Something that was rumoured to involve several nuclear explosions detonated by a few among the population unable to process the fear of Armageddon. Better to die in a huge explosion than by succumbing to a dirty pig flu, I suppose.

There were stories of greed and selfishness that made their way to us, naturally, but there were also stories of heroism and sacrifice. Like the one about the plane that had landed in New York City full of disease-stricken passengers and crew. This was still very early in the pandemic, and it still wasn't clear exactly what was going on, but the Captain seemed to know the stakes. He refused to open the airplane doors, either to let anybody get on to help, or get off and infect the city. Once he had enough gas, and with his own life failing, he lifted off again and crashed his death-plane into the ocean. It was pointless mind you. It gained the city an extra day or two, but the Captain couldn't have known that.

We didn't know everything that went on. Not really, because communication with the rest of world was gone by week three.

GONE. COMPLETELY.

A World Wide Web that had been designed to survive a nuclear attack, was completely out of our reach in less than a month. Of course, Oskar suspected that it had been sabotaged in some way, but I wouldn't hear that particular theory for a couple of years. For now, all that was left of the once great Internet were rumours that it was still out there somewhere, still operational in sequestered bunkers buried deep in the mid-west. But that didn't help us much. Our group of survivors were huddled desperately on an island in the Canadian Maritimes. We were still in shock, and, unable to go anywhere, we just stayed put, drank the Kool-Aid we were given, and thanked whatever God we worshipped that we were still alive enough to do even that.

It was perhaps a blessing that we lost all ability to communicate with our loved ones who were in the process of being mowed down by a ruthless virus on the mainland. I mean, how many times can you say goodbye, and apologize for being out of harm's way while you talk with somebody half a world away while you both wait for the inevitable to happen? It helped that both of my parents were already gone, and even though I never knew what happened to Patrick, it was a helluva lot worse for Suki. She was actually on the phone with her parents in Montreal when the lines went dead, and she spent months looking out over the Northumberland Strait as if hoping that they'd magically appear on the distant shore. And then, when the ships loaded with survivors started to arrive and were eventually allowed to dock, Suki and Mat were right there jostling with all of the other desperate families, pouring over the hand-written ship's manifest, looking in vain for familiar names.

I have to give a lot of credit to the Canadian government for how prepared it was and how well it managed the tragedy. They mobilized the population and got everyone working together to help one another. Existing food was efficiently distributed, and safeguards put in place so that those on the island who produced food (either through farming or fishing) could continue to do so as efficiently and as effectively as possible. Displaced people were eventually housed, first by filling any extra room on the island, and then through other means. Any building that could be used was appropriated, be it a shopping mall, a church, an arena, an old military base, or an empty warehouse. Even tourist buildings and museums were used to capacity, but still it wasn't enough. Not nearly. But we found a way. Perhaps it was the knowledge that there would be no international aid organization coming to our rescue that inspired us to get creative.

Once again, Mat, Suki, Wilson, and I were lucky. We had our rented RV to live in and, although we couldn't drive it out of the trailer park just outside Summerside since all of our gas had been commandeered, we could make space inside for three young people who had been celebrating their recent graduation with a bicycle trip across Canada. Perhaps it was the situation we were in, but it didn't take long for Donna, Vincent, and Celeste to become part of our family.

We all of us volunteered eagerly to pitch in to help the greater good. Mat worked on a local potato farm, Suki organized a local daycare, the kids distributed food on their bicycles, and I rigged the power grid that was feeding our park to operate more efficiently with the reduced flow of electricity that was now available. Then, when the underwater power feed from New Brunswick inevitably went dead, I located a turn-of-the-century hydroelectric power generating station near Freetown that had been turned into a museum, and spear-headed a team that managed to put the equipment that had been on display in the museum back into service. It wasn't much, but it allowed the electricity that was coming in from the thousands of wind turbines on the island to be directed to other areas of the tiny Province.

A third month passed with no real news that could be confirmed. Then, somehow, the virus made it across the Northumberland Strait killing most everyone in the West Cape area in a matter of days...

Well, I hate to dangle a cliff-hanger like this, but I hear a car in the driveway, and I really don't want to risk having to explain the fact that I'm suddenly keeping a journal to whomever it might be, so I will pick this up later.

SPOILER: I survive.

CHAPTER 8
The Jagoff and the Jag

H oly crap!
Something happened tonight that has changed everything. I mean *everything*! I found a temporal anomaly — an anachronism, if you will — and the implications could be huge!

It had been business as usual earlier in the day when I had finished journaling, in that I had yet to notice any differences between this 1985 and the 1985 that I had previously lived through. It had been around 4 PM when I had heard a car pull up in front of my parent's house, so I had finished my entry and then taken my journal upstairs to lock it in my desk. When I had come back downstairs a few minutes later, it was to find that both my parents were now home, having both apparently arrived coincidentally around the same time. Dad was over by the liquor cabinet grousing about the women in Mom's "coffee club," while Mom was pulling containers out of our saffron-coloured fridge, ignoring him. Because there was food involved, Chance was standing right behind her hoping for something edible to hit the floor.

When she saw me, Mom cut across my father to ask, "Are you here for supper tonight, Josh?"

I thanked her and explained that I wasn't because I had plans with Andi. "Oh, I didn't even think," I added. "Can I use the car?" I still hadn't gotten used to having a vehicle, much less having to have to ask for permission to use it.

"You asked already," answered Mom. "Last weekend sometime, remember? I'm still not planning on going out tonight, and if I do have to go somewhere unexpectedly, I'll get your father to drive me."

My father, who was in the process of pouring himself a rye and ginger, grunted a response that could have been affirmative but I couldn't tell for sure. My ability to interpret my father's non-verbal patterns of communication was woefully antiquated.

While Mom threw together something to eat for her and Dad, I sat at the table sipping at some kind of green soda from "The Pop Shoppe" (even as I imagined Scotty's voice telling me what flavour it was by saying, "It's Green"), while chatting with my parents and eyeing my father's drink covetously. The rye whiskey that Oskar served in his bar in 2025 had been made on the island and was a far cry from the drink that I had learned to love as an adult when I would prepare it just like my father had: mixed with Canada Dry ginger ale. As I watched Dad sip at his glass, it occurred to me that I should have had one this afternoon when I was alone. Surely, Dad didn't pay attention to the levels in his bottles, right? I was pretty sure that Patrick had a stash in his room as well, but I risked getting more than just a stern lecture if I stole booze from my burly brother.

As Mom started to serve supper for her and Dad, I excused myself and went upstairs to shower and get dressed for my date. Luckily the question of how to pay for my meal had been answered by a wad of five twenties that I had found earlier in the secret money envelope that I kept in my *Coca-Cola* nightstand. I seemed to recall that I had kept it there for emergencies, and, if shifting through time unexpectedly into the body of your younger self didn't qualify as an emergency, then it was beyond me what actually would.

I dressed in a pair of khakis with a short-sleeved, loose-fitting casual shirt with vertical stripes. Then, in adherence to 80s fashions, that I hoped I was remembering correctly, I flipped up the collar and fitted a loosely-knotted tie around my neck that was so thin that it might as well be emaciated. For footwear, I slipped on a pair of untied high tops. As I looked at myself in the mirror, I felt surprisingly comfortable and found myself smiling at the prospect of seeing Andi again so soon, even if I did have to endure an evening with her boorish friends to be with her.

When I got to Andi's a short while later, she was already outside and gesturing in such a way that made it clear that I shouldn't get too close to Brock's gleaming Jag, so I made sure to park on the street, a full hundred yards away. I'd no sooner got out of the car when Andi was on top of me, hugging me and kissing me.

"Thanks for last night," she said quietly in my ear. "And thanks for coming tonight. It means a lot to me. Phoebe and Brock are really looking forward to meeting you."

Andi had her long black hair pulled into a thick pony-tail, held in place by a ribbon tied to form a broad bow. She was dressed simply in a ruffled blouse with a skirt that would have been inappropriately short were she not wearing dark tights underneath it. The ensemble was capped off with leg-warmers that were the same green colour as the ribbon. It was, I had to agree, gloriously 80s.

As I hugged her, I could smell her favourite perfume that was, if memory served, called "White Linen." I was smiling in silly satisfaction at the whole experience, even as the young Greek woman broke out of the hug and started to pull me away from the car. Clearly, she was excited.

"Let's go, Josh! Phoebe and Brock are in the house!"

"Just a sec," I protested as I pulled the keys out of my pocket. "I have to lock the car." For a moment, Andi looked at me as I fumbled with the keys, instinctively—albeit briefly—trying to figure out where the lock button on the key fob was. Then, she reached over melodramatically, depressed the lock button on the actual car door and swung it shut.

I think she was muttering something about absent-minded professors when she grabbed my hand and pulled me up the driveway to the house's back door. Standing just inside that door were two of the yuppiest Yuppies I'd ever met. I mean, I could barely see past them and into the house because of the combined visual interference of their shoulder pads.

Once Andi had opened the door, Phoebe stepped forward, and the first thing I noticed about her, even as I heard Andi distantly introducing her, was her hair.

Holy guacamole, I thought as I shook her hand mechanically. *Did girls really do that to their hair in the 80s? How in heaven's name is all that hair able to stay up that high? Did Doug Henning style it? I once saw him on the Muppet Show make a little worm dance in mid-air. That's the only possible explanation.*

By the time I pulled my attention away from Phoebe's hair, I had enough time to briefly notice that she appeared to be wearing some kind of bridesmaid dress, before I became aware that Brock had been talking to me and had his arm extended expectantly.

I gripped his hand, remembering only as he was crushing my fingers, how he liked to overcompensate his firm handshakes, presumably to appear stronger and manlier. I ignored the discomfort as best I could, even as he jerked my hand around to pull me off balance, and told him that it was a pleasure meeting him and that it was a helluva nice car in the driveway.

"You dinn't park too close didja?" he asked almost predictably in his own particular version of the English language.

I assured him that I had given him plenty of room, before stepping back to take in his appearance. All in all, Brock appeared just as I'd remembered, dressed in a close approximation of one of the characters from *Miami Vice*, with a white blazer over a salmon coloured T-shirt and a five-o'clock shadow that was several o'clocks too shadowy. He sported an intricately wound gold chain around his neck, and had obviously made sure that a copious amount of chest hair was peeking over the top of his collar.

Off in the distance, I could hear Andi's parents yell a greeting to me from the dining room along with a directive to have a good time tonight. The only indication that Phoebe's parents were visiting was the smell of cigar smoke coming down the hallway, something that was uncharacteristically out of place in Andi's house. I called back to thank them, and then was following the other three out the back door as if they were in some kind of a hurry to get away from the adults. Little did they know that, in reality, I was pretty much more akin to their parents, at least in terms of age.

It was as I was climbing into the back seat of the Jaguar that another memory finally came back to me of what had happened the first time that I'd lived through this experience.

"Buckle up," I whispered to Andi beside me, as I located my own seat belt. I had just managed to clip the ends together and grab the back of the seat ahead of me for balance, when Brock peeled out of the driveway and squealed his way down the street.

Thus, began one of the scariest ten minutes of my life, as this pampered beer dynasty heir turned the normally quiet streets of Robertson into his own personal drag strip, by ignoring stop signs and passing slow moving traffic in areas where such things were most definitely not allowed. If I hadn't already known that I'd survive, I'd have probably considered going after the Carotid artery pressure point on his neck the next time he slowed down in the hopes that it would weaken his legs enough for us to come to a full stop. Of course, this course of action was just as likely to actually cause an accident, so I ultimately decided that it was far better just to weather the experience again and hope for the best.

As Phoebe screamed at her fiancé to slow down and stop showing off, I looked over at Andi to find her eyes wide with fear. I knew for a fact that she didn't much care for roller coasters, so knew that this wild ride must be particularly difficult for her. I reached out and took her hand, and she squeezed it firmly while fixing me with a smile that was one part positive and two parts apologetic.

It was as Brock was squealing into the parking spot in front of *Golden Sun* Chinese Food restaurant that I finally thought back to exactly how this approximation of *Mr. Toad's Wild Ride* had previously affected the rest of the night. I hadn't known it at the time, but everything about Brock—from his handshake to the way he drove when he had passengers in his car—was all about dominance. He consistently threw people off balance to show that he was in charge, and then took advantage of the resulting shock to fully assert himself.

This, most certainly was exactly what had happened the first time that I'd lived through this experience. I had exited the car fuming at what Brock had done, but hadn't wanted a confrontation, so I had spent the rest of the night withdrawn and sulking. Andi hadn't enjoyed herself either, having been too focused on trying to get me to cheer up. Even Phoebe had been aware of the tension, and had directed her obvious displeasure toward her otherwise oblivious fiancé.

All of this had allowed Brock to control everything about the meal—from what we ordered, to what we drank, and even to what we talked about. In the end, he had gotten what he wanted: attention. It may not have been positive attention, mind you, but it was attention nonetheless.

This time though, I knew what was going on, and was mature enough to suppress my irritation at the young man so that I could avoid playing the game his way again. Indeed, it was a perfect opportunity to make use of the biting wit that I'd spent a lifetime sharpening. So, when Brock opened the Jag door to let me out, a puerile smirk on his face, I complimented him.

"Well that was exhilarating, Brock," I said as I stood up beside him so that we were both on the same level. "You handle the stick-shift pretty well." Brock's chest actually puffed up noticeably at the compliment but, before he could say anything in response, I continued, "Now, I'm not an expert, but, if I'm not very much mistaken, it sounded like your clutch was sizzling a little. Is it possible that you might have been accelerating a bit too much between shifts?"

Clearly, this wasn't what the fatuous young man was expecting from a passenger who should be both shaken and stirred, and not challenging his manhood by telling him that he couldn't drive stick. Behind me, I could hear Phoebe helping Andi out of the passenger side of the car and apologizing.

"If you rush the transition between gears," I continued, straightening my tie and adjusting my clothing. "You risk getting snagged in the lever's gate. I'd be happy to show you some techniques and best practices later if you'd like."

Brock was about to open his mouth to respond when Phoebe interrupted, summoning him in terse tones.

"Be right there, honey," he said quietly as he scowled at me uncertainly. "Thanks," he finally said to me curtly before turning abruptly to stalk towards his fiancé at the door of the restaurant. Along the way though, he stopped to quickly polish the tiny chrome cat on the car's hood with a handkerchief that he'd pulled seemingly from nowhere.

By the time I joined Andi, she was already inside the restaurant where Brock was loudly asking anyone who could hear what kind of backwoods restaurant didn't have a maître d'. Andi's face was flushed and, when I put my hand on the side of her neck in a show of support, I could feel her pulse.

Damn. How could I have forgotten the car ride? I should have suggested that Andi and I meet at the restaurant so I could have driven here myself, and avoided all of this drama.

"You OK?" I asked Andi. Behind us, Mr. Wonderful was rejecting the table we'd been offered and demanding one by the window instead, so that he could keep an eye on his Jag. Andi's eyes darted to Brock and then back at me. "Believe it or not," she said quietly. "He's an improvement over the last jackass that Phoebe was engaged to."

I laughed. "Wanna walk home?"

This made Andi smile but, instead of answering, she just stared up at me. "How are *you*?" she asked finally, almost as if she too knew how I had reacted to the erratic car ride the first time.

"Me? Oh, I'm fine. I just prefer my roller coaster rides to be in carefully controlled conditions. With lap restraints." Andi was still looking at me, as if expecting more, so I added, "Brock's an asshat, but I'm not going to let his social dominance games ruin my night."

Wait. Was 'asshat' a term that was used in 1985?

Phoebe was calling to us, bidding us to follow her now that Brock had found a table that met his exacting specifications. Before heading off in Phoebe's direction though, Andi leaned up and kissed me on the cheek. "When did you get to be so mature, Mister? It turns me on."

As I followed her, I scanned the restaurant to look at the other customers. There were only a few occupied tables, all of them staring at us because of Brock's antics, but I didn't see any faces I recognized, thank goodness.

Brock was already seated at the table, scanning the menu. I held Andi's seat for her as Phoebe scowled at him for not doing the same for her, before eventually settling heavily onto the seat beside him. I knew that Brock was about to announce what he thought we should all eat so, before he could say anything, I spoke up, "Hey Andi, what's that specialty of the house that you liked so much the last time that we were here?" I was taking a chance, because I obviously had no idea when we'd last been here. I just knew that she had had a favourite item on the menu, but I just couldn't recall what it had been. The gamble paid off though.

"General Tso's chicken," answered Andi. "They make it regular or extra spicy."

"Oh, that sounds nice," added Phoebe, either unaware that Brock was about to speak or indifferent to it.

As Phoebe was still talking, I made a show of opening the menu to look like I was confirming something. "If memory serves," I lied, since I already knew from my visit here earlier today what I was about to suggest. "That dish is part of the *Dinner for Five* combination meal that the restaurant offers… Why, yes it is, there it is right there." I held my menu up so that the girls could see where I was indicating, but Brock could not. Conveniently, I was angling the document so that it was physically blocking Brock's line of sight, taking him out of the conversation and effectively leaving him out of the decision-making process.

When I eventually put the menu down, Brock was scowling at me again, as if suspecting me of usurping his unspoken authority. Last time, he had ordered a-la-carte and chosen a variety that hadn't been particularly inspiring, if even palatable. I don't think that even he had enjoyed the combination of tastes, especially with the special requests he had asked for, but it gave him a perverse pleasure knowing that we were being forced to abide by his choices no matter how much we had disliked it. But, now that Phoebe had expressed a desire to order what I was suggesting in lieu of what Brock wanted to decree, he was clearly taking it personally.

This meal hadn't been nearly this enjoyable the first time.

It got even more gratifying when it was Mr. Lin, the owner himself, that came to take our order instead of one of his wait staff. Apparently, my father had done a renovation on Mr. Lin's house last November, and the restaurant owner wanted to tell me how happy he was with it. As we chatted, I could tell that Brock was clearly itching to be the one to place our order, but I beat him to the punch in the course of my conversation with Mr. Lin. Then, once I had told the restauranteur what the four of us were celebrating, Mr. Lin even promised to send out a few extras on the house in honour of the young couple's engagement, including a round of his celebrated Won Ton soups. He would have offered champagne, he had said, but he knew that we were all too young, so it was the next best thing.

As the man spoke, I looked at him in rapt wonder. This whole interaction hadn't happened before, presumably, since I'd been in such a bad mood at the time and had clearly been sending off irate vibes. If I ever saw Oskar again, I'd be sure to tell him that his philosophy of life was definitely correct, now that I'd been able to see different results from the same situation when the only difference between the two was a positive change in attitude on my part.

After Mr. Lin had left us, Andi asked to see the engagement ring again, and Phoebe was all too happy to oblige, holding out her hand proudly so that Andi could get a better look. The rock on her finger was just as big as I had remembered, and just as spectacular—if you were into ostentatious displays of wealth, that was.

"Congratulations you two," I offered genially, lifting my glass of ice water by way of a toast. "You are about to embark on a truly amazing journey, being part of a team. It is truly a wonderful thing when we find a person that can both lift us up and make us feel grounded all at the same time. When we find somebody who not only sparks joy within us, but can light us up simply by smiling in our direction." Andi pulled her gaze away from the ring to look at me disbelievingly, as if this wasn't the kind of thing that I normally did or said. My eyes found hers as I continued speaking, "That kind of person is a rare thing. It's the kind of person that is worth falling backwards through time to find." Looking back at the couple across from me, I finished, "I wish the both of you continued health and happiness. May your joy be boundless, and may your life together be full of awe, and not the other way around."

If Andi was at all skeptical about my sentiment, Brock and Phoebe were eating up my attention and asking for seconds. We all clinked glasses. "That is an amazing rock, though," I added. "Don't hold it up to the light, you're likely to start a fire! Shouldn't you at least have a security officer following you around everywhere?"

"Who says dere ain't one around?" Brock offered lightly, glancing in pretend clandestineness over his shoulder.

I looked at him in shock for a moment. Had Brock just said something that I had found amusing?

Well, I'll be damned; miracles can *happen.*

We were all laughing good-naturedly at Brock's joke as the waiter delivered our drinks. This was actually another surprise in that, even though Brock was old enough to order alcohol, he was refraining from doing so out of respect for his three underage dinner companions. This too was something that differed from what had happened the first time, when he had forced us all to watch him drink a glass of expensive wine. We toasted again with pop instead of water, which was only slightly less lame.

This course of action appeared to be exactly what was needed to break the tension. As much as I would have liked to continue to yank Brock's chain, I also knew that this would upset Andi, and I really wanted her to have a good time. In fact, I wanted to enjoy myself too. I was still new to going out for a meal for fun, having been in basic survival mode for the last ten years of my life. Simply going out on an actual town that wasn't floating was a genuine thrill and, if the company wasn't one that I necessarily would have chosen, I was at least mature enough now to find ways to make it bearable.

This attitude carried me through most of the meal, even though I eventually found my focus slipping by the time that our complimentary desserts were being served, and just as Brock started to tell us all that he'd heard that the Phil Collins song *In the Air Tonight* was based on a true story.

"Yeah," Brock was saying. "So, like, Phil Collins was watchin' as this guy didn't do nothin'…"

That's about as far as I got in paying attention to Brock. I tuned him out in part because I'd finally had enough of his hideous mangling of the English language, but mostly because I already knew the story. From my perspective, it was extremely old news. The widely spread rumour in the early 80s was that Phil Collins had watched helplessly as somebody drowned when the one man who could have actually saved the guy had refused to help. The rumour further claimed that Phil invited this selfish man to one of his concerts, gave him a front row seat, and shone a spotlight on him as he sang the following lyrics from his new song directly at him:

```
Well if you told me you were drowning,
I would not lend a hand.
I've seen your face before my friend,
but I don't know if you know who I am.
Well I was there and I saw what you did,
I saw it with my own two eyes.
So, you can wipe off that grin,
I know where you've been,
It's all been a pack of lies.
```

The lyrics of the song were most definitely accusatory, and the wide-spread rumour went that right after the concert, knowing that whole world now knew about his cowardice, the man had gone home and killed himself.

As Brock chewed through his narrative with his unfortunate choice of vocabulary and diction, I sighed inwardly and looked wistfully out the window. Naturally, I'd heard the story before. *Many* times before, and knew from the perspective of fifty years that it was bullshit. Still, it made me wonder about how stories like this actually travelled in the days before the internet. In my youth, it had always amazed me how remote towns like Robertson were still up to date in so many things—current jokes, gossip, trends etc, yet information like the Phil Collins rumour didn't exactly spread by newspaper, TV, or radio. I grinned inwardly as I realized that I was sitting there looking at the answer to at least one of my questions, at least insofar as it concerned *In the Air Tonight*. This particular piece of gossip was being carried from the city of Toronto to a small town in Northern Ontario by a mouthy heir to a beer dynasty. Perhaps Brock was what Malcolm Gladwell would, years from now, call a "Maven."

But what about other such unsubstantiated stories? How had they travelled? I could vaguely recall that around this same time, my friends and I would be sharing the news that Cyndi Lauper's song *She Bop* was all about female masturbation, or that Ray Parker Jr. had stolen the tune for the *Ghostbusters* theme from Huey Lewis' *I Want A New Drug* (This last one especially funny because, in high school, I couldn't really see how the two songs were at all similar yet, years later, my eight-year-old son, Mat, upon hearing *I Want A New Drug* on an 80s flashback radio show, had told me that "it sounded an awful lot like that song from the movie with all the ghosts").

Then there were rumours that there were spider eggs in *Bubble Yum* chewing gum, or that Little Mikey's head exploded when he drank Coke with a mouth full of PopRocks, or that Richard Gere had gotten a little too "friendly" with a gerbil, or that Jamie Lee Curtis was really a man, or that Alice Cooper had bitten the head off a live chicken, or that Ozzy Osbourne had done the same thing to a live bat.

There were so many examples to list, all of them with no way for the kids of the 80s to prove or disprove them. This was the real fake news, years before Trump made the term a divisive political talking point, and without Web sites like snopes.com to settle the disputes.

Yet even access to the truth didn't always help, not in extreme cases of cognitive dissonance, where people with strongly held beliefs rejected ample evidence that contradicted those beliefs — even very obvious and irrefutable evidence. I'd often wondered if this was the root cause of the anxiety epidemic that gripped the majority of the population in the mid to late 2010s. In that era, people had started to get progressively more anxious, seemingly in direct relation to the amount of access that they had to the truth. For many, it wasn't so much that more information meant that there was more to be worried about, it meant that more information made it harder for them to justify holding onto their incorrect dogmas. Those who wanted to continue to fool themselves, got more and more anxious as it became harder to remain ignorant, and those who weren't fooling themselves got anxious when looking at the people who were.

I can recall being very frustrated at the trend of people like the anti-vaxxers or the climate change deniers who refused to accept any scientific evidence contrary to their politics, choosing instead to trust the conspiracy theory that it was all some kind of plot to deceive them. It was obvious that those who remained ignorant in the information age did so intentionally. Ironically, it got much easier for these people once the *Ensee* got control of information on the island and began subtly amending it to their own end. If alternative facts helped to reduce the anxiety level of a person like that, then it was simply amazing how quickly this person's memory shortened to accommodate it.

But then again, even before 2025, back when there actually was a full-fledged internet, it still wasn't always easy to establish a rumour's credibility. It certainly didn't help confirm that wild tale about Magnus Levenko, that the reason that he disappeared in the early 2000s was because he warned the American government about 9/11 before it happened, and was arrested shortly thereafter under suspicion of collusion.

Come to think of it, I haven't heard of Magnus at all since I shifted. As the wunderkind of the 80s, shouldn't he be all over the news? What was it he was up to in 1985?

In the background, Brock was still talking, and I tuned in suddenly to what he had just said because it was wrong—but not because it was fake news.

"…that's why da song says 'If you told me you was choking,'" he had just said. "It's, like… a reverence to de incident."

"I'm sorry," I interrupted, deciding not to tell him that he meant to say 'reference', asking instead, "The song says what?"

"If you told me you was choking," he repeated. So, I hadn't actually misheard him. "You heard da song ain't you Josh? It's on *Miami Vice* like every udder week."

"Drowning," I corrected him, thinking that he was screwing up the words of the song just as badly as he was transgressing against the English language. "If you told me you were *drowning*…" At this point, I stopped because it wasn't just Brock who was wearing an odd expression. All three of my dinner companions were looking at me now like I was crazy.

It was Andi who spoke next. "Josh," she began like she was talking to a toddler. "It's 'choking.' As in: 'If you told me you were *choking*...'"

What the bloody hell?

I froze for a moment as everyone scrutinized me. I knew, somehow instinctively, that there was something different, something significant going on. I immediately gave up even trying to argue the point, and instead chose to attempt a distraction. Looking out the window towards Brock's Jag, I told him that I thought I had just seen a bird defecate on it.

You would have thought a bomb had gone off. Brock stood up dramatically and ran out the door screaming bloody murder with Phoebe following right after him, calling out his name as if he had been heading off to war and had neglected to say good bye. Andi though, was different. She sat there looking at me, eyes slightly squinted, as if seeing me for the first time. I tried to ignore her by taking a drink of my pop as I narrated what Brock was doing outside the window of the Chinese restaurant.

"Oh look. He's actually got a special squeegee for bird droppings," I said. "I didn't know they made those. ... Wait. Is it gold? Brock's got a solid-gold squeegee, Andi! ... OK, now he's inspecting the car, and furiously scrubbing off anything that slightly resembles bird guano. ... Now he's looking up into the sky to see if maybe the guilty party is somewhere close by. I could be wrong, but I think that bird is long gone, but I'd be happy to volunteer to round up a few of the usual suspects if he wants."

Across from me, Andi's suspicious expression was slowly giving way to amusement thanks to the sports-broadcaster voice I was using to deliver my irreverent comments.

"...and now we can see that Brock's just pulled out a spray can and a cloth," I continued. "And he is now wiping down the car at random. ... Oh look, a crowd is gathering. It might just be this broadcaster's opinion, but Phoebe doesn't look at all happy, probably because Brock is taking questions. ... Oh wait, now he's chasing a small child away from the ornament thingee on the hood. What's that thing called again?"

"A hood ornament," answered Andi dryly, blinking languidly.

"Yeah. That's the ticket," I said in a John Lovitz impression that was obviously completely lost on my 1985 girlfriend. "Too soon?" I asked. It probably was. Guess I'd better not expect *Wayne's World* quotes to get recognized in this time period either.

"You're pretty pleased with yourself, aren't you?" Andi said dryly.

"I sure am... NOT." I replied cheekily. Andi looked back at me blankly.

Yep. Definitely too soon for Wayne's World.

By this point, Phoebe had finally dragged Brock back into the restaurant and back to his seat, but he was still restless and staring out the window even more than before.

"Thanks Josh," Brock said gratefully, his tough-guy attitude momentarily blunted for some reason. "Northern Ontario bird crap ain't de same as the crap in da South. It's more acidic. I was afraid of dis, it's why I axed to park da Jag underground but didn't know that this backwater ain't got no underground. I tole you I shoulda put da fabric cover on her, Phoebe."

As the two of them bickered, Andi rolled her eyes and jumped in to change the subject and direct it somewhere else entirely. She was really good that way. I was just happy that my mistake with the Phil Collins lyrics had been apparently forgotten. But *I* wasn't about to forget it though.

The rest of the night was a bit of a blur. I tried to stay present for Andi, but my mind was racing.

Why were the lyrics of that song different from what I remember them to be?

Admittedly, I hadn't really been listening to the music of the era very closely over the last three days. It was mostly because, unlike everyone else in 1985, I'd heard these same songs over and over again for the last five decades. To me, they'd become background music.

Now that I realized that there was at least one difference between this 1985 and the one that I had lived through, I was naturally wondering if there were others that I just hadn't noticed. So, through the rest of the evening, as we walked the downtown streets, and went to the local theater to see Madonna's first film *Desperately Seeking Susan*, I was looking everywhere for other temporal anomalies.

I didn't find any. Well, not at first, anyhow.

It was much later, when I had said goodbye to Andi and the others and was driving home, that I found my second altered lyric when I was listening to REO Speedwagon's *Can't Fight this Feeling* on the car radio. Although it had been the first song that I'd heard upon waking up in my own past just a few days earlier, I had understandably been a little preoccupied with being a teenager again to notice that it wasn't exactly the same as before.

Instead of singing "...and throw away the *oars* forever", like I remembered, the lead singer was now singing "...and throw away the *sails* forever."

Once I heard it, I began to tremble physically. Then, when the chorus repeated, and I heard it a second time, I actually teared up a little.

Am I losing it?

This was, in and of itself, worrisome since I'd had a tenuous grasp of late on whatever "it" was in the first place.

The first thing I had to confirm in my mind was whether this was an actual change, or whether I was simply misremembering it. Sure, the song was still new to this particular time period, but I was about to hear it over and over in the next few months as Andi would soon fall head over heels in love with it, and insist on playing it repeatedly during our fervent make out sessions. If that wasn't enough though, I would be forced to listen to it ad nauseum on oldies radio in the future where it would be repeated at least twice a day even forty or fifty years from now as well as in the playlist that Oskar insisted on playing in his bar, back on the *Pucks*.

No, I concluded. This wasn't a trick of my memory. I clearly remembered the old lyrics, having often wondered over the years, whenever I'd heard the song, about what kind of ship would use oars. Was it a Viking longboat? A slave galley?

I'm not mistaken, I'm sure of it.

Once I was confident in this assessment, I turned my mind to the other important question: Why are there differences? Sure, it was possible that time didn't necessarily have to flow the same way twice, but why would that manifest itself, as far as I could tell, simply in the alteration of a few song lyrics? Nothing else in this time period seemed out of place. The political leaders were all the same. Movies, songs, celebrities, people of prominence, headlines: they were all in keeping with what I remembered. It's not like I'd noticed any songs I'd never heard before, or movies I'd never seen, or people I'd never heard of. If this timeline was proceeding differently, then it should be obviously different, right? Not just in a, seemingly random, altered lyric.

When I got home, my parents had gone to bed but I didn't have any illusions that I'd be able to do the same thing myself. I went up to my room, pulled out the box that housed my collection of cassettes and started feeding them into my tape player one at a time. It was a task that would take hours, but I wasn't in any condition to sleep. While the music on the cassette tapes was playing as quietly as I could keep it while still reasonably being able to hear it, and, even as I listened carefully to the lyrics, I poured over anything in my room that might be obviously different from what I remembered it to be. This included my comic and magazine collection, my books, as well as my trading cards.

By three AM, I'd gone through ever piece of music I had at my disposal (most of my music was movie soundtracks which were still mostly orchestral in the 1980s, so I didn't really own that much in the way of 'Pop' music) and had even raided Patrick's cassettes. In about three and a half hours, I'd identified three more anomalies, all of them in the form of changed song lyrics. To help keep track, I'd used a ruler to draw a table on the last page of my new journal (man, I missed computer spreadsheets), and filled in the first few rows as follows:

	SONG	OLD	NEW
1	In the Air Tonight	If you told me you were DROWNING	If you told me you were CHOKING
2	Can't Fight This Feeling	OARS	SAILS
3	Every Breath you Take	I'll be WATCHING you	I will FOLLOW you
4	Straight from the Heart	Straight FROM the heart	Straight TO the heart
5	Wake me up before you Go Go	WAKE me up	GET me up

For the longest time, I sat staring at the table in front of me, a glass of rye whiskey gripped rather unsteadily in my trembling hand. About an hour ago, I had finally decided that I couldn't handle this change in the status quo sober, so had snuck quietly down to my father's liquor cabinet and helped myself, a clandestine activity that would have gone a lot smoother had Chance not thought that I'd come downstairs to play with her.

So, clearly, I wasn't imagining these changes. This was really happening. I had now identified five examples of things that were out of place in this time period. Five anomalies, or, more appropriately, since they were aspects (like myself) that didn't belong in this time period, five *anachronisms*.

Well, as Oskar liked to say: Fuck me, Jack Benny.

My geeky friends and I had always taken great pleasure in looking for anachronisms in movies that had been set in the past. These would be things that just didn't belong in the time period in which the movie had been set, such as the guitar that Marty McFly plays in *Back to the Future* which hadn't actually been released until three years after the year that he'd travelled back to, or the Canadian flag with the maple leaf that was shown in the *Untouchables* that wouldn't be created until some thirty years after the events depicted, or the *Apple* stocks that Forrest Gump bought in 1975 even though the company wouldn't go public until 1980.

Looking for such anachronisms in movies was one thing, but looking for them in real life? This was beyond weird. I took another sip of my drink, careful to go easy on a young throat that wasn't at all used to the kind of burn that went hand in hand with whiskey.

One anachronism might be explained away as pure chance, but *five?* And these were just the ones that I'd found so far. How many more were there? Was there a relevance to the fact that these are fairly minor changes to the popular culture of the day that would only really be obvious to somebody who had already lived through the era?

Holy awesome fuck, I thought as this fact sunk in. *I'm the only one who would know that they're different! I'm the only one who knows what they used to be.*

But why?

Even I was getting tired of hearing myself ask this question.

In an attempt to look at things differently, I pulled out a separate piece of paper and wrote down just the new words by themselves.

CHOKING

SAILS

FOLLOW

TO

GET

Well sure. Everything is much clearer now isn't it? I thought as I examined the words that looked almost like a message.

That's when it hit me.

What if they weren't just random words? Words formed sentences, right? And sentences formed messages. What if these words were actually some kind of a message?

Quickly, I pulled my pair of scissors out of the drawer of my desk and cut each of the words out so that I could try different combinations. It was only after another twenty minutes of fruitlessly trying to glean some kind of meaning from the various combinations of words, when another, perhaps even more important thought, struck me.

Maybe, I'm not alone!

What if somebody else came back too? What if they were making these changes to send a message to others, like myself, who had also been displaced?

There was a super simple way to test this theory: I was going to have to look for more. I was going to have to find them all.

END OF BOOK ONE

Dwayne R. James

FOR JOSH DONEGAL, THERE'S
SOMETHING OUT OF PLACE IN
THE 80s THIS TIME.

DON'T
WORRY!

THE
ANACHRONISTIC
C⊕DE

THE COMEBACK KID

DWAYNE R. JAMES

W ell, if I had any reservations about keeping the fact that I've traveled through time to myself, it came via a message from Weird Al.

Yes, *that* Weird Al.

The *Eat It* guy.

It's Thursday, April 25, 1985 today, and it's been a full week since I arrived unwittingly in my own past, waking up in a significantly younger body and in what appeared to be my childhood bedroom. Naturally, I was a little shocked at first, especially when I discovered that what I had first thought was just a hallucinatory dream, included people—specifically loved ones that I had lost years ago. Then, once it had become incontrovertibly apparent that what I was experiencing was genuine and that I really had shifted in time, I decided to try and fit into my own past until I could figure out what was going on, and how it had happened in the first place. Acting sufficiently natural not to draw any undue attention to myself would have been difficult enough, but I also had to make sure that my high school sweetheart, Andi, wouldn't notice that I was acting differently. Although it probably would have been wiser to keep the young woman at several arm's length, I soon came to realize that I was becoming a little infatuated with her all over again, something the 67-year-old inside of me had had a difficult time reconciling.

Then, only three days in, just as I had begun to feel comfortable enough to be enjoying the ride, everything changed. I had been out with Andi and some of her friends when I had noticed a temporal anachronism, a detail that didn't belong in this timeline—I mean besides myself, of course. The detail in question was a subtle difference in the song *In the Air Tonight*. The first time that I'd lived through 1985, the lyrics had been: "If you told me you were *drowning*." But now, in this iteration of 1985, for some inexplicable reason, Phil Collins was singing "If you told me you were *choking!*"

This had been last Saturday, and after a marathon session all night and into the morning, in which I listened to every piece of music I could get my ears on, I found *four* more anachronisms. Four more song lyrics that were not the way I remembered them to be. As I found each one, I wrote down the details in a spreadsheet-like table on the very last page of my journal. That table looked something like this:

	SONG	OLD	NEW
1	In the Air Tonight	If you told me you were DROWNING	If you told me you were CHOKING
2	Can't Fight This Feeling	OARS	SAILS
3	Every Breath you Take	I'll be WATCHING you	I will FOLLOW you
4	Straight from the Heart	Straight FROM the heart	Straight TO the heart
5	Wake me up before you Go Go	WAKE me up	GET me up

So, there were five songs that were different in this particular timeline, and it wasn't lost on me that these were not major alterations. They were small ones. Specifically, words. Words, I speculated, that could be combined to form messages. This had led me to believe that maybe, just maybe, the changes represented some kind of code.

Call it wishful thinking if you will, but until you yourself have been displaced in time into the body of your teenaged self with no idea how or why it happened, you've no right to judge me. The truth was, I knew from experience that humanity wasn't headed for a bright future. In 2025, billions and billions will be wiped out by a global pandemic, and the few who would be lucky enough to survive would eventually find themselves under the rule of an authoritarian corporation. If the existence of time-travel sounded at all ridiculous to the rational part of my brain, that part of my brain wasn't listening anymore. It was too busy grudgingly admitting that switching well-known song lyrics was an ideal way to get an accidental time-traveler's attention. I knew, from personal experience being inside my head, that certain lyrics stayed with us for years, especially the ones from the songs of our youth.

So yes, call it wishful thinking that the first explanation that I reached for to explain the anachronisms was that somebody else had come back from this same distant future too, and was trying to get my attention. And, to do this, they were sending out a coded message that could only be deciphered by people who had already lived through the 80s once, because they were the only ones who would know that there'd been a change in the first place. Still, I had to wonder about how much my own longings might be influencing my perspective on the situation. Was I being overly optimistic in thinking that the message might represent some kind of a way to keep a dystopian future from happening, or was I projecting patterns onto a timeline that didn't necessarily have to flow the same way twice?

There was only one way to know for sure: I had to find as many of the changes as I could, and then see if there was some kind of pattern to them. So, over the last four days, when I wasn't listening intently to the radio, I had been going through every piece of music I could lay my hands on.

I started in the most obvious place: home. I had listened to all of the cassettes in the house by Monday, and had then begun to wade through our modest record collection, which consisted mostly of my parents' albums and 45s from the 60s and early 70s. Almost immediately, I was reminded of how much work it was to listen to records! Beyond the 45s that contained just two songs (one to a side), a single side of an LP couldn't last more than thirty minutes! Coming from a time when listening to an endless variety of music was as easy as hitting the shuffle button on a music device, it was positively laborious to have to switch things up on the record player every twenty-five minutes or so!

I used to bore my kids with stories about how music had been changed by digital downloads. They were accustomed to simply being able to copy a vast song collection to the tiniest of players, or being able to go online at any time and stream whatever song you wanted to hear at any given moment. Even on the island, we still had the Strand's version of *YouTube* as well as the communal database on the Pucks library that offered free streaming of anything (copyright laws and broadcasting fees had been completely dismantled after 2025 in the hopes that familiar forms of entertainment could bring at least a little comfort to the survivors).

Dwayne R. James

Rewind to 1985 when this was certainly not the case. As a youth, I used to get very excited about collecting music, and I know I wasn't alone. It was a badge of honour to have friends over for a party and play music for them, so that they could get excited over the music you had access to and could play whenever you wanted (personally, one of the many reasons that I threw such terrible parties was because I just didn't have much in the way of popular music because most of what I owned were orchestral movie soundtracks).

The problem was that teenagers in the 80s just didn't have very extensive music collections, even the ones that thought they did. It was expensive to buy music, and it was relatively hard (at least by the standards of the future with which I was familiar) to listen to it once you had it. Sure, we had portable cassette players at the time, but the cassettes that fed them could never hold more than a couple dozen songs at any one time, and you had to listen to them in the order in which they had been recorded on the tape. Radio was by far the best way to hear a wider range of music than that which you owned, but even it was limited in that they only ever played what was current. 'Oldies' radio played mostly 60s music, meaning that there was a whole decade that hardly got any airtime at all. Sure, you could buy the multi-cassette compilations of 70s music that they were always advertising on TV, but, like I said at the beginning of this paragraph, that cost money that most teenagers (present company included) just didn't have.

This was the culture into which the mixed tape was born, with those tapes becoming a kind of currency in the schools of the time. If you could scrabble together a decent variety of popular songs and record them onto a cassette tape in a sequence of your own design, you could become a celebrity with your friends. You could trade copies of that tape for other things of value (usually a bag of Doritos or a couple of those cookies from our cafeteria that melted in your mouth before you could even swallow them), or lend the original out to friends so that they could make their own copies of it. And then, inevitably, that friend would lend it out to even more people until the copies that were being made were of such poor quality as to be virtually unlistenable. That was another problem of the era when it came to music. Few of us owned a stereo tape deck of sufficient grade to record copies off vinyl that came anywhere near the quality of the original.

Still, it was the further evolution of an era when kids stopped trying to use their own words to communicate with others, choosing instead to claim that, "this artist says it much better than I ever could in this song." It was a time when teenaged girls would hand their boyfriends a mixed tape with a special selection of music that she had specifically designed to tell him exactly how she felt, only to have him think that it was little more than romantic music to be played in the background while they made out.

Plus ça change, I suppose.

And then, there was the difference in sound! As I listened to these old LPs, I was reminded just how much I missed the subtle pop and hiss of the needle and the vinyl moving against each other physically. It just made it seem, I dunno, so much more real. Tangible. Palpable. It was like you were *feeling* the sounds as much as hearing them. I can remember hearing stories when the first CD players started showing up in cars in Northern Ontario, that the main reason the drivers could play that music so extraordinarily loud was because it was so clear that it didn't damage your hearing in the same way that analog music did.

Anyhow, I hadn't identified more than about ten anachronisms when I found one in Gino Vannelli's song *Black Cars*, and it occurred to me that a preponderance of the altered lyrics were showing up in Canadian songs. Beyond Vannelli's song, I had found a couple from Bryan Adams, as well one in *Tears are Not Enough* (now titled *Tears Just Aren't Enough* in this timeline), the Canadian answer to the Ethiopian fund-raising relief started by the United Kingdom's *Do They Know it's Christmas*, and followed soon after by the Americans with *We Are The World*. As I wondered why so many of the altered songs were Canadian, and if they had gotten much in the way of airplay outside of this country back in the day, it began to make a certain morbid kind of sense. If this was a message constructed by somebody who had experienced the future and was trying to contact others like me who had shifted in time, then that person would want to target Canadian songs, since we made up such a large percentage of the survivors of the events of 2025, thanks to our isolation on Prince Edward Island.

In any event, by the wee hours of Wednesday morning, I'd finally worked my way through my family's entire assortment of vinyl (I had been staying up well after everyone else had gone to sleep and was using a set of headphones that was tethering me to the stereo cabinet in the recroom in a manner that I had become unaccustomed to since the advent of *Bluetooth*). Although I had found a handful of differences in more modern recordings, I discovered that the effort to go through my parent's collection had been pretty much a complete waste of time. Every piece of popular music from that 60s (Dad loved classic rock and had most of a complete discography of the Beatles and the Stones, and Mom had had a bit of a Motown fetish in her youth) had been just exactly as I had remembered it all to be, and it had almost been the same for the stuff from the early 70s as well, with one huge exception. In the Tony Orlando and Dawn song *Tie a Yellow Ribbon Round the Ole Oak Tree*, the titular oak tree had been changed to an elm. So far, this had been the earliest anachronism that I had found, although I couldn't identify the exact year of its release, since dates were not often printed (or scratched) on records from that period.

After this, there was only one source of music left for me to explore at home: the box of ancient 8-track tapes in the basement. Yet, I knew that even this wouldn't be enough. I needed access to more music but, luckily, by now, I was getting a better idea of what songs to target.

Indeed, if I'd noticed one trend in the placement of anachronisms so far, it was that they were all in songs that were popular and fairly well-known. This made perfect sense, the more that I thought about it. If these clues were to be noticeable, they had to be packaged in *tent-pole* songs that would have an enduring impact of popular cultural over the next fifty years, ones that would become a part of the cultural zeitgeist and remain that way in the future. As luck would have it, I had a pretty decent idea of what that entailed, having lived through that future already.

This meant that I should be able to target my search by looking for specific songs, the only problem being that I couldn't always recollect when some of those songs had been released. Oh, sure, I could vaguely remember the timing of some of the huge successes based on where I had been when I first listened to them (like U2's *Joshua Tree* for instance, which I clearly remember being exposed to in University), but hunting specific songs that may or may even exist yet, just might be an exercise in futility.

Case in point: *Silent Running* by Mike + the Mechanics. If any song in the 80s had the obvious potential to contain an anachronism, I figured it was this one since it was all about a man sending a message back in time to warn his family about the impending collapse of society and the rise of a totalitarian regime. I hadn't heard it on the radio at all, so I tried a different media. I seemed to recall that my friends used to laugh about how the song was played during "intense" scenes on the soap opera *Days of Our Lives,* especially whenever some guy wearing an eye patch was on the show. So, I taped the show a handful of times, but as far as I could tell, that hasn't happened yet because the eye patch guy isn't around. On a related note, I find myself wanting to watch more *Days of Our Lives.* I'd forgotten how much fun it was, with its plot lines that involved secret agents, potions, formulas, codes, time machines, and androids. This wasn't a soap opera, it was science fiction, especially considering that one of the characters was John DeLancie, the guy that would eventually play 'Q' on *Star Trek: The Next Generation.*

All of this thinking about where I could expect to find anachronisms forced me to conclude one thing: I couldn't limit myself to music on the generic radio hit parade. I also had to examine other genres like popular Broadway musicals such as *Cats* and *Evita,* or popular movies like *The Rocky Horror Picture Show, Grease,* and *Saturday Night Fever* to name but a few. And, to do that, I had to call in some favours. So yesterday morning, I asked my friends at the geek window if I could borrow LPs and records, even mentioning a few specific ones by name. I told them that it was for a special mixed tape that I was compiling. A few of them were in the same boat that I was in, namely that most of their music was soundtracks and nothing that could be considered popular music. But a couple of them said that they might be able to help me out, especially if their parents or siblings were willing.

Later the same day, when I'd gotten home from school, and after Patrick and I had played fetch with Chance for a while, I'd pulled the monstrosity that was our ancient 8-track player out of storage in the basement and lugged it up to my bedroom where I put it under my desk. It made it a little awkward to sit at the desk, but I knew that it wouldn't be there for more than a day or two, and at least I didn't have to find a place to put its gargantuan 40W speakers, since I could just use headphones (even if those headphones were the size of halved coconuts). Then, I slipped an 8-track tape into the machine and embarked upon the most challenging part of my hunt heretofore. In fact, it was so frustrating, that I actually found myself feeling nostalgic for that long-ago time of just a few days ago when I'd been decrying records for being difficult to listen to because of their relative brevity.

The 8-track was the first real example of portable music, or at least music that was portable enough to play in your car. It consisted of a rectangular plastic cartridge containing a spool of magnetic tape that was wide enough for eight individual tracks of recorded music with each spool being split up into four programs of two stereo tracks each. Because you would pick up listening to a cartridge exactly where you left off the last time you had it in the player, you couldn't really control things beyond being able to switch from one Program to the other (which would just shift to whatever song was on the same position on the tape the next Program over). Much like the TV programming of the era, you were stuck with whatever was on, and had little choice in the matter. This is what made the process of looking for deviations on this media perplexing, because I couldn't change either the speed or direction of the magnetic tape. Meaning, that if I heard something suspicious, I couldn't rewind it, and I was forced to listen to the entire program over again before I could get back to the same point in the song and hear it again.

It's kinda why I'd left this particular media to the end, hoping that maybe I wouldn't actually have to do it, but the box contained a number of albums that I didn't have access to in the easier formats of vinyl and cassettes. On a side note, the box also held a number of Disco 8-tracks, but I wasn't really expecting much in the way of anachronisms from them though, because that style of music didn't qualify as "tent-pole", being fairly generic and largely forgettable, with the possible exception of the Donna Summer and Elton John songs from that era.

After all was sung and done though, my list remained the same. Most of the 8-tracks that my family owned were pretty obscure, so I wasn't familiar enough with their content to even be able to identify differences. So, when I finally went to bed, I had been a little downhearted, a mood that turned into what could best be described as erotically confounded by the content of one of my dreams. In said dream, Andi was dressed like Slave Leia from *Return of the Jedi,* and was telling me that I could do whatever I wanted with her, even as I told her that it was inappropriate in the wake of the #meToo movement of the late 2010s. I won't describe what she did to convince me that she was doing this consensually, but when I eventually woke up, it was with equal parts arousal and bewilderment, as well as the need to change the bedsheets. Again.

This morning at school, both Calvin and Reid had come through on my request for music. Reid brought three LPs for me today, including the very *Saturday Night Fever* and *Rocky Horror Picture Show* soundtracks I had been seeking, as well as one by Weird Al. Amazingly, all three had proven useful. Calvin's selections, not so much. It turns out that Calvin's favourite band was Rush, a group that I hadn't listened to much in my youth, so I was pretty much unable to figure out if any of the words had been switched. Although I thought there might have been something different about their song *Tom Sawyer*, so I noted it my journal with an asterisk.

This brought my list of anachronisms to more than a dozen, but the words still didn't make any sense to me in the context of a message, even with the new slip of paper I had made up for each one. Every time I tossed the pieces up to watch them land in new arrangements, I still couldn't help but wonder if this was all in my imagination.

Here is a list of the new words that I'd been putting on slips of paper to jumble them:

CHOKING, SAILS, FOLLOW, TO, GET, HOLDING YOU, MY, GLASS, JUST AREN'T, YELL, DARK, ELM, SOUL, YOUNG, NOWHERE, DO YOU DO...

Could it actually be a coded message?
Am I projecting my own hopes?
I finally got my answer thanks to Weird Al.

Weird Al's second studio album, *Weird Al Yankovik in 3-D*, was released in 1984. It was the one that truly established him as the premier parody artist of all time thanks in large part to the song *Eat It*, his version of Michael Jackson's *Beat It*. The album had eleven tracks, three of which were wholly original, while the rest were either direct parodies or songs in the style of a specific artist. One of those original songs, titled *Midnight Star* was all about the various crazy headlines that would appear in supermarket tabloids.

The following lyrics caught my attention:

```
Oh, Midnight Star, well,
don't cha know that I read it
I read it in the weekly Midnight Star
The UFO's have landed
and they say "Beware the Borg."
Midnight Star, I wanna know, I wanna know
```

Here's what my table looked like now:

	SONG	OLD	NEW
1	In the Air Tonight	If you told me you were DROWNING	If you told me you were CHOKING
2	Can't Fight This Feeling	OARS	SAILS
3	Every Breath you Take	I'll be WATCHING you	I will FOLLOW you
4	Straight from the Heart	Straight FROM the heart	Straight TO the heart
5	Wake me up before you Go Go	WAKE me up	GET me up
6	Heaven	when I'm LYIN' THERE in YOUR arms	when I'm HOLDING YOU in MY arms
7	Do they Know it's Christmas	Raise a TOAST for everyone	Raise a GLASS for everyone
8	Tears are not enough	Tears ARE NOT enough	Tears JUST AREN'T enough
9	When Doves Cry	Why do we SCREAM at each other?	Why do we YELL at each other?
10	Black Cars	BLACK cars look better in the shade.	DARK cars look better in the shade.
11	Tie a yellow ribbon 'round the old oak tree	... the old OAK tree	... the old ELM tree
12	Tom Sawyer *	... his MIND is not for rent??	... his SOUL is not for rent??
13	The Logical Song *	... when I was a BOY?	... when I was YOUNG?
14	Stayin' Alive*	...not goin' ANY-WHERE?	... not goin' NOWHERE?
15	Sweet Transvestite	How are you?	How do you do?
16	Midnight Star	???	The UFO's have landed and they say "Beware the 'Borg."

Now, if this were the mid-90s, this would clearly be a reference to the technologically augmented villains from *Star Trek: The Next Generation*. If this were the mid 2030s, where I come from (in a roundabout time-warped way), it's a reference to the *Ensee*, the multi-national corporation that was instrumental in helping those of us clustered on Prince Edward Island in the wake of the events of 2025. Colloquially, the *Ensee* had long been referred to as the 'Borg, thanks to the corporation's practice of absorbing and assimilating smaller companies into its larger whole, as well as the fact that it even called itself a *collective*. But this nickname took on a brand-new meaning around 2030. That's when graffiti started to appear on the island, graffiti that was eventually traced back to a burgeoning Resistance movement. It was the first public acknowledgment that the government that we had entrusted to keep us safe had become authoritarian and that the freedoms that we had given up willingly to keep us safe from a deadly plague were never going to be restored. "Beware the 'Borg" became a rallying cry for so many of the Island's population and, eventually, even for me.

But now, in this version of 1985, it didn't mean anything to anybody else but me, and I saw it for what it was: a warning. And because it was coming from Weird Al, in one of his parody songs (especially a parody song about the inane things that are published in a supermarket tabloid), it could easily be dismissed as another of the singer's many eccentricities. As a warning however, it was crystal clear. It was telling me that the *Ensee* existed in this time period, and if they figured out that there were people like me who knew what they were up to before they actually did any of it, then I was a potential threat. I might actually be in danger if I revealed myself.

This explained something else that I'd been wondering about: why were the changes so subtle? What could a person possibly hope to achieve by making such trivial alterations? Weren't there more obvious ways of getting the word out? And now I knew the answer.

The anachronisms were small because there might be somebody else watching, somebody who wouldn't necessarily want a person like me to find out that they weren't alone, especially if there were enough of us to gather in sufficient numbers to hinder nefarious plans. If the changes to the timeline were any bigger than what they were, then the *Ensee* might just catch on, so this was being done in secret. This *had* to be done in secret.

I finally knew that I wasn't imagining things and even had a pretty good idea that I was on the right track.

And I owed it all to Weird Al.

Thanks, Weird Al. Big fan.

I 've said it before and I'll likely say it again: access to information in the 80s sucks.

Or wait. Maybe it blows?

I honestly can't recall the slang that the kids are using these days. Perhaps I should be saying that it, like, gags me with a spoon or some such. I dunno. In my sixties, I had just finally got comfortable using the term 'dude' and now I'm a couple decades too early to use it here.

But I digress.

So, I've been in this version of 1985 for just over a week now, and I'm beginning to think that it might just well be permanent. If I had access to the Internet, I'd be finished gathering all of these anachronisms by now, I'm sure of it. Instead, I'm forced to look for opportunities and keep my eyes and ears attentive to everything, even as I maintain what so often feels like a pointless charade to imitate my previous life, especially at school. On the bright side, I'm pretty much caught up with schoolwork, except for the courses that I had continued to study in University and Grad School, in which case, I'm actually way ahead. And not just ahead of my fellow students, I'm ahead of our teachers! Not that I can point that out though.

Fitting in with my peers has gotten easier, now that I'm back in the swing of things and I haven't done anything else to draw attention to myself. Ironically, my outburst at Hamm has given me a reputation in the hallways that I didn't have my first time here, and my week-long detention has given me cred with some of the 'behaviour' kids. I'd actually begun to tutor some of them while in detention, and have promised to continue it during my spares next week. It's weird how things work out.

So yes, my attitude has been greatly improved. It helped, I think, finding that there were anachronisms in this timeline. I'm not so much obsessed over questions of *why* I'm back (although the *how* of it still hangs there like a ripe fruit just begging to be picked), now that I've got a purpose and an overarching motivation, so to speak. This isn't just a chance to relive my teens, it's a chance to change the future too.

I hope.

As for my relationship with Andi, well… it's as steady as I think it should be. I'm still trying to be a little stand-offish, but that's getting more and more difficult the more I get to know the young woman again. I can see her looking at me occasionally when she thinks I don't know, and it's like she's trying to figure me out. And it makes sense too. If anybody is going to notice a difference in my behaviour, it's a loved one who knows everything about me. Or, at least everything about who I *used* to be.

I can tell that she's frustrated that I'm not spending as much time with her as I used to and, when I am, I'm distracted. Add to that the fact that I've got new moves when we're being intimate and, from the perspective of an insecure teenaged girl, I wouldn't be surprised if she thinks that there's another woman. More than once, I'd wondered if it was possible to let her in on my secret.

Now, don't get me wrong. It's not that I'm still feeling guilty that I'm dating her — I feel like I fully resolved that issue last week. Sure, I still think of both Heather and Celeste occasionally, but lately it's been my children who have been on my mind the most. Especially when I see a little girl who looks like Wren, or even when I catch my father in a certain light and am reminded of how much he could have been Mat's twin. It's one thing when you're missing somebody that you had a romantic relationship with in the future, because there's always a chance that you might meet them again in the past and fall in love all over again. But your unborn children? That was a lot more uncertain.

I didn't know how time-travel worked, but I was pretty sure that the chances of the same offspring being born to me just like they had been the first time were astronomically hopeless. This meant that I was a man who had lost each and every one of his children and grandchildren. And yes, when I'd left the island on Oskar's fool mission, I had said goodbye to them with the expectation that I might not ever see them again, but there had still been a possibility that I might have survived and found my way back to them. Now that possibility was gone, and even the prospect of living some of my best years all over again was cold comfort at best.

So, to try to keep my mind off these thoughts, I've been keeping busy. When I haven't been obsessing over my search for anachronisms, I've been supplementing my meagre finances by picking up as many extra hours at *Duckies* as my school work will allow. I've also been wracking my brain, trying to think of other ways to bring in extra money. Briefly, I'd contemplated soliciting contracts for some made-to-order computer-programming— maybe try and set up a few local businesses with some computer-driven point-of-sale systems—but my BASIC programming skills are inexcusably rusty, and JAVA and C++ were still years off. Hell, it would even be nice to get into fixing broken electronics and such, but, beside the fact that it would be suspicious that I suddenly possessed the necessary skills, Dad's workshop just wasn't quite up to snuff for something like that.

It's not like I'm insulting Dad's garage set-up, it's just that, whenever I think about my father's workshop in a gently competitive way, it brings to mind how Heather had first reacted to the fully-equipped, state-of-the-art studio that I had built in Haliburton after we'd moved there in 2000.

"Your father will be proud," she had said as she looked around at the space in wonder, with its shelves packed with every kind of electronic device, and the separate enclosed space with its smooth concrete floor jammed full of all manner of woodworking machinery, all of it linked together by an elaborate dust collection system.

"I don't want to make him proud," I'd replied in jest. "I want to make him jealous!"

It's funny how my feelings of that memory have flipped around now that I'm in my teens again. The last time that I had revisited it in my mind, I had been in my tiny hovel of a marine workshop on the Pucks (the space had once been a U-Haul moving van before I'd floated the box and installed a large retractable floor over a hole in its bottom so that I had a makeshift moon pool), it had been bittersweet, since both Heather and my father were long gone, and it had just made me miss them all the more. Now, I was back in a time period where they were both alive, yet, somehow, I was still grieving for their deaths in a future that hadn't happened yet. It is perhaps a blessing that brains don't have their own Check Engine lights, because I'm pretty sure that the paradoxical strain that my time-shifting had put on my own brain would have had my own such light blinking by now. Rapidly.

On Saturday, Andi met me at *Duckies* at the end of my afternoon shift and we picked up a few supplies from the grocery store downtown, before driving out to my house to get ready for the night's festivities. There wasn't really much involved in getting set up for a Video Recital, beyond putting out a bunch of snacks and clearing a big area in front of the TV set in case things got animated. Mom and Dad were going to be out late tonight at some function at the Legion, and Patrick was off in Sudbury for the weekend, so we didn't have to worry about disturbing anybody if things got as loud as they usually did.

Calvin was slated to arrive around 5:30 with a carload of geeks and enough pizza for the entire group, with his copy of *Blade Runner* scheduled to go on around 6. I'd taken the opportunity to watch the movie last night to brush up on Deckard's narration. Although I'd revisited the movie a number of times during my sleepless mornings on the Pucks, it had been the director's cut without Harrison Ford's unnecessary voice-over and with the re-insertion of the unicorn sequence, so I wanted to make sure that I was keeping up with the times, so to speak.

Andi's choice in movies was scheduled next, and she had surprised us all by not insisting on something like a John Hughes film. Instead, she had selected *Monty Python and the Holy Grail*, in the process introducing the eminently quotable Monty Python films to our geek tradition. She had been correct last week when she'd told Calvin that he would love her choice because he, along with everyone in the group, was excited about the prospect of boisterously quoting Python out loud along with the dialogue on the screen and in the appropriate accent.

If all went according to the timetable, we'd be finished the movies around midnight, which was perfect timing, since Andi wasn't expected to be home until 1-ish, although her parents were pretty flexible when they knew she was doing something that they considered to be "wholesome." In fact, when they'd heard about the concept of the Video Recital, they'd been halfway tempted to come along, and I'd been halfway tempted to invite them, especially if it meant having another adult or two in the room besides myself.

It was obvious within an hour that Andi's first Video Recital was shaping up to be an absolute triumph for her. How she had managed to memorize *Blade Runner* in just a few days was beyond me. In fact, she was so good, that several of the other participants simply dropped out as we neared the end of the first movie (although they did rejoin us during *Holy Grail* simply so as not to miss out on the fun of imitating the Knights who say "Ni", or the entirety of the Black Knight's dialogue, or the instructions about how to use the Holy Hand Grenade of Antioch).

The only thing was, I kept reminding myself even as I acted out the movie along with my friends, *this hadn't happened before. None of it.*

I'd read about a chaos theory called *The Butterfly Effect* that was applied to time-travel in an old story by Ray Bradbury. The idea being that even the tiniest of changes while in the past—like killing a butterfly by mistake for instance—can have significant impact on the future, and I'd just experienced my second such incident (the first was Mr. Lin, the owner at the Chinese restaurant, giving us free food). In my original timeline, Andi had never attended one of the Video Recitals. I'd successfully managed to keep my two worlds separate in order to keep them from colliding, as George Costanza would say. But, on the morning I had time-shifted last week, I changed things when I hadn't meet Andi at her locker. That simple act of her coming to find me at geek window and overhearing Calvin talk about the party, had been enough to pique her interest and ask to come. Now she was quoting a movie in time with the actors on the screen like a pro, and closing in on winning the crown, and it was changing everything. This shit was a lot more complicated than killing a butterfly in the past.

The competition during the *Holy Grail* was frenetic and the big winner was almost too close to call. Calvin did a fair job, but I was much better since Grail had been another one of those movies that I had re-watched in the future when I couldn't sleep, even going so far as to program it into the OVUM simulacrum so that I could fully immerse myself in it. Ultimately though, it was clear that Andi was the clear victor, and I even suggested that she win a special award for nailing each and every one of the many accents in the film.

For me, the evening had been a welcome reprieve from thinking about anachronisms, and I had managed to keep my mind off them completely and stay fully present in the festivities, until something happened near the end of our last flick of the night, *Superman: The Movie*. It was just before Lex Luthor revealed to his mistress, Miss Teschmacher that, because his bumbling assistant Otis had screwed up while programming the missile directional coordinates into the Army rocket that they had hijacked, her hometown was going to be blown up, along with her mother who lived there.

On the TV screen in front of the group of us gathered in its glow, a Kryptonite-weakened Superman pleaded with Lex Luthor. "You don't ... even care where the other missile is headed, do you?"

"I know exactly where it's headed," we all mimicked along with Gene Hackman just before he tossed the helpless Christopher Reeve into a pool of water, and as he revealed the destination of the Army bird.

The only thing was, as I said "Hackensack, New Jersey", the name of the city as I remembered it to be, everyone else in the room said something else. We all stopped talking, and every head turned to stare at me. I covered quickly, laughing out loud to indicate that I had been goofing around, and returned as much of my attention as I could to the movie, and everyone else followed suit. Everyone, that was, except Andi who, between the dialogue, was sipping at her pop while she stared pensively at me, just like she had in the restaurant a week back.

Not much later, Andi was wearing the crown, and waving goodbye to everyone in Calvin's car, who were all responding with enthusiastic thumbs up. Although Calvin had told me last week that he hadn't wanted to lose the crown to a girl, he was more than happy to put it on Andi's head since he'd had a lot of fun.

"Your girlfriend's excellent memory has finally given me the challenge I've been waiting for, Donegal," he told me as he was packing up to leave. I wasn't even insulted by the back-handed slight because, once again, I was marvelling at how things had turned out differently, and in a manner that was much better than the original circumstances.

After everyone else had left, Andi offered to help me clean up before I drove her home, something that hadn't taken all that long since there were just a bunch of chip bags, bottles, and empty dip containers to gather up. It felt really weird putting so much of it directly in the garbage though, because there wasn't anything in the way of a recycling program in 1985.

Andi didn't say much as we worked, and the drive into town was equally quiet, with her resisting all of my light-hearted attempts to make her laugh. I had a sneaking suspicion what she was hung up on, and sure enough, she confirmed as much when we were approaching the fountain in mid-town, when she finally looked over sharply at me and said, "Do you mind telling me what's going on with you?" It wasn't an angry or concerned tone of voice. It was actually more like she was curious.

"Whatever do you mean?" I asked, feigning ignorance, even as I pulled into the parking lot beside the fountain and put the car in park. This wasn't a conversation that I wanted to have while driving.

Andi didn't miss a beat. She'd obviously been thinking about what to say, and it all came flowing out. "You're not really... well, *you* anymore," she gushed in an embarrassed tone, as if she realized how ridiculous it sounded. "I mean you are, but there's something different. You spend so much time on your own now even when you're with other people. You're always deep in thought and ignoring everyone else as you write in that notebook of yours, the one that you refuse to let anybody else see. And there's your attitude too. I mean twice in the last twenty-four hours alone, I've heard you use the phrase 'I could be wrong, but...' That's not you at all, Josh!"

I laughed at this, but only lightly, sensing that it wouldn't do to appear to be mocking her in any way just now.

"I know this sounds crazy," she continued. "But you talk and act like an adult now, when you used to be over-the-top melodramatic. You're not even walking the same—you used to walk kinda hunched over, and quickly. Now you're standing tall and *strolling*! Hell, you even eat differently. The other day, when you had soup in the cafeteria, you took the crackers *out* of the package first instead of leaving them inside it and crushing them into a powder with your fist."

I couldn't tell for sure, but it seemed like Andi was shaking. I wanted to reach out and steady her, but I was too busy trying to figure out how to respond. Ironically, I was actually glad that she had so much to say, because it was giving me more time to think.

"You're a lot more confrontational too. In the entire time I've known you, you've never talked back to anyone, let alone a teacher! Hamm still avoids you in the hallways."

Andi stopped talking for a moment, and looked out the window as if she couldn't stand looking at me for what was coming.

"And … well, you kiss like a pro and well, that's not the only new skill you suddenly know." She blushed a little, apparently thinking about our *makein* session the other day. "But that's not all. You're forgetting things. Things we talked about just last month. Then you're forgetting where you sit in school, or how to read music, or how to play a clarinet. And if you're not forgetting things, then you're remembering them wrong, like in that Phil Collins song, or with that movie tonight." I swallowed, inwardly cursing myself for letting it come to this. It was just as I had feared. If anybody was going to notice my being different, it would be somebody who was closest to me. Somebody like Andi.

"I know you Josh," Andi continued, looking straight at me again. "You know that Superman movie backwards and forwards, you kept quoting it when you made me watch it with you on our third date. There's no way you would have messed up something so obvious. And for both of those slip ups, you didn't just forget what they were, you were *adamant* that they were something else. I memorized that movie to get ready for the party tonight. There's no way it was that place in New Jersey that you said. It's always been Mansfield, Ohio."

I spun my head to look at her. "Mansfield, Ohio?" I asked. In all the confusion earlier, I hadn't made out the city that everyone else had quoted.

Andi narrowed her eyes as she answered. "Yes. Why?"

Why did Mansfield, Ohio sound familiar? Why was it significant?

I had been back and forth between Cleveland and Columbus, Ohio in the mid 2000s for business, and I'm sure that Mansfield had been part of trip somehow, but I couldn't think of…

"Are you even listening to me Josh?" Andi barked, angry for the first time in this conversation. "There you go again. Like I just said. Your mind is off somewhere else, and your eyes…" All of a sudden, Andi was crying. Quietly at first, but it didn't take long for it to become great big racking sobs. I reached out to touch her and, as I leaned in, she grabbed my face and held it so that our gazes locked. "It's your eyes that are the worst, Josh. They're not the same. When you look at me now, there's something… something new. And I've seen eyes like them before…" Her voice broke again, and it took a few deep breaths for her to bring it back under control.

"I don't remember if I ever told you, but when my Grandfather died in 1982, I helped take care of him. I spent days by his bedside because somehow, I felt that I had to. His memory... well, it was spotty and the family never knew when he was lucid or talking gibberish. I knew though, because I learned to read his eyes. I knew when he was there, and when he wasn't. But there was something else in his eyes too. Something I could never figure out until he told me a story."

Letting go of my face, Andi leaned back and pulled a tissue out of her purse. Wiping at her eyes and nose, she continued. "Papou grew up in Greece and was in his mid-twenties during World War Two. He and my Grandmother had been married for a few years by then, and my father would have been... um, about two at the time—too young to remember any of it, which is probably why he never told me about it himself. Anyhow, Papou, along with his father, brothers, and uncles were members of the Greek resistance, and they were involved in a number of skirmishes with the German army." She took a deep breath and tried to swallow the lump in her throat. I stayed quiet, not wanting to interrupt her story in any way. "Anyhow, in 1943, the Germans wanted to punish the resistance fighters in my Papou's village, so they looted and torched it. Then they gathered all the older boys and men, over four hundred in total, and used machine guns to ... to mow them down."

I gasped. The car suddenly feeling a lot colder than it actually was.

"It became known as the Kalavryta Massacre. There were only about a dozen survivors, and they lived because they got buried under the dead men as they collapsed. My Papou was one of those survivors, but he almost wished he hadn't been. When he was finally freed from the bottom of the pile of bodies, he found that he'd lost his father and three brothers to the German guns, not to mention about a dozen or so uncles and cousins, and his ancestral home had been burned to the ground. His wife, son, and mother were fine, thank goodness, or at least as fine as you could be after something like that.

"They tried to rebuild, but it wasn't easy. Eventually, it was just too much for my Great-Grandmother, and she died before the war had even ended. After that, well my Papou didn't want to live in a place that reminded him of what had happened, so he gave up, and left Greece entirely, and found a new life in Canada."

Andi pulled out another tissue and blew her nose before continuing. "His entire village had been destroyed. Every male member of his family had been slaughtered. He lived because he was buried under a bloody hill of dead men, most of them his own family. He was never quite the same after that. It changed the way he looked at the world." Andi was looking at me again. "It changed his eyes. It was after he had told me about the massacre that I finally figured out what it was that I had always seen in his eyes. It was loss. Deep unfathomable, ancient loss, one he had spent a lifetime trying to get over." Through a breaking voice, Andi finished. "That's… that's what I see in your eyes now … Josh. It's not you anymore. You act kinda the same, and try to be light and funny and amusing, but you're hiding something. I can see it, even if nobody else can."

We sat in silence for a time. I turned to look out the front window at the fountain as I gripped the steering wheel. Funny how it had to be here at the fountain where we were having this conversation considering it was where we had met.

Dammit. Why didn't I run away the moment I woke up in my own past?

I had only been thinking of myself. I never considered how my playing along would affect other people. How others might get hurt. What should I tell Andi? Could she handle the truth? Would that be any worse than simply breaking up now and leaving?

I looked at her again. Andi was a bright young woman. One of the smartest people I ever knew. It sure would be nice to have somebody to talk to about this whole experience. It sure would be nice to have a little help gathering the clues too…

"Are you sick, Josh?" Andi asked suddenly. "Like a brain tumour or something?"

I laughed out loud despite the gravity of the question. "It's not a toomor," I replied in my best Arnold Schwarzenegger impression. In response, Andi just looked at me, her eyes wide and looking even more concerned than before.

I apologized, suddenly realizing what I had to do. "Let's go for a walk, OK?"

A moment later, we were standing beside the circular fountain, and I was holding her hand. It was a beautiful night, and despite the late hour, there were still a few people out and about. There was a waxing moon above us, and the riverside had never looked lovelier.

I took a deep breath and let it out. "I'm going to tell you something Andi, and please keep an open mind." Beside me, Andi tensed, her grip on my hand suddenly rigid.

I swallowed before continuing. "This fountain. It's where we met last year. It's where I fell in love with you ... head over heels in love." She laughed rigidly and leaned into me. I used this contact to turn her body so that we were facing across the river to the bandstand on the other side. "And that's where, in the summer of 1987, I will make one of the biggest mistakes of my life ... and break up with you." Andi tensed again, gasping abruptly for breath and then not letting it out. I kept talking, afraid to stop now that I'd begun. "I'll rationalize it at the time that, since I'll be going to Western and you're going to be spending a year in Greece on an archaeological dig with your aunt, that there's little point in even trying a long-distance relationship." I shifted our position again towards an area where the Robertson River flowed into the Groundhog.

"That tree over there, the one that hangs out over the water. It's where you and your husband and kids will pose for the town's seemingly obligatory Robertson tourist picture sometime in the late 2000s. You'll show it to me on your smartphone at the big twenty-fifth high school reunion in 2012, when we finally see each other for the first time in twenty years."

I paused for just a moment, and assumed that, because she hadn't run away yet, Andi was tolerating me at least enough to let me continue. At least she was breathing again, although it was pretty rapid and shallow. I turned and pulled her towards me so that she could see my eyes again, hoping that she could perceive the truth in their depths, along with the unfathomable loss she had just been speaking of.

"But before all of that happens, we'll get to know each other a lot better in the next few years. You'll tell me things that you've never told anybody. Like your mother's alcoholism, and how it got much worse after she lost a son in childbirth about five years after you were born. And how your father's narcissism made doing anything about it all but impossible."

Andi gasped and finally pulled away from me. She buried her face in her hands, and started crying again. "I've never told anybody that," she spat. "How the fuck could you know any of that about my parents? How could you possibly know about my aunt wanting me to spend a year in Greece? She only just talked about it as a *possibility* last month. I hadn't told *anybody* about it. Not even Mom and Dad."

"I'm sorry, Andi. But I know something else about you too. I know what your real name is. It's something that you kept from me until much later in our relationship because you despised it, and resented your mother for insisting on giving it to you." In response, she lowered her hands and glared at me, a mixture of anger and what I could only hope was curiosity. "Truly, I am sorry ... Andromeda," I continued, her head jerking back like she'd just been slapped the moment that I had said her real name.

"How could you possibly know things like my real name? How could you possibly know what's going to happen ... unless..."

I saw the final pieces click into place for her. Her eyes widened in shock as what I could only imagine was an impossible thought occurred to her.

"You've been watching way too many fucking time-travel movies, Donegal! You can't honestly expect me to believe that you're... that you've... I can't even say it." She turned again and walked away from me, putting the entire fountain between us before stopping to glare back at me, her arms crossed in front of her.

"I'm sorry, Andi," I repeated. "But, you're right. I'm not the same person I was last month. I haven't been that person in about fifty years, and you'll have to forgive me if I'm a little out of practice."

When Andi spoke, her voice was low and delivered in a hiss that was clear, even from across the tumbling water. "Are you actually making jokes about this, Donegal?"

I smiled weakly and lifted my hands in mock surrender, knowing that she only ever called me by my last name when she was truly upset. "They take this fountain out eventually, y'know," I continued unabated. "To widen the intersection. Patrick, who comes back to Robertson for a few years after a successful career in the Ontario Hockey League, managed to keep a piece for me since he knew how important it was to me because of our history with it. I kept it framed in a shadow-box in my study for years. They finally replace the bridge in the mid-2010s as well, and the bandstand burns down in the mid-1990s during a Victoria Day Celebration when they set off fireworks too close to it. Eventually, they use it as the location for a new fountain. Oh, and they demolish the old public school too and put an addition onto the high school instead. It made bussing all the kids easier."

"That's enough Josh!"

"I get married for the first time in 1992, and my son Mat will be born in…"

"I SAID THAT'S ENOUGH!" Andi had sprinted around to my side of the fountain to face me, but she wasn't angry. She grabbed me by the elbows and, her voice suddenly quiet and still quivering, she said, "That's enough. I believe you."

"Believe what? I haven't told you anything yet. *You're* the one who mentioned time-travel."

Despite everything that we'd just discussed, Andi just laughed in response, almost hysterically. She was also shivering, deep racking vibrations. The spring night was a tad chilly, but she was clearly in shock too.

"Let's go to the car," I said gently as I put my arm around her and guided her to the parking lot where I held the car door for her so that she could climb into the passenger seat. Then, I went to the trunk to grab the emergency blanket that my father made sure was always present in all of our vehicles—a habit I had also picked up on in later life. I got into the driver's seat and covered Andi in the blanket as best I could, in the same gentle way that I'd used when I'd tucked my kids into bed when they were sick or upset. Then I started the car, and turned the heat on high.

We sat in silence for a few minutes.

Andi believes me! I thought to myself as I stared at her in wonder.

Even as I said it though, I realized that I wasn't all that surprised that she had accepted the truth so quickly. One of the things that would make Andi an excellent journalist in the future was her ability to sort through facts quickly, separate the useless ones from those with significance, and then reach a conclusion. The thing that made her an outstanding journalist was her ability to discard even those conclusions almost immediately when better evidence presented itself. She had always had an innate ability to discern the truth, no matter how uncomfortable or, (at least in this situation), farfetched it might seem.

Finally, her teeth still chattering, Andi simply asked, "How?"

"Did I come back? I don't know."

"Why?"

"No idea either."

Andi snorted. "Ok then. When?"

"When did I come back from?"

Andi nodded.

I sighed. "2035," I answered quietly.

"Shit." Andi was laughing again as she did the math in her head. "That's, um … fifty years from now? So, you're what, … 67 or 68?… Fucking hell. You're old enough to be my … my Grandfather."

"Just my mind," I countered, while I laughed in time with her.

"Like that fucking matters." She grabbed another tissue. Her body wasn't shaking as badly now, but her head was, lightly back and forth—a nervous habit of hers when she was thinking. It was a clear indication that she was evaluating everything that she'd observed over the last week, pairing it with what I'd just told her, and figuring things out. "It was that Thursday morning just over a week back wasn't it? When I found you at the window with your friends when you were supposed to meet me at my locker. You seemed distant somehow, like you didn't recognize me. But then you kissed me…"

"Ah yes. Sorry about that. I was trying to distract you."

Andi scoffed. "And the bird shit on Brock's car, after you got the words to the song wrong. Was that a distraction too?"

"Yes. I wanted to divert attention away from my mistake so that I could figure out why the song was different in this timeline."

Andi stiffened. It was like her radar had detected something of interest. "What do you mean?" she asked.

I took another deep breath and found myself gripping the steering wheel again. "This timeline is slightly different than mine," I told her. "You saw another example of that tonight with the movie. The first time that I lived through the 80s, the lyric for *In the Air Tonight* was most definitely 'drowning' instead of 'choking', and Miss Teschmacher's home town was Hackensack, New Jersey."

"They're different?"

"Yes."

Andi thought about this in silence for a moment, her head rocking slightly from side to side. "Well, there's no guarantee that the timeline would go exactly the same way each time, right?" Then, she stopped and had a good laugh. It was a genuine laugh too, and it went a long way towards relieving the unacknowledged tension between us. "I can't believe that I'm discussing time-travel rationally," she admitted as he wiped at her nose with the back of her hand. "Like it's actually a real thing."

"It took me a while too," I said. "I also wondered the same thing about timelines, and how much they might differ when repeated, but, well... I've been spending the last week looking for as many anomalies as possible — it's why I've been distracted whenever the radio is on. I've found a bunch of them, but nothing before the early 1970s. All the classics, like the Beatles and the Stones and Dylan, they're all exactly as I remember. It's like the changes only started in the last fifteen years."

"Why?"

I laughed out loud again, more of an amused bark than anything else. "I don't know exactly, but the best I can figure is that... well, it's some kind of code." I stopped, and glanced over at Andi sidelong to gauge her reaction. It was strange how telling her about me having travelled through time was actually easier than revealing that I suspected that there was some kind of conspiracy theory behind it all. When she didn't react in an untoward way, I continued, "I've found about a dozen anomalies since our date with Brock and Phoebe, and have been trying to figure out if the words combine into some kind of message. It's been challenging trying to access the variety of music I need to listen to in order to find more."

Andi looked at me and blinked as she contemplated my words before saying, "It's a little needlessly complicated no? I mean, if it's a puzzle, then how many people would actually know what Miss Tessmacher's hometown was? It's such an insignificant detail, one that only a dedicated geek like yourself would remember. And who would be sending you a message like that? And how? If somebody else came back in time with you, why wouldn't they make it more obvious?"

"What? You mean rent out a billboard that says 'If you're a time-traveller, call me'?" I asked through a silly grin.

"Well, yeah," Andi replied slyly. "That would work. Most people would just think it was a stupid publicity stunt or something. Wouldn't they?"

"I've been wondering the same thing myself. It may be that they don't want certain parties to know that it's happened."

"'Certain parties'," Andi parroted me, smiling suddenly as if what she was saying were nothing more than a ridiculous cliché. "What? D'you mean, like the *bad guys*?"

I sighed again. Part of me heard Doc Brown's voice telling me that no person should know too much about their own future. But then, I knew that this quote was just a plot device put there by the writers to create a challenge for the characters in order to make the movie more dramatic for the audience. Now that I was actually talking about being a bona fide time-traveller out loud, it was becoming instinctively clear to me that this kind of thing just didn't matter in the long run. I knew that I had to tell Andi everything.

For the longest time, I just looked at her as I chewed on my bottom lip. Ironically, now that I had decided to actually open up to Andi, I didn't really know where to begin.

"What?" Andi said. "Josh, what is it? Why are you looking at me like that? It's freaking me out."

In response, I took her hand as gently as I could, looked at her and swallowed. She stiffened, as if sensing that this wasn't going to be easy to either say or hear. Once I started talking, it didn't take very long. I knew that, since it was getting pretty close to 1AM, I didn't have much time before I had to drop her off, so I condensed it as much as a person could condense a story that involved the death of the vast majority of the Earth's population and the corporation that had pretty much successfully enslaved the survivors.

By the time I was done, Andi was crying again. Pushing the blanket off her body, she leaned forward and pulled me into a hug. For a time, we just stayed that way, our bodies shuddering against each other, me drawing strength from her warmth.

"Your eyes," she said finally. "I understand now. That's why they're like that. The billions … who died…" Her voice faded as she started crying again. She tried to speak a few times, I could hear her mouth opening and closing, but clearly, she couldn't find the words.

Finally, in a tiny distant voice, she said. "You lost so much, Josh. How… how could you have possibly gone on after… after something like… that?"

"I'm sure your Papou would have said the same, but it's because you don't have any other choice," I eventually answered, as if I'd rehearsed it. As if I'd said the same thing to myself countless times in the last decade. "You're never the same, but… well, you're alive. It helped that we didn't really know what was going on, being disconnected from any form of global communication. We could hold on to hope, no matter how irrational, that somewhere there

162

were other pockets of humanity that had survived just like we had." I paused for a moment as I watched a droplet of condensation roll down the inside of the windshield. I wondered how much to tell her about what I'd discovered about what had really happened to the rest of humanity in my last few days in the future, just before I had been inexplicably shifted into my own past.

I looked over at Andi who was looking at me, eyes wide with shock and beginning to water again. "And let's be honest," I continued, deciding not to go into unnecessary detail — there would be time for that later. "The human mind is pretty myopic anyhow. After the initial shock, we all began to focus on the group of us that were left, and there seemed like there were a hell of a lot of us, especially when it came to feeding everyone. Our minds couldn't really grasp the concept of 'billions of deaths,' not when there were just over two million clinging to the island just trying to survive."

I took another deep breath. I hadn't really gotten into my personal life in what I'd just told Andi. It wasn't easy telling your high school sweetheart about the love life that you would have without her in the future. It was almost as difficult as telling your wife about the relationships that you'd had with other women in the past. Perhaps, in the end, it was pretty much the same thing.

"As for me, well ... I hadn't exactly lost everything." I exhaled as I felt a lump gathering in my throat as my chin began to quiver. "I, at least still had my family ... Mat, Suki, Celeste, and the kids ... that is ... until now..." For the first time since I had shifted back in time, I broke down and, in Andi's arms, I wept at once for the life that I'd never see again and for being reunited with loved ones I'd lost a long time ago. I wept knowing that, even though I might currently be reunited with those loved ones, I could already feel my path leading me away from them, because I was pretty sure that, if there was a coded message after all, it wasn't going to say "Stay put and have fun."

Andi held me for a good long time in silence. I could tell that she was crying too, but she was struggling not to be at all obvious about it, probably so as not to risk making the moment about her. She stroked my head and held it to her chest and I could hear her heart racing.

Finally, I sat up and looked at my watch. It was five minutes before 1 AM.

"We'd better get you home," I said. Andi didn't argue, she just held my right hand as I drove with my left, and stared at me silently the whole way to her street. When we pulled up in the driveway beside the Petras house, I could see a light on in the kitchen window and watched as Andi's mother looked out at the car. Now that her parents could see that she was home, I knew that it gave us a few extra minutes.

Andi was staring at me strangely now, an odd look on her face. Swallowing, she said. "You were married in the future? On the … um, island? Where is she now?" Her voice was tighter now, constrained.

"Who? Celeste?"

"Was that her name? Then yes," she swallowed again. It was obvious that Andi was trying to be supportive by asking about my future relationships.

"Ah, well," I started sheepishly. "She hasn't exactly been… ah, born yet."

Andi blinked a few times, her supportive manner morphing into something bordering on indignation. "Please don't tell me that you turn into one of those old men who have to prove that they're still virile by marrying young wives."

I couldn't help but laugh. "Hardly. It wasn't really my choice. Not to put too fine a point on it, but the future of society hinged partly on the survivors being able to produce viable offspring. As luck would have it, there were fewer young men on the island when the authorities started encouraging us to hook up, and Celeste got stuck with me."

For the longest time, Andi glared at me, as if she were unsure whether or not to believe me.

"Wait. You said you got married earlier than that. In… um, when was it?"

"1992." I answered, amazed at her ability to remember something that was said when she was upset and being bombarded with impossible facts. "I … um, well, I marry a woman named Heather Hudson just after University and we have … er, *had* a son in 1995. That's why we were on the island in the first place. Heather … well, she dies of breast cancer in 2024, and Mat and I travel to her ancestral home in PEI to spread her ashes. Mat's wife and my Grand-daughter Wilson were with us too."

Andi blinked as she absorbed what I'd just said. A few times, she opened her mouth to say something, but then thought better of it.

"I have so many questions," she said finally.

"I can imagine."

"Are there things you're not allowed to tell me about the future?"

I smiled. "It's not like I'm bound by any time-traveling conventions or anything," I replied. "This whole thing is a mystery to me as well. It helps that I can talk about it, and I appreciate you being so understanding. You can ask me anything you want. I'll leave it to you to decide whether or not you really want to hear what I tell you. A lot of things can happen over fifty years, and I had the benefit of experiencing it all slowly, and in sequence. If I tell you everything all at once, and out of context, it might be a bigger shock to your system than what I've already told you tonight."

"As if that's possible," Andi muttered as she looked back towards the kitchen window. "I don't want to leave..."

"I know. The timing is lousy. If only I had a time machine..."

Andi laughed lightly. "You work tomorrow afternoon?"

"Yes."

"Can we pick this up then? I'll meet you there after?"

I took her hand and said, "I like pink very much, Lois." It was a quote from *Superman*, and Andi caught on right away, knowing that it was my way of saying "yes." She leaned in towards me as if wanting to kiss me, but stopped halfway, as if suddenly unsure of herself.

"It's OK," I said, reassuringly. "I understand if you can't..." The rest of my words were cut off by the sudden pressure of her lips. They lingered for a moment, moving against mine gently and tenderly. Pulling away a few inches, those same lips breathed, "I love you, Josh Donegal. No matter what. Do you understand that?"

I was crying again as I repeated the sentiment.

Then, Andi was out the door and running up her driveway. I had just started the car and was putting it in reverse when I spotted her running back towards me. She was approaching the driver's side window, so I rolled it down in time for her to lean in.

"Just one last question about the future before you go, OK?"

"Shoot."

"I just need to know," she said breathlessly. "Brock's gay right?"

"Like you wouldn't believe."

CHAPTER 11
Blowing Bubbles

T he moment I got back home, I went downstairs where the *Superman* videotape was still in the VCR, and rewound it to the second scene in which Miss Teschmacher's home town was mentioned. This took place after Lex had dropped Superman in the pool, when we found out that Miss Teschmacher had overheard the whole conversation about where the Army missile was headed.

"But Lex," I watched Valerie Perrine, the actress who played Lex's mistress, say. "My mother lives in Mansfield." In response, the heartless super criminal simply glances at his watch, before shaking his head dismissively and walking away.

I rewound the tape to the beginning of the scene, and watched it again to see if the movie had been overdubbed or something. After repeating this action three more times, I was finally convinced that Valerie's lips matched the words that were coming out of them. Then I went back even further and re-watched the section before it, the one in which I'd first got the detail wrong during the Video Recital. I couldn't see any evidence of post-filming trickery, like had been done in the scene in *Galaxy Quest* where Sigourney Weaver's lips can be seen mouthing the words "Well, fuck that" even though what is actually heard is, "Well, screw that," thanks to some looping that was done after the fact to make the film more family-friendly.

To be honest, I didn't really know why I was being so thorough. After all, each and every one of my friends (including Andi) were in complete and total agreement with the Lex and Miss Teschmacher of this alternate 1985. It was just that this was different from finding modifications to songs. With the added visual aspect, it was possible to determine if these changes were being made with some fancy sound editing equipment after they'd been recorded, or if the words were actually said (or sung) by the actors (or artists) themselves in the first place. Seeing an anachronism in a movie made it pretty clear that it was the former and that however this change had been initiated, it had obviously been made before the movie itself had even been filmed. Possibly as far back as when it was being scripted.

Turning off the TV set and VCR, I did one last sweep of the room to make sure that it was clean. I made a mental note to vacuum the carpet tomorrow (although Chance had taken care of all of the most obvious of food crumbs), before going upstairs to my room to get my notebook so that I could document this new anachronism. Mom and Dad had apparently gotten home while I'd been out dropping off Andi, but, once again, I was in no mood to sleep, not now that I'd found another media to explore for alterations. It was close to 1:30 AM, but maybe I could watch at least one more movie tonight.

When I got back to the recroom, I had a green tea (I'd managed to find some at one of the local grocery stores earlier this week) and a dog that was very excited that I was spending time downstairs with her again rather than going to bed with everyone else. As I scanned my VHS movie collection, I thought again about the anachronisms that I'd found so far and how they had been in songs that were well known. Would the same strategy apply to movies?

I couldn't help but laugh at myself, because this theory had already been proven wrong before I'd even fully articulated it. *Superman* may have been a blockbuster movie, but Andi was right when she had said that not that many people would be able to remember a trivial detail like Miss Teschmacher's home town.

It is way too late at night for these kinds of internal debates!

And, besides, I was still a little wound up from the way my conversation with Andi had gone. Best then to pick a movie that could both distract me from thinking about Andi and test my theory that blockbusters would be bigger targets for anachronisms. So, I found my VHS copy of the biggest blockbuster I could think of, and fed it into the VCR.

As *Star Wars* began, I updated the table in my journal with Mansfield, Ohio, even as I wondered why it sounded so familiar. I was sure that something important, at least insofar as pop culture was concerned, would happen there, but damned if I could remember what it was. Since an Internet search engine wasn't an option, I'd have to check into it the next time I was at the library.

Closing my journal and sipping my tea, I settled in with one of my favourite movies. Like many of the other genre movies that I would collectively perform with friends at our Video Recitals, I knew this one backwards and forwards, and not just the dialogue. I was a definite content expert insofar as the visuals were concerned as well. From the dice hanging in the cockpit of the *Millennium Falcon*, to the time that Chewie appears to check out the ass of a droid that was walking by as Luke and Han (disguised as stormtroopers) were ushering him onto an elevator. Like *Holy Grail*, I'd programmed this particular movie into my OVUM simulacrum on the island, and had spent many hours exploring it in much greater detail than could be done by watching this criminally low-resolution video tape on the convex screen of a 70s era TV set that wasn't getting any of the colours right.

I was getting a little sleepy as *Star Wars* reached its climax, but I was jolted alert the moment that I found the anachronism. It was on Luke's last trench-run targeting the Death Star's exhaust port, when a pursuing Darth Vader says, "The Force is strong with this ONE." Only, in this timeline, the dialogue had been changed to "The Force is strong with this BOY."

Like with the *Superman* movie just a few hours earlier, I rewound the movie a few times just to make sure that I'd gotten it right, even though I couldn't match up the spoken words with moving lips, for obvious reasons. Even if this particular line of dialogue was a little hard to make out in the movie itself, I had heard it countless times in the *Star Wars* coin-operated video game (one of the first to use actual dialogue and music from a movie), that broadcast the line (along with Obi-Wan's pleading voice saying to "Use the Force, Luke") from speakers behind the player's head inside a mock-up of an X-wing cockpit. In addition, I was also pretty sure that this wasn't something that George Lucas himself had changed "in post," since he wouldn't start meddling with his greatest creations until sometime in the late 90s, when, among other things, he would use CGI to make it look as if Han had shot Greedo in self-defence and that, for some inexplicable reason, Anakin Skywalker had no eyebrows.

It was getting close to 3:30 AM, and I was exhausted, but I watched the rest of the movie anyhow, just to be thorough. When I hadn't noticed anything else out of place with the film, I went to bed satisfied that it had been worth it. Even though I was absolutely exhausted, I felt secure in the knowledge that I would be able to make up for the late night by sleeping-in in the morning.

This, unfortunately was not to be, said the narrator.

Blame it on the tea that I'd had after midnight, but I was compelled to wake up earlier than I'd wanted to on Sunday morning by the overpowering urge to pee. I never made it back to bed afterwards either, having been ultimately enticed downstairs by the seductive aroma of Mom's French toast. Walking into the kitchen, I said, "Yes, please," before my she even got the chance to ask if I wanted any. Then, I asked what I could do to help.

"You can put the strawberries in a bowl, dear," she replied. "And ask your father to bring up some maple syrup from the cold cellar. Somebody finished the jar in the fridge."

Sheepishly, I did as I was instructed. I didn't want to tell her that it had been me that had polished off the maple syrup not long after I'd discovered it mid-week. It was also something that had been in short supply on the island, and I'd been enjoying pretty much a shot glass a day just to celebrate the fact that I had access to the magical elixir again.

It was amusing that, before I'd inexplicably shifted back to 1985, the closest I'd ever come to time-travel was anytime I either smelled or tasted maple syrup. Without fail, this simple act would always transport me right back to my youth when I would be helping my father gather sap and boil it into syrup on Grandpa's farm in Kanata. If I closed my eyes, I could see my Grandpa handing me an old tin cup full of warm, half-boiled sap, and sense it light up my taste-buds as I drank it. Sometimes, if I was really focusing, I could even feel the old man lifting me up on his shoulders so I could get a better look at the evaporator, and watch the golden water roiling and bubbling and producing a thick maple steam that hung so heavy within the tiny wooden shack that it would coat my face with tiny droplets of sweet liquid that ran down off my lips and onto my tongue.

Those trips to the family farm were magical. It was something that we tried to do every March break, no matter how busy my father may have been at work. In fact, it always amazed me how my father was able to make as much time for leisurely pursuits as he did, especially when those pursuits involved me or Patrick.

The three of us were sitting at the breakfast table now, tucking in to another spectacular spread of French toast topped with strawberries and served with breakfast sausages. As my parents discussed their plans for the day, I continued to think about the things my father did to be present for his family. He would take us on week-long camping trips, fly us into remote fishing camps in the Northern-Ontario wilderness, or take us out on day-long ice-fishing trips where we'd get a big fire going in the middle of the lake and bomb around on ancient ski-doos while he watched the lines. During each of these trips, he would always make time to teach us how to make snares, or build shelters, or live off the land. The wilderness still scared me back then, but never when I was with him.

On weekends when we were at home, he'd always be pushing us to play board games, or to sit with him and watch *Doctor Who* (one of his favourites), or go to a movie, or sit and listen to music with him so that he could tell us what made *The Beatles* the best rock band of all time. If I ever had something I wanted to build, he'd push his own projects aside in the workshop to make room for mine and would be right there to help me no matter how long it took.

My father was connected to his children in a way that few other fathers were in that era, and I always felt I did a poor job in living up to his standards. Surely, he had been just as passionate about his work as I had been with mine. How had he managed to put it aside so easily?

I was watching as Mom got up to get some more coffee for herself when it occurred to me that I had just been thinking about something important, specifically how it was that I used to watch *Doctor Who* with my father. Indeed, it could be said that I owed my love of all things sci-fi to him, as he'd introduced me to all of the classics like *The Day the Earth Stood Still*, *Forbidden Planet*, and, of course, *Star Trek*. It was just now dawning on me that, in a roundabout way, he was the one who had introduced me to the sci-fi trope of time-travel in the first place and not, ironically, through *Doctor Who* or *Star Trek*. Although both those shows were all about time-travel, the themes they explored just never seemed relatable, because they always seemed to take place in outer space and involve aliens and monsters.

No, the first time that I can recall ever being absolutely enthralled by the concept of time-travel was in *The Final Countdown*, a movie that I saw in the movie theater in the late 70s with my father. It was all about a modern aircraft carrier that got mysteriously sent back in time to the WWII era, and the characters had to decide whether to stop the attack on Pearl Harbour and risk changing history.

There were characters who got left in the past, and showed up back in the present at the end of the movie, and that concept just blew me away.

As I contemplated this, I found myself staring at my father, and the way he chewed on the tiny seeds from the strawberries on his French Toast. Was it actually possible that he, of all people, might be able to understand what was happening to me? Now that Andi knew, could I risk letting other people in on the secret too? For her part, Andi seemed to have accepted it a lot more readily than I had expected, but I knew instinctively that I would need to jump through bigger hoops to convince my father. I couldn't, at the moment, imagine what those hoops might be, so I would have to continue to think about it and remain open to inspiration.

It was at this moment that my internal contemplation about my father was interrupted by the man himself. He was telling me how impressed he had been with the improvement in my behaviour of late. "You were playing my records the other day," he was saying. "And you put them all away the way you found them! Then, after you had borrowed tools, I found them back where they belonged!" I'm pretty sure I was blushing once I figured out that he was being sincere instead of sarcastic. What a feeling knowing that I was revelling in the praise that my father was giving me even though I was technically his senior. How could I possibly tell the man that I finally understood how it felt to have your son go through your things and leave them in a mess, or scatter your tools through the house so thoroughly that you had to send out search parties to collect them every time you wanted to start a project. It had only taken me about thirty years, but I finally understood what I'd put my father through, and it had happened in exactly the way he'd predicted all those years back whenever he'd say, "One day, I hope your kids do it to you so that you'll know how it feels!"

After breakfast, I had a couple of hours before I had to leave for work. Mom and Dad were going to visit some friends for the day, so, after I'd seen them off, I went upstairs where I took some time to go through my Tai Chi movements before enjoying a long, hot shower. Then, I grabbed some leftover coffee, warmed it up in the microwave, and took it down to the recroom, Chance in tow. I knew that I didn't have time to watch a full movie this morning, so I wanted to test another theory in relation to TV shows. This theory was that I would be unlikely to find anachronisms in regular television programming since most of them, with the possible exception of the *Star Trek: The Original Series* (or TOS, as it would be known colloquially once there was more than just one *Star Trek* series to refer to), wouldn't have the same level of quotability as would, say, a popular movie. But it was a different story altogether with the theme songs, and I was confident that, if any changes had been made to the theme songs of these TV shows, I'd be able to pick up on them. Especially the ones from the 60s and 70s that took upwards to a full minute to set up the premise of the TV show before an episode of it even began. Kids in my generation used to know all of those theme songs by heart, especially the ones from *The Flintstones, The Brady Bunch, The Beverly Hillbillies*, and *Gilligan's Island*.

Unfortunately, I couldn't test this theory with those particular shows this morning, but I did know a few other ones that I could check out. If memory served, I had a bunch of video tapes with recordings of my favourite TV shows like *Greatest American Hero* and *Knight Rider* and others like them, as well as the must-see-TV lineup from Thursday nights. I could scan through these recordings pretty quickly, paying special attention to the theme songs, and see what I could find.

Before I'd left for work an hour and a half later, I had about a half-dozen theme songs running through my head, and another anachronism in my book in the form of a change to the *Cheers* theme song. In my original timeline, the song had famously asked, "Wouldn't you like to get away?" but in this new and improved 1985, it had been changed to, "Wouldn't you like to just escape?"

True to her word, Andi showed up at *Duckies* about ten minutes before my shift ended. She was smiling brightly, if exaggeratedly, but her eyes looked red and puffy as if she'd been crying. While I was with my last customer, she pointed out the window at the park across the street indicating the riverside park bench where she'd be waiting for me when I was done.

Fifteen minutes later, I was sitting on the bench beside her. It was an overcast day, but not all that chilly. Even so, Andi was wearing a thick sweater with a turtle neck to keep the out the Spring chill. For a time, we didn't really know what to say to each other beyond pleasantries, and I couldn't really blame Andi for being uncomfortable with me. Although she had left last night's conversation in good spirits, I suspect that had changed not long after the shock of what I'd told her had worn off. I wondered how much sleep she had managed to get.

"I have something for you," I said as I reached into the pocket of my wind breaker, handing her a small cylindrical plastic container.

"Bubbles?" she asked when she'd read the label.

"Bubbles." I replied. "They never fail to break the tension."

"Josh…" she began.

"Seriously, try it," I implored as I took the bottle and opened it up. As I held up the wand in front of my face, I said, "I'm not sure if you're aware of this but the first rule of blowing bubbles is always to blow. Never to suck. I cannot emphasize this enough. It's an ugly lesson to learn, although it does freshen the breath surprisingly well." She giggled at this, if a little anaemically, as I blew a few tentative bubbles out in front of her. Then, I was holding the wand in front of her face asking her to do the same.

Andi pursed her lips and directed a strong targeted lungful towards the tiny hoop, and several large bubbles formed on it before finally breaking free and floating off. After we'd watched them dance away on the breeze, she looked over and smiled at me and, for the first time today, her smile reached her eyes.

I blew a few more bubbles, and they were floating out over the river when I said, "I'm sorry, Andi. I never should have told you."

"Josh, please. You had to," she answered as she grabbed the wand from me to take her turn. "It's not like you could have kept it secret much longer. Not from me, anyhow. I knew something was off and it had me so worried last week. I kept thinking that you were sick, or worse, that you were thinking of breaking up with me."

"Wait, What?" I interjected. "Me breaking up with you is worse than me being sick? That girl has got to sort out her priorities," I said to nobody in particular in a mock British accent, paraphrasing a line from Ron Weasley from the first *Harry Potter* film.

Andi grinned toothily at that, even as she said, "Let me bet. That's from some book or movie that hasn't been made yet."

I nodded as I blew some more bubbles, realizing in the process that I had actually missed this simple activity. "Let's just say that you're gonna love the books. One of the characters is just like you."

Andi took her turn with the bubble wand, but otherwise didn't say anything. After she'd handed it back to me, she moved her backpack off the bench where it had been creating a natural barrier between us, and slid a little closer to me.

"I, ah… well, I didn't get much sleep last night," she said, confirming my earlier suspicion. "I kept going back and forth on whether or not to believe you."

"Oh, sorry," I said as I exhaled in short, quick breaths, trying to make a bunch of small bubbles. "And what did you finally decide?"

"Well, I'm here aren't I? I decided to believe you."

"What tipped the scales?" I asked, partly out of curiosity, but mostly as direction as to how to present the concept to my parents if the need arose.

"Well, if it was just the stuff you shouldn't have known … like my real name," she said turning her head away from me slightly so that I couldn't see her face redden. "Well, I might have just thought that you were a psychic, like my Great-aunt Phaedra. But, you've been acting differently too. Acting like an adult." She turned back towards me again, tucking a length of her hair behind her left ear. "But, like I told you last night, what really convinced me, Josh, were your eyes."

"I see." Oddly, this was a bit of a disappointment for me, at least insofar as if informing me on how to present my situation to my parents. I couldn't very well see me telling them to look me in the eyes because they'd changed. "When did you get so mature?"

In response, Andi just smiled and kissed my cheek. "And, the more I think about it," she said. "The more I think that you're right. This has got to be some kind of message, and you have to figure it out. And you're going to need my help."

I laughed as kindly as I could. She didn't mean what she had just said arrogantly, it was just her confidence speaking, that same confidence that had attracted me to her in the first place. She wasn't wrong either; she had always had a way of tackling problems that was inspiring. Maybe she *could* suggest possibilities that I wouldn't be able to think of myself.

"And I'll prove it to you," she finished as she pulled her backpack up on to her lap and started rooting through it. "Yesterday, you were telling me that you've been having a difficult time getting access to a wide variety of music. I've got a solution." With that, she produced a couple of magazines and set them on my lap. I picked one up, for a moment not knowing what I was looking at. Then it hit me. It was a song lyrics magazine!

"Andi! You are a wonder!" I exclaimed as I started flipping through the pages. I'd completely forgotten, but long before you could look up the lyrics of any song on websites that acted as repositories for such information, song lyric magazines served that purpose. Often, these magazines were divided into sections for current hits, oldies, and even different genres of music. They were, bar none, the absolute best way to see the words for songs that just didn't get much in the way of airtime anymore, like *American Pie* or *Hotel California* for instance. Now that I was holding it, I was reminded of long school field trips with a bunch of us crowded around one of these magazines while we belted out songs for which we knew the tune, but not the words.

The issue that I was looking at now had a huge Golden Oldies section, so I flipped to the lyrics for *Tie a Yellow Ribbon Round the Ole Elm Tree*, and confirmed that what I had heard last week hadn't been my imagination. Just seeing the anachronism in print made if feel different somehow. Like it was suddenly that much more real. When I looked up at Andi, I had tears in my eyes and, when she saw them, she started crying too.

"This is really happening," I choked out. "I mean, I knew it was, but now... well, it's just more tangible."

"Show me," she said quietly, her voice cracking under the strain.

Holding the magazine up for her to see, I pointed to the words of the song and said, "This is actually the earliest change I've been able to find. In my timeline, it was an oak tree that they tied the yellow ribbon to."

Andi reached out and stroked the pages thoughtfully, as if looking for evidence that the page had been altered. "For me, it's always been an elm tree. Weird." She was lost in thought for a moment, her head rocking gently back and forth in contemplation. "Show me another one."

I flipped to the front of the book to the index and located the section with Current Hits and scanned the songs listed there. The magazine was about a year old, but it didn't take long before I'd located a change that I'd recently identified on the radio.

"This one," I said, pointing to a song by Culture Club. "I know it as *Do You Really Want to Hurt Me.*"

"I've always known it as *Do You Really Have to Hurt Me,*" Andi said, pausing for a moment as she thought about the nature of the differences. "I think I like your version better."

"Me too," I said, as I flipped some more. "But I might be biased."

"Both of the ones you just pointed out. The changes were in the actual titles. Are they all like that?"

"No, not all," I answered. "But I'm finding that they're mostly in either the title or the chorus. The parts of the song that are the most well-known. The ones that get sung the most often. I suspect that this is on purpose."

"Makes sense," she agreed.

An idea struck me, and I flipped back to the index of the issue that I was holding. When I couldn't find what I was looking for, I checked the other two as well.

"What are you looking for?"

"Classic TV theme songs," I said. "But I don't see any sections for them." Closing the magazine, I looked at Andi. "How well do you know classic TV theme songs."

Andi grinned. I knew that answer already. That girl had a memory like a proverbial steel trap. "You're going to ask me to sing, aren't you?"

"I'm going to ask you to sing."

We spent the next half hour singing songs from our youth and comparing them for differences. Eventually we moved to the footbridge that spanned the Robertson river at its thinnest point, feet dangling just above the rushing water, flipping through the magazines, and circling every anachronism that we came across.

Every once in a while, Andi would ask me a question about the future, and I would answer it, and all the discomfort we'd felt from my shocking revelation the evening before seemed to disparate entirely as we both adjusted to the new nature of our relationship.

When I eventually dropped Andi off at her home, she kissed me without any hesitation at all, our lips lingering protractedly. Before she got out of the car though, she told me, "I still don't know how to feel about you. About this whole time-travel mess. On one hand, I feel selfish in that something's been stolen from me because the Josh I fell in love with is... gone. No offense." I shook my head to indicate that I wasn't bothered by her words. "Somebody took him from me. But, on the other hand, I now know that it was going to happen anyhow, I mean in that we break up after high school." She swallowed. "Like I said, I'm confused. I also know what the future holds too, and it makes me feel better knowing that you have a chance to change it all, and I have a chance to be a part of it."

I hugged her again while I reassured her that hurting her was the last thing I would ever want to do. Even as I said it though, I knew, in the very back of my mind, that I would very likely be doing that very thing if I ever solved this fucking clue, because it was exceedingly likely that it would lead me away from Robertson, and away from her. I couldn't tell her that though. Not yet. So, instead, I walked her to her door, and kissed her good night.

I got home just in time for a late supper with my parents and Patrick, who had just arrived home from his weekend away. He looked exhausted and, I was pretty sure, still a little drunk. Afterwards, I went to my bedroom where Andi's lyrics magazines helped me add no fewer than a half-dozen new anachronisms to my list. In addition, I was able to use them to positively confirm a number that I'd already found. These magazines had proven to be the most efficient way to spot temporal variations and I only wish that I'd thought of them earlier.

Later that night, after everyone had gone to bed, I stayed up and popped *The Wrath of Khan,* the second (and still the best) *Star Trek* motion picture, into the VCR. In the process of watching it, I was rewarded for staying up later than I really should have with the discovery of another alteration. The famous philosophical interchange between Kirk and Spock that occurs twice in the movie used to be: "The needs of the many outweigh the needs of the few. Or THE one." Now, it was: "The needs of the many outweigh the needs of the few. Or JUST one."

When I got to my bedroom around 1:30AM, I made up some new slips of paper for the new words that I'd found today and tossed them around with all the other ones. After about a half hour of looking at various phrase combinations, none of which made any sense at all, I finally gave up and went to bed.

These were all the changed words I've found so far:

CHOKING, SAILS, FOLLOW, TO, GET, HOLDING YOU, MY, GLASS, JUST AREN'T, YELL, DARK, ELM, SOUL, YOUNG, NOWHERE, DO YOU DO, HAVE, MANSFIELD, BOY, JUST ESCAPE, WISH I KNEW, CRUSH, BENEATH, COME WITH, ON MY OWN, FLOWERS, JUST LIKE YOU AND ME, JUST...

Dwayne R. James

And the latest entries in my table at the back of my journal now looked like this:

	SONG	OLD	NEW
17	Do you really want to hurt me?	Do you really WANT to hurt me?	Do you really HAVE to hurt me?
18	Superman: The Movie	Hackensack, New Jersey	Mansfield, Ohio
19	Star Wars	The Force is Strong with this ONE.	The Force is Strong with this BOY.
20	Cheers theme	Wouldn't you like to GET AWAY?	Wouldn't you like to JUST ESCAPE?
21	Margaritaville	How it got here I HAVEN'T A CLUE	How it got here, I WISH I KNEW
22	Don't Fall in love with a Dreamer*	He'll BREAK you every time.	He'll CRUSH you every time.
23	Arthur's Theme	...BETWEEN the moon AND New York City	...BENEATH the moon IN New York City
24	Follow you, follow me	I will FOLLOW you, will you follow me	I will COME WITH you, will you follow me
25	Hello	I've been ALONE with you inside my mind	I've been ON MY OWN with you inside my mind
26	Season in the Sun*	Pretty GIRLS are everywhere?	Pretty FLOWERS everywhere?
27	Islands in the Stream	THAT IS WHAT WE ARE	JUST LIKE YOU AND ME
28	Wrath of Khan	...needs of the few. Or THE one.	...needs of the few. Or JUST one.

178

CHAPTER 12
A Youthful Optimism

The weekend had been so eventful for me that it took longer than usual to get used to going back to school on Monday. If I had been distracted by the search for anachronisms before, I was doubly distracted now that Andi was in on my secret. It wasn't that I was concerned that she would blow my cover by asking a question at an inopportune time, it was just that … well, I was feeling responsible for her now. I had just changed the young woman's life by letting her know that the future held an unimaginable catastrophe. Mercifully, she had yet to ask about her own fate, but I knew that it was just a matter of time, even if I didn't have the foggiest notion of how to answer such a question. I didn't have much of a choice in my being back in the past with a full memory of what was in store for everyone, but I did have a say as to who I impacted with that knowledge, and how.

As for Andi, well, she seemed to be taking the impossible change in our status quo in stride, and didn't seem to be at all out of sorts on Monday. She'd shown up at my locker with a duffel bag full of cassettes, LPs, and 45s. "I would have brought it yesterday," she explained. "But I needed to be able to sort through it first so that I wasn't giving you something you already had."

For the longest time, I didn't know what to say. This was above and beyond, even for Andi. Finally, I told her how much I appreciated her help, but admitted that I was concerned. "I've been obsessed with the search, and it's been a distraction for me, but I don't really have a choice in the matter. I don't want the puzzle to become a distraction for you too, especially if it starts to negatively impact your school work."

Andi scoffed at the suggestion. "First, stop sounding like my parents, old man," she was speaking softly enough so that nobody in the hallway chaos around us could hear. "And second, this is me, remember? I've been getting a little bored of late anyhow. I needed the challenge."

My suspicion that Andi was exaggerating in her boast was borne out later that day when we were sharing a table in the library during a spare period. She was studying for an upcoming test in Algebra and I was looking through some *Popular Mechanics* magazines looking for some mention of Magnus. I had been to the town library the other day to check on him as well, and so far, I hadn't been able to find anything of note. I was distantly scanning an article about how engineers were hoping to be able to refloat the *Titanic* when it was eventually found, when it abruptly occurred to me that I finally had an ally who knew even more about this era than did I.

"Do you mind if I ask you a question?" I said.

Andi looked up from her textbook and grinned. "That'll be a change of pace," she said. "Sure."

"What's happened to Magnus Levenko?"

"Who?"

I had been afraid of an answer like that. It indicated another change to this timeline, and it was a significant, especially since it represented the complete absence of a high-profile celebrity. "He was a wunderkind in his youth," I answered. "Kinda like Mozart. At the age of seven, he was performing concerts where he would flawlessly play one instrument after another. From the piano, to the cello, to the trumpet, he played them all. His father was a famous music producer, so it was said that it came to him naturally. Before Magnus had turned ten, he'd released an award-winning orchestral album on which he had performed each and every instrument in a sweeping symphony that he had composed himself."

"Oh right. That does sound familiar! Yes, I do remember him now, kinda. Didn't he die, like really young?"

"Hmm. Well, not in my timeline."

"Did he do something important in your future?" she asked quietly, even as she looked around to make sure that we couldn't be overheard.

"You might say that, but in the 80s that I lived through the first time," I found myself looking around as well as I spoke, "his celebrity grew when he moved beyond his music and got into computer programming, science, and electronics design. He was a regular Elon Musk."

"Who?"

"Oh right. I'll tell you about him another time. As for Magnus... well, imagine Michael Jackson's fame but with a scientist. You name it, his name was either on it or he was promoting it. He should be here. I'm really surprised that he's not. Some of his inventions appear to be, but he should be all over the news with his exploits and adventures."

"You mean like Tony Stark?"

I laughed at this. "You really are a geek. Did you know that?"

"Shh," she hissed back. "Don't let it get out. I don't want to upset my platinum standing with the cool kids."

I went back to skimming through the article on the *Titanic*, amused that they were still expecting to find the sunken ocean liner in one piece, while Andi went back to her textbook. This didn't last long though and, about five minutes later, she was pushing the book away from her, as she hissed in frustration.

"Are you having a problem with Algebra?"

In response, Andi just hissed again.

"Have you tried turning it off and back on again?" I asked, in my best *IT Crowd* imitation.

Ignoring me, Andi just said, "Please tell me that math gets easier in the future."

"Not really," I said, not looking up. "But there is a big math revolt in the early 2020s"

"What. Really?"

"Yeah, all the numbers that we borrowed from in high school come back and demand to be repaid with interest."

As I picked the pencil off my lap that she'd just thrown at me in response to my flippant remark, I asked, "Would you like some help?"

I spent the rest of the spare tutoring her on the finer points of Algebra and using some real-world examples from my own experience (aka the future) to drive the point home. Afterwards, as she gathered up her books to get ready for her next class, she thanked me. "I gotta say, having an older and experienced man in my life is kinda appealing." Then, she kissed me and slipped out of the library door ahead of me, before seemingly floating off down the hallway away from me. Reflectively rubbing my cheek where she'd kissed me, I made my way towards my next class. I wasn't so much feeling out of place in this timeline anymore; it didn't really feel like I was reliving my past so much anymore. In fact, it was honestly beginning to feel like an extension of my lifespan already in progress, and that was all kinds of crazy.

At school, I was definitely trying harder in all my classes, even when that didn't always work out the way I would have expected. So often, I'd encounter the problem where I knew better than my teachers, specifically when I would provide answers that, though technically correct, either weren't in the Grade 11 curriculum or were based on research that hadn't even been done yet. Worse, I couldn't necessarily argue my point because I shouldn't really know what I knew, and there was no way I wanted a repeat of my confrontation with Hamm. So, I learned to keep my mouth shut, and lived with the cards the way they fell.

The gatherings around geek window were expanding a little bit more every day. Andi was there with me every morning, the younger geeks positively worshipping her as if she were her new Queen, and she was bringing some of her female friends with her. When we weren't singing old TV theme songs like *WKRP, Happy Days,* or *Laverne & Shirley* (naturally, this had been my idea), Calvin was gleefully explaining the finer points of *Lord of the Rings* mythology to a surprisingly captive audience. Earlier this week, Calvin had also gotten ahold of a list of movies that were coming out this summer, and he was getting excited about such titles as *The Goonies, Red Sonja,* and the *Mad Max* sequel, as well as a little movie called *Back to the Future.* But, for some inexplicable reason, the movie that he was most enthusiastic about was the forthcoming *Pee Wee's Big Adventure* because it was being directed by the up and coming Tim Burton.

My reaction to the news was almost visceral, something that I thought I had disguised pretty well until Andi and I were walking towards our home rooms later, and she asked me teasingly, "I take it you're not a Pee-Wee Herman fan."

I laughed. "Oh God, that's not it," I said. "It's Tim Burton. I still haven't forgiven him for Batman."

"What'd he going to do to Batman?"

"He directs a big-budget movie in ... I want to say, the late 80s, or something. The movie was OK, but he asked Prince to write a song for the soundtrack. That video still haunts my nightmares, and it hasn't even been made yet."

I had spent the last few evenings working my way through the selection of music that Andi had provided (which had resulted in a couple of excellent anachronisms including one that switched the phone number in the song *867-5309* to *867-9305)*. On Tuesday night, once my family had gone to bed, I'd re-watched *The Empire Strikes Back*, and then on Wednesday it was *Return of the Jedi*. Neither one appeared to have been altered in any obvious way, although it had been nice to watch the original versions without any of the changes that Lucas would ultimately make, even if the quality of the pan and scan transfer onto video tape had been generally poor. Add the widescreen format on home videos and a flat screen TV set that could handle it, to something else that I missed from the future.

On Thursday night, I found what was perhaps the most unique anachronism yet in Spielberg's *Close Encounters of the Third Kind*. The classic five note motif played during the communication between the humans and the alien ship on top of Devil's Tower was different in that the same musical notes were played in a different order. Once I was able to play the theme on my clarinet the next day, I figured out that the original tune was: B flat, C, A flat, (change octaves), A flat, E flat and that the new motif was: B flat, A flat, C, (change octaves), E flat, A flat.

It was this change in *Close Encounters*, perhaps more than any other one that I'd gathered thus far, that threw me. I could kind of understand the concept of drawing attention to changed words because they could potentially be combined to form messages. But musical notes? Why on earth would the notes of what was arguably the most recognizable five-note melody in the world require rearrangement?

I decided right then and there that I was going to solve this geedee puzzle if, for no other reason, than to know the answer to this question.

This morning, just as Calvin was leaving geek window, it occurred to me that it was Friday May the 3rd so, I said, "Have a Happy *Star Wars* day tomorrow, Calvin."

In response, he looked about as confused as I'd expected he would be, so I explained it to him slowly, emphasizing certain words and using helpful hand gestures, "It's the fourth of May tomorrow. So... May ... the ... *fourth* ... be with you."

Calvin blinked a few times as he processed what I'd just told him. I knew that this particular play on words wouldn't reach the tipping point into the collective consciousness until the mid to late 2000s, but I just couldn't resist introducing it early to such an ardent *Star Wars* fan like Calvin. I figured that, if he was at all like me (and I knew that he was), he would rejoice in being able to confuse others with the greeting, at least until they began to catch on and do it themselves. At that point, the thrill would wear off, once the mainstream figured out what it meant, and every Tom, Dick, and Multinational Conglomerate was tweeting about it and trying to promote their products through brand name association.

Finally, the young man's face lit up and he smiled broadly as he clapped his hands in delight. "That's perfect!" he said. "I love it. May the Fourth be with you too, Josh."

As Calvin disappeared down the hallway in the direction of his home room, he was greeting pretty much everyone with an enthusiastic, "May the Fourth be with you." Perhaps predictably, not too many faces were registering comprehension.

I knew that it was time for me to head to my own homeroom, but something about those youthful expressions caught my eye. This wasn't the first time that I'd been struck by the mood here in 1985, and, indeed, it was getting harder and harder not to notice it the longer I was surrounded by it. There was an energy here, an optimism. Not the kind of optimism that makes you feel as if everything will turn out OK no matter what happens, but the kind that makes you feel that the world is full of *possibilities* and you're poised to take advantage of each and every one of them. It's like you can go anywhere. Do anything. Be anything.

I'd almost forgotten about the awareness and appreciation of life's potential that I'd had in my youth, and I honestly have no idea when I stopped feeling it. I mean, I can certainly recall a certain malaise that epitomized my fifties in a way that I hadn't felt in any of my previous decades. That's when it first started sinking in that my options in life were suddenly limited somehow. I was the product of all of my choices theretofore, and further opportunities were rapidly drying up, and I found myself feeling that I'd made my bed a long time ago, and would continue sleeping in that one and only bed for the rest of my life, never to buy another bed again.

It was both comfortable and depressing, and I wasn't the only one feeling it either. Although, this was still a few years before the events of 2025, so many of my peers were feeling stuck, isolated. The threat of terrorism, civil unrest, and climate change kept so many of us close to home and unwilling to risk international travel. Naturally, this changed after the pandemic and our isolation on the island of P.E.I. when we went from not wanting to go anywhere to being unable to. The fact that we were simply lucky to still be alive, after a time, didn't measure up in the face of a lifetime of being limited and confined.

And now, here I was, back in a past full of kids who hadn't learned to stop reaching. Who'd been raised on a steady diet of being told that they could do whatever they set their minds to. It was, well… there was no other word for it but, *intoxicating*. The kids all around me had dreams and hopes. Oh sure, most of them were childish fantasies that revolved around either writing a hit song or getting discovered by a talent agent and becoming famous enough to buy a big luxury car that they could drive around Robertson with the windows down, waving at all of their old friends. But they were still *positive* fantasies. *Happy* dreams.

Still, as invigorating as this was, and no matter how happy I allowed it to make me in the moment, there was still something dark and menacing underneath it all. I knew where humans on this planet were headed, and it wasn't at all a pleasant destination. The senior citizen in me wanted to sink into despair and start yelling at clouds, but these kids were reminding me that there was an alternative. Call it a youthful optimism or remembering what it was like to be awash with potential, but it was contagious. Yes, I know where we're going, but they were making me feel more and more every day that it just might be possible to change our future direction, especially if the anachronisms I was noticing turned out to represent what I was hoping they did.

At the end of the school day, I drove downtown with Andi for our weekly date at the *Golden Sun*. Normally, I would have had to work, but I had apparently switched my schedule around sometime before my temporal displacement so that I could attend what promised to be the high school dance of the year: our first ever Video Dance party!

It should probably go without saying that, in the MTV era that I found myself revisiting, music videos were all the rage. Music videos were so popular, that we would often get together in groups just to watch them, especially for events like the world premiere of

Michael Jackson's *Thriller* video, even though that wasn't always easy. In Canada, before our own music channel, *MuchMusic*, came along, our only source to watch videos was a weekly hour and half program called *Friday Night Videos*.

The idea of having these videos as a backdrop to a dance wasn't exactly new, it was just that nobody had figured out how to do it properly. The obvious problem was that, at the time, television was broadcast in mono, and you couldn't just record a video off a TV broadcast and expect to play it through huge speakers for an auditorium full of kids and expect it to sound halfway decent. A DJ service in a nearby town had claimed to have found a solution.

They hadn't, said Ron Howard's *Arrested Development* voice.

Although the DJ's set-up certainly looked professional enough — with a big screen TV on the stage surrounded by all sorts of high-tech looking equipment and speakers of the appropriate size — the moment the dance started, we noticed the issue: the music that they were playing didn't actually match the video that was being projected! The problem wasn't that the vocals were out of synch with the movement of the singer's mouths, it was that the song was a different song altogether, by a different artist. Now, to the DJ's credit, he did, every once in a while, play a video that matched the music, but for the rest of the night it was just a regular dance with the DJ playing whatever music or video that he wanted while simultaneously ignoring the shouts from the dance floor to synch things up.

The first time I had experienced this particular event, I can remember being disappointed that it was pretty much a regular dance but, this time around, I was just happy to be getting an opportunity to listen to a variety of music that I might not necessarily have heard yet. As I danced, I listened as intently as I could, and was rewarded for my efforts with an anachronism in David Bowie's song *Let's Dance*. The words were now "Out in the moonlight" when, in my timeline, it had been "Under the moonlight."

There was also another difference about tonight that hadn't happened before or, for that matter, any time I'd ever graced a dance floor. In my teens, I'd always felt a little out of place in such environments because I'd always been very self-conscious in that I was clearly lacking in any kind of moves that could be considered halfway coordinated, but not tonight. Oh sure, I still didn't have any of the moves, but for the first time in my life, I simply didn't care. I'd been back long enough now that I was finally familiar with all my old friends again, and I was having a blast bouncing off each other on the dance floor while we sang along in time with the music (unlike the figures on the TV screen, our mouths actually matched the singer's voice) and jumped whenever Van Halen told us to.

And then, there was Andi.

It had been about a week since I'd told Andi my secret and, I'd been trying to keep a respectful distance to give her the time she needed to adjust, but it was pretty clear by the way she was kissing me on the dancefloor as we held each other to Madonna's *Crazy for You*, that she'd had all the time she'd needed.

"Have you heard any… what do you call them… *anachronisms* yet?" she asked in my ear.

"One," I answered.

"Did you want to look for more, or do… um, something else?"

I smiled. "What'd you have in mind?"

Twenty minutes later, after we'd snuck out of the school dance as discreetly as we could, we were parked on the ledge overlooking Hermann's gravel pit. There weren't as many stars to be seen from the window of the hatchback tonight because it was so overcast, but we didn't care, because we barely looked up anyway. We'd both of us come full circle. I'd finally adjusted to the fact that I was an occupant of 1985 again and didn't need to feel beholden to a life that hadn't happened yet, and Andi had accepted the fact that, even though my eyes had changed, I was still at heart the same person she'd fallen in love with. In fact, if there was still one thing to our relationship for me to adjust to, it was that it was so casual, at least in comparison to a marriage. I wasn't used to having a partner that I didn't see more often, or one that I didn't get to sleep beside every night or wake up beside every morning. Or worse, one that I would have to bid goodnight to under the light beside the back door of her parent's house so criminally soon after we'd shared such a tender moment together.

The next morning, I was up early again to eat breakfast with Mom and Dad. As I spread the ketchup liberally on my bacon and eggs, I broached a topic with them about an idea that had just occurred to me the day before.

"So, I was looking at the calendar yesterday," I started. "And I see that the Victoria Day holiday is coming up in a few weeks' time. Not sure if there's anything planned, but I was wondering if maybe we could arrange to visit some family in Ottawa."

My parents exchanged curious looks. "Which ones?" asked Mom.

"Why, all of them or course," I answered.

Even as I said it though, I had to wonder: was the entire family still talking? I mean, relations between my Mom and Dad's in-laws had always been cordial and everything, but I was more thinking about my Mom's side of the family. When had her brothers and sisters fallen out over petty squabbling about inheritances? Well, obviously not yet, since both of my grandparents were still alive in 1985. What a thrill it would be to see them all again, especially considering they'd still be younger than I had been before my temporal displacement.

Neither one of my parents got a chance to respond to my request however, because we were all interrupted by the unexpected entrance of Patrick, who was actually home this weekend, and was uncharacteristically getting out of bed before noon to join the rest of us for breakfast. This was a huge surprise, but the ulterior motive for his early awakening was made obvious about twenty minutes later when his friend Geoffrey showed up at the front door. Apparently, the two of them had a long ride planned on their motorcycles today, and they'd wanted to get an early start. Mom absolutely adored Geoffrey, and positively spoiled him anytime he was over. Naturally, she fussed over both of them as they got ready, making sure that they had packed enough to eat and were wearing the right clothes for the rain that had been forecast to fall for most of the day.

Mom watched them worriedly out the window as they sped off down the highway on their bikes, a thick spray of mist in their wake. I wanted to reassure her by telling her that I knew for a fact that nothing bad would happen to them today, simply because I knew that they both had a solid future to look forward to. But, I knew I couldn't play my hand, at least not like this. So, instead, I simply said, "They're both excellent drivers as well as responsible young men. I'm sure that they'll both be just fine."

In response, my mother just looked at me and blinked a few times before turning to begin the breakfast clean-up. Dad had already slipped out quietly to the workshop, so I knew that it was pointless revisiting the earlier conversation about the impromptu family reunion that I had proposed until I could get them both together again. I'd planted the seed. I had a few days to spare to see if anything grew from it.

Once breakfast was put away, I went upstairs and spent the rest of the morning catching up on homework and going through a few of the cassettes that my friend Dean had leant me earlier in the week, before taking Chance for a walk through the fields and forests behind the house. It was funny how I'd been so afraid to go anywhere near these woods as a kid, and only really learned to appreciate having such easy access to them after I'd moved away and no longer had easy access to them. I'd always despised the line from the Joni Mitchell song that went: "you don't know what you've got 'till it's gone," because I'd always thought that, if you were paying attention, you knew what you had, and you could appreciate it without having to lose it. Instead, I'd long known that you could know what you had before you lost it, to the point that, when it did disappear, you just missed it that much more. This was never more obvious to me as I climbed over logs and ducked under branches with Chance bounding excitedly around me through the bushes. I'd *always* loved having an environment like this in my own backyard, even when I had been too scared to go anywhere near it.

My afternoon was spent working at *Duckies* before coming back home around 6 so that I could have a quick bite to eat and get changed for Andi's party. It had been Tuesday at lunch when she had announced that she wanted to have some friends over to her place on Saturday night to "listen to music." She had even gone so far as to encourage everyone to bring along at least six albums or cassettes or 45s, in as many musical genres as possible, "Y'know, to broaden our musical horizons," as she had put it. Then, privately, she told me that I could be in charge of playing the music, and that I should bring a bunch of blank cassettes in case I wanted to make some recordings for my "research."

The fact that she had made it sound like the motivation for the party had been entirely for socialization, and only made mention of it helping my "research" after the fact, made me appreciate the young woman even more. Andi was certainly living up to her promise to help me figure out what the coded message was by coming up with ways to get access to music that hadn't even occurred to me. Blame it on my stubborn independence, but I'd always approached problems as if they had to be solved alone. I wasn't one to ask for help with anything, especially in an endeavour as secretive as this, but, thanks to Andi, I was quickly discovering the advantages in getting others involved.

Before I left for the party, I sought out my parents to say goodbye for the evening. Mom was in her sewing room mending some of Patrick's sports jerseys and Dad was in the recroom, Chance at his feet, eating a slice of apple pie (with cheese) and watching a classic episode of *Doctor Who* on the TV Ontario channel. Glancing at my watch, I decided that I had enough time to sit down and watch a bit of it with him. Some of my fondest memories of my father were sitting in the recroom like this, bonding over our mutual love of cheesy British sci-fi, even if, when he'd first introduced me to *Doctor Who*, I had dismissed it as being laughable because of the awful special effects that weren't nearly as spectacular as those on other TV shows of the time like *Battlestar Galactica*. But then, once I'd started to watch the Doctor, I was impressed not only by how intelligent it was, but also by how the writers made it seem conceivable that tense situations could be resolved with little more than a witty argument, a robot dog, and a marked lack of guns.

The episode that Dad was watching involved the fourth Doctor (the one with the scarf) and his assistant Romana being trapped in some kind of time loop and, even though this kind of thing happened pretty much every episode, I actually remembered this one. In fact, I was surprised by how many of the details were coming back to me as I watched it. I'm not claiming to have some kind of photographic memory or anything, it was just that, at the risk of sounding like I'm saying that my generation was better than younger ones, kids of my era actually were better at remembering such things. Ask any child of the 70s about something that they had once watched on TV or in the theaters, and I'll bet you credits to croissants that they could still tell you almost everything about it. They remembered it so vividly because, at the time, they didn't have any other choice. There were no VCRs or a home video market and, as far as they knew, they would only have but that one opportunity to see the TV show or movie.

Years later, when the world was obsessed with multi-tasking, and it was impossible to do just one thing at a time, I wondered why it was that I could remember scenes I'd seen only once years ago better than the scenes in current movies that I'd just watched the night before. I was pretty sure that it was because that, once movies got to the point where we knew we could see them again in a few months, and then be able to rewind an individual moment over and over, we stopped paying attention, especially when something interesting was also happening on your smart phone.

When I was in a darkened theater in the late 70s, I was watching everything closely; soaking it all in, not sure when, or if, I'd ever be seeing it again. When I was watching a new movie in the 2010s, I knew in the back of my mind that I'd be able to read a post online the next day pointing out all of the things I had failed to notice.

Oh, back in the day, we did try and find ways to experience the movie again, at least in part, on our own schedule. For example, whenever my favourite movies were finally broadcast on TV, before we had our first VCR, I did the next best thing, and recorded the movie's audio on cassette. People talk about how television and movies ruined books because they destroyed people's ability to use their imagination to create the scenes that they were reading about. I disagreed, because I was having my imagination stimulated by following along with the audio track from a movie I'd seen only once or twice, my eyes closed, trying desperately to remember how the scenes looked that one or two times I'd witnessed them.

Neither was I alone in this kind of behaviour. In fact, I can recall hearing stories about the very first *Star Trek* convention in the early 70s. It took place not long after the series had been cancelled, and just as it was finding a huge new audience thanks to syndication, but the crowds still went wild when Gene Rodenberry brought along some 16mm films of a few of the episodes for them to watch because there really weren't any other viewing options. It was a different world at the time. The producers of the show were just beginning to figure out that *Star Trek* was a show that wouldn't die, and there wasn't much in way of memorabilia available as a result, so fans made their own. These fans were desperate for some kind of a way to be able to experience their beloved show now that it was no longer on the air. Some (like I had done with my favourite movies) had recorded the audio off their TV sets during the original broadcasts, while others had taken pictures of their TV screens. Not surprisingly, copies of these pictures, fuzzy as they were, sold out at the convention even though they were neither sanctioned or autographed.

"I'm going fishing on *Lost Otter* tomorrow," my father said, breaking in on the thought process that had been distracting me from the TV program in exactly the way I'd been bemoaning in that very thought process. "Weather permitting of course. Supposed to be nice though. There's room in the canoe..."

He left the invitation open ended. As usual, by not having actually asked me explicitly, he was leaving it up to me to make the next move. It was yet another of the irritating character traits that I'd inherited from the man. It wasn't until I was in my forties that I finally realized that, like my father before me, I would often subtly manipulate people into asking to do things with me so that, if things went south, I wasn't strictly to blame. "I'd love to come along," I answered. "If there's room. I work tomorrow night though. Will we be back in time?"

"If you don't get us lost again," he answered playfully between mouthfuls of his pie.

Chance had finally given up on getting any stray tidbits from my father, and had come over to hop up on the couch beside me. I was scratching her behind the ears as I responded. "If memory serves, you asked me to drive home on the backroads, and then you promptly fell asleep in the passenger seat without giving me directions." The experience was still clear in my mind, even this many years later. By the time Dad had awoken, it was getting dark and I had no idea where we were. He took over the steering wheel and managed to find a landmark that he recognized after about a half hour of driving. Naturally, he was a little upset at the time, but it hadn't taken long for the story to become a funny anecdote in our relationship. One that we would jokingly revisit many times over the years, especially when I would buy him his first GPS in 2002.

"You gonna have an actual map in the truck this time? Or a compass?" I asked. My comment was rewarded with a chortle from a man who rarely smiled. "When do we leave?"

"Six. Shouldn't be a problem for you lately."

I grinned. "Sounds good. I'm off to Andi's for a party. See you tomorrow morning then."

The party in the Petras' basement was an ideal follow-up to the school dance the night before, and was an even better setting in which to catch up with old friends who didn't know that we'd spent any time apart. Andi's parents had an excellent stereo system with huge speakers, a turntable that was suspended from the ceiling, and a state-of-the-art double cassette deck. I spent most of the party hovering over the stereo system and switching up the music while keeping track of the selections mentally. By the time I was on the way home four or five hours later, I had three whole cassettes of music—most of which I hadn't really been able to pay attention to at the party—as well as one anachronism from Billy Idol's song *Dancing with Myself*, which, I'm pretty sure, had been changed to *Dancing by Myself*. I say that I'm "pretty sure" since tiny changes like that were hard to be unequivocal about, so, when I got home, I noted it in my journal with an asterisk that indicated that I could be wrong about it.

The next morning, I was up before my father, and even had his coffee ready for him in his favourite thermos. I'm guessing that he'd gotten used to this kind of behaviour from me of late because he didn't even look at me funny when he finally came downstairs to the kitchen.

Two hours later, I was sitting backwards in the bow of a cedar rib canoe facing my father in the stern with a slightly restless Golden Retriever between us. With one hand, Dad was steering the tiny 2HP outboard motor clamped to the gunwale, while his other held a fishing rod, the line played out behind him. He was wearing a wide-brimmed hat, clip-on sunglasses, and had the white tip of a smelly Old Port cigar clamped firmly in his teeth. I was pretty sure I could hear him humming some classic Rock song as he played his rod like the expert he was. The man was in his element out here, trolling around one of the thousands of deep lakes that were ubiquitous to northern Ontario, with a bottom that dropped away into absolute darkness only a couple of feet from shore. There were so many of these lakes that a lot of them didn't even have official names, which is why my father and his friends had assigned the labels themselves. Today, we were on *Lost Otter*, named for the time an otter had climbed out of one of their ice fishing holes, looked at the men gathered around it, and grabbed a fish that had been caught earlier before disappearing with it back down the hole.

This was my father's paradise. It was the reason he'd moved his family from his father's farm on the outskirts of Ottawa to this remote area of the province. So that he could be in an environment where he could strap the canoe to the top of his truck, drive an hour, drop that canoe in a crystal-clear stream, and paddle up and out into a secluded lake where you might not see anybody else for the better part of a week.

When I had been much younger, I would be curled up in the bow of this huge wooden canoe, warm sun on my face, mostly asleep, but alert enough to notice if anything tugged on my line even if, most of the time, it was just my father pranking me by pulling on it from the stern. I was a little too big to sink down behind the bow seat today though, which was just as well because, as we found out pretty much right away, the fish were eager to feed us today. I'd completely forgotten about the magical feel of a tug on the line and the expression on my father's face that went with it as he watched me reel in a fish, like he was living vicariously through me.

Yet, as much as I enjoyed it, the raw emotion behind it always made me feel like I had disappointed him by not truly appreciating his other great passion: hunting. Oh, I had *tried* to appreciate it, certainly, more than Patrick, who had simply rejected it outright. It hadn't been easy for me though because I had always been a sensitive child, and the wilderness, with the myriad ways in which it could kill you, had always scared me, and I didn't much relish the idea of being forced out into it. It didn't stop my father from putting a gun in my hands anyhow, although I think we can all agree that his idea one autumn of getting behind the prey to flush it out through the forest in the direction of a frightened kid with a loaded firearm had been a bad idea.

And then, just as I thought that I'd figuratively dodged the bullet that represented his expectations, the Ontario Ministry of Natural Resources initiated its first ever moose lottery in our area. Before this, you could shoot whatever moose happened to wander in your sights, irrespective of its gender or age. Now, with the new restrictions, there would be a limited number of females available and, as I understood it, only two bulls in the entire region of Robertson. Imagine my surprise when my father, in breathless excitement, congratulated me one day and told me that I'd won one of the bulls.

"But I didn't even enter the lottery!" I protested as much as a person could after learning he'd won a contest.

"I know," he had answered. "I put your name in for you!"

Naturally, this became another funny anecdote in our relationship that we would revisit on multiple occasions over the years. At the time though, it initiated one of the most uncomfortable six weeks of my youth. Every weekend, my father would drag me out of bed early, dress me in bright orange, thrust a powerful gun in my hands, and force me out into the same forest that I'd spent so much of my childhood theretofore avoiding. I spent the entire time that I was "on the prowl" for big game praying that I wouldn't find any. What's more, I resolved that if I did see a moose, I would pretend that I hadn't, and, if Dad happened to spot it and tell me to shoot at it, I would miss on purpose. Luckily, the opportunity never presented itself, and I spent much of the time sleeping in the passenger seat of his beat-up truck as we drove around the backroads of Northern Ontario looking for opportunities.

As for fishing, his second big passion, my attitude was more in line to his, but only marginally. I didn't mind catching a fish, even if I still didn't much like having to watch it slowly asphyxiate to death on the floor of our canoe, or on the ice beside the hole. Nor did I enjoy having to bait my hook by thrusting a sharp point up under a minnow's chin and out through the top of its tiny head.

As I got older, I finally began to appreciate that going fishing with my father was one of the best ways to spend quality time with the man. So, that's why, on one Christmas holiday when I was home from University, I happily agreed to go ice fishing with him even though I had no desire to... well, actually ice fish. As we sat in a rented ice-shack that was bigger and warmer than my first house, he didn't know that I had concocted a plan to make sure that I didn't catch any fish that day. When he wasn't looking, I'd dropped my hook down the hole in the ice without any bait! It was a couple hours later without either of us getting so much as a nibble, that I was shocked to see my ice fishing rod dip down in a clear indication that I'd caught something. I can remember staring at it for the longest time, not sure what to do. Finally, it was my father who urged me to act by asking, "Are you going to get that?"

When I pulled at the line, I was met with a significant amount of resistance and I responded instinctively by hauling ass, getting caught up in all the excitement despite myself. After a fair amount of pulling and a whole lot of encouragement behind me from my father, I pulled an immense Whitefish out of the ice.

Upon closer inspection, it appeared that the fish had happened to snag the hook in its gill as it swam by, because that hook suddenly dislodged just as the beast's head cleared the top of the hole. I could have let the fish go, but I figured that if the universe was letting me catch a fish without using bait, then dammit, the universe wanted me to have that fish. So, I reached down and grabbed the fish by the gills before it could manoeuvre its way back down a hole that was almost too small for it, and pulled it up over my head triumphantly as my father cheered me on.

That was one of my best memories, and it had only happened because I had wanted to spend time with the man. And here I was, back in time doing just that, in this case, for the first time. I couldn't recall joining him on this particular excursion on my first trip through 1985, but I was certainly glad to be here now. In this moment, I didn't care that there was a seemingly impossible puzzle waiting for me back home, as long as I could have more of this perfect sunny day in a canoe with my father as we trolled around this peaceful northern lake.

I kept looking for something to say. These fishing trips had always been pretty quiet, not out of fear of scaring the fish, but due mostly to the fact that we hadn't really had that much to say to each other at the time. That status-quo had now changed, understandably, and I had a whole laundry-list of topics I wanted to broach now.

"So how was the episode of *Doctor Who* yesterday?" I finally said.

"Repeat," Dad answered simply. "Tom Baker left the show last year, but TVO is showing repeats of his final episodes. They're still a few years behind the BBC though."

"How's the new guy?" I only ever knew the fourth Doctor in my time watching the show with Dad, but my father had been a fan since the beginning, watching the episodes as well as he could from Canada.

"Not bad. It's different every time there's a regeneration. I'll get used to him. Eventually."

"Hey, can Time Lords change into women?" I asked, as if the question had just suddenly occurred to me. I, of course, already knew the answer, thanks to Jodie Whittaker's most excellent performance on the show in the late 2010s.

Dad just grunted in response in a way that wasn't clear whether he was for or against the concept. It was still foreign to me how he could go from being talkative one moment, and monosyllabic the next.

I watched him as he reeled in his line, check to see that there was still bait on the hook, and then toss it out again into deeper water, all while guiding the small motor with his left knee. Between us, Chance stood up and looked wistfully out into the thick brush gliding by on the shore.

"You're not going for a run out there, girl," cautioned my father. "That's how we lost Prince." Prince had been a beagle that we'd owned when I'd been about five. I could still remember the trauma I'd felt when I'd found out that Dad had lost her on a hunting trip, when she'd taken off after some animal, never to be seen again. Chance looked up at the man in the stern, and then back at me with a forlorn look in her eyes, as if asking, "What did I do?"

Any further discussion was interrupted by a sudden jerk on my line indicating a bite. I pulled it back towards me quickly to set the hook and, over the next few minutes, fought to land what turned out to be a fair size northern pike, a species of fish that my father and friends referred to as "snakes." I looked over at him a few times as he prepared to deploy the net. He was using a full-sized one now, ever since that time when I'd been about ten and the collapsible contraption that he had brought with him folded up on him just as he was about to land what must have been a good ten-plus pound pickerel at the end of my line. The fish had gotten away, and he had never forgiven himself for losing what would have been a prize-winning fish.

After we'd added the pike to the already burgeoning stringer dragging behind the canoe, and once I'd rebaited my hook and tossed it overboard, I decided to ask the man another question. It wasn't that I was trying to get him thinking about time-travel to lay any groundwork or anything, it was just a topic that, for reasons that should be obvious by now, were foremost on my mind. I thought it was also a great way to introduce a proposal that was just now percolating through my brain cells.

"Hey Dad," I said. "Remember that movie we saw a couple years back. What was it called? *Final Countdown*?"

Dad grunted in affirmation. "Yeah," he said out the side of his mouth, the diminishing cigar still tight in the teeth on the other side. "What about it?"

"Oh, I dunno. I was just thinking about it. *Doctor Who* got me thinking about time-travel."

"Hmmmmph," he grunted. And then, surprisingly, instead of letting the topic die, he kept talking about it. "That movie seemed more like an advertisement for the American Navy than anything else. But it was one of the few time-travel movies that got it right by side-stepping all that time-paradox bull crap."

This was a surprise. Dad had read some of the sci-fi classics like Asimov, Clarke, Bradbury, and Heinlein, but, like me, most of his experience in the area was based on TV shows and movies. We'd talked sci-fi a lot over the years, but I'd never heard him talk so disparagingly about time paradoxes. "How do you mean?"

My father pulled the Old Port out of his mouth and cleared his throat to make it easier to speak. "Those two characters, I've forgotten their names, they get trapped in the past, right? They get stranded on an island in 1941. But, it turns out that they're the ones who funded the construction of the aircraft carrier in the first place. They were in the story from the beginning, we just didn't know it. They couldn't go back and change what had already happened, because they were a part of what had already happened, because the time portal had already made them a part of it." He flicked ash off his cigar and put the plastic stub back in his mouth. "Time's fixed. Every event is pre-determined because it's already happened. When people travel into the past, they've already been there. That's why you can never go into the past and be surprised when you meet yourself, because you'd have remembered doing it in the first place."

"Fascinating," I mused out loud. What he was saying was wrong of course — my presence in the body of my younger self being the most obvious proof — but it was still a fascinating concept.

"That same thing happens on *Doctor Who* all the time too," he continued. "There are fixed points in time. Things that just can't be changed no matter how much you fiddle with the time stream."

Now, that was something that I'd been spending a lot of time thinking about already when I'd been contemplating whether it was possible to change the course of future events. "It sounds like you've given this some thought."

My father grunted again, a sound that I interpreted to be his way of saying, "A little bit."

"The other day, my friend Calvin brought a movie magazine to school," I said, launching into the proposal that I'd been toying with. "He was talking about an upcoming time-travel movie that looks interesting. It comes out this summer. We should go see it."

Dad looked at me. I couldn't really judge his expression with his eyes hidden behind his dark shades, but he seemed to be assessing me again. He was sucking at his bottom teeth in thought, a reminder of where my own habit of doing that had come from.

"That sounds like fun," he said finally, a loose smile on his face as he went through the motion to cast his line out again. "We should definitely do that."

Because we'd caught our limits pretty quickly, we were home well before supper. As I was looking in the mirror to get cleaned up for work, I realized that I had neglected to put on sunscreen while I'd been out in the canoe, and my skin had definitely gotten a little too much sun. So, I grabbed some vinegar from the kitchen and splashed it on the affected areas. I might smell like a French fry for the rest of the night, but at least my skin would feel better and wouldn't blister or peel.

Later that night, after I'd locked up, I called Andi from the store's phone and we told each other about our respective Sundays. Everything lately had been about me, so I was making a concerted effort to ask how she was doing. It took some prodding, but she eventually revealed to me that things had been stressful for her at home of late. Her mother's behaviour was becoming increasingly erratic, and her father was dealing with it by not dealing with it. Once Andi got going, she really opened up, and told me things that I'd never actually heard before. Chalk it up to another impact that my new empathetic attitude was having on this particular timeline. I would never have asked these questions of my high school girlfriend before, because they wouldn't have had much of anything to do with me.

As Andi spoke, I didn't really know what to say, so I mostly just listened, interjecting only rarely, and then just to offer encouragement. At one point, I reflexively said, "It'll work out," because that was the kind of thing that you said in conversations like this.

In response, Andi stopped talking. Then in a tiny voice, she asked, "Will it, Josh? Will it actually work out?"

I froze. It was one thing to reveal to the people of this time that a dark future awaited and that we might be able to work together to keep it from happening. It was another thing entirely to tell somebody that another kind of dark future waited for them that was very personal and likely couldn't be avoided.

"Andi..." I said hesitantly.

She interrupted me. "No, Josh. Don't... I'm sorry... I shouldn't have asked. Whatever it is. I... I just don't want to hear it. Not yet." With that, she switched subjects entirely and started telling me about a phone call that she'd had with Phoebe today.

I was only half-listening as she spoke, because the bigger part of my brain was realizing, perhaps for the first time, that having this level of knowledge about the future was an awesome power. Not surprisingly, it was Peter Parker's Uncle Ben that I heard next, and he was telling me what having awesome power meant. The old man wasn't wrong, almost like he knew things he shouldn't have known.

Had he been a time-traveler too?

I continued my active search for anachronisms on Monday night by re-watching one of my favourite sci-fi television shows of all time: Douglas Adams' *The Hitchhikers Guide to the Galaxy*, a series of six half-hour episodes that had been broadcast on the BBC in the early 80s. I had recorded it off TV Ontario on video tape when it had been shown in Canada not long afterwards.

Like so many other geeks of my generation, I'd fallen in love with Douglas Adams and his irreverent and subversively intellectual sense of humour. The TV series had been my introduction to his seminal sci-fi creation, and I'd immediately gone out and gotten ahold of as many of his books as were available at the time, as well as recordings of the radio plays on which they had been based. Over the years, I had been constantly amazed at how many other people were familiar with his ideas, even if they'd never actually read the books or seen the TV show. Everyone, for example, seemed to know that the answer to Life, the Universe, and Everything was 42, and that the helpful phrase on the cover of the electronic guide book (which, not surprisingly, would later be not unlike an internet-enabled smart phone) was "Don't Panic."

Only, as I discovered when binge-watching the episodes again, those two facts weren't exactly the same anymore. According to my videotaped version, the ultimate answer was now 36, and the phrase had been changed to: "Don't Worry."

I was pretty sure that a few purists would be upset and livid at how the ultimate answer had been changed, since many of them had used math (specifically base 13) to prove that 42 actually was the perfect number, and that Douglas Adams had been a genius for using it. As for Adams though, he had maintained until his death that he had simply picked the number at random and had used it because it was smallish, could be divided into two to suit his narrative, and was pleasant enough to be the kind of number you could "introduce to your parents."

Personally, I didn't like 36 any better than 42, but then, I'd spent the last fifty years knowing it to be one way. This was just another example of something I was just going to have to get used to.

When I was finished watching the video, I went up to my bedroom to the corkboard behind my desk to look for something. I had to move a few pictures and scraps of paper out of the way first, but I finally found it: the novelty button that had come with my *Hitchhiker's Guide to Galaxy* computer game. The button had been one of several bonus items that had been included in the packaging, but this one had probably proven to be the most enduring. It was a round red disc about two inches in diameter with blocky yellow text that had, at least in my memory, once read: "Don't Panic." Now though, the large friendly letters spelled out much different words and, even though they were now telling me, "Don't Worry" I was most certainly not feeling the urge to heed the advice.

Sighing deeply, I turned to open my closet door and pulled the paperback versions of the novelizations off my shelf and flipped through them. Sure enough, both of the changes that I'd noticed on the TV shows were in print as well. So, now books were a source of anachronisms.

Great. This search just got bigger!

I sighed again as I noted the newest changes in my journal before getting ready for bed. As I settled in to sleep, my mind was a tad unsettled. My search parameters just kept getting bigger and bigger and I was increasingly at a loss to explain how the components that I'd already identified fit into the temporal puzzle, much less how to organize it into a form that actually made sense. There had to come a time when I could stop collecting clues and figure out how to put them into the correct order to form a message.

Right?

At school the next day, things certainly got interesting in Mrs. Cooper's English class when we turned our desks into a semi-circle so that we could have a final discussion on George Orwell's *1984*, the book that we'd been reading over the last few weeks. For me, this had been the first book that I'd read concurrently with everyone else in the class since coming back in time. It was also a topic that was very personal for me, since I was most definitely the only teenager in the semi-circle who could claim to have experienced a world that was halfway reminiscent of the one described in the book. In fact, as I read Orwell's most famous creation, I kept being struck by how much it paralleled what the *Ensee* had done, to the point where I was actually wondering if they had used it as a fucking manual. If life on the island under *Ensee* rule wasn't exactly like the government of Big Brother in the book, it was only because it hadn't been around long enough.

With every chapter of the book, phrases and snippets kept leaping off the page at me, and not necessarily the ones that I'd seen in memes over the years whenever one world government or another seemed to abusing its authority. Two passages from the book resonated in particular. The first was fairly early-on in the narrative when Winston wrote in his journal: "it was not by making yourself heard, but by staying sane that you carried on the human heritage." For me, it was appropriate considering that I was now in a reality that had several times made me question my own sanity. The other line that stood out for me was: "The best books are the ones that tell you what you already know." This excerpt seemed prescient somehow, seeing as I'd come back to a time where some of the things in books that I thought I knew had been somehow altered.

I shared both of these quotes with the class during our discussion, but kept some of my musings to myself for obvious reasons. I also shared that for the first chapter, I kept thinking that the use of the term "Big Brother" actually felt like a bit of a cliché. I explained that, it was because I'd seen it used so often in movies or stories or news articles that wanted to imply that a government or a group was authoritarian, and I had to keep reminding myself that this was where the very concept itself had originated.

After I'd spoken, it was Tina Blanchard's turn, and she was trotting out the tired old argument that such a thing as "The Party" from *1984* could never rise to power in today's modern society. It was tired because I'd heard the same thing so many times in my life, especially during the Trump era, when it was clear from the administration's first-ever press conference, when the press secretary's opening statement in reference to the size of the crowd at the new President's inauguration, was to express something that wasn't true (a point of view that would very soon be defended as an "alternative fact"), that the administration was trying to establish its own version of *1984*, or, at the very least, *1984-lite*. To me though, what they had tried to do had always come off as *1984 For Dummies*, since the administration had tried to strongly assert its own version of the truth, but simply couldn't enforce it like Big Brother did in Oceania, namely by destroying all evidence that contradicted their assertions. It got so ridiculous that anytime Trump tweeted a typo (and he tweeted a lot of them) or any time he misread a cue card, or anytime he got somebody's name wrong, it was immediately defended by his White House minions as being absolutely correct (or doubleplusright) in a use of Newspeak that would have made Orwell's totalitarian government proud.

It was only after the Trump administration was long gone would it finally be revealed, to the surprise of nobody, that the man had been an unwitting puppet the whole time. He had been put in power through the clandestine machinations of a larger meta-organization who needed a distraction and, in that respect, they had unquestionably got a helluva lot more than even they had bargained for. Although the things that Trump had said were more ludicrous than even his puppet-masters had expected (when it had become lucidly clear that there was no such thing as either "rock-bottom" or "over the top" for his inanity), those puppet-masters hadn't moved to stop him because the increased attention that he was getting actually served their purposes all the more. Only later would it be revealed that what they had been planning would have dire consequences for the whole world, and Trump never once clued in that he had been a key part of it all.

Tina was now saying that, in her opinion, the primary reasons that a totalitarian state like the one in *1984* couldn't work in today's world was because of the technology. The idea of Big Brother being able to surveil members of the Party twenty-four hours a day was predicated on the existence of "telescreens" that could both broadcast and monitor, and that technology just didn't exist.

"Yet," I said, just as Tina was looking at Mrs. Cooper as if seeking the ratification of her theory. All heads turned towards me, even Mrs. Cooper's, which I took as permission to continue. "Your argument that it can't happen because we don't have the technology is short-sighted at best. What you should be saying is that it can't happen *yet*." I knew I couldn't very well expand on this and tell her that there would be a time in the not-too-distant future when everyone would have a webcam on their computer that could be used to spy on them. But, ironically, even that webcam wouldn't be necessary to keep tabs on individuals, because most every user on the network would be giving the milk away for free by ecstatically broadcasting every seemingly frivolous detail about their lives, from what they had eaten for lunch to when their children had last had bowel movements, on social media.

For the longest time, nobody said anything. The only sound in the room was the noise of clothing moving against itself as the students swiveled in their seats or leaned all the way forward to get a better look at me. Obviously, none of them had been expecting a genuine debate today, much less a challenge from a boy who they knew had a mind, but, heretofore, had never spoken it.

The thing was, I didn't feel that I was talking down to children anymore, given my actual age. Of late, it had actually been getting easier and easier to treat these kids like peers. Not because I was getting used to looking like one of them, but because now that the initial shock of my time displacement had worn off, I was actually starting to treat them like the adults that I would know them as in the future.

Case in point: Tina. Like so many of my generation, I would lose touch with people like Tina Blanchard after high school, but we would rediscover each other years later through social media where we would get to know each other all over again. In most cases, relationships picked up pretty much where they had left off post-graduation but occasionally, new aspects of our personalities would emerge, inflamed, no doubt, by the sense of impunity that the internet afforded. Tina, for instance, (when she wasn't, for some reason, reminding me privately much she hated my old friend Calvin), would use these social media platforms to complain loudly and bitterly about the younger generation of the time. She would criticize them endlessly about how lazy they were, how they were destroying everything that her generation had built, and that all they wanted to do was drink and party. It got so bad that I eventually couldn't take it anymore and I unfriended her outright, something I rarely did.

So, even though I knew that I wasn't arguing with the bitter woman that Tina would become, it didn't make me want to restrain myself that much, knowing that I was instead debating a smug, entitled teen who was a fixture at the huge drunken pit parties that happened pretty much weekly. It was hypocrisy at its most ironic that young Tina epitomized the very teenage stereotype that old Tina would one day vilify online.

"I mean, even beyond technology that hasn't been invented yet," I went on. "Why couldn't a Big Brother state happen? What if a catastrophic event happened? The most important detail in the whole story isn't more than a couple of lines long. It happens when Winston is reading Goldstein's book and the manner in which the three Global states gained power is detailed in the briefest of terms. In less than a paragraph, the author states that, in the late 40s, hundreds of atomic bombs are dropped in strategic places around the world, effectively destabilizing society. Any countries left standing were told to obey, or they'd be more bombings. It's such a small point, but an important one. If you can destroy entire governments, then a well-organized group could conceivably subjugate whoever remains by offering themselves up as their saviour and their one best hope for survival. And by giving them advanced tech to dazzle their senses and entertainment to soften them up. The one thing that *1984* got wrong was that you don't subjugate a people with fear and scarcity, you do it with distractions and superfluity, much like the World Government did in *Brave New World*." It had been a calculated risk mentioning Huxley's book in this discussion, since the class had read it a few months back and it would therefore be a lot fresher in everyone else's memory.

Luckily, Tina didn't chase the soma down that particular rabbit hole when she said, "You're talking about science fiction, Josh! Be realistic!"

"Is it? What if I told you that it's already started? One of the central tenants of Orwell's book is that the second group of people he talks about have to be kept stupid. If they get too smart, then they start to question those in charge. Well look around you at every student here. Each and every one of us is proof that they just can't do that. We're all too smart. When they finally realize that they can't keep us stupid, at least in the short-term, they'll ultimately conclude that their only other option is to kill us off. Well, most of us anyway."

There was the briefest period of silence, and I was just opening my mouth to continue when Mrs. Cooper spoke up, clearly eager to redirect this particular topic of discussion before it progressed much farther. "Well, um... that's an excellent point Josh. But it well… well, it's beyond the scope of the discussion. Let's talk about the actual content of the book and not, um… conjecture. Can somebody else tell me the significance of doublespeak?" She looked away from me to the other side of the semi-circle making it abundantly clear that she really meant it when she said "somebody else."

Part of me wanted to jump in on the discussion anyhow, but there were two things holding me back. The first was Andi's fingers on my arm, urging me to restrain myself, and the second was the promise that I'd made to myself that I wouldn't repeat the mistake that I'd made with Hamm. Reaching over, I grasped Andi's hand and squeezed it gently by way of showing her my gratitude. Then I went back to listening as the students missed the point of Orwell's book entirely. Not that I could blame them really. When I'd first read it at their age, I'd failed to grasp its significance too.

If those who cannot learn from History class are condemned to repeat it, then people who fail to heed the warnings in what they read in English class are condemned to experience them.

Part of the problem, I realized, was myopia. I had admitted to Andi the other night that is was one of the things that made dealing with the trauma of a worldwide pandemic easier when we were isolated on an island so far apart from it all. But, ironically, it was also how the *Ensee* had been able to impose its own extreme form of corporatocracy on the residents of the island.

I'd always thought that if a "utopia" was an idyllic society, and a "dystopia" was one that was broken, then a "myopia" would be one in which the people in it think they're in a paradise when they're not, because those in charge have put mechanisms in place that encourage the residents not to see past their own personal experiences. A population that is trained and enabled not to care about what's happening around them out of concern that it might interfere with the entertainment on their streaming feed is not likely one to rise up in protest.

When I got home from school that night I was beginning to feel frustrated again. After supper, I continued to go through the tapes I'd made at Andi's party on the weekend, and identified a few changes that I'd missed during the festivities. This brought my total number to over forty of the fucking things, which should have been a cause for celebration, but felt instead like a hollow victory.

Surely there's a message in them, right?

I mean, I feel like I've got enough to write an entire novel! What's the next step? How do I figure out how to arrange them into the correct order?

The list of my more recent anachronisms was as follows:

	SONG	OLD	NEW
29	Sweet Dreams	ALL OF US looking for something.	EVERYBODY'S looking for something.
30	867-5309	867-5309	867-9305
31	Hard Habit to Break	YOU replaced with SHE in entire song.	YOU replaced with SHE in entire song.
32	Glory of Love*	could never make it ALONE	could never make it ON MY OWN
33	Close Encounters theme	B FLAT, C, A FLAT, (CHANGE OCTAVES), A FLAT, E FLAT.	B FLAT, A FLAT, C, (CHANGE OCTAVES), E FLAT, A FLAT
34	Let's Dance	UNDER the moonlight	OUT IN the moonlight
35	Livin' on a Prayer	Ohhhh, we're ALMOST there...	Ohhhh, we're HALF-WAY there...
36	Dancing with myself*	Dancing WITH myself	Dancing BY myself
37	Jack and Diane*	let's run off BEHIND a shady tree	let's run off BESIDE a shady tree
38	Pink Houses*	There's an BLACK man	There's an OLD man
39	Owner of a Lonely Heart	Much BETTER than a..	Much DIFFERENT than a..
40	Hitch-hikers Guide to the Galaxy	Don't PANIC	Don't WORRY
41	Hitch-hikers Guide to the Galaxy	Answer to Life, Universe, & Everything: 42	Answer to Life, Universe, & Everything: 36
42	Karma Chameleon	Red, Gold, and Green	Gold, Red, and Green
43	Cum on Feel the Noize	Girls ROCK your boys	Girls SHOCK your boys

And these are all the changed words I've found so far:
CHOKING, SAILS, FOLLOW, TO, GET, HOLDING YOU, MY, GLASS, JUST AREN'T, YELL, DARK, ELM, SOUL, YOUNG, NOWHERE, DO YOU DO, HAVE, MANSFIELD, BOY, JUST ESCAPE, WISH I KNEW, CRUSH, BENEATH, COME WITH, ON MY OWN, FLOWERS, JUST LIKE YOU

AND ME, JUST, EVERYBODY'S, 867-9305, SHE, ON
MY OWN, OUT IN, HALFWAY, BY, BESIDE, OLD,
DIFFERENT, WORRY, 36, GOLD, RED, AND GREEN,
SHOCK...

And then there were the maybes, the anachronisms that I wasn't all that sure of, and the chaos that they had the potential to introduce. At least six of the song titles on my list had an asterisk beside them. How was I to know whether they actually were part of the coded message? Not knowing one way or another with those words meant that every time I threw my words slips onto the floor, there was a good possibility that many of them were muddying the water, so to speak.

I went to bed in a disheartened mood. I'd always felt that things had a way of working out, given time. I had held on to that belief my entire life, through the uncertainty with my career, with Mat's difficult teen years, and even with Heather's death. The only time I'd really lost track of it was on those first few years on the island when I surrendered to abject hopelessness. It was Oskar that had finally brought me around. First, by pointing out that I couldn't argue with the philosophy that things will work out if I was alive in a world where so many others had died. And second, by showing me how to find my way in an uncertain future by staying in the moment and looking for opportunities and inspiration.

But now, well, it wasn't so much that I was having a difficult time staying in the moment or even recapturing a feeling of hopefulness, especially in the optimistic era I had been returned to. It was just that, I had just been shown in a very roundabout way that my philosophy about life was true when I had been returned to my own past from a dystopian future. So yes, things always did work out, *given time*. But it was those last two words that were the fulcrum upon which the entire philosophy was balanced. You had to be patient.

Well, fuck that, as Sigourney Weaver would almost say.

I knew this fact instinctively but, to be blunt, after close to 70 years, I just didn't know if I had the patience anymore. I was on the verge of some big discovery, I could feel it, and I was damned if I was going to wait another ten fucking years to figure out what the hell it was!

CHAPTER 14
The Obligatory Fart Joke

S o, it's been two weeks since I'd found my last anachronism. My frustration with the lack of progress is still there, but it's been blunted somewhat by all of the distractions that have been going on around me. In those two weeks, for instance, Andi hosted another music listening party, the school band had a big end-of-year concert, I've been fishing with Dad a few more times, and we celebrated Mother's Day, as well as my father's birthday. In addition, Patrick and Geoff even invited me to go on a motorbike ride with them. They borrowed a much smaller bike from a buddy of theirs for me and, even though they spent much of the trip teasing me that I couldn't keep up, we had a great time. We drove across the border into Quebec and went to a bar where they didn't check ID (to be fair, the legal drinking age in "La Belle Province" was 18, so I was only just a few months shy of it—at least physically). I couldn't have more than a single beer because I was driving, but damn it was delicious. Much better than that swill that Oskar passed off as beer on the Pucks.

I also spent a fair amount of time on the phone running up long-distance charges (seriously, calling long-distance was ridiculously expensive before cell phones and the internet changed things), communicating with various family members about getting together on Victoria Day for a multi-family reunion. I was gratified to see that there was a lot of interest in it, especially from all four of my grand-parents, who were in agreement that the family just didn't gather enough anymore since my father had move up north.

Now, the concept of getting the two sides of my extended family together at an event outside of a wedding wasn't all that strange in my case, because it wasn't like the two sides of my family were strangers to each other. Mom and Dad had been high-school sweethearts growing up in, what then had been, the rural west-end of Ottawa. Dad had been raised on a farm, and Mom was a city-girl through and through, but both of their families had gone to the same church and had been prominent families in the congregation. When my parents had gotten unexpectedly pregnant in their late teens, it had naturally caused quite a stir (but not *that* big a stir since unexpected teenage pregnancies were actually a family tradition on *both* sides of the family, stretching back generations). But, rather than be outraged by it, both families had agreed to put all their judgemental differences aside for the good of the children, providing, of course, that those two children married pretty much immediately. As a result, I had been raised in a loving group of relatives that had always put family first and had made it clear from a young age that I would always have somebody that I could count on.

That's why it didn't take a whole lot of convincing to get every one of them behind the idea of a party, even though that was the traditional weekend to open my maternal Grandparent's cottage. So, fast forward to Victoria Day weekend in 1985, and I was standing up in front of well over two dozen members of my extended family in the banquet room of the *Golden Palace* Chinese restaurant on Carling Street in Ottawa, proposing a toast.

"There are no doubt better words that can be used to commemorate a gathering like this," I said loudly enough for everyone to hear. "But I don't think there are any that are much better than those three simple words of which we're all familiar: Family is everything."

I swear to God, my maternal Grandmother actually started crying as I spoke, even as everyone (with the exception of Aunt Maggie who thought, after all, that opening the cottage *was* more important) just stared at me wide-eyed. Once again, the shy seventeen-year-old that I had been shouldn't be hugging and greeting everyone like he hadn't seen them in years, and as if the most recent memories that he had for most of them had been the last time he had seen their weathered gravestones.

Over the course of the meal, I moved from table to table and engaged each person in conversation, one after the other. Patrick was sitting at a table with a number of the cousins of our generation and, when I eventually joined them, I referred to it as the "kids' table." For some reason, he thought that this was the funniest thing that he'd ever heard. Still, he looked at me kinda curiously as I left to continue my reunion tour.

When I got to the table with my father and his brothers, Dad was in a serious conversation with Uncle Frank, who had taken over my their father's finances now that Grandpa was aiming to retire from farming. A developer was offering what seemed like an insane sum of money for the property as it was prime land on the very outskirts of the city.

The only thing was, I knew better.

It may have seemed like a large sum of money, but in about six months, they would find out that their neighbour, Mr. McGillivray had held out for almost five times as much. This would create a rift between my father and his brother, who would always feel that my Uncle had been short-sighted and miss-managed the funds of a man who, it turned out, was exhibiting the initial symptoms of dementia. I had never much liked the fact that the family farm had been turned into a sub-division but, if it was going to happen, at least my family could do a better job benefitting from the transaction this time around.

"They'll pay more," I said so that they could hear, looking into my glass of soda pop as if I were revealing a big secret. "At least five times their initial offer. They always do. Just ask old man MacGillivray."

"I knew it!" exclaimed my Grandfather at the adjoining table as he smacked Frank in the back of the head. "Don't' piss in my ear and tell me it's raining, boy! Old Jacob Mac knows what he's doin', he was always a better businessman than he was a farmer. We're holding out for more, and that's my final word on it."

Uncle Frank scowled at me a little, his face a close approximation of my father's when it was recriminating. My father, on the other hand, had an air of approval on his face, even if it was mixed with a certain measure of incomprehension. My Grandfather though, wore a gigantic grin as he tipped his glass towards me in a salute, winking. For just a moment I wondered, from the way he looked at me knowingly, if perhaps he had come back from the future as well, but I dismissed it as unlikely almost as soon as it flitted into my head, seeing as he was destined to pass away within the next five or six years. The last time I would visit his grave in the early 2020s, it would be with the realization that he'd been dead for almost twice as long as I'd known him alive. I went over and hugged him, and it seemed to me that his boney hands didn't want to let me go.

For the rest of the weekend, when we weren't visiting family who hadn't been able to make it to the meal (except for Aunt Maggy who, in true overblown martyrdom style, told us that she couldn't possibly spare a moment for a visit since *all* of the work of opening up the cottage had fallen on her shoulders), I spent some time doing research, the kind I couldn't have done in a small town like Robertson. I went to book stores and flipped through anything that I thought might be relevant to my search. I went to record stores to look at the rows of LPs, looking for inspiration. I scrutinized newspapers, billboards, bus advertisements, and even the posters plastered to the sides of poles around town (in this case, I wasn't so much looking for anachronisms, but messages from other time-displaced people like myself). The problem was, if I was lucky enough to spot an anachronism, it was always one that that I'd already found. I just couldn't seem to find anything new, or figure out just what the next step towards solving the code was.

I was still in a bit of a funk about my lack of progress a few days later when I was sitting in the cafeteria at school, dipping my sandwich in my soup, and looking around while pondering the nature of my environment. I found my mind wandering a lot more of late, something that was likely a defense mechanism to keep me from getting frustrated with my stalled search.

As I observed each of the other tables in turn, it was occurring to me that, in every movie about high school that I'd ever seen, there were always specific cliques and groups that never mixed one with the other, especially in the cafeteria. I blinked a few times as I tried to remember how many groups there were, and what they had been called in the movie *The Breakfast Club*. Normally, I'd have consulted my smartphone to find out, but, in this time period, I had a much better source for that particular information in the form of Andi, a self-avowed expert on all-things John Hughes. During a break in the conversation she was having with her friends, I leaned over and quietly excused myself as I asked. "What were the cliques in the *Breakfast Club* movie?"

To her great credit, mostly because she was used to this kind of behaviour from me of late, Andi answered just as quietly, "There are five of them," she said as she flipped up a different finger for each of the characters that she listed. "Anthony Michael Hall was "the geek", Emilio Estevez was the "the jock", Molly Ringwald (I absolutely adore her by the way) was "the princess", Judd Nelson was "the criminal" and Ally Sheedy was "the basket case". That what you need?"

"Thanks," I answered. "Once again, above and beyond."

So, according to that movie, there were five basic stereotypes of people in high school, and it took a weird weekend detention to get them to interact with each other, because they just couldn't do that normally, like for example, in the cafeteria at lunch. I'd always wondered if perhaps I was too self-involved to have noticed those disparate groups in my youth, but here I was back again watching those teens, and I just couldn't see any evidence of exclusive cliques. Sure, the kids seemed to sit in the groupings that felt the most comfortable because of mutual interests, like the ones that played chess every lunch, or the ones that got a card game going, or the ones like Patrick and his buddies who sat together in groupings that corresponded to their sports teams. Until recently, when they'd started sitting with me and Andi and her friends, several of my geek friends used to sit by themselves so that they could work on the comic book that Calvin and Reid had created called *The Sky Lords* (Calvin had thought of the title when he'd heard the words "in the sky, Lord, in the sky" in the gospel song *Will the Circle be Unbroken*). But the locations for these groups changed frequently, and there was always movement back and forth between them. There was also a constant open communication, and it seemed to always be fairly cordial too.

Except for right now apparently.

At pretty much that very moment, I became aware of an exception to the very thing that I had just been thinking, because Jeb Grant, who was sitting two tables over, was currently in the process of loudly telling a rude joke at somebody's expense. Even as I was thinking that John Hughes had been wrong about the number of social groups in high school, because he had clearly forgotten about "the bully," I became acutely aware that the person for whom the joke was in expense of was, in fact, me.

"… so Josh asks the hitchhiker, 'Do you mind if I fart?' The guy says OK, so Josh lets one rip." At this point, Jeb imitated a protracted sound that was a lot like a very loud lawn mower cutting a very big, and very wet, yard. The kids at Jeb's table laughed and started looking over at me to see if I was aware that I was being disparaged. I already knew that this joke was going to imply that, because I farted loudly, I was a homosexual with an ass loosened by gay sex, and I was instantly weary. In high school there had long been rumours that I had been gay because of a close friendship that I'd had with a boy named Eddie in grade school. Eddie had moved out of Robertson back in Grade eight though, but that hadn't put a stop to the insinuations, and they really had bothered me at the time. Even after I'd started dating Andi openly, the rumours had persisted, and Patrick would once tell me that it was because of idiots like Jeb on his sports team that he and Monique would pretend to be a couple for as long as they had. This wasn't the first time that Jeb had publicly taunted me on the subject either, and he was doing it loudly enough so that most of the lunch crowd had, by now, stopped to listen.

I remembered this day! This was Grade 11? Here I thought it would happen next year.

"So anyhow," Jeb continued, relishing the increased attention. "A few minutes later, the hitchhiker asked Josh and his boyfriend, 'Do you mind if I fart?' and when Josh says sure, the guy makes a noise like this:" At this, Jeb made the sound of a tiny, and very constricted, raspberry before finishing the joke with, "So Josh looks at his boyfriend and says, 'He must be a virgin.'"

The kids in the cafeteria erupted in a loud, sustained laugh even as everyone looked over at me to gauge my response. Now that he'd finished speaking, Jeb was cackling tauntingly amongst his friends while he looked directly at me expectantly, as if saying 'what you gonna do?'

The first time that this had happened, I had been angry and embarrassed at losing face in front of the whole school so, naturally, I had heatedly responded with something that had been equally immature. This had led to a verbal war of words in the cafeteria, but nothing physical because of the teachers in the hallway. But, it hadn't ended there. Later, Jeb had jumped me as I was leaving school and had given me a black eye and a bloody nose before throwing me into a muddy ditch. The injuries were admittedly minor, but my pride had flat-lined as a result, because of having to be seen by my friends bruised, bloodied, and covered in mud. I had tried to press charges, but there hadn't been any witnesses. I was able to procure a restraining order through the OPP though, one that Jeb had simply flaunted until his family moved away a few months later at the end of the school year.

The laughter in the cafeteria was fading slowly, even though the tension remained, as I stared at Jeb in wonder and chewed my sandwich. It was an odd feeling, like I was outside my body. I wasn't embarrassed this time, not in the least. I was decades past caring what teenagers thought of me. Right now, in that instant, reliving one of the most embarrassing moments in my memory, I was fascinated. I was a scientist observing Jeb, his friends, my own friends, and the collective group around us. It was only as an afterthought that I realized that everyone was now staring at me, waiting for me to respond.

I glanced around the room at all the eyeballs. Nobody behind those tiny orbs said a word, or gave me any kind of hint as to what was expected of me. I'd been away from teenaged drama for so long that it was still foreign to me.

"Oh, this is the part where I speak," I finally said, clearing my throat. "Let me make sure I got this straight. Jeb just told a joke that has cast doubt on my heterosexuality by implying that I am, in fact, a homosexual. Am I correct to assume that I am now expected to scream my denial and respond in kind with some kind of equally-weighted insult?"

People were looking at each other now, dumb-founded. This was not how teenaged drama of this nature was supposed to play out. There was supposed to be angry insults. A fight even. Not this.

"Fine," I continued, rubbing my hands together. "Let me see… Um, OK Jeb, you really shouldn't wear that shade of plaid. It clashes with your ruddy complexion." I looked around at my friends, to see that Calvin had just snorted milk out of his nose. "How was that?"

Nobody got a chance to answer. A muted murmuring laugh was just beginning to spread through the room when it was interrupted by Jeb's very angry voice. He didn't know exactly how, but he was sure he'd just been insulted. "You're a faggot, Donegal. Everybody knows it."

I stared at Jeb again for a moment before responding calmly, "I honestly don't care what you, or anybody else thinks, Jeb, if, for no other reason, then there's absolutely nothing wrong with being gay, and most of the people in this room are eventually going to figure that out."

Beside me, Andi tensed, and I could hear her breathe my name quietly. "Josh… careful."

"It's OK," I whispered back even as I reached over the lightly squeeze her leg.

"As for those who preach that homosexuality is wrong … well, a word of advice about that. You're going to find that the people who are often the loudest about projecting suspicion onto others are often hiding that very same thing themselves. It's appropriate, in light of the offensive joke that Jeb just told, but it's very often true that he who smelt it, dealt it. Isn't that right, Jeb?" I dipped my sandwich in my soup, took a bite, and then added through a mouthful of food, "Not that there's anything wrong with it."

The cafeteria openly erupted in laughter, but I knew it obviously wasn't in response to the *Seinfeld* reference. I was already kind of regretting the fact that, in one breath I was lecturing on accepting homosexuality and in the next insinuating that Jeb was gay, knowing full well that it would elicit the response that it just had.

Jeb was on his feet in a second, his face glowing red. He was taking a step towards my table when Mr. Lowry stepped into the cafeteria to make his presence known, as had Patrick, who, at the far back of the cafeteria was slowly lumbering towards Jeb, cracking his knuckles. Jeb stopped briefly to look at the opposition building against him before ultimately turning around and walking out of the room, flinging the door open violently as he went. Patrick looked at me as if wondering if I wanted him to follow the bully, and I shook my head. Shrugging his shoulders, Patrick returned to his seat. Rack up my brother's actions to something else that hadn't occurred the last time this had happened.

When Jeb came at me that afternoon, I was ready. In fact, I had been ready for about fifty years. After Jeb had managed to beat me up the first time, I had vowed that I would never let that kind of thing happen again, so I had immediately enrolled in self-defence courses. Over the years, I had studied dozens of different fighting styles and had even won a few tournaments in the process.

So, when Jeb jumped me from behind the same parked car from where he'd taken me by surprise the last time, I stepped deftly to the side and, as he went sailing past me, I jabbed at him with the index finger of my right hand, making just enough contact with the pressure point on his left leg to pretty much disable it. As he tumbled to the ground in a heap behind me, I just kept moving forward as if nothing had happened. I kept walking, whistling a happy tune and ignoring Jeb as he hurled threats and insults at me even as he tried limping after me, eventually tumbling, cursing into the same muddy ditch where he had dumped me the first time.

I probably shouldn't have been enjoying this as much as I was. Even beyond that time he had physically assaulted me, Jeb had made large parts of my high school experience miserable with his bullying, and had in turn inspired me to go a little overboard on learning my self-defence to the degree that I had. When I had first started my training, I used to fantasize about meeting him again as an adult and having my revenge, but I never did (after his family moved, I never saw him again) and eventually, I matured enough that I stopped caring. Still, listening to him slip and slide around in the mud behind me, knowing that his left leg would be numb for the next half hour, filled me with a childish, giddy glee.

When Jeb came at me again a few days later, once his limp had faded enough for him to forget about how he had gotten it in the first place, I took out his right arm for the afternoon. The next day, I put pressure on a muscle on his neck that's connected directly to his groin, making him feel like he'd just been kicked in the testicles. As I walked away that time, I said over my shoulder, "Next time, Jeb, I go for the nerve that shrinks dicks." There was no such nerve, but Jeb didn't know that. He steered well clear of me after that, and I only ever saw him at a distance, glaring at me. My threat had been far more effective than had been the restraining order.

I didn't know it at the time though, but I was being watched.

CHAPTER 15
Excerpt from Josh's journal

Nobody else in this alternate 1985 appears to have memories of Magnus Levekno, but I certainly do, especially about how he single-handedly saved all of us on Prince Edward Island from the YELLOW DEATH.

It happened just a day after it was reported that the virus had somehow made it across the Northumberland Strait, close to West Cape on the north-west end of the island. Of course, we'd heard about the infection almost immediately, since it had more or less been expected. All activity pretty much halted as a result, as we collectively resigned ourselves to the inevitable, and quietly tried to find what little peace might still remain for those of us who were left. The island had been our last best hope; there really was nowhere else to run to. While the pandemic had, apparently, killed everything in its path on the rest of the globe, we'd survived here because the island was far enough away from the mainland to keep an airborne disease from spreading, and small enough for the Canadian government (that had set up shop here not long after they had realized just what they were up against) to effectively manage and defend.

Just as nobody knew how the virus made it onto the island, nobody was entirely sure how Magnus got through the blockade. It was said that he just suddenly appeared in the middle of a crowd in downtown Charlottetown, carrying a case full of medical vials with some kind of glowing purple concoction in them. Everyone recognized Magnus of course—such was his level of celebrity in my timeline. But, before anybody knew what was happening, he'd handed the case over to a couple of cops in full view of a very confused crowd of onlookers, told them that it was a vaccine for the Yellow Death, and that they should get the case to the appropriate medical authorities immediately. Then, just as mysteriously as he had appeared, Magnus vanished into that same, now frenzied, crowd. Some say he seemed to be pulled skywards to disappear behind some tall buildings, others that there was an actual puff of smoke before he sunk into the ground, and a handful of reports even claimed that he transformed into an old woman and hobbled slowly away. Public accounts of actual events had been notoriously inaccurate even before the threat of Global extermination. Afterwards, they had become positively ridiculous.

If the authorities were wary, it didn't last long. With the virus already on the island, what choice did they have? If they waited even a few hours, it would mean certain death for hundreds, if not thousands. Within a half day, the inoculation was being used even as it was being replicated (thanks to the thorough set of instructions that Magnus had provided with the case). The vaccine worked, with the majority of the population that remained on the island being saved, while the absent Magnus (who was never heard from again) became an instant hero.

Naturally, we celebrated with a joy that none of us had felt for months, even if that joy was tempered significantly by the extreme depth of our communal loss. The Government increased our rations, and revealed that, now that we were apparently safe from the disease, it was working on plans to begin exploring the mainland for survivors, once the threat level could be properly assessed, with the ultimate goal of getting us off the island. I was still living in our rented RV with my son, Mat, his wife, Suki and their daughter Wilson, while sharing the space with Donna, Celeste, and Vincent, three young cyclists who had been celebrating their graduation from University with a bike tour of the Maritimes. It was cramped, but we at least got along, and we knew that it wasn't going to be permanent, especially with the prospect of being able to return to the mainland imminently.

Before any of the Government's plans could happen though, the NAFFARIUM COLLECTIVE arrived in a of huge cargo ship called the *Marie-Rose*, and told us that leaving the island was nothing but a pointless endeavor. They brought with them news about the rest of the world, and it wasn't remotely good. The death rate was unimaginable and pretty much universal. If there were isolated pockets of humanity, nobody knew where at the moment, what with communication systems inoperable.

Crop lands on the mainland were useless, they told us, as were the cities. Quite simply, it was the rotting bodies that were the problem. They were perfect petri dishes for the plague to fester and mutate. Yes, we'd been protected from the initial strain, but the only way to make sure we didn't get infected by something different—something potentially worse—was to stay put. Honestly, with everything we'd all just been through, it didn't take much to convince us otherwise.

According to the NC (as we had started to call them before that short form became the word unto itself that was the *Ensee*), we shouldn't even be alive (reports also said that they were shocked to hear that we had a cure for the disease, and Oskar had always wondered why it was that they'd only seemed to ask us to share that cure with them as an afterthought) and there was a good chance that we were the largest group that was left. An island of less than a million people on a planet where, just last year, there had been billions.

The *Ensee* had been preparing for just such a catastrophe. They had resources where we had none, advanced technology we could only dream of, and they were basically giving it all to us with no strings attached. Magnus may have saved us from the pandemic, but it was the *Ensee* that gave us our first real hope.

It probably goes without saying that the first year was the hardest, as the Canadian Government and the *Ensee* collaborated to expand infrastructure and streamline the food distribution systems. A wage-based economy wouldn't work anymore, and privilege didn't mean anything in a world where money didn't have value. Everyone was taken care of though, and work was found for everyone who was able.

The population of the island just after the pandemic was a little over a million. Over the next first six months, the government abruptly reversed its policy of repelling newcomers from our shores and actively started looking for them and offering them refuge. The *Marie-Rose* left with the mission of scouring the most isolated regions of the continent for survivors and, over the course of several trips, she brought back hundreds of thousands of them, each and every one of them wide-eyed with shock.

But our new government didn't stop there. With no other form of communication seemingly working, they began broadcasting radio messages on all frequencies and monitoring any other media that had the potential of being used to send or receive messages. The desperate ploy worked. Within months, there was a steady influx of all manner of people who had taken to the sea to escape the plague in whatever vessel they could find that could even half-way float. This included all manner of fishing cruisers, houseboats, yachts, sailboats, ferries and even three separate cruise ships, each one packed to the rafters with desperate, mostly starving, people. A steady trickle continued from locations all over the world and, within the first year, our numbers on the island swelled to about two million. The message from all of these new arrivals was a stark one. Our island refuge was the only substantial gathering of survivors anywhere in the world. We were truly alone.

With the burgeoning population, the experts appointed by the new Government were tasked with figuring out exactly how much land was needed for farming and livestock to feed everyone, and the rest was used to build all manner of shelters. Still, there just wasn't enough land for everyone, even in a province as sparsely populated as PEI, so some of us were forced to move out onto the water.

And so it was that, by the year 2029, I was living with my new family on an aquatic farm, one of hundreds of transparent hexagonal domes that were officially called

Hexagonal Hydroponic Pods, or HEXAPODS for short. Each one was about an acre square, collectively proliferating en masse into the Northumberland Strait from a central hub, somewhere in the area of Summerside. Not long after the project was started— nobody is exactly sure how it happened—but, being Canadian, the whole community of Hexapods got nicknamed the PUCKS, and, even though they looked nothing like the familiar round black disk, the name stuck.

The living quarters on our aquatic farm, like most of the construction material that made up the Hexapods, was recycled. Celeste and I were using two school buses welded together at their butt ends at a right angle. Mat and Suki were close by in the RV that we had driven to PEI in the first place (conveniently, the rental company had never asked for it back), and because I was one of the few civilians allowed to do maintenance on the Pucks themselves, I was allowed the privilege of a tiny workshop in the form of the back of a U-Haul moving van. Vehicles were made buoyant through a combination of trapped air and the same futuristic construction material that was used to float the entire agricultural complex. Suspended firmly in the space between each of these former vehicles, there was a large flat platform about the size of a tennis court that acted as our family's outdoor common space. It's where we gathered for meals when we could, and where we'd fashioned a small garden for things like assorted berry plants, tomatoes, carrots, and fresh herbs. We even made use of the space underneath us too, maintaining our own oyster and mussel beds on the seabed to supplement our protein intake.

This was a pretty standard residential configuration on the Pucks actually, although the nature of the living quarters varied. By far, the most popular space to use for a dwelling was an old bus with the seats removed, but there were still a fair number of old train cars and shipping containers pressed into service, and even the odd houseboat. Large vehicles were a popular choice to engineer into a living space because, once the gas ran out on the island, they were otherwise useless. What's more, there were a whole bunch of them that could be fished out of the water under what remained of the Confederation Bridge, if you could get past how they'd gotten there in the first place, and what might still be inside them.

No matter the construction though, or the limitations on space, the units were each multi-generational. That meant that there were ten of us on our farm: my new family.

Sounds like the perfect segue to tell you all about them.

It was sometime in 2027 when the new Island Authority (the final vestiges of the Canadian Government had been dismantled the previous year in favour of a more adaptable autonomous collective made up of council members from all over the Island), had decided to "encourage" procreation. Existing couples were urged to reproduce and it was "suggested" that non-couples should basically join in on the fun as well. We were being thrown together by a fledgling island government that had just seen the impossible happen, and knew that we all had to pitch in so that we could rebuild a Global society.

Oh sure, they found a much nicer way of saying it than I'm documenting here, but it still boiled down to the same basic message: everybody get fucking, now!

Like I said, there was no official decree, but there certainly was a lot of pressure to conform, and it came for all corners of Island society. If humanity was to survive, we needed more children, and, what's more, it was felt that a loving family unit offered the best chance of raising well-balanced kids, or at least as well-balanced as could be expected post-apocalypse.

This was before we'd moved onto the Pucks, and the first of us to heed the call close to home (or should I say close to RV), were Celeste's friends Donna and Vincent. It wasn't too much of a stretch for them, since they were already dating, but we celebrated their coming together anyhow. True to its promise to reward all unions for the sake of procreation, the Island Authority arranged for new living quarters for the new couple not far away. Mat and Suki followed suit, and were expecting again within two months, but they opted to stay with me in the RV.

It was actually Celeste that suggested our own union because she'd grown to trust me while we had been sharing the RV as a living space. Still, it didn't help that we were pretty much forced into it, matched, like so many others at the time, based on our potential for fecundity. And, since there just weren't as many men her age to go around, she got stuck with fifty-nine-year-old me. By the time our first child (Wren) was a year old in 2029, we were all settling into our new life as aquatic farmers on the Pucks. Jean-Patrice was born in 2030, and Franklin in 2032.

It took me several years to start to accept Celeste as a wife, in part because she was so very young, but mostly because I had just lost Heather, and still felt married to her. Having said that, Celeste and I did eventually grow to be fairly close. She was a bright young woman, and an exceptional mother.

So, a little over a decade. That was all it took to build a new society on the island out of the ashes of the old one.

Like I've already said—I think more than once in this journal—everyone had a role to play in that new society. Agriculture was, of course huge. Although PEI was known for its potato crops, it would have been too much of a single variety of food for the new island population, so a portion of the farms were transformed as needed. Sea food collection, whether it was in the form of fishing, trapping lobster, collecting jellyfish, or farming mussels or oysters, continued pretty much undisturbed.

One of the first challenges that the Island Authority encountered was the lack of building materials on the island, since PEI didn't really have much in the way of forests appropriate for logging and saw-milling. The answer, it was discovered, was literally washing up onto the island's shores in the form of seaweed. Scores of residents were assigned to collect the strands that littered the beaches. Then these strands were dried, before being processed into a compound not unlike plastic, through the use of another one of the *Ensee*'s astounding new technologies. This new organic compound was then used in one of two ways: it was either pressed into building material like modular walls or bricks that had a considerable amount of strength thanks to the fibrous nature of the seaweed, or it was turned into long cords that fed construction-grade 3D printers that would literally "print" buildings.

And then, there were the Pucks.

When I described our residence as being a farm earlier, perhaps I wasn't specific enough. We weren't growing food, exactly. One of the other new technologies that the *Ensee* gifted us with was a new, genetically engineered form of free-floating algae that was capable of sucking carbon from the atmosphere during photosynthesis and turn it into methane that was shipped to our new automated offshore power plant. This took care of one of other problems that the Island Authority encountered very quickly: the lack of electricity. Although PEI produced power through the use of hundreds of windmills around the island, it still wasn't enough to meet the greatly increased demand of a population of over two million people. So, the government managed to secure a, now vacant, offshore drilling platform and convert it into a power-generating station that ran off the methane that was produced naturally in the domed Pucks.

The other problem that the algae solved was fresh water. Not surprisingly, the fresh water supplies on the island were pretty much at risk within even a couple of years of such a profound population explosion. Enter the *Ensee's* super algae and the Pucks that were specifically engineered to grow it.

The aquatic farm actually created fresh water twenty-four hours a day. During the sunlight hours, seawater evaporated, and the water droplets were caught in the fine mesh of the segmented dome where it eventually wicked down into reservoirs. At night, this process was further continued through the process of cellular respiration, where the water emitted from the algae was caught by the same mesh on the dome, feeding the same reservoirs. Eventually, these tanks would overflow, and the effluent would mix with the fluid from all of the other Hexapods, providing the island community with a constant, and substantial, source of fresh water.

Even more amazing, there was still one more thing that the algae was useful for. When it was eventually spent, we collected it using large rakes and sent it to our local farmers so that they could use it as a very effective fertilizer.

My electrical engineering skills didn't go to waste during my time on the Pucks, and I made good use of the plethora of advanced technology being distributed by the *Ensee*. My favourite creation was my Personal Flotation Device, or PFD.

It's likely not the kind of PFD that you're thinking of.

This device consisted of a flattish, lighter than air 'inflatable' about the size of a Zodiac with four high-speed, maneuverable propellers embedded at strategic locations upon it, just like you'd see on a drone.

Using a full body harness, much like the ones that they used in special effects movies to make it seem like people can fly, I could hang beneath the balloon, suspended from three guy wires attached to winches. The PFD was buoyant enough to support my weight, and the winches worked in concert with the propellers to move me through the air quickly and smoothly. What's more, all of the electronics and servo-motors were controlled by vocal commands that were communicated via the PFD's internal A.I. (nick-named "Jerome").

Out of all the various technologies that I was being forced to live without now that I was back in 1985, it was perhaps my PFD that I missed the most. Although, I used it primarily for hard-to-reach repair jobs on the Pucks, whether those places were up high or out over the water, I also greatly enjoyed being able to jump great distances with little effort (the voice command for this manoeuvre, naturally, was "Jerome: up, up, and away!"). Let me tell you, my kids and Grandkids loved it when I took them for rides. Celeste and Suki, not so much.

So, yeah, life was kinda simple on the Pucks. We lived a quiet family life, our evenings spent with our children and a surprising amount of leisure time. We could travel to the Island for some things, but most of our needs were met on the Hexapods complex. There was a large floating communal area close by, one of a dozen or so distributed around the entire Hexapod network. This one contained, among other things, the school that the kids attended, a couple of small shops, a co-op, a health clinic, and a restaurant. My typical destination was Oskar's bar (the *PuckStop*), which was made from four over-sized shipping containers floating side by side and fused together with the shared walls in the middle removed to create a rectangular space. It wasn't huge, but it was big enough for a few booths, a pool table, a dartboard, and a couple of rooms in the back for Oskar's living space—all of it made accessible for his wheelchair.

About two months after the *Ensee* had arrived, once the priorities such as food and accommodation had been sorted out, they re-established local communication. *Ensee* proprietary technology was used to blanket about 92% of the Island (and the surrounding Puck complexes) with a solid Wi-Fi signal, and every survivor was provided with a device of some kind with which to access it. This didn't give us access to the World-Wide Web or to satellites, mind you, because both of them were apparently no longer functional. Instead, it provided a Local Area Network of sorts that became known as the "Strand" (as it was just a small portion of what had once been a web), and was comprised of whatever could be rescued from what was left of the internet, mostly data that had been backed up on local servers and the like. It wasn't too bad, to be honest, and it was certainly better than nothing. Beyond the inability to communicate with anybody who wasn't on the island, the Strand contained most of the information and the entertainment that we'd come to rely upon as a people over the last few decades. It, more than anything else helped the displaced population on the island deal with everything that had just happened, by giving them a forum on which to either vent or watch cute cat videos (cat videos, by the way, are the digital equivalent of cockroaches in that they are able to survive pretty much any kind of cataclysm—no pun intended).

The Strand quickly became our primary source of entertainment, mostly because there wasn't much in the way of direct competition. Hollywood didn't exist anymore, and there was no real cinematic counterpart on the island, just the basics for news and local broadcasting. Fairly early on, an administrative department was tasked with collecting all of the Blu ray and DVD collections that could be found on the island, digitizing everything, and putting it up for public consumption on a central database. To their credit, the Island Authority didn't try to charge for this entertainment, they just made it all readily available for streaming on the Strand. They figured that it was the best, and cheapest, way to improve morale—by encouraging everybody to sit down in front of a screen and zone-out to happier times.

This zoning-out was made even easier with another of the *Ensee*'s premiere inventions, the Ontological Visualization Undercasting Matrix (OVUM) simulacrum. The best way to describe this device is to liken it to a miniature planetarium about the size of a semi-circular pup-tent under which the user would sit cross-legged on a low swivel-chair mounted on a large, flat, circular platform. The platform had dozens of lasers that could spin around its circumference while casting their beams out onto the inner surface of the "tent".

This technology took the concept of Laser-Floyd—where lasers drew intricate designs on the inner surface of a planetarium dome in time with Pink Floyd's music—to the next level. For one, the OVUM lasers were multi-coloured and could animate complicated, fully-rendered graphics in high-resolution. For another, the nature of the walls of tent gave these graphics depth.

The standard OVUM tent wall was about a foot thick and was comprised of multiple semi-translucent membranes that were positioned at various distances from each other. The inner skins—those closest to the user—were arranged within inches of each other, and the furthest one was suspended a good six inches on its own behind the rest. The lasers operated at different frequencies, and so could "draw" on whatever layer they wanted. This allowed them to create a 3D effect in their animations, one that could be enhanced even further with special polarized glasses, not unlike the ones that were used for 3D movies from the late 2000s onwards.

The virtual environment that the matrix created was made fully interactive through the use of a sensory bar along the bottom of the semi-sphere. This bar used infrared sensors to monitor the position and motion of the user's body and track eye-movement, so that it knew exactly how you were moving and where you were looking. If the user was equipped with motion-sensitive haptic gloves, they could "handle" the objects that were drawn by the lasers and then put right out in front of them using the polarized lenses.

It probably shouldn't come as too much of a surprise that I referred to my own OVUM simulacrum as my "personal TARDIS" since, when it was activated, it looked a lot bigger on the inside. Although it wasn't fully immersive in that I could still see the floor around me, I was told that the *Ensee* had some spherical rooms—like hamster balls—in the larger centers that you could enter and were so realistic that it honestly felt like you were in another world. Was it any wonder that, when I first woke up in this version of 1985, I thought that perhaps it was this technology that was being used to fool me?

The diversionary possibilities that the OVUM offered were, quite literally, endless. It was the ideal technology for a displaced population longing to forget about the disaster that had befallen them, and so, naturally, many people used it to recreate familiar environments to ease their troubled minds, and simulation files were traded back and forth like the comic books of my youth. What better way to spend a night in a cramped van floating out in the middle of the Northumberland Strait in the dead of winter than in an expansive virtual environment that looked and felt exactly like the place you spent your honeymoon twenty years ago? Personally, when I wasn't watching retro shows and movies from my youth projected onto what looked like a huge cinematic screen, I was programming my all-time favourite motion pictures so that it felt like I was actually inside of them. Same difference I suppose.

OK. I lied. I really miss this particular technology too, about as much as the PFD.

It all sounds pretty idyllic doesn't it? Well, it wasn't. Not exactly. Nobody was sure exactly when it happened, but the *Ensee* went from being a benevolent corporation to an autocracy (or, more specifically, a corporatocracy). But that's a topic for a future journal entry when I'll document how Oskar finally lifted the curtain on what was really going on, and set me on a path that would flip my life around even more than it had been flipped by the events of 2025.

T he old sailors describe a doldrum as a spot on the ocean without any wind. In other words, a state where no forward motion can be made.

That pretty much described the state that I'd been in for the last couple of weeks. It was now early June, and I'd only recognized two new anachronisms in as many weeks. I was still making a slip of paper for every new word that I found, but tossing them around still wasn't working all that well. Finally, it occurred to me to put what little I remembered about BASIC programming to use, and I wrote a program on my Commodore 64 to randomly scramble the words for me. I did this by using a data array to assign each word a numerical value, and then getting the computer to spit out a different order of these values each time, and display the corresponding words on the screen in sentence form. The hard part was coding it to figure out what values had already been chosen so that they wouldn't be selected again.

After several days of programming and consulting with my teachers and fellow nerds at the high school, I finally had a functioning program that successfully rearranged the words for me at speeds that were both lightning fast and totally useless. It didn't matter how many times I ran the program, or how many permutations of the words I looked at, none of it made any sense to me whatsoever.

The lack of progress was bothering me, to be sure, as were the painful memories that my frequent journaling was dredging up. But, if there was one saving grace to the whole sorry state of affairs, it was that I was really starting to enjoy being a teenager again. Like a whole lot.

When I wasn't working, I've been enjoying time with friends, all of us excited that the school year was winding down and that summer vacation was nigh. We've gotten together a handful of times at *PJs* where we've spent time losing quarters in the coin-ops (well, me at least) when we weren't sitting around tables eating burgers, chicken fingers, and some of the best poutine I've ever tasted. We've had house parties (a lot tamer than the ones you might have seen in the movies), and gone on a few road trips to Timmins, including one to go see a double-feature at the drive-in movie theater of *Rambo: First Blood Part II* and *A View to a Kill*. I'm happy to say that I successfully resisted the urge to reveal random bits of trivia about the movies, or recite bits of dialogue in time with it. It might have amused Andi, but I'm not sure how the other people in the car would have felt about it. Well, maybe Calvin might have appreciated it, in a competitive kind of way.

But, as for deciphering the coded message, I was at a dead-end.

And then, finally, I got a break.

It was a Saturday night in early June, and Andi and I had just come out of the movie theater where we had seen *The Goonies*. She was so excited that the main girl in the movie was also named "Andy," that she was practically vibrating.

"I'm not the only one anymore!" she said through a broad grin as we passed by the local *Radio Shack* store.

When I had been much younger, this had been where I had taken advantage of their *Battery of the Month* promotion, and it was where I had bought all of the necessary parts to build my three-stage rocket when I'd been about ten, and then the electronics to build my first remote-control plane at twelve. It was also where I picked up all of my computer games, as they had a great selection of disks and cartridges for the Commodore 64.

Andi was revealing to me just how much she had hated her name (which had not been a surprise to me), mostly because she was dead tired of hearing people ask, "Isn't that a boy's name?" She was just in the process of telling me that she had even looked into the process of having it legally changed (again, not a surprise), and had been planning on proceeding with it once she figured out how to broach the subject with her mother, when something in the window of the electronics store caught my eye.

On the bottom edge of the window, just below eye-level, was a poster advertising the *Hitchhiker's Guide to the Galaxy* computer game, a busy poster that proudly proclaimed it to be the biggest selling video game of the year. I knew the poster well, considering that it was, after all, how I'd found out about the game in the first place. The advertisement had obviously been in the window for a while, because the bright yellow background was getting a little bleached, but there was a detail on it that I hadn't noticed until now, meaning that it was likely new to this timeline. In the upper right corner, written in text angled at a forty-five-degree angle in relation to everything on the rest of the poster, were the words: "Special Time Warp Edition!" Moving closer, I saw that there were smaller words beneath the tagline that explained that this particular game had fallen through a time warp from the year 2035.

That can't be a coincidence!

I quickly scanned the rest of the poster looking for anything else that might stand out. Along with large blocks of text that would be out of place in modern advertisements that trended more towards striking visuals, the poster showed each of the "feelies" that came with the game. In the early 80s, *Infocom Games* tried to draw more attention to their entertainment software by including a number of promotional items in the box that were each of them related to the theme of the game. They had called these items "feelies," and, for the Hitchhiker's game, this had included such things as some pocket fluff, an empty plastic bag purported to contain a microscopic space fleet, and a red button with the words "Don't Panic" on it in large friendly yellow letters. Only, as was evidenced by the picture of the button I could see on the poster, as well as my own discovery a few weeks back, the big friendly letters now read: "Don't Worry."

I was scanning the text quickly to see if there were any more details about what made this "Time Warp Edition" special, not even cognizant of the fact that, after I had stopped short in front of the store, Andi, who had been in mid-sentence, had continued on down the street without me. She, was now back beside me asking, "What is it? Another difference?"

"Yes," I answered. "Not sure what it means though. I have a copy of this game at home. This advertisement actually identifies the year that I shifted from."

"Special Time Warp Edition from 2035," read Andi. "That can't be a coincidence."

I smiled at how she had so closely echoed my thought process. "My feelings exactly," I said as I checked the hours on the door even though I knew that the store would have closed up shop much earlier this evening. "I'm going to check my game tonight and, if it's not the right version, I'll come back tomorrow and pick one up."

"On a Sunday?"

"Oh right." I forgot that most stores were still closed on Sundays in the 80s. "Then I'll have to do it on Monday then. Let's hope the copy that I already have is what I need, because I've been waiting for a break like this for a long time and I don't really feel like waiting any longer!"

Apologizing to Andi for the rush (I needn't have worried, as she was just as excited as I was about this possible hint as to the puzzle's solution), I took her back to her house immediately, and sped home to mine. When I got there, I went straight to my bedroom and pulled the *Hitchhiker's Guide to the Galaxy* game disc out of the drawer of my desk. Sure enough, along the bottom of the disk's label were the words "Time Warp Edition!"

With shaking hands, I booted up my Commodore 64 system and slid the floppy into the drive. As the program loaded into memory, I started to think back on what to expect. The program was a classic text-based adventure in which the user interacted with the game-play through a limited number of text commands in order to solve puzzles and collect items to put into inventory. There were no graphics, forcing the user to rely on his or her imagination, something that, in my humble opinion, made it much better than even the best and most high-resolution graphic-based games of the future. This particular game was designed in part by Douglas Adams himself, meaning that it was revolutionary for its time and, like Adams, irreverent as hell.

As for the plot, well, my memories were slightly vague, but I seemed to recall that most of it was based on the events from the radio, book, and TV incarnations, but at least a chunk of it had Arthur Dent travelling through time into the past consciousnesses of his shipmates. I couldn't help but notice that this particular aspect was suspiciously similar to what had happened to me. Could that be the part of the game that will be significant to helping me solve the code? If so, then how long would it take for me to get to that part of the game's narrative again? Although I'd logged hours and hours playing this game as a teen, and died dozens, if not hundreds of times, in the process, I was a little rusty and would have to figure a lot of it out as I went. I found myself wishing for an internet connection so that I could look up a walkthrough guide.

Finally, the file was loaded and ready, so I ran the program, and the first lines of the narrative scrolled onto the screen, along with a chevron and a flashing underscore, indicating the prompt where my input was expected.

```
You wake up. The room is spinning
very gently round your head. Or at
least it would be if you could see
it which you can't.

It is pitch black.

>_
```

Ah yes. Now it was coming back to me. I glanced at the instructions to remind myself of how to play. These text-based games accepted a limited number of commands, and then would respond accordingly. I had seen this particular screen quite a few times in my youth until I finally figured out that the correct command was the most obvious one. So, I entered:

```
> Turn on light
```

In response, more text scrolled up and onto the screen. I read it all very carefully, trying to be cognizant of even the smallest of things that might be different.

```
Good start to the day. Pity it's
going to be the worst one of your
life. The light is now on.

Bedroom, in the bed

The bedroom is a mess.

It is a small bedroom with a faded
carpet and old wallpaper. There is a
washbasin, a chair with a tatty
dressing gown slung over it, and a
window with the curtains drawn. Near
the exit leading south is a phone
with a Post-it note on the receiver.

There is a flathead screwdriver
here. (outside the bed)
```

```
There is a toothbrush here. (outside
the bed)

>_
```

I almost didn't see it at first. This had also been a screen that I'd spent a lot of time reading those first few hundred times I'd played the game. I had often had to start it all over again when the later clues proved too difficult to solve because I'd apparently missed something. Most famously, for instance, if you failed to get the babel fish early in the game you wouldn't be able to decipher the Vogon text on a later puzzle.

So yes, I knew this screen well, even all these years later, and I was willing to bet my house (even if it was about to be destroyed to make way for a bypass), that the original game made no mention of there having been a Post-it note on the phone.

Excitedly, I typed:

```
> get Post-it note

You lunge for it, but the room spins
nauseatingly away. The floor gives
you a light tap on the forehead.
```

Oh right, Arthur Dent has a hangover, and I can't do much of anything else until I take the necessary steps to deal with it. With some slight difficulty because I was rusty with the commands, I took my character through the process of standing up, getting the dressing gown, putting it on, opening the pocket, and ingesting the analgesic that he found there. This cleared up my hangover-induced headache enough to interact with the smaller items in the room, like the Post-it note.

```
> get Post-it note

You pick up the Post-it note. There
is a message on it.
```

OK yeah. This is definitely new.

```
> examine Post-it note
```

```
It is like every other Post-it note
you've ever seen except for the
message in what looks like your
aunt's handwriting. It says, "Jenny
called."
```

Jenny? Who the hell is Jenny? Am I supposed to call her back?
I told the game to pick up the receiver, and was rewarded with
the same message that I'd always gotten whenever I'd picked it up:

```
You pick up the receiver. A moment
later, the dialing tone is suddenly
cut off. Glancing through the window
you can't help but notice the large
old oak tree of which you are
particularly fond crashing down
through the phone cable.
```

I tried a few combinations that involved Jenny, and received a
variation of answers telling me that I was obviously on the wrong
track.

```
>call Jenny

I don't know the word "jenny".


>dial jenny

I don't know the word "dial".


>get phone

The cable is down, remember?


>pick up phone

The cable is down, remember?
```

```
>dial phone

I don't know the word "dial".


>use phone

I don't know the word "use".


>phone Jenny

I don't know the word "jenny".
```

Eventually, I ran out of both options and time when I got a message telling me that my house had been destroyed with me inside it. It was not an unfamiliar note.

```
Better luck next life.
```

I restarted the game. This action was also not something unfamiliar to me since, as I've already said more than once, I couldn't count the number of times that I had died while playing this game! Perhaps predictably, the second run ended the same as the first. Afterwards, I sat for a while staring at the message telling me that I'd lost, but wishing me the best next time around.

This was ridiculous!

I finally get a break with deciphering the coded message, and this is how it ends?

I restarted one more time, and decided to see if there were changes later in the game, but I was so unfamiliar with everything beyond the first screen that I may as well have been playing it for the first time. After four more tries, I hadn't really made much progress, when my frustration, coupled with the certainty that the message on the Post-it note was exactly what I had been looking for all along, finally convinced me that it was pointless. Dejectedly, I powered everything off and got ready for bed. As I lay there in the dim light of the moon through my open curtains, I thought about the Post-it note in the game.

246

Who in the hell is Jenny?

I searched my memory for all the women named Jen or Jenny who were, or would be, famous in the 80s, 90s, and beyond. I could only think of a few, like Jennifer Aniston, Jenny McCarthy, Jenny Jones, and Jenny from Forrest Gump.

Wait, the Tom Hanks movie was based on a book, right? Has the book been written yet? Maybe there's a clue in it or something.

I fell asleep convinced that, even if I wasn't onto something, at least I still had some options left.

The next morning, I got up early, still excited that I was finally making some headway with the decoding of the message, even if I didn't know exactly how to make it work yet. I went downstairs to let Chance out for a run and then came back inside to get some coffee going for Mom and Dad. I was part-way through making some French Toast with strawberries and sausages, when they both wandered down the stairs and into the kitchen around 7. This was much later than usual for my father, and I was sure that my earlier suspicions were true and he was starting to take advantage of my getting up earlier than him.

As we ate, I asked them if they knew whether or not the library was open on Sundays.

"I'm not sure," answered my mother. "Why not call them. Maybe they have a message?"

"Nice idea," I said, even though I knew that her suggestion could be hit or miss, since answering machines that delivered an outgoing message to callers outside of business hours were still kind of new in this era. I got lucky though and was greeted with a friendly message a few minutes later once I'd located the library's number in the phone book. The chipper voice in the receiver told me that the building was currently closed, but listed their hours. They would be open at noon today.

Smiling as I hung up on the phone, I had to admit that I had a really good feeling about today. After I'd helped to clean up after breakfast, I called Andi to let her know that I was going in on my bike about an hour earlier than we had planned to meet up so that I could go to the library. In a quiet voice, she told me that she would meet me there. She also said that she was anxious to hear how it had gone with the game, but it was obvious from the raised voices in the background that we couldn't talk about it now.

"Gotta go," she said abruptly in the middle of my reply, and the line went dead. I stared at the receiver for a while before finally hanging it up. I felt kinda guilty not feeling worse than I did about Andi's tumultuous home life. I knew that it was a very difficult time for her right now, but I also knew that it all worked out for her, eventually. I just didn't like the fact that my sudden impossible revelation was making things more difficult for her no matter how much she might claim to need a distraction.

There were still several hours before the library opened, so I decided to check out a movie in the recroom. When I didn't find any changes in *Wargames*, I put *Raiders of the Lost Ark* in the VCR, even though I knew that I would only have time to watch a little less than the first hour before I had to get ready to leave.

I was standing outside the door to the library when it was unlocked at noon, and I went directly to the card catalogue. There was no book called *Forrest Gump* in the obvious categories, and I was standing there trying to figure out if the book might have had a name that was different than its movie interpretation and, if so, where else to look, when a librarian I didn't recognize asked if she could help me with something.

"I'm looking for a book," I began, realizing too late that I probably could have avoided stating the obvious. "I'm not sure that it's even been published yet, or who the author is, but I'm pretty sure that it's called 'Forrest Gump.'"

"Forest Gomp?" the young woman confirmed.

"Yes," I replied, deciding against correcting her pronunciation. "I heard them talking about it on the CBC," I lied. "But I didn't catch them say when it was coming out. I thought I'd take a chance and see if it was already available."

"Well, I've never heard of it, but let me check the list of new and pending arrivals," she offered.

Andi was walking into the library a few minutes later just as I was walking out.

"How'd it go with the game?" she asked as we moved back out into the sunlight. She was wearing dark sunglasses, but I was pretty sure that what I could see of her eyes looked puffy.

I didn't answer her. Instead, I pulled her into a hug. She resisted for a moment, her body tense and rigid. And then she melted into me as her arms found their way around me to return the embrace.

"How are you?" I asked.

She didn't answer at first. "I need to get my mind off it. Tell me you have good news about the game."

"Good and bad," I answered. "I have the right version, I think. There's a new aspect to the gameplay that wasn't there before. But I can't figure out how to make it work. I had a possible solution. That's why I came here, but it was a dead-end."

"What's the new aspect?" she asked as she pulled away from the hug and bent over to unlock her bike.

"There's a message on a Post-it note on a phone that wasn't there before, and it says 'Jenny called.'"

Andi stood up quickly and gave me a look that got gradually more patronizing the longer it persisted. It felt very much like she was staring at me in pity, like you would at a dull child.

"What?" I asked.

"Josh, there's now a *phone* in the game with the words *'Jenny called'* on it?"

"Well, strictly speaking, the phone was there already. It's just the Post-it note that's new. But, yeah, so?"

"Whatever. The implication of the note is that you should call this *Jenny* back, right?"

"Yeah, so?" I repeated. "I tried that. It didn't work. I don't have her phone number."

Andi actually rolled her eyes in exasperation to this. "Most of the changes that you've found to the timeline have been in songs, right?" she explained a little slower than she had to, I thought. "So, logic dictates that you should probably look to a song for your answer, right?"

"I love it when you talk like Spock, by the way. Please continue."

"Jenny's got the most well-known phone number in, like, ever. In fact, the song was on one of the cassettes that I let you borrow last month."

I blinked a few times, still not clear on what she was getting at. I couldn't be positive, but it sure seemed like she was enjoying knowing something that I didn't.

"867..." she began in a sing-song voice.

"5309!" I finished loudly.

"9305," Andi corrected.

"Yeah, whatever," I said. "Wait, that's *Jenny's* phone number?"

"Yeah, her name's in the song," she said. "You never noticed? It starts out, like, 'Jenny, Jenny'."

"Oh," I said. "Is that what the words are? I thought it was 'Jelly, Jelly.'"

"Jelly, Jelly?"

"Yeah, it's always confused me. I thought the singer really liked jams." I was getting really excited now, and feeling very far away from both home and computer. "When I logged the anachronism in my table, I listed the title as the phone number because that's what I thought it was."

Quickly, I unlocked my bike, swung my leg over the bar, and settled onto the seat. "Wanna come over and solve a time-travel code with me?"

"Like you even have to ask."

It didn't take us long to zip out to my house on our bikes, and I swear I heard the song that I now knew was called "Jenny" playing by way of a soundtrack the whole way. My parents were just finishing lunch when we got there. Mom greeted Andi like she was a member of the family, and asked her if she wanted something to eat, while I swept by everyone as politely as I could, heading in the direction of my bedroom and the computer that waited there. Andi arrived several minutes later, holding two plates of steaming lasagna and with a very excited Golden Retriever following very closely behind.

"I told your Mom that you were excited about a new computer program," she explained as she put a plate down beside my keyboard. I'd already worked my way through the initial stages of the game, and had just gotten to the point where Arthur Dent was feeling well enough to pick up the phone with the Post-it note on it.

First, I tried using the number from this timeline.

```
>phone 867-9385

The cable is down, remember?
```

Beside me, Andi froze, her fork still coming out of her mouth and her face mid-chew. I was just as tense, but we weren't out of options yet.

"OK," I said as optimistically as possible. "That obviously isn't it. Then how about the original?"

```
>phone 867-5309
```

This time, the screen cleared completely and at the top were the following words:

```
WELCOME TO THE ANACHRONISTIC CODE,
TIME-TRAVELER.

You are the ultimate comeback kid,
having fallen into a time warp and
into your own past. Undertake this
side-quest, and solve the coded
message to save the future!

Enter your first name to continue

>_
```

"Holy fucking fuck," said Andi, a girl who never swore. She was shaking. I hugged her because I was shaking too and I was hoping that it would at least steady me a little.

This is actually happening. I hadn't imagined the whole thing after all!

"This is actually real! Yayyyyyyy!" I said as I flailed my arms in the air like an excited Kermit the Frog. Then I fished my keys out of the front pocket of my jeans and unlocked the drawer where I kept my journal, and turned back to the screen to read the message again. I was impressed. The text that had come up in response to my entering Jenny's original phone number looked like nothing more than the kind of side-quest that would be very popular in console games a couple of decades from now. If somebody happened to chance upon this, they probably wouldn't think anything of it.

I hesitated in entering my name at first, afraid that I'd be identifying myself to a hacker, but then I remembered that this game was in no way connected to the internet. It was completely standalone, so that made anything I entered completely private for the obvious reason that it couldn't be anything except that. Unless, of course, this computer was like the arcade game in *The Last Starfighter* and could transmit an interstellar signal out into space.

But that's ridiculous. Right?

Placing my journal to the left of the keyboard, I entered:

```
>Josh
```

And the game responded:

```
Hello Josh!

To complete this side-quest, you
must first find clues in the real
world in the form of anachronisms.

Have you noticed any anachronisms?

Y or N

>_
```

"The game is calling them anachronisms too!" I exclaimed to Andi. "This just kept getting better and better." I entered "Y".

```
Excellent.

To begin, tell me about the
anachronisms you've noticed and I'll
help you put them in the correct
order.

Enter Y to continue...
```

Andi and I exchanged an excited glance. I keyed the "Y" again, and was surprised at the sentence that scrolled up onto to the screen in response.

```
But first, a side-quest within a
side-quest, just to make absolutely
sure that you are who you say you
are, Josh!

Enter Y to continue...
```

The tone of the text was surprisingly chipper, all things considered, and in the style of the game in which it found itself, making me wonder if Douglas Adams had had something to do with it. I typed "Y" again, and a graphic scrolled up onto the screen, pushing most of the previous text off the top edge.

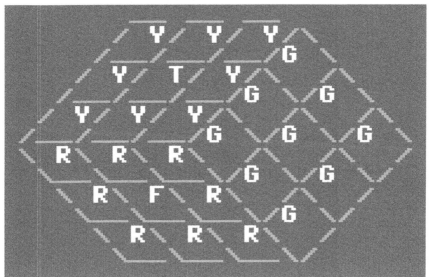

It appeared to be an ASCII image of a Rubik's cube, with 'Y' for yellow on top, 'R' for red beneath that, and 'G' for green to the right. There was a 'T' on the yellow face, an 'F' on the Red, and nothing on the Green. Under the cube was a series of letters and numbers that I recognized as standard cube turning instructions, where R was the face on the right of the cube, F the front, T the top, B the Bottom, and, lastly, L representing the left face.

```
R+ F2 R- T2 L+ B- R+ T- B- R+ L+ B-
```

Beneath this was the phrase:

```
Hold the cube like you see here and
follow the instructions. Don't forget
what Chameleons do, and know the
pattern that you will need can be
found where Jack and Diane used to
run.

Enter Y to continue...
```

"My cube! Where's my cube?" I said mostly to myself as I stood up and walked over to my bedside table where my Rubik's cube had remained untouched since my return a number of weeks back. It was jumbled and, as I returned to where Andi was sitting, I admitted out loud that I no longer knew how to solve it.

"That's no problem," she said brightly as she took it from me. "It's about time I made a contribution."

"Are you kidding?" I said as I sat back down. "If you hadn't told me that 867-5309 was Jenny's phone number (as I spoke, Andi reflexively corrected me by saying "9305"), I'd still be knocking my head against the wall just trying to get into the game in the first place!"

I went back to reading the clue a second time as Andi flipped the cube around in her hands, manipulating it deftly.

"I wondered about that song!" I exclaimed as I sorted through my journal to the table on the last page.

"Jack and Diane?"

"Yeah," I found the row in the table where I'd written the title of John Cougar's popular 80s song. "It was one of the songs that I wasn't really sure of, since I wasn't all familiar with it in the first place. In this timeline, Jack says: 'Diane, let's run off *beside* a shady tree." I held up the notebook so that Andi could see where I was pointing. "In my memory though, I was pretty sure that they ran off *behind* a shady tree, but I was iffy about it, so I put a little asterisk beside the song's title. Now, this side-quest makes it clear that I was right."

Andi interrupted me, seeing where I was going. "So, we follow the instructions to jumble the cube in a specific way, and then flip the cube over to see what the pattern is *behind* the cube? Like the back of it?"

"That'd be my guess," I said. "I expect that the specific pattern of colours will create some kind of QR code,"

"A what?" She was doing well with the cube, having gotten the top and the sides, and was now working her way through the final move combinations to solve the bottom.

"Futuristic bar code," I answered. "The position and colour of the dots within a square pattern can contain text and messages when interpreted by an app."

"What's an app?"

"Heh. Long story. Kind of like a specialized computer program. In this case, it's one that would interpret the QR code and tell you the message that is embedded within it. Usually, it would be a web address, but it could also contain text."

"What's a web address?" Andi asked almost absent-mindedly as she held up the solved cube with a self-satisfied grin.

"Another time," I answered "Nicely done, young lady."

"Call me that again, old man, and I'll hit you with it."

I smiled as I scanned the instructions again. "The moves look pretty straight forward, it's the orientation that we need to be careful of. I'm guessing that, because the text mentions 'Chameleon' that it's referring to the Culture Club song." I looked to the table in the back of my journal again, and scanned the list of songs until I found what I needed. "Yep. Just as I thought. The new lyrics say that Boy George's dreams are gold, red, and green, but in my memory, they were listed in the order of red, gold, and green. Assuming that gold represents the yellow of the Rubik's cube, then my guess is the instructions are telling us to do what Chameleons are famous for, and change colours. Specifically, we're supposed to switch red for yellow."

I looked over at Andi who was already holding up the cube so that red was on top and yellow was facing her, having obviously reached the same conclusion that I'd just expressed, likely before I'd even begun to express it. "Gotcha. Which would make red 'T' and yellow 'F', just the opposite of how it's labeled. That puts the green on the left instead of the right, which is probably why it's not actually given an orientation in the graphic. OK, feed me the instructions."

"First, I want to repeat how brilliant this is!" I said through a smile. "If somebody from your timeline followed these instructions without switching the colours, they would end up with a completely different cube! Then, on top of all that, they wouldn't know enough to flip it over to read the backside. I'm impressed! It's the perfect way to give everyone the exact same instructions that only a select few can actually successfully follow!"

"Yeah, yeah. I get it. You want to rent the instructions an apartment and visit them on weekends. C'mon old man, the clock's ticking!"

As I read out each move listed on the screen in turn, Andi flipped the corresponding side of the cube. After a couple of minutes, we were done. Before she did anything else, I pulled a marker from the top drawer of my desk, and wrote a small F on the yellow cube in the center of the side that was facing her.

"OK, flip it over," I instructed. When she had, I marked the white square on the opposite side with a little star. "That should make sure that we don't get confused, as long as we remember that red is always the top."

Together we looked at the pattern. It was little more than a jumble of coloured squares. It didn't make any sense to me at all, and, from the look on Andi's face, it was clear that the confusion was mutual.

"Did I get it right?" she asked.

I pulled a large index card from the second drawer of my desk and quickly sketched out two nine-celled square tables, one for the back of the cube, and the other for the front. Then, I put the first letter of each of the colours in their respective squares.

"Ok, can you do the sequence in reverse, and then do it again from the start?" I suggested. "Then we'll see if it's the same."

BACK

Y	B	Y
R	W	Y
O	B	O

FRONT

W	G	O
O	Y	O
B	G	Y

"Good idea," she replied as she started twisting the cube following the instructions from the bottom, each action in the opposite direction of the one listed. When she got back to the beginning, the cube was in its solved state.

"So far so good," she said, as she started working her way through the sequence of moves from the beginning again. When she was finished, we compared the cube to the drawings that I'd made, and it matched perfectly.

"Now, if this side-quest they're talking about is anything like the game that it's embedded in," I said as I folded up the index card and slipped it into my wallet. "Then I know enough not to leave information like this behind. I'm going to keep it on me just in case I don't have the cube if I ever need the patterns again."

Once again, I hit the "Y" key to get to the next screen.

```
On the next page, you will need to
choose the cube with the correct
pattern, Josh.

Get it wrong and you're more than
just out of luck. This disc will be
reformatted and the program will
modify a memory module on this
computer so that you will never be
able to run the game on it again.

But no pressure, right?

Choose wisely.

>_
```

"Wait, is that actually possible?" asked Andi. "Modifying a memory module?"

"Damned if I can remember, but I really don't want to take any chances…"

The next message that scrolled up onto the screen was a colourful one. It showed four columns and three rows of nine-squared cubes, each with a different colour combination, and each one labelled with a number.

"So, we look where Jack and Diane used to run, so we look *behind* the cube," I narrated out loud. As I spoke, Andi flipped the cube so that we could see the face that I'd just marked with the little star, and held it up beside the TV set that I used as a computer monitor.

I was in the middle of narrowing my choices down to three by looking for all cubes with a white center, when Andi interrupted my thought process.

"One," she said excitedly, her words coming out in an uninterrupted stream. "It's the first one. Enter the number one, Josh. The answer is 'one'."

I looked over at the young woman with an amused grin. If it was possible, she was actually more excited about this than was I.

I quickly compared the face of the cube that Andi was holding up towards us to the first option on the screen. Sure enough, Andi had been correct. The colours were an exact match. So, slowly, as if moving too quickly might scare the information on the TV set, I typed '1' and moved my finger to hover over the RETURN key.

"OK," I said, taking a deep breath. "Here goes…"

"Oh for God's sake, Josh," Andi said as she reached over and pressed down on my poised finger. "You take way too long, y'know that?"

Nothing happened for the longest time. Any other time I'd entered something or hit a key in this game, new text scrolled up from the bottom immediately. That wasn't happening this time though. I looked over at Andi before positioning my finger to hit the RETURN key again.

"Did I break it?" Andi asked, a note of fear in her voice.

I was about to respond when text screen finally scrolled into view.

```
FATAL ERROR!

 .

 .

 .

DOES NOT COMPUTE. . .

 .

 .

 .
```

Andi actually screamed and I was just about to press the RUN/STOP key to see if I could halt the program, when more text appeared.

```
 .

 .

 .

SORRY. Just goofing with you.

Welcome to the WONDERFUL WORLD OF
WAS, time-traveler!

Hit any key to continue
```

First, I started breathing again, then Andi retracted what felt like sharp talons from my upper arm that I hadn't even felt attach themselves in the first place, and said, "*Wonderful World of Was*? Cute alliteration. Does that make you Dorothy?"

"I'm pretty sure that I'm the Wizard," I said as I hit the space bar. "I'm *always* the Wizard. Unless we're playing Monopoly. Then I'm always the car." Together, we took a few calming breaths as we watched the screen scroll.

```
Now what say I help you make sense
of those pesky anachronisms...

Draw a grid on a piece of paper with
7 columns and 4 rows and then put
letters above the columns and
numbers beside the rows, like an
Excel table.

Hit any key to continue
```

I grinned at this little revelation of just how real this was, since the graphic version of Excel that would match what the game was directing me to draw wouldn't exist for a couple of years. Grabbing my journal, I flipped to another page at the back, where I used a whole page to draw the table as instructed.

As I was doing this, I could hear footsteps in the hallway approaching the room. I did a quick scan of the desk to make sure that nothing was improperly exposed, even as I heard my Mom's voice call, "Is everything OK in there?" I was spinning around in my chair to greet her just as she was entering the room. Beside me Andi was straightening up in the way that most kids do when an adult enters the room, as if they are expecting to be scolded for slouching. "I heard a scream," Mom stated.

"Oh sorry, Mrs. Donegal," answered Andi. "That was me. We're playing a new computer game, and I got really excited."

"That must be some computer game," said my mother as she cleaned up the used lunch plates, and headed back towards the bedroom door. "I'm making cookies, if you want any."

"Making?" I asked. My ears perking up. "As in you haven't *baked* them yet?" I was on my feet in a second, beckoning Andi to follow me as I walked after my mother down the hallway towards the kitchen and the cookie dough that awaited there. It should go without saying that my mother made the most amazing cookie dough, and the cookies that they produced were pretty good too. I suspect it was the obscene amount of butter and sugar that she used.

We spent almost an hour in the kitchen. I made some green tea for myself and Andi, while my mother answered Andi's questions about the finer points of making cookies, a skill that she had never learned from her own mother. Dad wandered in from the workshop to see how the baking was going, and we ended up sitting around the table for a while, chatting. It was a nice distraction, and one that made me realize just how keyed up and intense Andi and I had become as a result of the game. Although I was anxious to get back to the side-quest, now that we were actually making progress, and especially just as we were about to start sorting the clues, I also didn't want to pass up any opportunities to bond with loved ones like this. I was also enjoying watching Andi interact with my mother. I didn't want to ever compare her to Heather, at least out loud, but she had a relationship with my mother that my one-time wife, for whatever reason, would never enjoy.

When we finally got back to my bedroom with a plate of cookies and two mugs of steaming tea, I sat down in front of the Commodore 64 and pressed the space bar. The program had been waiting patiently this whole time, and immediately presented the next step in the instructions:

```
HERE ARE SOME BASIC WORDS TO GET YOU
STARTED, JOSH...

AND: D2

A: F3

OF: B4

AM: F4

Oh, and you might as well put a big
X in cell G3. It's empty. Or at least
it will be until you put an 'X' in
it.

WHEN YOU ARE READY, HIT ANY KEY TO
CONTINUE.
```

I added the words in the locations listed. When I was done, the clue looked like this:

	A	B	C	D	E	F	G
1							
2				AND			
3						A	X
4		OF				AN	

I stared at the words for a moment and shook my head. This was the most complicated *Wheel of Fortune*-like puzzle I'd ever seen, with so many empty cells and only a handful of articles to work with, there were way too many blanks to make any sense of it. At least for now.

Beside me, I could hear Andi's heated breathing in my ear. It had a very impatient nature about it, as it unassumingly informed me that I was taking too long to get on with it. Smiling weakly at my girlfriend, I hit the space bar, and a new screen appeared with the following text:

```
WHAT IS THE SOURCE OF YOUR
ANACHRONISM:

(S)ong or (M)ovie?
```

Without even asking, and before I even had a chance to settle my notebook on the desk in front of me again, Andi pulled it away from me.

"Song," she offered perfunctorily.

My hand shaking again, I typed 'S.'

Beneath the existing text, another question appeared

```
WHAT IS THE NAME OF THE SONG?

>_
```

Beneath the question mark, and just to the right of a chevron, a flashing vertical line indicated that this was where I was expected to input my answer. I didn't even need to refer to my list, so I used the keyboard to type *In the Air Tonight,* and hit the RETURN key.

The game's response was immediate.

```
CORRECT.

However, that song is not part of
this clue. Please try again.

Hit any key to continue, or 'Q' to
quit.
```

Andi and I exchanged a look. For the first time since we had found this side-quest hidden within the larger *Hitchhiker's Guide to the Galaxy* game, I was concerned.

Why would this anachronism not be in the clue? Was there an error in the program?

"Do you ... um, want the next one?" Andi asked me helpfully.

"Uh, sure," I said optimistically. "It does say to try again."

"The next song on your list is *Can't Fight this Feeling.*"

I hit the space bar. This brought up the question about whether the anachronism was in a song or a movie. I answered appropriately and then typed the song title into the input field again and entered it. Once again, the message telling us that the song wasn't part of the clue scrolled up onto the screen, along with the helpful command to try again.

"I haven't been told to try again this much since the last time I played *Roll up the Rim* at *Tim's*," I said sardonically. The way that Andi was looking at me blankly made it clear that she was long past asking what particular future detail I was referencing. Before I had a chance to say anything else though, Andi was feeding me the next song on the list.

"*Every Breath You Take,*" she said, perched on the edge of my bed, knuckles gripping my journal so tightly that they were white. She was clearly just as anxious about this as was I, so I didn't waste any time doing as she suggested. This time, thankfully, we got a different response.

```
CORRECT.

Please enter the NEW word in that
song in cell E2.

Hit any key to continue, or 'Q' to
quit.
```

Andi flipped to the page with the table and I handed her a pencil.

"Interesting that the game is very specific that it's the NEW lyrics and not the old ones," I mused as she was doing as instructed and writing the word "FOLLOW" in cell E2 in the makeshift spreadsheet.

The table now looked like this:

	A	B	C	D	E	F	G
1							
2				AND	FOLLOW		
3						A	✕
4		OF				AN	

Andi didn't waste any more time. "Next one," she demanded. "Hit a key already."

I couldn't help but laugh. Our personalities certainly differed in how we handled situations like this. I wanted to take it slowly and contemplate every action, analyze every command, and thoroughly strategize every move before we made it. Andi, on the other hand, didn't want the journey to get in the way of the destination.

Instead of doing as she commanded though, I reached out to touch the young Greek woman's leg, impelling it to stop its nervous twitching. "Andi," I began.

"I know," she answered immediately. "I get a little intense when I'm trying to figure something out, especially something as monumental as this. I'll reign it in. I promise."

"Works for me," I said as I turned back to the desk and pressed the space bar on the computer's keyboard. Text scrolled, and once more, we were looking at the first question:

```
WHAT IS THE SOURCE OF THE
ANACHRONISM:

(S)ong or (M)ovie?
```

And so, over the next hour and a bit, we worked through my list of anachronisms, inputting them into the game one at a time, with it telling us where to put each word in our faux Excel table. Aside from a couple of entries, most of the words that the game told us to use were the original lyrics – the ones that only I would know. Sometimes, the cell number was followed by the command to punctuate the sentence, and other times we were told either to pluralize the entry or to use the present tense, and there were even instances when the same word was used more than once, such as with the word "clue." In cases where the anachronisms were several words instead of just one, the instructions would tell us which word to use.

And, more than once, we'd see the following error message:

```
I DON'T KNOW THAT ANACHRONISM.

PLEASE TRY AGAIN - TYPE CAREFULLY.
THINGS AREN'T FUZZY FOR ME.
```

The first time we saw the text, just after I had entered the song title *Stayin' Alive*, Andi had said, "Fuzzy? Do you know what that means?"

"Yeah," I had answered. "Computers in the future will use something called 'fuzzy string matching.' Basically, it means that an algorithm will be able to figure out what the user is trying to type even if the user isn't all that clear, or makes a spelling mistake, or only has half the word. This 1980s software doesn't have that, so we have to precisely match what it's already programmed to know."

"Ah," she said. "Is it possible that it can't handle the dropped 'g'?"

"Exactly what I was thinking," I said as I typed *Staying Alive*. This time, the program accepted the title, and promptly informed us that it wasn't a part of the clue.

"Well that was worth the extra effort," I quipped sarcastically.

We saw this error message quite a few times as we moved down the list, mostly because of issues with capitalization when upper- and lower-case letters had to be inputted exactly as the game expected, especially for such titles as *Don't Fall in Love with a Dreamer*. But this wasn't the only reason we saw it. Sometimes I just had the title of the song wrong, and other times I struggled with punctuation (like *Wake Me Up Before You Go-Go* which, I found out after three attempts had to include the hyphen). Coincidentally, that's also when I found out that, in cases where the anachronism was actually *in* the song title, I had to enter the current title, or the program would throw the error again. Naturally, this made it more difficult to confirm whether the songs that I'd marked with an asterisk actually were legit. It would take several tries, and numerous different combinations, before we could conclude that I'd been wrong about an anachronism. Andi kept track of all of the variations that we'd tried on a separate piece of paper, and only after we'd felt that we'd exhausted every possibility would we eventually cross a song off the list completely.

As we worked through the code's solution, I kept marvelling at its brilliance (in fact, I did so out loud so many times that Andi eventually started ignoring me completely). None of the words in the message that we were assembling ever actually appeared on the TV screen, meaning that none of those words were actually stored anywhere in the computer program. I suspected that the code behind the game was organized using scattered ASCII values, proxies, and aliases so that the song titles weren't directly associated with the numbers and if somebody was able to hack it, they wouldn't be able to piece it together.

Indeed, the only way that *anybody* could figure out the actual message, was for them to put the words in the proper order using this side-quest—and the only way that they could actually do this was by knowing what had been changed and how! This is what added the extra layer of security, because, for the vast majority of the clues, I was being asked to use the *original* lyric, not the one it was replaced with in this alternate timeline. That meant that a codebreaker had absolutely no way of knowing what the vast majority of the words in the clue were unless they themselves were similarly time-displaced. Nobody native to this reality had any chance of breaking this code. It was simply astounding!

The last time I'd expressed this opinion, Andi muttered something about how I should marry the code if I was that much in love with it, before demanding (moderately politely) that I enter the next piece of information.

When we'd finally entered the last of the anachronisms on my list and pressed 'Q', the following message scrolled up from below:

```
THANK YOU FOR PLAYING THE
ANACHRONISTIC CODE, TIME-TRAVELER!

REMEMBER, if your message is missing
words, keep looking.

The number of anachronisms out there
will align with the original answer
to Life, the Universe, and
Everything.
```

"So, there's a total of 42," I said, matter-of-factly.

"I still can't get used to it being anything other than 36," stated Andi. "42 just sounds weird!"

"I feel the same," I said. "But the other way around." I was scanning the table of anachronisms to count them, while mentally subtracting the ones that we'd crossed off. "So, we've got 38, right? That means we're four short of the total. If I've done my math correctly."

"Makes sense to me," answered Andi while shrugging her shoulders as if to say that not much of any of this made much sense to her in the first place. "What about those anachronisms that the game told us were real, but weren't in this clue?"

"I've been wondering about that. Maybe there are a few in there just to throw 'certain parties' off the scent. There's a chance, no matter how slim, especially if they had access to a really powerful computer, that somebody might be able to scramble the words randomly enough to make some kind of sense of them. And then, there's the possibility that some of the unused anachronisms might have other uses—like Jenny's phone number that got us into this side-quest, but isn't part of the actual clue."

"Or maybe there are a few phony anachronisms just to bring the number up to 42?" Andi suggested.

I laughed again, even though I had barely been more than a breath away from laughing giddily since we first entered Jenny's number and found the side-quest a couple of hours ago. "I do tend to over-complicate things," I offered. "Heather used to tease me about..." I stopped, having sensed that, beside me, Andi had flinched.

"I'm sorry," I said.

"Josh," she said, her voice clipped a little. "It's alright. I'm still getting used to it. I've just never ... well, I've never dated a boy who's been married twice ... in the future."

At this, we both laughed at the ludicrousness of it all. I reached over and pulled her into a hug. "Thanks again for this," I said. "I really appreciate your help. I couldn't have done it without you."

"You're just being kind," she said. "You coulda done it. It probably would've taken you an extra few months, and it wouldn't have been as much fun alone, but you would've gotten there, eventually."

Ignoring Andi's good-natured taunting, I sat down beside her on the bed, and she opened up my journal between us so that we could both see the table. Now that I was no longer focused on the struggle to enter words into the computer in such a way as to make the game understand them, I was finally able to truly look at the message. It was four lines of text, comprised of a total of twenty-seven words, four of which were missing.

	A	B	C	D	E	F	G
1	YOU	ARE	NOT	ALONE.		EVERYONE	WITH
2		FROM		AND	FOLLOW	THE	CLUES.
3	GET	THE		CLUE	UNDER	A	✕
4	ROCK	OF	BLACK	GLASS	BENEATH	AN	OAK.

I was in tears reading it, and so was Andi. I hugged her again.

I'm not alone. There are others who came back!

I mean, it was something that had been pretty much obvious since I heard Weird Al's warning about the 'Borg a number of weeks back, but this… well, somehow this made it seem that much more real. I still couldn't discern exactly what the message meant, especially with some key words missing, but part of the message was clear: there were more clues to find beyond this one, and this message was leading me to one of them, by telling me that it was hidden "under a rock of black glass beneath an oak." I narrowed my eyes as an absurd idea occurred to me.

As gently as I could, I extricated myself from Andi's embrace and took the journal and the pencil from her. Then, to the side of the makeshift Excel table, I wrote down the message again so that it would be easier to read without the distraction of the lines and labels.

You are not alone. _____ everybody with

_____ from _____ and follow the clues.

Get the _____ clue under a

rock of black glass beneath an oak.

Staring at the last line of the message again, I repeated the thought that had just run through my brain.

That's it? Isn't that, like, a little too obvious?

I'd kinda expected that the solution would be a little more complicated to be honest. I mean, somebody had obviously gone through an impossible amount of effort in hiding the anachronisms in plain sight, and then making it very difficult for the average person to put them together, only to give it all away with a clue that was way too obvious to be clever.

Right?

Am I missing something? Could it really be that ... well, easy?

END OF BOOK TWO

The story CONTINUES in:

The ANACHRONISTIC CODE
BOOK THREE: MEMORIES from TOMORROW

It's 1985, and Josh Donegal is seventeen ... again, and he's being watched.

Josh may have decoded enough of the first message from the future to have a rough idea of where the next clue might be, but he's about to find out that he's being followed by a group that doesn't want him to succeed. That may not be his biggest challenge though. He still has to figure out how to say goodbye again to the girl he'd left behind the first time.

Now Available!

Watercolour artist and author **Dwayne R. James** lives just outside Lakefield, Ontario where he writes and paints as often as he can, that is when he's not spending time with his daughter, twin sons, and his very forgiving wife.

Dwayne has a Master's Degree in archaeology, something he claims is definitive proof that he knows how to write creatively. "Indeed, the most important skill I learned in university," he posits, "was the ability to pretentiously write about myself in the third person."

After spending close to a decade as a technical writer at a large multi-national computer company, Dwayne opted to look at their Jan 2009 decision to downsize him as an opportunity to become a stay@home Dad for his newborn twins, and pursue his painting and writing whenever the boys allowed him to do so.

It is a decision that continues to make him giggle with wild abandon to this very day.

Visit Dwayne online:

His personal Web page:
www.dwaynerjames.com

His virtual art studio and store:
www.resteddy.com.

His Facebook page:
http://www.facebook.com/dwaynerjames

His Twitter page:
https://twitter.com/restEddy

Made in the USA
Monee, IL
25 February 2021

60993170R00154